THE
HOUSE
WITH THE
GOLDEN
DOOR

THE WOLF DEN TRILOGY

The Wolf Den
The House with the Golden Door

THE
HOUSE
WITH THE
GOLDEN
DOOR

ELODIE HARPER

An Apollo Book

First published in the UK in 2022 by Head of Zeus Ltd,
part of Bloomsbury Publishing Plc

9 7 5 3 1 2 4 6 8

A catalogue record for this book is available from
the British Library.

ISBN (HB): 9781838933579
ISBN (XTPB): 9781838933586
ISBN (E): 9781838933609

Typeset by Divaddict Publishing Solutions Ltd

Printed and bound in Great Britain by
CPI Group (UK) Ltd, Croydon CR0 4YY

For my dearest son Jonathon,
I love you with all my heart

AD 75

PARENTALIA

1

Man alone of living creatures has been given grief... and
likewise ambition, greed and a boundless lust for living.
Pliny the Elder, Natural History

The painter stands balanced on a wooden platform, his brushstrokes hidden from sight as he brings the goddess to life. Amara watches him. The rest of the fresco is complete, a hunting scene encircling her small garden. Only Diana's face is unfinished. She breathes in deeply, enjoying the scents of spring. Narcissi lie scattered at her feet like white stars, and the air is sweet with them.

"Nobody could do justice to her beauty," the painter remarks, standing back briefly from his work to scrutinize it, before busying himself with the brush again.

Amara knows he does not mean the goddess Diana. She could have hired anyone to paint a god, but she chose this man, Priscus, because he was once the lover of her friend Dido and the only artist capable of drawing her likeness. "I know that you will," she replies. Or she certainly hopes so. The rest of the painting has been done by his craftsmen at a far cheaper rate. It cost ten times as much to hire Priscus, the master of the firm, to immortalize her friend.

"She was the most exquisite woman," Priscus says. "There was a lightness to her unlike anyone else. I can still remember the way she sang."

Dido has barely been dead three months and Amara feels tears prick her eyes. She blinks, not wanting Priscus to notice. It is strange to have him in her home. The last time they had met, she and Dido were enslaved. Priscus had been a regular customer, paying their pimp to spend the night with Dido, while his friend Salvius paid for Amara's company in the bedroom next door. Now she is a freedwoman paying for *his* services. She suspects neither of them quite knows how to treat the other after this change in fortune.

He stands back from the wall again, looking over his work. "I believe it is finished."

Amara steps forwards. "May I see?"

"Of course," Priscus climbs down from the platform, finally leaving his painting in view.

Dido is standing with one hand to her heart, the other pointing across the garden. Amara gazes at her dead friend. Priscus has captured the perfect symmetry of her face, the softness of her mouth and, most of all, her eyes, dark with a sadness she could never hide. Grief hits Amara then, and she turns away. Priscus reaches out before dropping his hand, perhaps afraid his touch will offend her. It is a while before she trusts herself to speak. "I can never thank you enough for this."

"It has been my pleasure," he says. "It gives me some comfort to think her beauty is not entirely lost." Priscus stands next to Amara, leaving enough space between them to show his respect. "But can I ask you something? Why did you choose to remember her like this?"

He gestures at the walls surrounding them, and Amara takes in the scene, so different from the woman he has just painted. A stag with a human face is being ripped apart by hunting dogs, their muzzles slick with blood, teeth sharp in wide open mouths. Through the stag's mangled body, white ribs are poking, showing the red of his heart. It is Acteon, transformed into a stag by the goddess Diana, only to be torn to pieces by his own hounds. The price he paid for seeing the goddess naked. Diana points at him as he dies, turning Dido's melancholy into a mark of cruel indifference.

"She had the purest heart," Amara replies. "Who else could Dido be but the virgin goddess?"

They both know she has avoided his question. Priscus bows his head in agreement, too polite to press further. "Of course."

Amara waits while he collects his paints, packing them carefully into a box, his apprentice taking apart the platform to carry it back to the workshop. Afterwards she walks them both across the atrium to the door. There is no need to hand over the money now. Rufus, her patron and lover, can be relied upon to pay an account at his own leisure. At the doorway, Priscus hesitates. "I hope you will not mind if..." He trails off, then collects himself. "Salvius asked me to pass on his good wishes for your health, and his heartfelt thanks to the gods for your good fortune. He holds you in great esteem."

Amara's face betrays no sign of the turmoil she feels at this reminder of her old life. She is conscious of Juventus, the porter, no doubt listening to every word, even as he stands silent at his post. "That is kind of your friend. Please pass on my thanks and good wishes for his own health." She nods, polite but distant, and walks away before Priscus can say anything more. The mention of Salvius has flooded her mind with unwanted memories. His hands on her body, his nakedness, the weight of him, and then worse, not Salvius, but the fear and darkness of her old cell at the brothel, the violence and the pain. Her past is the whirlpool Charybdis, pulling her down under the waves where she cannot breathe.

Amara walks swiftly up the stairs to her private study, trying not to run, and shuts the door. Her legs are trembling. She sits down at the desk, hands flat on its wooden surface, trying to crush the rising panic. Her mind is playing tricks on her again, giving her the sense that she is not here, where her eyes tell her she is sitting, but back there, in Felix's Wolf Den. Blood thuds in her ears as she searches in the drawer for the box that always calms her. It is heavy in her hands. She sets it down and opens the lid. Inside is all the money she has earned since she came to live here, a mixture of loans she has collected and the generous allowance Rufus gives her. She runs her fingers through the coins, feeling their reassuring weight, listening to the sound of them drop, like the gentle patter of rain.

She arranged this room to be as unlike Felix's study as possible, placing the furniture at unfamiliar angles, making everything look different. The walls are white not red, small cupids balance gracefully at intervals along the walls, one with a harp, another with a bow. Every small, pale figure, each careful brushstroke on their bodies, is more finely drawn than anything in the Wolf Den, yet somehow, the images are less vivid than the bulls' skulls and black plinths she remembers. If she closes her eyes, Amara knows she will see them. There is something about sitting behind a desk that always makes her think of her old master. Even in her dreams, this is how she remembers him. The sharp lines of his body bent over the books, the tilt of his head glancing up, the strength in his hands.

A knock at the door startles her back into the present. "Who is it?"

Martha enters. Amara smiles, but her maid only looks at the floor. "Shall I get you ready to see Drusilla, mistress?" Martha's accent is so strong Amara sometimes struggles to understand her.

Martha's shoulders are rounded, her whole posture hunched. At first Amara had thought the girl was shy, but now she recognizes it as the deliberate withdrawal of the unwilling slave. She herself used that same reticence against Felix. Amara has to stifle her irritation. *The girl does not know how lucky she is to be here in this beautiful house, not there, in the brothel.*

Martha is Hebrew, captured in Rome's recent offensive against Masada – or so Philos, the household steward, told Amara. It was Philos who chose which other two slaves should join him here on behalf of his master. Rufus, who owns Martha, has not said anything about her. Slaves are not people to him. He 'loaned' all the servants to Amara along with the furniture, and it would no more occur to him to explain their different personalities than he would waste his time describing a history of the tables or lampstands. Amara only hopes Rufus never slept with Martha, although the girl is pretty enough. It might explain why she is so unfriendly.

"Thank you," Amara says, rising from the desk. "You are good to remind me."

They walk downstairs to the first of Amara's private rooms off the atrium. Martha has already set out the dressing table. It is impossible for Amara not to think about her friend and fellow she-wolf Victoria when she takes her place in front of all the perfumes and cosmetics. She remembers all the cheap bottles Victoria used to line up so carefully on her windowsill at the brothel, the pains she always took to look her best. Victoria is so vivid in Amara's memory, the tumble of black curls over her shoulders, her husky laugh and the drawl of her sarcastic remarks, that it seems impossible she will not walk into the room, demanding her own turn at the table. Martha starts to comb out her mistress's hair. Amara picks up a delicate glass jar, shaped like a flower, unstoppers it and holds it to her nose. Jasmine. It is the only scent Rufus likes her to wear. Martha huffs as Amara puts it down again, and the maid pulls at the comb. All this movement is ruining her attempts to style her mistress's ringlets.

When she has finished, Martha holds out the silver mirror. Amara always prefers to do her own make-up. She takes the kohl, redoes her eyes where it has smudged, but doesn't smear any paste on her skin. It was unaffordable while she worked at the brothel, and now Rufus is used to seeing her bare-faced. The only time she painted herself for him, he had hated it. All the words he uses to describe her – *lovely, delicate, naive* – she takes as instructions rather than compliments. It doesn't matter that she worked in a brothel, that she outwitted the most violent pimp in Pompeii, or that she could move mountains with her rage. This is not what her lover wants to see, so she hides it all.

"Thank you," Amara says. "You can start work in the kitchen now."

"But don't you need me to come with you?" Martha looks nervous. "Master said it's better you don't walk out alone."

It is one thing having to put up with a discontented maid; Amara does not want a spy as well. "The streets do not frighten me," she replies, with a cold smile, knowing the girl will understand her. "I am quite used to walking them."

Martha bows her head, cheeks flushing, no doubt cursing the day the Romans dragged her from her homeland to serve a *whore*. Amara leaves her and walks across the atrium to the huge wooden door. Juventus hesitates a moment before letting her out unaccompanied, glancing round to see if Philos, the steward, is there to grant permission. "Philos is with the Master today," Amara says impatiently. "Perhaps you will let me out to attend the harp lesson Rufus has paid for?"

"Of course, mistress," Juventus says, stepping aside.

It's a quieter street than the one she used to live on – the brothel stood at a fork in the road, facing one bar and a stone's throw from another – but even so, stepping out onto the pavement always makes Amara feel like she has slipped from a still pond into a fast-moving stream. She weaves her way past the billowing cloths that flank her doorway, strips of red, yellow and orange fabric flapping in the breeze. The house Rufus rents for her is fronted by a clothes store, one of several on the street. The shopkeeper, Virgula, nods as she passes, unperturbed at having a concubine for a neighbour. After all, they both share the same landlord – a friend of Rufus who Amara is yet to meet.

The road is narrow, but Amara owns her space on the pavement, her gaze cutting through to the middle distance, forcing others to let her pass. A man weighed down with an armful of leather goods huffs but stands aside. Amara does not acknowledge him. The days when she had to meet any man's eye on the street are over.

It's not long before she reaches Drusilla's house. Pompeii's most desirable courtesan does not live far away – her road runs parallel to Amara's. It's why she knows Rufus will tolerate her making the journey alone. This house is not rented; Drusilla owns it outright, and the beautiful glass workshop that fronts it is also hers. Amara lingers, looking in. The glassware becomes increasingly intricate the further inside you venture. Plain cups and scent bottles stacked on the counter give way to jugs shaped like fishes and an urn dripping in green grapes, a pair of nymphs acting as the vessel's arms. Amara's eyes are always drawn to the same place. A shelf carrying small statuettes of the gods. She thinks of the beautiful glass Pallas-Athene from her parents' house, wonders who owns it now.

Amara feels her heart lift as she steps across the threshold into Drusilla's atrium. The porter inclines his head as she enters – she is always welcome here.

"There you are!" Drusilla calls down, leaning over the indoor balcony, her face dimpled in a smile. Amara beams back. Drusilla is – bar Dido – the most beautiful woman she has ever known. The pale-yellow linen tunic she is wearing brings out the warmth of her skin, and her black hair frames her face like a laurel wreath. *She could be Hesperia,* Amara thinks, *goddess of the setting sun.*

Amara hurries up the stairs. She always enjoys Drusilla's company, even more so when they meet without their lovers present, when she knows everything her friend says is genuine. They embrace on the balcony, admiring one another's outfits, then head to Drusilla's bedroom where she keeps her harp.

"When is he going to buy you your own?" Drusilla asks, as they sit down together, Amara positioned to play the instrument, Drusilla close beside her to instruct.

"Today, if I let him," she replies, with a sigh. "But I'm not good enough yet; I don't want him to hear me."

"But you could practise every day with your own. You would improve more quickly."

Amara knows it is true. She is finding the harp harder to master than she anticipated. Every time she plays the lyre for Rufus, however beautifully or skilfully, all he wants to know is when she will entertain him with the harp. There's no malice in the way he asks; it's all eagerness like a child, but his insistence makes her feel insecure. She wishes he could enjoy the instrument she already plays. "I'm not sure why he's so set on this," she says, patting the strings.

Drusilla strokes her lightly on the back, brushing her hair over one shoulder. "I think it's an encouraging sign," she says. "He's making his mark. Turning you into the perfect concubine to suit his tastes. If he invests enough money in you, he won't look elsewhere."

Amara feels a flicker of anxiety. It's a constant shadow, the worry of losing her patron's interest. "Let's try Sappho again," she says. "I nearly had it last time."

They play for an hour or more. Amara is a dedicated pupil, never complaining when Drusilla gets her to practise the same chords over and over. For her part, Drusilla is an exacting teacher, not only passing on her musical knowledge, but also her advice on how Amara should hold herself to look as attractive as possible when she plays.

"I think that's enough for now," Drusilla says, running her hand along Amara's arm. "You are getting tense. I was serious earlier. Let Rufus buy you your own instrument. You will learn faster."

Amara follows Drusilla to the couch. The maid, Thalia, has left them some wine and pastries. "All this effort," Amara remarks, helping herself to a bun, telling herself she will eat less later. "Can you imagine Rufus and Quintus spending their afternoons deciding how to please us?"

"Not Quintus, certainly," Drusilla says with a frown.

"But he adores you."

Drusilla shakes her head. "A man like Quintus will inevitably want the excitement of something new, sooner or later. And I worry it might be sooner." She toys with her wine glass. It is blue, no doubt bought from the shop she rents out, the red of the wine shining purple through the glaze. "I'm not in love with him, as you know, but a new man is always a disruption. I'm used to Quintus now."

Amara is not entirely sure she believes Drusilla when she says she does not love Quintus. It's hard to dedicate so much attention to pleasing a man without ending up feeling some affection for him. "I keep having to remind myself to ration out the tricks I learned at the brothel," Amara says, raising an eyebrow. "Leave Rufus a *few* surprises."

Drusilla snorts. "That one manoeuvre you told me about! I think even Quintus was shocked when I tried it."

They both laugh. Amara settles back onto the cushions, enjoying the freedom of friendship, the licence to say what she likes. Her apprenticeship at the brothel was brutal, everything Felix forced her to learn coming at the highest possible cost, but now she has escaped, it can almost seem worth the pain. "Priscus finished the painting today," she says.

"How do you think Rufus will react? When he realizes it's Dido?"

"Philos says he won't even notice," Amara shrugs. "She was just a slave to him."

"You discuss Rufus with Philos?" Drusilla's voice is sharp. "Is that wise?"

"Philos was my friend before, when we were both..." Amara hesitates, not wanting to say the word. "When we were both enslaved."

"But now *you* are not, and *he* still is. Philos belongs to your lover. Be careful what you say. He might feel bound to repeat it to his master."

"I trust him," Amara says. "I don't believe he would do that to me." She hopes it is true. She feels too ashamed to admit the truth to Drusilla. That she is so lonely she cannot bear to be distant with Philos, to admit that he is Rufus's servant and not her friend. Who else is there in the house for her to talk to? "How is Primus?" she asks, changing the subject.

"Oh!" Drusilla claps her hands, face shining with delight. "He's doing so well with his letters! Such a clever boy. Come, come, I'll take you to see him. He will love to show off to you." She leaps off the couch, holding out her hand. Amara takes it and lets Drusilla lead her down the stairs.

They cross the atrium, heading out into the garden. Primus is roaming through the flowers, prattling about a bee, waving a small chubby hand, watched over by his nurse. He looks so like his mother. The same dimples when he smiles, the large, dark eyes. Drusilla flings her arms out and the little boy runs over, hugging her round the knees. Amara smiles. She didn't even know about the existence of Primus until a month after Rufus freed her. Drusilla guards her child from all but her closest friends.

"What have you learned today?" Drusilla is asking him. "What can you tell Mummy?"

"Bees live in palaces of wax!" he declares, looking up at his mother and then at Amara, as if daring her to contradict him. "They turn flowers into honey!"

Drusilla gazes adoringly at her son as he relays his three-year-old's wisdom with a great deal of self-importance. Amara had been shocked when she learned who the child's father is. Popidus is a Pompeiian grandee, one so ancient Primus must be many years younger than his father's legitimate grandchildren. The old man does not recognize Drusilla's son as his own.

Sitting with her friend, watching the child play in the garden, Amara can almost imagine that her life is now one of blissful security. But even though he is absent, she can still feel Rufus's hands holding her up... and knows he has the power to let her fall. It is his money which brought her here; he pays for Drusilla's time, and Amara knows she would never have won such a valued place in her friend's life if she had had a less prestigious lover. When they meet at the Venus Baths, Drusilla is always surrounded by other, less powerful concubines. Amara is just one of many women in her orbit.

Time alone with Drusilla is precious, but Amara doesn't dare linger. She needs to prepare herself for Rufus's visit in the evening. He has been busy this past fortnight with his family, celebrating the Parentalia – a domestic festival commemorating the ancestors – which has left him little time to see Amara. The festival has been an uncomfortable reminder of her peripheral position in Rufus's life, and her own orphaned, rootless status.

She rises, murmuring her excuses about Rufus to Drusilla who accompanies her to the door. Drusilla leaves Primus behind with some reluctance, even though she will be free to join her son again in a matter of moments.

"Do you think Rufus would be pleased if you gave him a boy?" Drusilla asks the question just as Amara is poised to step out onto the street.

"I'm not sure," she says, startled. "I don't think so." It is hard for her to explain why, but she is almost certain Rufus would not like to see her as a mother. She is still scrupulous at avoiding pregnancy.

"It is always a gamble." Drusilla nods, no doubt thinking of the heartless Popidus. "Don't forget to mention the harp tonight. Go well, my love."

Drusilla slips back into her home. Amara stands on the threshold, loneliness creeping up on her. When she was enslaved, she would visit Drusilla's house with Dido. They would leave together too, walking the streets hand in hand back to the Wolf Den. The grief hits her so hard that, for a moment, she doesn't think she will be able to keep her composure. *I have my freedom now*, Amara tells herself. *That's all that matters.* She strides out onto the pavement, her face cold, betraying nothing of the loss she feels.

2

"They're slaves," people say. No. They're human beings.
"They're slaves." But they share the same roof as ourselves.

Seneca, Letters from a Stoic

The water is barely tepid as Martha splashes it on her skin. Amara has stripped off and is washing herself, making sure her legs are completely smooth, removing any stray hairs. Having a wash at home is not as pleasant as soaking in the heat of the Venus Baths, but it's the only way to ensure she is fresh in the evening for her lover.

When Amara is satisfied that she is clean, she sprinkles distilled jasmine onto her palms, and rubs it over her whole body. The scent is overpoweringly sweet, but she knows it will have faded by the time Rufus arrives, adding to his enjoyment of her.

"Did you make sure you bought the cheese he likes?" Amara asks, as she slathers jasmine over her upper arms.

"Yes," Martha replies, staring at the floor.

"And the stew? You didn't overcook the beans?"

"No."

"He wasn't happy last time."

Martha says nothing. She has to share cooking duties with the porter Juventus, and neither of them are especially good at it. Amara normally sends one of them out to buy something from the cook shop on the corner and heat it up again at home. She stretches out her hand for the diaphanous silk that she always wears to entertain Rufus when he visits alone. Martha hands it to her then helps pin the material in place. The dress leaves very little to the imagination. Amara wishes Victoria or Beronice were here instead of Martha. Then she could ask how she looks and get an honest answer.

When she is dressed, Martha re-styles her hair. A last flick of kohl round her eyes, and Amara finally makes her way to the dining room to wait for her patron. She never eats in here when she is on her own – it would be far too grand. Martha has lit the oil lamps which rest at the top of tall bronze columns, illuminating the paintings with their flames. Jupiter's unfortunate mortal lovers sprawl over the walls in various states of undress. Io is being transformed into a cow by the door, while Leda embraces a swan above the couch where Amara is sitting. She never feels at ease in this room. The paintings remind her too much of the brothel, even though the scenes are drawn in finer taste.

The house is silent. Nobody is here but her and the two slaves who belong to her lover. Juventus will still be sitting in his cubby hole by the door, Martha warming the bean stew in the kitchen. The February air is chill, and Amara has draped a shawl round her shoulders to keep herself from shivering. Her heart beats fast with nerves and anticipation. She would love to tuck into some bread, to settle her stomach enough to start drinking the wine. It could be a while before Rufus arrives. She stares through the doorway into the darkening atrium, willing her lover to appear so she can eat.

Her stomach rumbles. That settles it. Better a fat concubine than a revolting one. She takes a piece of bread off the plate, tearing into it. Aside from the sweet bun at Drusilla's, it is all she has eaten today. The last time Rufus was here, he tried to encircle her waist completely with his hands, but his fingers no longer came close to meeting round the back. He has always held her like that, complimenting her on how slim she is, and she never thought anything of it, didn't imagine he was actually *measuring* how fat she was. "At least nobody can say that I'm starving you, little bird." He had laughed, letting go of her.

Amara had been mortified. Then furious. What did he expect? That she would stay as thin as she had been at the brothel when she could barely afford one meal a day? But she had swallowed her anger. *Rufus is not unkind*, she tells herself. She is lucky to have such a devoted patron. And maybe it wasn't even a criticism. Maybe he was just noticing. Making an affectionate joke even. Still, she has decided to eat less, to be on the safe side.

The clank of the door rings out, the murmur of male voices. Amara drops her bread and flings off the shawl, swinging her legs up on the couch, trying to make herself look as seductive as possible. A figure is approaching. It is hard to see clearly when the room is so bright and the atrium so dim, but even so, she can tell it is not Rufus. The man is too slight, and his tread not heavy enough. Amara sits back up again, heart thudding with disappointment, as Philos walks into the room.

"The Master says he is very sorry not to make it this evening." Philos does not come too close to her, instead lingering by the door. Unlike Juventus who never misses a chance to eye up his master's girlfriend when she is in the transparent dress, Philos keeps his eyes on Amara's face. "He had to have dinner with Helvius."

"Oh," Amara says, reaching for her shawl to cover herself again. "And that was *definitely* the reason?" In another life, when Felix still owned her, it was Philos who had told her about Rufus having a second lover. He promised her back then that the affair with the serving girl meant nothing to his master, and he had been proven right.

"I promise," he replies. "He really was *very* disappointed not to see you."

Amara breathes out with relief. She can see Philos step back, knows he is about to leave. "Won't you stay and have something?" she blurts out, not wanting to be alone.

"Here?" Philos asks, incredulous. They stare at one another, Amara's cheeks burning with embarrassment. He lowers his voice. "You know I can't. What sort of slave eats his master's food in his own dining room?" *With his own concubine*, he might add, but doesn't.

"You're right," she says. "Sorry."

The pair of them remain in awkward silence, Amara sitting on the couch, Philos standing by the door. She suspects he is just as lonely as she is, for all his protests about propriety. "If you wanted to have a drink in the garden," he says, speaking slowly, as if feeling his way, "then I could stay a while and tell you about the Master's day. I think that's an acceptable thing for a steward to do." She cannot tell if he is being humorous with his last comment. There used to be such an ease between them. She can still remember his words when he picked her up from the brothel one night to take her to his master. *Who'd be a slave, eh? When you're young they fuck you, and when you're old they fuck you over.*

The memory of Philos swearing brings a slight smile to her lips. She picks up two wine glasses, motions for him to take the jug. "Very well," she says.

Amara walks through to the garden, and he follows. Dido is lost in shadow on the wall. They sit on a stone bench, the wine jug and glasses between them, along with a very sizeable gap left by Philos who is taking up as little space on the seat as possible. He refuses the wine, as she knew he would.

"So what are Rufus and Helvius meeting to discuss this evening?" she asks.

"The celebrations," he replies. "Rufus has offered to put on a show at the theatre after the campaign. Helvius is happy enough to be spared the expense but is less generous about taking his name off it."

Helvius is standing for election as aedile in Pompeii this year, and almost certain to win. The role is as much ceremonial as administrative, with the expectation that those elected will spend their own money providing free entertainment for the public. Amara's lover Rufus is planning to stand for election next year and wants to get some support in early.

"Can't they both take some credit?" Amara asks.

"I'm sure it will come to that eventually," Philos says. He reaches out towards one of the plants growing by the bench and breaks off a sprig, crushing it between his fingers, releasing the scent. Thyme. The smell takes Amara back instantly to her childhood, her father preparing draughts of the herb with hot water and honey to ease a patient's cough. *It helps digestion. Also good for melancholy.* Philos is taking the sprig apart, piece by piece, dropping each scrap on the ground. "How did it go with the harp?" he asks.

"Drusilla thinks I should let Rufus buy one so I can practise at home," she replies. "I'm not sure I'm ever going to be very good at it though." She drinks the wine, feels its warmth spreading through her. "And after the music lesson we saw Primus. He was learning his letters in the garden."

"Oh," Philos exclaims. "I remember doing that as a boy. In the house where I was born." The light is fading, but it is still bright enough for her to see he is smiling at the memory. He has stopped shredding the thyme.

"Were you once free?" she says, surprised into asking a personal question. She had been so sure that Philos was born into servitude.

"No, I've always been a slave," he replies. "Just a well-educated one." She stares at him, wanting to know more without liking to intrude. He smiles again. She realizes he is enjoying her curiosity; there is mischief in his grey eyes. He looks more how she remembers, back when they were truly friends.

"*Tell me about a complicated man,*" he says, switching to Greek. "*Muse, tell me how he wandered and was lost when he had wrecked the holy town of Troy, and where he went, and who he met and the pain he suffered in the storms at sea.*"

"You learned Homer?" Amara is surprised.

"A *little* bit of Homer," Philos corrects her. "To be honest, that's almost all I can remember. I barely got a few hundred verses into *The Odyssey* before the Master's children objected to me reciting it."

"Why would they do that?" Amara asks.

"Because I was good at it," he replies. She is expecting him to go on, but instead he looks uncomfortable, as if aware he has said too much about himself. "I'm sorry, I don't..." He stops, not finishing whatever it is he wants to tell her. "I should go and ask Martha to save the dinner. Rufus said he will call on you as soon as he can. Maybe tomorrow. Goodnight."

He gets up and hurries from the garden, disappearing into the dark atrium. Amara watches him leave, a heavy feeling in her chest. She isn't sure if the ache inside is hunger or loneliness. It would have been more sensible to ask Martha to bring out some stew, no need for *her* to miss dinner simply because Rufus hasn't turned up, but she is reluctant to call Philos back. A few months ago, she was a lower order of slave than anyone else here. Now they all have to wait on her. She can easily imagine what the others might say about their brothel-whore-mistress behind her back.

It is painful to think Philos might share the disdain. She knows he will soon be going to his room – or rather his cell – a tiny, dark, cupboard-like space underneath the stairs. Smaller even than her cell in the brothel. But then, he doesn't have to entertain anyone in there. She pours herself more wine. Amara is aware that Philos must lead a much lonelier life here than he did at Rufus's house where he no doubt has a whole network of friends, the alternative 'family' every slave builds up in service. Perhaps he resents the change to this half-empty house. She has even less idea what the other two think. The porter Juventus will be hunched in his cubby hole all night, unable to leave his post, even for sleep. Martha will bed down in a tiny room upstairs. In her mind, she can see the storeroom at Felix's flat, the one Rufus paid for her to take as lodgings, rather than let her suffer every night in the brothel, in the months before he bought her. *Paris must still sleep there,* she thinks, picturing her old roommate hunched on the floor. She never cared for him much. Felix's slave boy and part-time prostitute was very far from being a friend. In fact, Paris and Amara spent most of their time in that room squabbling, but she finds herself thinking of him now with something approaching affection.

"Don't be a fucking idiot," she mutters, free to swear because she is alone. Amara takes another swig from her glass. The wine burns. It is not Paris she misses. Her friends from the brothel are so vivid in her mind they almost feel more tangible than the garden she is sitting in. At this hour, she knows they will be getting ready for the onslaught of customers, joking together to lighten the darkness. She wonders if Beronice still has a pot of gold paste to smear over her eyes, whether she managed to steal any time with her lover Gallus today, or whether Victoria still teases her about it. Amara grips the stem of her glass more tightly. *Victoria.* The two of them are bound together, not only by love, but a blood debt, a bond as sacred to the gods as it is to men. Without Victoria, Amara would not be alive. It was Victoria who risked everything for Amara, killing a man to save her life. And Amara has never repaid her. Instead, she abandoned her friend to become a rich man's mistress, leaving Victoria to rot in the brothel.

Guilt sweeps through her, as hot as the wine. She looks at the painting of Dido, little more than a dark shape above. The shadow blurs as her eyes fill with tears. "Goodnight, my friend," she says to the wall. Amara drains her glass then stands up, leaving everything on the bench for Martha to clear away in the morning.

The study is red. Felix has his back to her, but it is only a matter of time before he turns. She opens her mouth to scream but makes no sound. She wants to run, but her legs are like lead. She cannot move them fast enough. He is beside her, holding a knife, the one he wielded on the Saturnalia, the night Dido died. She knows he will rape her, that she can do nothing to stop him. Felix points the blade at her eye. "I missed you."

Amara wakes, gasping for air. Her face is wet with tears. It takes her a moment to remember where she is. Then she burrows back under the blanket, desperate to sob into it, digging her nails into the palms of her hands, clenching her fists. Even in the grip of panic, she knows she cannot risk ugly, swollen eyes. "It will pass," she murmurs to herself, smothered in the darkness, refusing to cry. "It will pass." Nightmares torment her more now, when she is safe, than they did when she was enduring the horrors in her waking life.

It is stuffy under the covers. Amara surfaces, forcing herself to get out of bed. The tiles on the floor are cold. She stretches, willing the fear away, as if she might be able to shake it from her fingertips. Her bedroom is small, with no room for anything more than a bed and a linen chest, but it is calming. An internal window into the tablinum provides the only natural light. Frescoes of flowering branches circle the narrow space, giving it the soft glow of apple blossom. Oil lamps rest in alcoves cut into the walls. When they are lit at night, Rufus says they look like stars shining through the treetops.

The thought of her lover is soothing. She rests one hand over her heart. Rufus will protect her from Felix – he always has done.

Amara starts to get dressed, preferring to do it herself rather than call Martha in to help. She picks out her favourite outfit from the chest: the white robe Pliny gave her. It is still the loveliest dress she owns, even though the fabric is getting a little worn. If he had not signed over all his rights to Rufus, then Pliny, the Admiral of the Roman Fleet, would have been her patron instead. It was Pliny who gave her both her freedom and his name. Amara doesn't think she will ever tire of those four words, especially the last. Gaia Plinia Amara, *Liberta*. She fastens the white dress at the shoulder, whispering her new title like an incantation. She hopes she will see the admiral again one day, to thank him for all he has done.

Amara unlocks her door and steps out into her second chamber. Martha is already there, sitting on a stool, waiting for her. She looks tired. As soon as she sees her mistress, she heaves herself to her feet.

"You've no need to get up so early," Amara says, embarrassed. "Please. You can rest until I call you."

"Master said I was to wait on you," Martha replies, moving over to the dressing table, gesturing at Amara to sit down so that she can style her hair.

The two women are silent while Martha works, teasing the comb through Amara's curls where she has slept on them, making her look presentable.

"Were you a maid back in your hometown?" Amara eventually asks. "In Masada?"

Martha stops so abruptly, the tug on her scalp makes Amara wince. "Who told you that?"

"You must have mentioned it," Amara says, not wanting to reveal that she heard it from Philos.

"I was not a maid, no. I was married." Martha's voice is flat. She resumes her brushing.

Amara realizes then that Martha might also have been a mother, that perhaps she has just intruded on another woman's deepest agony – the theft or murder of her children. "I'm sorry," she says. "It is hard to be taken from your home. And your family."

"It is as God wills," Martha replies. "Not for me to question." *And not for you either*, is the implication she leaves unsaid.

Amara gives up. Let Martha keep her secrets. After all, the maid owns nothing else. She closes her eyes, imagines that it is her friend Victoria dressing her hair instead, that the fingers she can feel belong to someone who loves her. Victoria always used to wake everyone at the brothel by singing in the morning, however dark the night before had been. Even the memory of her sweet voice makes Amara smile. Martha finishes styling her hair in silence, then holds out the mirror for Amara to draw her eyes. When she is done, mistress and maid part company with what Amara suspects is a mutual sense of relief.

She walks out into the garden. The bench is empty now,

the jug and wine glasses all cleared away. Above her, the sky is the pale blue of a new day, the sun not long risen. She can smell the dew, still fresh in the air. Water falls into the fountain with a gentle murmur, a small marble Venus reclining at the edge of the pool. Amara feels a wash of happiness. This is what it means to be free, to have all this to enjoy.

She bends down to inspect the thyme Philos mangled yesterday, to discover what other medicinal herbs might be growing alongside it. All these months, she's been here and not paid proper attention.

"You have no need to fear the flowers. You put them all to shame."

She jumps up, startled by his voice. "Rufus!"

Her patron is standing at the edge of the garden, watching her. She runs over to embrace him.

"I'm so sorry I disappointed you last night, my darling," he says, crushing her in a bear hug. "I came as soon as I could."

Amara gazes up at him, exuding adoration. Her fear of losing his protection is as real as if she truly loved him. "I'm just so happy you are here now," she says, letting him kiss her. "Though I'm not sure I can forgive Helvius for keeping you."

Rufus flops down on the bench with a groan. "Such a pompous man!" Amara perches beside him, and he rests his hand on her knee. "You won't believe what he's planning. He wants to hold the Taurian Games at the end of May, to appease the gods of the underworld."

"But why?" Amara asks, alarmed.

"That tremor we had in January. He's convinced another Great Earthquake is coming."

"But that was barely anything!" she says, remembering the way the ground had quivered, a rumble like distant thunder. The whole event had been over almost before Amara realized what was happening, though it had caused a surprisingly large crack in the atrium and left the pavements outside littered with roof tiles.

"You weren't here for the disaster in the Year of Marius and Afinius," Rufus says, sounding a little pompous himself. "We're still repairing the damage." He waves a hand, as if dismissing an imaginary Helvius. "But in any case, I'm quite happy for him to throw his Taurian Games. Only now, he's suggesting that a festival of theatre for the Floralia just before will cheapen it. Ridiculous. Even *Cicero* threw one. And he's not even been elected yet! Imagine how much more pompous he will be after that."

"You will win him over – I know you will. And when you are aedile next year, you can do as you like." Amara twines her fingers through his, trying to hide her nervousness, wondering if now is a good moment to weave herself more tightly into his life. "I was thinking," she says. "Perhaps you could invite Helvius *here* one evening? I could put on a musical entertainment for you all. Let him see how important performance is to you. I was going to suggest that I buy a couple of musicians. You could sponsor them as your own."

"You want to buy musicians?" Rufus asks, surprised. In her former life, Amara and Dido were rented out by their pimp to sing at dinner parties. It is how she met Pliny. Music was seldom the only service she was obliged to offer.

"I'm not suggesting that *I* perform anywhere but at this house," Amara says quickly. "But I did so enjoy arranging poetry to music with Dido; I should love to entertain you that way. Drusilla would be very interested in sharing the cost, if she could also use our musicians from time to time. We were thinking maybe flautists?"

"Oh, so you girls have been plotting, have you?" Rufus laughs. "Well, let me think about it. Perhaps I will buy them for you once you can play the harp for me." Philos arrives with a tray laden with sweet wine, bread and the crumbling white cheese Martha bought in specially yesterday. He sets it down on the small table on Amara's side of the bench. She tries to catch his eye to thank him, but he is not looking at her. Philos leaves as silently as he arrived. "What did Drusilla say at your lesson yesterday?" Rufus continues, not acknowledging his slave. He has not noticed Dido painted on the wall either. "Are you getting better at it?"

"She thinks it would help if I had my own instrument at home, to practise," Amara says, handing Rufus a glass of wine.

"But that's what I've been saying all along!" he exclaims, rolling his eyes. He takes a sip.

"I worry you might not like my playing yet," Amara says. "I don't want to disappoint you."

"Nervous little bird," Rufus says, leaning over to kiss her again. "How could I do anything but adore you?" Amara smiles at him, inwardly wincing at the nickname. Rufus started calling her this after he freed her, a joke based on a letter from Pliny comparing her to a bird that cannot sing in captivity. Her patron sets down his wine, pulling her closer. "I don't have much time this morning, my love," he murmurs into her hair, his hands sliding into the folds of her dress.

"Just give me a moment," Amara replies, thinking of all the jasmine she did not sprinkle on her body earlier, and worse, about the contraceptive she never likes Rufus to see her use.

"Don't be long," he replies, letting go. Amara walks from the atrium, giving him the deliberate backwards glance that Victoria taught her, the one she knows he cannot resist. His eyes meet hers, and in that moment, she feels invincible. It is impossible to imagine a time this man will not desire her.

After Rufus has left, she spends some moments alone at her dressing table. Her hands shake slightly as she picks up the bottle to reapply the kohl. She puts it down again. It had been an act of overconfidence to try that particular move to impress Rufus, the one Felix always demanded, the one fraught with dark memories. She is fortunate her lover had been too caught up in pleasure to notice her falter. At least her gamble served its purpose.

Amara picks up the kohl again, and this time, her hands are steadier. She props up the mirror for herself, not calling for Martha, and draws the dark lines around her eyes. Her reflection stares back, braver than she feels inside.

Juventus and Philos are laughing together when she walks into the atrium. They are speaking a local dialect she does not understand, leaning against the wall, enjoying some private joke. Juventus is a much burlier man than Philos, with a thick beard where the steward is clean-shaven, but in moments like this, they look as familiar as brothers. Amara knows the porter owes his position to Philos, and she notices he is holding a hunk of bread. Philos must have brought it for him from the kitchen. The two men fall silent at her approach.

"Is anybody here for me today?" she asks.

"A woman is waiting on the bench outside," Philos says. "Neither of us have seen her before. Metella from the Venus Baths."

Amara nods to Juventus. "You can let her in."

"Will you need me to draw up a contract?" Philos asks.

"Give me a little time alone with her first," Amara replies. "Maybe you could bring in the tray from the garden?"

"Of course."

Metella walks in. She is the sort of respectable married woman who would once have refused to acknowledge Amara on the street. Now she steps into her home, looking both nervous and defensive.

"I'm so glad you could call on me," Amara exclaims, embracing her. "I'm sorry you were kept waiting."

Metella returns the smile but still looks wary. Amara keeps up a stream of pleasantries as she steers her guest towards the tablinum, her public study for entertaining guests, prattling about Julia Felix, their mutual friend and the owner of the private baths where they both met. By the time the two women are sitting opposite each other and Philos has left the food and wine on the table, Metella seems more at ease.

The tablinum is one of the finest rooms in the house. A large window is set behind Amara, letting in the air and scent of the garden. The walls are yellow, and birds fly from panel to panel or perch on flowering branches. A peacock is painted opposite the window, his tail fanned out in a glorious display behind Metella's head, and doves rest on the door lintel. Amara does not get down to business straight away. She shares the wine, asks about Metella's family, gushes over her guest's children's accomplishments and nods sympathetically at tales of a tyrannical father-in-law. The whole time Metella talks, Amara is attentive. Learning about a client's life is a trick she learned from her old master. Felix's skill with moneylending was always exceptional. His shadow lies across these meetings, but Amara's memories of him are not wholly unwelcome. She wears his easy charm like a cloak, hiding their shared passion for making a profit.

"And your patron knows about... your business?" Metella asks, finally coming to the point. She looks around at the bright walls, at the delicate swallows painted in flight behind her host's shoulders, calculating the value Rufus must place on his concubine. His family is well known in Pompeii, even more so now he is following his father Hortensius into politics.

"Oh!" Amara says, waving her hand. "It's not a *business*. I would hate you to think that. I just help friends out from time to time. Where I can."

"It's not a large sum," Metella replies. "Just fifteen denarii. I will have no difficulty repaying. But I would prefer this to be discreet. My husband might not like to be bothered by it."

Amara understands from this that the husband will not be told. "It's a trifle between women," she agrees. "No need to involve anyone else."

Metella unfastens a bracelet from her wrist, setting it down slowly on the desk. "This is very precious to me," she says.

"I promise to look after it," Amara says, picking up the

bracelet and examining the engraved bronze with a suitable show of reverence. She places the jewellery carefully in a small box so that Metella will not be distressed by the sight of it. "And my rates are not unreasonable. Five per cent interest per month. An extra five per cent on top of that if it is not paid within three months."

Metella nods, looking less pleased by this information. "Very well," she replies.

Amara gets up and crosses to the door, opening it as the cue for Philos to enter. He is in the room almost before she has sat down again. She murmurs to him as he bends to take up the tablet from the desk, letting him know the sum. It had surprised Amara when Philos declined her offer to take commission on the loan agreements he writes. She herself cannot imagine refusing money from *anyone*, ever.

Amara continues to chat to Metella as Philos writes out the agreement. He hands it to them both to sign. Metella hesitates for a moment before marking the wax. Five per cent is nowhere near as high as the extortionate rate Felix used to charge, but then, Amara does not have a violent protection racket to call upon to back up her claims. Not that she can imagine ever having the need. All her clients are women, and she has long suspected they are a more reliable market.

Once the agreement is signed, Metella seems eager to leave. Amara knows this is not uncommon after a deal. She follows Metella back into the atrium, making a point of showing off the garden, chattering about the narcissi, trying to soothe her guest with the pretence that this is nothing more than a social call.

"What an extraordinary painting," Metella remarks,

looking a little uncertain at the savage hunting scene surrounding her.

Amara smiles. "The house came already decorated," she says.

After a few more awkward exchanges about the fountain, Amara walks her client to the door, ignoring the ragged old woman now sitting by the stairwell in the atrium. The hunched figure could easily be mistaken for an elderly house slave, unworthy of notice.

As soon as they have said their goodbyes, and she is sure Metella is safely out of sight, Amara turns back to the old woman. The figure stands up, pushing the hood from her face. It is Fabia, the brothel dogsbody, a former prostitute and Felix's oldest slave.

"Thank you for coming," Amara says, taking Fabia's outstretched hands in her own. "I've missed you."

3

And all this time the poor slaves are forbidden to move their lips to speak, let alone to eat. The slightest murmur is checked with a stick; not even accidental sounds like a cough, or a sneeze, or a hiccup are let off a beating.

Seneca, Letters from a Stoic

Amara and Fabia sit in the garden, last night's bean stew and a heap of bread on a table beside them. They both eat like wolves, Fabia ravenous from near starvation and Amara from her self-imposed fasting. She knows what they must look like – an old whore and a young one, slaking their appetites, stew dripping from their chins, but she doesn't care.

"That's good, that is," Fabia says, rubbing another hunk of bread around her already polished bowl. "A good cook you have there."

"I'll tell Martha you liked it," Amara replies.

"Look at you," Fabia says, sitting back slightly and squinting at her, finally able to focus on her companion now the edge of her hunger has been blunted. "How well you've done! I can hardly believe it."

The painting of Dido is behind Fabia, and Amara is pleased she has not seen it yet, that she does not have to confront Fabia's grief. "How is everyone?" she asks. "How is Victoria? And Beronice? Is she still with Gallus? Is Britannica doing any better?"

"All the same," Fabia replies, helping herself to yet another piece of bread and taking a slug of wine. "Beronice still thinks Gallus will marry her. Maybe he will, who knows. And the boss finally got replacements for you and Dido. A couple of Greeks. A girl and a boy, so my Paris is pleased, less time in the brothel for *him*. Though they're a bit young for it, if you ask me. Put Victoria's nose out of joint."

"Does Felix still have her stay nights upstairs?"

Fabia nods. "Such a bastard. He'll keep her up there a week at a time, like some sort of wife, then back she goes to the brothel. Victoria's a strong girl, but it's enough to break anyone's spirit, having your hopes dashed all the time. It's a trick he learned from—" the old woman stops herself.

"His father?" Amara asks.

"You know I can't," Fabia mutters.

Amara pours her more wine. "My friend, I promise you, Felix has no spies here."

"I suppose so," Fabia says, knocking back her glass. "Yes, he learned it from his father. It's what the old master did to Felix's mother. To Felicula." The name is like the brush of cold fingers on Amara's skin. She can remember it, carved into the brothel walls. *I fucked Felicula here.* "How that silly girl loved the old man," Fabia says, with a sigh. "Always making pathetic excuses for him. She was a tiny little thing, surprisingly popular with the customers. I could never understand it. Not very sharp."

"Where did Felix live back then?"

"Wherever his mother was," Fabia replies. "Always hanging off her, like a squirrel. I know he's a shit now, but he was the most *beautiful* child. Those big brown eyes." She sets down her empty wine glass, and Amara tops it up again. "Even prettier than my Paris at that age, if I'm honest."

Amara knows that if Fabia starts talking about her son Paris, it will be impossible to get her off the subject. "What happened to Felicula?"

"Is there any more stew?" Fabia looks at Amara and understanding passes between them. They are not just two old friends meeting up. Everything has its price.

"Of course," Amara answers. She lifts the lid from the large tureen Martha left them, ladling out a third portion.

"Felix can't find out that I've told you all this," Fabia says, watching her bowl fill up. "More than my life's worth."

"You weren't followed, were you?"

"No," Fabia replies. "I always check. Not that anyone really bothers where I go, not some old bag like me." She pauses the conversation to eat. Amara watches her. Fabia's hunger is a reminder of what her life could have been if Rufus had not rescued her, the disgrace and destitution of a prostitute once her looks have gone. Helping the old woman is a way of acknowledging her own good fortune, a reminder of the knife-edge they all live on. And of course, if it weren't for Fabia, she would have no way of knowing what is happening to her friends, or what Felix is up to. Amara is not sure what purpose all this information on her old master will ever serve, but she still feels compelled to gather it.

The last few beans are gone, and Fabia scrapes her spoon

around the side, determined not to miss a drop. "That's so good. Keep me going all week, that will." She glances up at Amara. "It's a long time since I've thought about Felicula. Why are you so interested in this old stuff anyway?"

Amara shrugs. "So what did happen to her?"

"If you think Felix is bad, you should have known the old master." Fabia shudders. "That poor little boy saw his father beating his mother, and who knows what else over the years. Felix was even there when she died." Amara is about to ask what happened when understanding hits. Fabia nods, seeing the look on her face. "I don't suppose the Master *meant* to kill her, but she was such a frail little thing. He broke her neck."

In her mind's eye, Amara can see Felix kneeling on the floor, staring at his father's desk, and remembers what he said about his mother. *She died when I was ten.* The horror is too much for her to speak. She stares at the fountain, letting the gentle murmur of the water drown out the pulse in her ears. Pity is the last emotion she owes Felix, but her heart is heavy thinking of all he must have suffered, the pain he must still carry.

"I thought he might have turned out different," Fabia says, helping herself to the wine when it's clear Amara is too distracted to pour. "Felix, I mean. His mother was such a sweet girl, and he did dote on her. Trailing round after her everywhere. But his father took him on after that – I don't know whether it was guilt or what. Made Felix into his own image. Beat any kindness out of the boy, I shouldn't wonder. And now, he's doing it all over again with Victoria."

The mention of her friend startles Amara. "Do you think Felix would ever hurt Victoria? I mean, *really* hurt her?"

Fabia looks troubled. "I think he hits her more than he used to," she admits. "He's been more violent since you left. More unpredictable."

"Since *I* left?" Amara asks, surprised. "Why? He got paid a fucking fortune!"

"Well, I don't know what went on upstairs between the pair of you," Fabia says, picking up the last piece of bread from the table. "All that time you spent alone with him. Not *my* business."

"Nothing went on. I just did his books."

Fabia raises her eyebrows, unconvinced. "Maybe it was Dido dying then. But I always thought it was you he was sweet on." She waves the bread at Amara, dropping crumbs. "And all the questions you ask about him! I thought that was why. Some sort of lover's thing."

Fabia's words take Amara back to the red study. She is facing Felix again, his voice in her head. *I missed you.* Perhaps she has always chosen not to understand what he meant. "There was never anything like that," she says, dismissing the memory, shutting out the shame. "Perhaps you would like some fruit now? And then you must tell me what Paris is up to."

Fabia's visits always last hours. Eventually, Amara is forced to invent an excuse for her to leave, claiming Rufus is due for an assignation. She lets Philos escort the old woman to the door, keeping up the flimsy pretence that these meetings are purely out of charity not friendship. She can hear Fabia exclaiming as she crosses the atrium, trying to eke out her stay a few moments longer, and the murmur of Philos's indulgent replies. He is always unfailingly polite to Fabia, calling her *mistress*, as if she were a respectable woman. Fabia titters in delight whenever he uses the term, as if forgetting she is no longer a pretty, young flirt.

Amara is left alone with Dido. She looks at her friend, but the painting's gaze is directed instead at the dying stag. Dido will never meet her eyes again, not even as a shade. Before she was freed, Amara had promised to do everything in her power to buy Dido, to bring her to live in this house. Now she is dead. But Victoria is still alive.

"Your old friends doing well, are they?" Philos is cheerful as he wanders back in to clear up the lunch. Fabia always seems to amuse him. Amara instinctively gets up to help, but he recoils when her hands touch his.

"Sorry," she says, sitting back down again. "I don't like…" She trails off. Amara finds it hard to explain why she finds it difficult to watch Philos serve her.

"If it makes you feel better, I wait on you because that is what Rufus has commanded," Philos says, stacking the bowls. His face is impassive, impossible for her to read. "Just as *you* live here at his pleasure. Nothing for either of us to question. Or feel bad about."

Everything he has said is true, but Amara does not find it comforting. "You must wonder why I still see Fabia."

"Not at all," Philos says, looking up at her. His expression is kinder this time. "Why shouldn't you help an old woman? Not her fault she's hungry. Most natural thing in the world, friendship."

"That's true," Amara says, his words adding weight to the idea forming in her mind. She gestures impatiently at the tray. "Can you leave that? There's a purchase I need to discuss with you."

"Now?" Philos is startled by her change in mood.

"Yes, I need your advice." Amara stands up again, agitated. Having decided what needs to be done, her sense of urgency is overwhelming. "Right away." She hurries upstairs to her private study, and he follows.

Philos stands in the doorway, looking on, as Amara drags her money box out of the drawer. She flings open the lid, rifling through it, counting up the total even though she already knows it by heart.

"What is this?" His voice is low, and now they are alone, his manner is more familiar. "What are you doing?"

"Fabia told me Felix is becoming more violent with Victoria. He takes her upstairs for a while and then sells her again. Exactly as his father did to his mother." She holds up a pair of earrings Rufus gave her, squinting at them, trying to guess their worth. "Felix saw his father kill his mother – did you know that?" She glances back at Philos. "Imagine what he might be capable of, what he might *do*."

Philos sits down on a chest without permission, an unthinkable liberty he would never take with Rufus. He looks completely calm in the face of her anxiety. It is infuriating. "I'm sorry to hear that about Victoria," he says. "But it doesn't mean Felix is going to kill her. He is not his father."

"He's a fucking monster!" Amara shouts. Her hands are shaking too badly to continue counting the money. She puts one hand to her throat, remembering the pressure of Felix's fingers. "You don't know what it's like to be owned by someone like that." As soon as she has said the words, Amara realizes that Philos does, in fact, know exactly what it's like. All the years of abuse he endured when his owner was not Rufus, but Rufus's grandfather, Terentius.

"Felix does not own you now," Philos replies. He is looking at her with such sadness it makes her want to weep. "You are safe from him. You are safe here. He cannot hurt you anymore."

"But he is hurting Victoria."

Philos does not contradict her. "That's not your fault. Or your responsibility."

His acknowledgement of Victoria's distress does nothing to allay her own. Amara turns away, trying to calm herself. She needs to convince Philos, not cry over him. "I owe my life to Victoria," she says, her voice colder. "I would be dead without her. It's a blood debt. I have no choice."

"No," he says, already understanding. "You can't do this."

"Why not? I told Rufus I wanted to buy some musicians. He didn't say no. Victoria is a great singer!"

"You said flautists."

"You were *listening*?"

"I'm not a doorpost," Philos says, with irritation. "I have ears, and you were talking."

"Rufus never pays that much attention to me," Amara replies. "He won't remember. And why should he care anyway? What difference does it make to *him* whether it's a singer or a flautist?" Philos frowns, and she remembers Drusilla's warning about where his loyalty might lie. "I meant no disrespect—" she stammers.

"I know that," he says, cutting her off with a look of

distaste at the fawning tone to her voice. "I'm not going to *report* you; I'm not your jailor."

"So you agree he might not mind?"

"It's not about Rufus," Philos says. "Even though I don't think it's clever to make a show of independence – he doesn't much like that sort of thing."

"What is it then?"

"It's you!" he says, exasperated. "Think of how hard you've worked to be free of Felix. And now you want to be *in debt* to him." He gestures at the coins and jewellery spilled all over the desk. "Felix is never going to agree a reasonable price. And then what? You have to troop round to the brothel every month to pay him off? What sort of risk is that?"

"Rufus might pay," Amara says, wavering.

"I doubt the price Felix will demand is one you will want to admit to Rufus."

"Maybe I could ask for half?"

"Please don't do this."

"But I *love* her. Can't you understand that? What is my freedom worth if I don't help somebody I love?"

"You cannot buy everyone you once cared about as a slave."

"Not everyone, no. But I might be able to rescue Victoria. If you were free, isn't there anybody you would buy? There must be *someone* you love that much."

The obvious distress on his face almost makes Amara wish she had not asked. "My sister," he says.

"I have no family left. Dido is dead. Victoria is my sister."

Amara and Philos stare at one another. He is the first to look away. "I still think it's a bad idea," he says. "You

44

might be safe from Felix *now*, but what happens when you invite him back into your life? If you owe him all that money? It could ruin everything. Think of how much he frightens you."

She runs her fingers over the coins, but the usual feeling of reassurance does not come. The thought of spending all that precious security – even on Victoria – gives her the urge to pile every last piece back in the box and lock it. "You think I'm a coward."

"No!" Philos exclaims. "That's ridiculous. *I* would be afraid of him, if he had been my master. Do you think I wasn't afraid of Terentius? That I'm not *still* afraid of him, even though he's dead?"

Amara thinks of the nightmares, the constant weight she carries, the burden of all Felix did to her. She feels her resolve falter. "Does it never go away?"

Philos does not ask her what she means. They have never discussed it, except fleetingly, when he covered his past suffering with a joke, but she knows that he understands what it is like to be physically powerless, to be *used* by another. His silence is her answer.

"I will think it over this afternoon," she says, rising from her chair, angry with him for forcing her to confront her own vulnerability, "and let you know what I decide tomorrow."

4

We can tell she has been in a pimp's house – she is a wheedler.
Seneca, Declamations 1.2

Darkness still falls early on the February evenings. Amara retires to bed, not wanting to sit up alone in the empty house. She avoids the garden, with its shadowy imitation of her friend. Dido's absence feels wrenching tonight. The loss always hits Amara that way, unpredictable in when it will strike. She sits on the bed, hugging her knees, as if she might be able to hold in her grief, prevent it spilling out in an ugly flood, like the guts from her painted stag.

If only Rufus's visit today had not been so brief. She thinks how much easier she would feel if he had come back again this evening. Perhaps if she saw more of him, the lack of companionship would not affect her so deeply. Amara resolves to practise the harp for hours when it arrives, anything that might succeed in luring him here and fill her days with purpose. And yet even if he visited every night, she knows Rufus could never mean half as much to her as Dido did. Amara can picture her friend, sitting in their old cell. She imagines calling Dido's name, seeing her turn and smile, the affection in her eyes. The knowledge that she was loved, completely, by another.

You escaped the Wolf Den, Amara tells herself. *You are free! Be grateful for what you have.* She lies back on the bed, watching the light flicker over the apple blossom from the single oil lamp. She keeps it burning at night to chase away the darkness. Thanks to her generous lover, she can afford to waste the fuel. The air is cool here, the space peaceful. Her door is locked, but even if it weren't, she knows nobody is going to stumble in and maul her, this is not the brothel. All those nights she schemed for her freedom, desperate to escape to somewhere like this. How is it that now all she can think about is the friends she left behind?

She can imagine them here, how they would laugh together, filling the garden with their voices. She turns over on the bed. It is not only out of guilt that she wants to free Victoria, although the guilt is crushing enough. The thought of her friend in this house gives Amara a sense of joy almost as great as her fear of Felix. She knows Philos understood, even though he tried to persuade her otherwise. It was plain from his face when he mentioned his sister. She stares up at the shadows dancing on the ceiling, knowing that he will be lying alone now too, perhaps thinking of his family, just as she is thinking of Victoria. She hopes she did not hurt him by reminding him of his losses. Or maybe that is all he thinks about, every night.

The covers are suffocating, and Amara pushes them off, sitting up again. The image of Philos lying so close by disturbs her. He is a much slighter man than Rufus, yet somehow, his presence in a room always registers; she is constantly aware of him, of where he is in the house. *I'm just lonely*, she thinks. *That's all it is. Loneliness.*

Amara breathes out and closes her eyes. She tries to think of Rufus. In her mind, she counts up his kindnesses, much the same as she counts the coins in her money box. The gifts he has given her, the house he has rented for her and, above all, the freedom he granted her. She lingers on the last, but her memory of the Saturnalia, the night she gained her freedom, is slippery. Images slide from Rufus's face, to Dido, to her lover's cold response to her grief. And then there is Menander.

That night was the last time she saw him. Where the image of Rufus feels hazy and difficult to grasp, all her memories of Menander are as sharp and clear as glass, and just as cutting. She humiliated the man she loved, brutally and publicly, rather than risk losing her wealthy lover. Even thinking about it now makes her want to sink into the ground. She tells herself it was her only choice. Menander is enslaved – they could have done nothing for one another – whereas Rufus had the power to transform her life. But the knowledge of what the decision cost, makes her feel older and wearier than Fabia.

Amara slumps back on the bed again. Freedom has already exacted a heavy price. She cannot give up *everything*, or she will have nothing left of herself.

Amara is conscious of Philos approaching with the tray before she turns towards him. The morning is chill, too cold to be sitting in the garden, but it is the public part of the house where she feels most at ease. She is swathed in an expensive red cloak, another gift from Rufus.

"Have you decided?" Philos asks, setting down the food.

"Yes."

"And I really cannot persuade you otherwise?"

"No."

She thinks he will argue, but instead, he sighs, as if this is no more than he expected. "Then we'd better think about how it's done."

They sit together on the bench, the tray between them, discussing the matter in low voices. Amara had resolved last night to be more distant from Philos, but in his presence, she finds this difficult. He is holding his arms, and she realizes that he must be cold sitting out here in just a tunic. She regrets not suggesting they sit in the study.

"It's important that you tell Rufus as much as possible," he says. "That you are honest with him. My preference is to ask his permission."

"But if he says no, I cannot then go against him."

"I wish you wouldn't say things like that."

"Like what?" she replies, tilting her head and widening her eyes, a pose copied from Beronice at the brothel. "That I will always be obedient?"

"You know *exactly* what I mean," he says, looking away to hide his smile. "In that case you will have to hope his sympathy for a tale of love and loyalty outweighs his annoyance at not being consulted in advance. It just might, I suppose. As long as Victoria really *is* a good musician."

Amara nods. "He will love her singing."

"And she's not too... coarse?"

"No," Amara says, suddenly embarrassed, hoping Philos does not see *her* like that.

"You must have an upper limit in mind when you negotiate with Felix."

"I have."

"What is it?"

"You wouldn't like it. If I tell you, it will put me off. But I promise I can afford it."

Something hardens in his expression. It looks like resentment. "And you are sure this is how you want to spend your money?"

She is flustered by the coldness of his question. Amara thinks of the money box upstairs. The heavier it gets, the safer she feels. In front of her, the fountain continues its merry patter, the stone Venus lying peacefully at the water's edge. The air is fresh with the scent of spring's earliest flowers. All this is hers: the quiet, the safety. Perhaps she is a fool to be risking it, even for Victoria.

She realizes Philos is watching her and feels exposed. "You don't have to do this," he says.

"I do though," she replies. "If I am ever to live with myself." He is silent, and it occurs to her that perhaps he is not thinking of her at all, but is afraid for himself. "I can tell Rufus you didn't know," she says. "I can tell him I lied to you, that you believed he had given me permission. If that makes it easier."

Philos frowns. "Why would you do that?"

"Why should you get into trouble? Not very fair, is it? Victoria isn't *your* friend."

Amara can tell she has unsettled him.

"You don't have to lie for me. I would never ask it of you.

And besides..." She waits, while he struggles to find the words. "I don't agree with your decision," he says, finally. "But I understand it. And you were right yesterday. If I were free, I would do the same. Or at least, I hope I would." He stands up without looking at her. "Tell me when you want to leave. I will accompany you."

Amara suspects Philos may have paid her a compliment, but she doesn't know how to respond.

When he has left, she walks over to the painting of Dido. From this low angle, looking up, her friend is distorted, eyes narrowed and hard. "I would have done this for you," she murmurs, laying her hands at Dido-Diana's feet. "It's only right I do the same for Victoria, isn't it?" She follows the goddess's melancholy gaze to the half-human stag. Amara did not dare paint the face of the man she most wanted to see in Acteon's place, the man she blames for Dido's death. Hatred wells up hot in her heart. "You are right," she says. "It will hurt him to lose her."

Virgula greets Amara as she and Philos leave the house. The fabric seller is hanging up a rack of freshly dyed linens – or rather her slave is hanging them up, while Virgula supervises. Amara notices the girl's hands are stained orange, and wonders if the colour ever scrubs off. Neither Philos nor the servant girl say anything while the free women speak.

"If you ever want a gift for your man," Virgula is saying, "we have some new linen in. Pure white. Perfect for a celebration, if his candidate wins." She smiles, nodding to the election slogan painted on her shop wall, proclaiming

Helvius as the best choice for aedile. Virgula clearly knows how to ingratiate herself with those who matter.

"What a wonderful idea," Amara replies. "Lay some aside for me, please. I will be in later to choose it." She nods and walks past, Philos behind her. When they have reached the end of the street, Amara waits for him to walk by her side. It is the mirror image of the courtesy he used to pay her, when he collected her from the brothel. Though it would be unthinkable now for him to offer his arm, or for her to accept.

They walk along together, leaving a dignified gap on the pavement that makes others trying to pass them tut or swear in frustration. Soon, they reach the grocer at the crossroads with the Via Veneria, which Amara always views as the edge of her new neighbourhood. Once they have picked their way round its barrels of slick green olives and pushed through the shop's dawdling customers, she starts to feel more apprehensive.

"I don't want to be trapped inside with Felix," she says to Philos. "We need witnesses. I think it's best if I ask Paris to bring him to the square outside The Sparrow." Felix's women are all well-known at The Sparrow, a tavern around the corner from the Wolf Den. The landlord Zoskales is Amara's almost-friend, and his waiter Nicandrus was Dido's almost-lover. She realizes she has not seen Nicandrus since the night of Dido's murder. The thought of how sharp his grief must be brings an ache to her chest.

"Wherever you meet," Philos says, "you know Felix is going to do everything he can to distress you. You have to prepare yourself."

Amara almost wishes she had not made her hostility to Felix so obvious after Dido's death. "I know," she says.

"I don't just mean because he's a shit," Philos adds, surprising her by swearing. "He will upset you to try and put you off your negotiating. Don't let him." Philos is closer to her now, and some of his deference has dropped. "It's a while since anyone has spoken to you the way he once did. You will always be a slave to Felix. I hope you won't budge on that maximum price."

"If I have to walk away, I will."

"Even if Victoria begs you?"

Amara swallows, hating the thought. "She wouldn't do that. Victoria never begs."

"Do you think there's *anything* a human being won't do when they are that close to tasting their freedom?"

"If Felix knows I will walk away, he won't push me that far. He will want the money."

They are getting closer to the old familiar part of town. It is easier for them to walk together on the wide pavements of the Via Veneria. The road rises up the hill. At the top sits the Forum which Amara knows will be ringing with hawkers' cries and the hammering of building work on the nearby Temple of Venus. A wagon stacked with masonry rattles past, and Philos steers her to the side, shielding her from the dust.

They keep walking, at last arriving at the piazza outside the baths. Amara hesitates. She used to tout for business here. *Fishing*, as Victoria calls it. She sees the men sauntering out of the gateway, faces shining from the heat of the steam room, and feels a stab of fear.

"We can go back," Philos says, noticing her increasing agitation.

"I can't leave her," Amara replies. "I *can't*."

Philos looks troubled, and for a moment she thinks he is going to argue, to force her to go home. She almost hopes he will.

"As you wish," he says.

They set off again, passing in front of the baths, taking the narrow road that leads to the brothel. She lets her feet guide her, abandoning her will to the habit of her body. Then they round the corner, and it's there. The Wolf Den. The building hangs over the street at the fork, its shadow falling towards her. She wants to take Philos's arm then, whatever the impropriety, but forces herself to carry on alone.

At the door to Felix's flat, they stop. She knocks hard on the wood. There is the thud of steps down the stairs, a scramble at the lock, then Paris answers.

Felix's young slave stares at her, amazed, and in that moment, she sees herself through his eyes. Her hair piled up on her head in intricate curls, the expensive cloak Rufus bought her, the air of wealth she now wears, like the scent of distilled jasmine on her skin. She is not Felix's slave anymore. The thought gives her courage.

"Is your master in?"

Paris darts his eyes nervously between her and Philos. "Might be," he says.

"Tell Felix that the admiral's freedwoman is here to make him an offer for the slave known as Victoria. I will be waiting outside The Sparrow."

Paris nods slowly and closes the door. Amara turns to Philos. "No going back now," she says. "Stay with me."

"I'm here," he replies.

5

The things slaves say; the squalid snark; the filthy slanders of a
street vendor's tongue.

Martial's epigrams 10.3

The Sparrow is smaller and seedier than she remembers. It seems impossible that she spent so many hours of her life here, that it was ever somewhere she felt safe or comfortable. There is a shocked silence as she approaches the bar with Philos. The only women who set foot in a tavern like this are prostitutes. It takes Zoskales a moment to recognize her.

"Amara!" he exclaims, then draws back, unsure how to greet her. He looks at Philos. "Is this your…" She can tell Zoskales is baffled, unsure whether Philos is her patron or her minder.

"This is my patron's steward, Philos," she says. "Please, I don't have much time. I'm here to buy Victoria. Will you be my witness?"

"Are you crossing Felix?" Zoskales says, his face less friendly. "You know I won't help you there."

"No!" she says, forcing herself to laugh. "As if I would dare! I just need a witness. Nothing more."

The landlord nods warily. "Very well. I will ask Felix if he minds. And now, I think it best if you wait outside. This is no place for you."

"Is Nicandrus not here?" she asks, trying not to feel hurt by her old friend's reaction.

"I sold him," Zoskales replies. Amara puts her hand to her mouth. It is like losing another part of Dido, to lose the man who loved her. Zoskales sees her distress and relents. "It was for his own good, my love," he says, lowering his voice. "I was afraid of what he might say to Felix, after Dido died. He works at Asellina's place now, on the Via Veneria."

Amara nods. "Thank you." She and Philos walk outside. The crowd in the square parts slightly, leaving them some space, looking at them both with a mixture of curiosity and aggression. Amara begins to worry it might have been safer to have done the deal in Felix's study after all.

She stands at the edge of the road, looking towards the brothel. His shape, even his walk, is so familiar, that when Felix appears, it is almost like seeing an old friend. Then he gets nearer, his face coming into sharper focus, and Amara's hatred blazes into life. *Dido took the knife meant for this man.* She steps back and feels Philos brush his fingertips against her arm. It reminds her of the way she and Dido used to communicate, the silent gestures between slaves. *But I am free now*, Amara reminds herself. *Felix does not own me.*

Beronice and Victoria are walking behind their master, and the sight of her friends squeezes Amara's heart – she has missed them both so much. It is all she can do to stop herself from rushing over to embrace them. Felix wastes no time with greetings, nor does he leave a respectful space. He comes so close to her she can sense Philos tense up by her side.

"Which one do you want then?" Felix says, gesturing at his women. "Or are you here for both?"

Amara looks at Victoria and Beronice's hopeful, desperate faces and feels a rush of anguish. Felix has immediately wrong-footed her. "I came..." She falters. She cannot admit the truth to Beronice. "I came for both of them."

"That will be fifteen thousand sesterces then," Felix says. There is laughter from the men standing on the square, seeing the pimp put the posh girl in her place.

"Don't be a fucking idiot," Amara says, anger making her more like her old, coarser self.

"Too high?" Felix raises his eyebrows. "They aren't worth that much to you? Look at *you*, putting a price on friendship." He turns back to his women. "Seems she doesn't love you after all."

Felix is looking sidelong at her, expecting her to crumble, and anger numbs her to the pain. "Nobody ages faster than a whore," she says, her voice as cold as his. "That's what you once told me. This pair are going to do nothing but lose their value with each passing year, and you know it. So I wouldn't stand there sneering. Not if making a profit is still important to you." Amara cannot bear to see her friends' reactions, so she keeps her eyes fixed on Felix instead. A slight twitch betrays that he is clenching his jaw. Nothing will annoy him more than being disrespected in front of an audience.

"Like I said, the price is fifteen thousand."

"Three," Amara replies, choosing the amount she had

hoped Felix might agree to accept for just one of the women.

"Now who's the fool!" Felix laughs at her. "You clearly can't afford them both, don't waste my fucking time. Which do you want?" He pulls Beronice forwards by the elbow. "This one's younger. She'll last me longer. But she's also lazier." Beronice fingers a cheap cameo at her neck, a present Amara remembers her getting from her lover Gallus. The look of hurt bewilderment on her face makes Amara want to cry. "Or you can have my hardest working whore." Felix jabs a thumb towards Victoria. He addresses the drinkers who are now all crowded round, listening, enjoying the show. "If anyone thinks they've had better cunt after fucking *that* one, they can have their money back." A couple of men laugh, one shouting out what the women can expect to get from him later.

Amara looks at Victoria. In her memory, her friend is always laughing, irrepressible, *unconquered*, like her name. Now Victoria looks tired, and heartsick, and somehow smaller. Amara used to envy the way Victoria wore her clothes, but in this unforgiving light, all she can see is how cheap they are. Victoria is looking back at her, almost out of hope, and Amara knows then that she would give up the wooden box, and all it means to her, a thousand times over to set her friend free.

"Victoria," she says, her voice breaking. She cannot look at Beronice.

"Nine thousand," Felix replies.

"You said fifteen for both! That's more than half!"

"This one's worth more to me."

"I will give you three and a half."

"Eight"

"Four."

"Six," Felix says, and the sudden drop, where she was expecting seven, takes her by surprise. He smiles at her, and she understands. Six is the price Pliny offered him, when the admiral bought her for Rufus on the Saturnalia. It is also a thousand sesterces above the upper limit she set herself, one that will see her sink deep into debt.

"Five," Amara says. "That's already far more than you'd get for her on the open market."

"No lower than six thousand," Felix replies, and she knows that he won't back down. Not now he has declared it to the crowd.

"In that case I want Britannica too. As part of the deal."

"*Britannica?*" Felix frowns, surprised and suspicious. "Why do you want the Briton?"

"Because she's my friend, and I don't want her to die here. We both know she was a bad investment for you; she makes nothing but a loss."

"What if I say no?"

"Then I walk away."

Felix stares at her, assessing whether she means it. She keeps her face still, giving the lie to her wildly beating heart. "Done," he says at last. "Good luck putting the British bitch to any use. Though I'm sure your *patron* will be delighted to have yet another greedy whore to feed."

Amara turns to Philos to take the tablets from him. His face is inscrutable, but she knows he must be afraid of what his master will say about *two* brothel slaves, not to mention how she is ever going to pay back this enormous debt. "Before I sign," Amara says. "There is one last condition. The sale will only mention Britannica. I want you to free Victoria, not sell her to me. The six thousand will compensate your generosity."

Victoria cries out, almost falling to her knees with shock. Philos steps forwards, grasping Victoria's elbow to steady her. Felix says nothing. Amara cannot tell if she has surprised him or not. "Why not free her yourself?" he asks, even though he knows the answer. "But of course! You were too recently a slave yourself to do that." Felix clicks his fingers at Amara, the way he did when she was still his property. "Sign for the money first, and I will free her."

"Free her and then I sign."

"If I may suggest," Philos says, stepping in, before Amara and Felix can begin haggling again. "I will write up a different contract. The payment will be both for transferred ownership of the slave known as Britannica and to compensate Felix for granting the slave known as Victoria her freedom. That way both the money and the gift of freedom are legally binding. If the payment is not made, Felix will take back both women. If Victoria is not freed, or Britannica not handed over, no payment will be made."

Amara can see Felix does not like taking suggestions from a slave, but Philos is looking at her old master with a mild, unchallenging expression that gives no trace of the dislike she knows he feels. *He looks at Rufus like that,* she realizes.

"Write it," Felix says to Philos. "And when we have both read it and signed, I will free her."

"I would like to call Zoskales as a witness," Amara says.

Felix shrugs in answer. "Call whoever you like." One of the drinkers staggers off to fetch the landlord.

Felix and Zoskales sign first, then Philos hands the tablet to her. She scans the agreement, trying not to focus on Felix's extortionate rate of interest, and signs. Philos does too, then stamps it for her.

Felix turns to Victoria and takes her by the hand. Amara can see she is trembling. "Victoria, in front of witnesses, and in the sight of the gods, I grant you your freedom," he says. "You now take my name as Gaia Terentia Victoria, Liberta." Victoria starts to cry, overwhelmed. Amara remembers the moment Rufus freed her, the way time stopped, her heart unable to take in the magnitude. Felix pulls Victoria closer and kisses her. "And now you are free," he says, tenderly stroking the hair from her face. "Will you be my wife?"

There is a shocked silence. Victoria gazes back at Felix, and in that terrible instant Amara knows she will say yes.

"No!" Beronice screams. "No!" She grabs Victoria, tearing her from Felix's astonished grip. "Don't do it!" Beronice shouts, shaking her by the shoulders. "Don't throw it away, don't do this to me!" She points at Amara. "She chose *you*. I could have gone with her! It could be *me* leaving now. It could have been me!" Beronice breaks down, sinking to the ground, sobbing, and Amara rushes forwards.

"I'm sorry," she cries, taking Beronice in her arms. "I'm so sorry. I *owed* her. I had to choose her, I had to."

Victoria looks down at them both, her two friends weeping in a heap, Amara's expensive cloak now crushed in the dirt. Then she looks up at Felix. "The answer is no."

6

He still feels his master's slap and wants to give
himself a good time.
Petronius, The Satyricon

Amara stares at Victoria. The kohl around her eyes is
smudged with tears, and she looks terrified, yet she is
still managing to hold Felix's gaze. Victoria has loved him so
long and endured so much cruelty, it seems impossible that
she has finally found the courage to let him go. Amara can
scarcely believe it. From the expression on his face, it seems
Felix cannot believe it either. A few men in the crowd titter
to see the pimp rejected by his whore. Amara is afraid then,
knowing her former master will never forgive the humiliation.

Felix does not acknowledge Victoria's answer. Instead,
he bends down to wrench Beronice to her feet before
slapping her hard on the back of the head. Amara cries out,
and Philos steps forwards, as if to intervene. Felix turns on
him, giving Rufus's slave a look of vicious contempt. Philos
steps back. They all know Beronice's lawful owner can do
whatever he likes with her.

"Don't be late with your payments, Amara," Felix calls

as he leaves the square, dragging Beronice along. "I will expect to see you here *in person*."

Amara feels as if she might be sick. In her head, she can still hear Beronice's words. *I could have gone with her.* Victoria takes her hand, and Amara realizes Victoria is trembling, unsteady on her feet. "You're safe now," Amara says, embracing her, trying to focus on the friend she chose, not the one she abandoned.

Philos leans towards them both. "We need to collect the other woman and go," he whispers. "Before things turn." Amara looks round. A number of men are still standing about the square, watching. She has just revealed herself as having several thousand sesterces to spare, an inviting target for robbers.

Zoskales seems to share their anxiety. He flaps his hands at the men still milling about. "Show's over," he declares, shepherding customers towards the tavern. "Plenty of drink left inside."

Philos takes advantage of the distraction, hurrying her and Victoria down the road to the brothel. Thraso, Felix's henchman, is standing guard at the door. The sight of him there, exactly how Amara remembers, is like walking round the corner to her past. Behind him, the building is a malevolent presence, saturated with unhappiness, the stench of soot and the sense of fear. She can hear Beronice sobbing inside.

"The Briton?" Thraso says, shaking his head as she approaches. "You want the fucking *Briton*?"

"Give her to me," Amara says. She cannot bear to stand here at the threshold of her nightmares, listening to Beronice's suffering, for a moment longer. "She's mine."

Thraso stares down at her, until the memory of his slap is so acute, she can almost feel it on her skin. "Wait here."

A few moments later, Britannica emerges blinking into the daylight. She is almost as tall as Thraso and even more unkempt than Amara remembers. Her red hair has been hacked short like a man, and a ragged tunic exposes her pale, muscular arms. Britannica's face breaks into a grin when she sees Amara. "You come for me," she rasps out, barging past Thraso to join them on the pavement.

"It *talks*?" Thraso exclaims. Britannica's refusal to speak a word of Latin had always been one of her many forms of resistance to life in the brothel.

Britannica spins round, bristling with aggression. "Yes, I *talk*." She spits at his feet. "Fuck you."

If she did not have the advantage of Thraso's complete astonishment, Britannica would undoubtedly have felt his fist in her face. Instead, Philos uses the split-second of surprise to yank her out of harm's way. They break into a run, ignoring the threats Thraso bellows after them. Amara looks back. He is not following, staying instead at his post on the brothel door. Felix must have given orders to let them go.

The Wolf Den disappears as they round the corner, joining a crowd of women queuing to get into the baths. They weave their way through, trying not to trip over anyone's feet or trailing hems. In the crush, Amara can feel hysteria rising in her chest like a bubble seeking air. Her horror at leaving Beronice is fading, overwhelmed by a growing sense of elation at their escape. She grips Victoria's hand. The enormity of freedom is just starting to sink in, she can see it in the drunk way Victoria is staring at her surroundings, as if only just noticing them, understanding that her life now belongs to her.

On the Via Veneria, people turn and stare at the strange trio of women, with Philos trailing after them. A group of customers emerging from the bakers openly point and laugh. Amara finds she doesn't care. Ever since Rufus freed her, she has enjoyed all the luxury of being a kept woman but also its isolation. Now she is no longer alone.

They turn into her street. She is delighted by Victoria's look of wonder at all the fabrics on display as they reach the row of dress shops. "Here? You live here?" Victoria says, running her fingers along the length of some fine red wool hung from the entrance to Virgula's store. Virgula comes out to greet Amara then stops, perturbed by the state of her neighbour's new companions.

Philos is standing in the doorway, waiting for them, gesturing at Amara to hurry. Brass studs, protruding from the half-open wooden door, gleam golden in the light. Amara apologizes to Virgula, promising to return, and leads her friends into the narrow hallway. As soon as they are inside the atrium, Philos orders Juventus to lock up, then turns to face her. He looks wrecked. "What have you *done?*"

"What I planned to do," she retorts, not liking his tone.

"*Six thousand sesterces?*" he says, his voice rising. "That's twice what they are worth and twice what you own!" Philos gestures at Victoria. "Do you think she will ever be safe now she's made an enemy of Felix? Do you think any of us will? And how do I explain...?" He stops, lost for words to describe Britannica. "Rufus will be *furious*. You've made a fool of him!" Amara has never seen Philos angry before, and she is surprised by the passion in his voice.

"I'm sure I can talk Rufus round," she says, dismissing his temper with a shrug. "And I didn't mean to deceive you. Britannica was an afterthought."

"You are *not* the mistress of this house," Philos replies, lowering his voice so that Juventus cannot hear. "You have nothing. Everything here belongs to him, including you. All you own is his love, and you are squandering it." He walks off, too enraged to speak further. She watches him leave, feeling her anxiety rise.

"Well," Victoria says, raising an eyebrow in the arch way Amara loves and remembers. "Charming slave you have there."

"He's not *my* slave," Amara says.

"No," Victoria agrees, solemnly. "He just made that point." Amara can't help smiling, even though the joke makes her uncomfortable. "All I can say is it's very *fine*, this house that you don't own." Victoria turns to gaze round at the atrium. Amara sees it with her, as if for the first time. The ceiling high above them, with its small square open to the sky, the shaft of sunlight falling on the pool of rainwater beneath. On the walls, painted columns deceive the eye, and scenes from the life of Venus sit in small squares between them. The pool is not marble but lined with shards of amphora pots, and the house is tiny compared to the grand homes where she and Dido used to perform, but Amara knows it is a palace compared to the brothel. "When we've explored the place," Victoria says, eyes shining with excitement, "maybe one of the servants who aren't yours could get us a drink? And then we can enjoy our non-existent freedom?"

"Drink first." It is Britannica. They jump at her voice, with its harsh, unfamiliar accent. She is standing in the doorway, legs akimbo, unmoved by the mosaic of stars under her feet. Behind her, Amara can see Juventus staring, unable to hide his curiosity about the strange woman.

"Is she coming with us?" Victoria whispers, taking Amara's elbow, trying to move out of earshot.

"Of course," Amara replies. "We can go to my rooms, have some wine, get you both new clothes. Then we can see the house."

Victoria raises her eyebrows but doesn't complain. Britannica strides over to join them. Amara feels uneasy that, even now, on a day which should bring nothing but happiness, the pair cannot hide their antipathy. She calls for Martha, asking her to bring water for a bath, then heads to her rooms. Her two friends follow.

Amara's first room is just big enough to receive guests, with a couch and side table, as well as the dressing table where Martha does her hair. She looks at the black frieze running round the walls. Pale nymphs gambol along it, singing and playing the lyre, swirls of pink and yellow silk circling their limbs like smoke. The nymphs are the reason Rufus told Amara he chose the house, to celebrate her skill as a musician. Showing her friends inside, she feels a swell of gratitude and affection for him, followed by an undertow of unease. Surely, it's impossible her lover could be as angry as Philos fears?

Victoria shrieks in excitement at the sight of the dressing table. "You have a mirror! A silver one! And look at all those bottles! Can I try your scent? What is it? Oh, let me see!" She unstoppers the bottle without giving Amara a chance to reply and dabs the distilled jasmine on her wrist. Martha, returning with a tub of water and a bundle of cloths draped over her arm, looks startled to see a stranger handling Amara's things.

"You can leave that, Martha," Amara says. "We will help ourselves now. If you could just bring us some wine and pastries in a little while." Martha nods, clearly disappointed to be abandoning such a rich seam of gossip. As soon as the maid has gone, Victoria and Britannica strip off, splashing themselves with water and rubbing their skin with the rough cloths to get clean. Amara goes into her bedroom and opens the clothes chest, fetching out two of the three dresses Pliny gave her. She is more attached to them than all the robes Rufus has bought her, but she cannot risk offending her lover by handing his gifts away.

"I'll have the yellow one," Victoria says, able to spot the finer garment from across the room. "Red will suit Britannica's hair better."

Britannica heads over to inspect her new robe, lifting it from the couch with a doubtful expression. Her naked body reminds Amara of Felix – she is all muscle and hard edges. A rough leather amulet is hanging from her neck, a dark stain against the chalk-white skin. It is the gift Amara chose for Britannica on the Saturnalia, a token dipped in a gladiator's blood. She remembers buying the amulet with Dido and has to suppress the thought that follows. *If only Dido were here instead.* Britannica bunches the red material of Pliny's robe against herself, her movements awkward, then puts it down. "Tunic?"

"This is nicer than a tunic, though," Amara reassures her.

"Tunic better for me," Britannica insists.

"She *is* a slave. She's right, a short tunic might be better," Victoria says. "Maybe Philos has a spare."

"Yes! Much better," Britannica says, misunderstanding the teasing. "I ask him."

"No, please don't," Amara says, horrified by the thought of a naked Britannica hunting down Philos to demand his clothes. Victoria is helpless with laughter. "I will ask Martha to buy you a new one. In the meantime, please try wearing this. Look, I'll help you." She fusses around Britannica, folding the material, pinning the red robe into place. The hem barely reaches her calves.

Victoria, in the meantime, has dressed herself in the yellow outfit. It is more flattering to her figure than it ever was to Amara's. Victoria holds out her arms to see how the material falls, stroking the fabric, and Amara realizes that she is struggling not to cry. She remembers how her own freedom first caught her like that, the sudden moments of joy and disbelief.

"You look beautiful," she says.

Victoria puts her hand to her heart. "Thank you," she says. "For everything. I can never, *ever* repay you."

Martha returns with the tray and almost drops it when she sees Britannica sitting on the couch. "I thought…" she stutters. "Sorry. I thought it was a man."

"I would hardly have a strange man in my private chambers, would I?" Amara snaps. "Just leave it, please." Martha fumbles with the tray, clanking it down on the side table, spilling some of the wine. Then she hurries from the room.

Victoria is almost hysterical with laughter, and this time, Amara joins her. Even Britannica smiles. "I look like *man*," she says, standing taller to show off her strength.

The three of them drink the wine together, growing ever

giddier with excitement. Britannica does not speak much, clearly understanding more than she can say, but Victoria asks Amara endless questions, desperate to know all about her life. Most of all she wants to know when she can finally meet Amara's patron.

"What a generous man he must be! To let you buy me!"

"He doesn't know yet," Amara admits. "I told him I was thinking of buying some musicians. I thought you could sing for him."

"Of course I will!" Victoria says. "I can sing every hour of every day if that's what he enjoys. Will he want anything else from me?" Her tone is matter of fact, making it clear her body is no less at Rufus's disposal than her voice.

"No," Amara says, not liking the suggestion. "Rufus is a romantic. I think that would offend him."

"Well, you can ask," Victoria shrugs. "I don't mind."

"I mind," Britannica says, folding her arms.

Victoria snorts, but Amara senses Britannica's fear. "I know," Amara says. "And I will never, *ever* force you to lie with a man, I promise." She places her hand on the Briton's arm. "That part of your life is over. Nobody will touch you." Britannica clenches her jaw, unwilling to show weakness, but Amara can see tears of relief welling in her eyes.

"I hope that part of *my* life isn't over," Victoria says, pulling a face.

"Not if you don't want it to be," Amara says. "I'm hoping you might catch the eye of one of the guests Rufus brings here."

Victoria leaps up from the couch and spins round and round in her new dress, laughing. She grabs hold of Amara's hands, spinning her round too. "The rest of the house!" Victoria cries. "Show me the rest!"

The three of them run from room to room like children. Amara has not felt such abandoned joy since she came here. She takes her friends to the tablinum, the dining room off the atrium, and then they head to the three rooms upstairs. "This can be yours," Amara says to Victoria, walking along the inside balcony. "We can fit it up better over time." The room is white, like her private study, and almost empty save for an old couch and a side table that was too tarnished for elsewhere, but Victoria looks thrilled. Amara leads them to one of the much smaller rooms next door, not much bigger than the cell at the end where Martha sleeps. She smiles at Britannica, feeling a little embarrassed by the obvious difference. "And maybe this for you?" Britannica nods.

"And what about the garden!" Victoria exclaims. "I can't believe you have a fountain!" She rushes down the stairs before Amara can warn her about the painting. By the time Amara has caught up with her, Victoria is already standing, frozen, beneath the giant figure of Dido. She turns to Amara, eyes wide with shock. "What have you done?"

"Remembered her."

"But Dido never looked like *this*!" Victoria gestures at the wall, and its gruesome carnival of death. "She was gentle and kind. This is horrible! Dido never hated anyone, still less wished them harm!"

"How do you know what her shade would wish?" Amara says. "Does Dido have no right to vengeance?"

"But Balbus is dead!" Victoria says, speaking of the murderer who meant to kill Felix, and hit Dido instead. She points at the stag. "So who is that?"

"You know who it is," Amara replies. The two women stare at one another, until Victoria quails in the face of Amara's coldness. She heads back into the atrium, towards Amara's dressing room, shoulders hunched with distress.

Britannica catches Amara's arm, preventing her from going after Victoria. "Leave her." Felix's two remaining women stand side by side in the garden, looking up at their former companion. Amara remembers how Britannica held Dido in her arms while she died, how she risked her own life trying to save her. Britannica is looking at the painting with an expression of grim satisfaction, and Amara senses that here, at least, is one person who truly understands what she has done. Then Britannica turns to her. "What is *afterthought?*"

Amara opens her mouth to explain the meaning, before realizing that Britannica already knows.

7

The three women have dinner in Amara's private room. It does not take much to win Victoria round after the shock of the painting; she is too happy at being free. Britannica, on the other hand, seems to grow warier the more Victoria relaxes. Amara can sense the Briton's increasing withdrawal. She leaves soon after eating and heads to her small cell where Amara knows Martha has laid out a straw pallet and a new tunic.

Victoria dismisses Amara's unease. "Oh, don't be ridiculous." She sighs, leaning back on the couch beside her. "She's lucky to be here! Why on earth did you buy her anyway?"

"Felix wasn't going to give me Beronice. I thought I might be able to persuade him to part with Britannica instead."

"But what will you *do* with her," Victoria persists. "I can't imagine she's very musical. Unless it's to bellow out a soldier's marching song."

"I trust her," Amara says. "She's here for my protection.

And yours. I used to watch her in the brothel; she knows how to fight. I'd like to learn how to protect myself."

"You've got *men* for all that though," Victoria grumbles. "It would almost be kinder to sell her on. And you'd make back some of the money."

Amara sits up abruptly, jolting Victoria from where she was leaning against her shoulder. "Don't ever say that again!" She is prepared for a row – she and Victoria clashed often enough in the brothel – but instead, Victoria just rolls her eyes.

"Fine," Victoria replies. "You're the boss now."

"I didn't mean it that way," Amara says, not liking the feeling of outranking her friend. "I'm asking you not to say it, because it upsets me. Not ordering you."

"Sorry," Victoria says, reaching out to embrace her. "I didn't mean to be a bitch." They hold one another, and when they pull apart, Amara can see tears on Victoria's face. "I'm so happy and grateful," she says. "I can't *tell* you how grateful I am for what you've done. I can never repay the debt."

"It's already paid," Amara says. "A thousand times over." They look at one another. It is the unspoken secret they will always share – the man Victoria killed to save Amara's life. Neither of them know the man's name, only that he was sent by Felix's rival Simo to avenge the attack Felix had ordered on Drauca, Simo's most valuable whore.

"Let's never speak of it," Victoria whispers, and Amara squeezes her hand. Victoria sighs, still close to tears. "I cannot believe I'm free. It's all so overwhelming."

"I understand. I've felt like that too, sometimes. In fact, every day since I left the brothel."

"You feel afraid of being free?"

"A lot of the time, yes."

Victoria wipes her eyes. "Maybe I'll feel better when the men arrive," she says, her tone brighter, and Amara knows she is trying to lighten the mood, the way she always does. "At least I know I'm good at that."

"You can't have Rufus," Amara teases, not really worried that Victoria will ever be her lover's type. "But I'm hoping you can entertain Helvius, the candidate he wants to work with. Charm him with your singing. Though you'll have to tone down the chat a bit. Apparently, he's very pompous."

"Oh, I can do pompous!" Victoria exclaims. "And you're wrong about toning it down. *All* men want to be told how wonderful they are. I'll just have to praise his marvellous skill with something other than his cock. At least over dinner." They both laugh. Amara reaches for the wine, topping up their glasses. Victoria sips it, her expression more serious. "*Almost* all men are like that," she says. The two women stare at one another. Amara knows which man Victoria is thinking about.

"I'm sorry for all he did to you," Amara says. "But now he can *never* hurt you again."

"The look in his eyes when I refused him today. I thought he was going to kill me." Victoria is trembling, and Amara takes her in her arms again, holding her tightly. "He's been so frightening since you left, you have no idea."

Hatred burns in Amara's chest. "I wish I could kill him for you."

"I wouldn't want that. It's so hard to explain, but I don't think he can help himself. And his life... The things he has suffered."

"It doesn't excuse anything." Amara is unwilling to admit all she knows about Felix's childhood, not wanting to feel any sympathy for him. "Whatever he might have suffered, he doesn't have to torment everyone else for it."

"He used to beg my forgiveness, afterwards, and tell me how much he loved me. And I used to believe him. But the last time he hurt me, he told me it was my fault. That only an idiot would put up with what he did to me. That I was pathetic for loving him."

"But you didn't put up with it. You left him. And I'm so proud of you for that." Amara disentangles herself from their embrace, taking Victoria's face in her hands. "I know it hurt you to leave him. But he is a monster. He never, *ever* deserved you. I hope he pays a thousand times over for everything he did to you. I hope he dies in the street like a dog."

Victoria flinches at the violence in Amara's words. "I know I have to forget him. I know I do. But I still can't bear to think of him suffering. So please don't say things like that."

Amara is about to object, but then she sees the anguish in Victoria's face and thinks of the courage it must have taken to leave Felix behind. "Of course," she says, kissing her on the forehead. "I'm sorry. I'm only glad you are safe now."

They stay up a little later, plotting the songs Victoria might sing to charm Rufus when she first meets him, the more modest gestures she will need to learn, but Amara can see that Victoria is exhausted. She insists on sending her to bed, escorting her across the atrium. Amara watches from the foot of the stairs as the flame from Victoria's oil lamp climbs upwards, illuminating the hall, chasing over the rafters, before the light disappears, along with her friend, behind the darkness of the closed door. She hopes the room will not be too cold. She had asked Martha to add some extra blankets.

Amara stands alone in the centre of her house. She looks up at the dark ceiling. It is a clear night. In the square of deeper black which marks the opening to the sky, she can see the stars shining. Outside, the streets are almost silent. The loudest sound now is the murmur of the fountain. Amara wraps her cloak around her shoulders and heads into the garden. The patter of the water guides her. She watches the spray fall, gleaming as it catches the moonlight, before sending ripples of silver across the black pool beneath. Amara stoops down and dips her fingers in the water, then takes them back with a splash, shocked by the cold.

From the corner of her eye, she senses movement. Terror is followed almost as swiftly by relief. Even in the dark, she knows his shape.

"Philos?"

He is instantly still. "I did not mean to disturb you." She cannot see him clearly, only hear his voice from the shadows.

"There's no point hiding in a corner," she says. "This is ridiculous."

He walks towards the fountain. His face is lit by the moon's reflection on the water and Amara knows then, looking at him, what she has always known but chosen not to see. He is a more attractive man than Rufus. She takes a step back. "I'm sorry about earlier," she says, flustered. "I promise I didn't lie to you about Britannica. I really didn't plan it."

Perhaps because it is night, or because her chaotic actions have upended the usual hierarchies, Philos does not simply make his excuses and leave. Instead, he looks at her, the way she might look at Victoria, as an equal. "I realize that," he says. "I was angry earlier. I'm still angry, but not with you."

"With who then?"

"With myself. For letting you do it."

"Don't patronize me," Amara says. "I'm not a child, to be saved from sticking my hand in the fire. I know what I'm doing."

"You have no idea."

"You're worried Rufus will be angry? I think you're wrong, I think—"

"I think you have no idea who Rufus is," Philos replies. "And for some reason, you have blinded yourself to what it means to owe Felix this much money." Amara says nothing, but she can feel fear seep into her skin, damp like the chill night air. "I don't blame you for choosing to forget your old life," Philos says. "But I haven't forgotten it. It was *me* who had to go to the brothel and collect you every week, only to take you back again. Leaving you in that place was agony, Amara. Rufus left you there for months." He stops. Again, the only sound she can hear is the splash of the fountain, but this time, it does not soothe her. She cannot speak. "Rufus could have bought you at any point," Philos continues, "and he chose to wait until the Saturnalia, because it was more enjoyable for him. *All that time*, Amara. All that time, he left you with Felix who he knew was violent. When he was supposedly in love with you. You would be a fool to feel complacent about your influence over a man like that."

"But this house! All the money he's spent moving me in

here. The harp lessons, the clothes. Setting me free! That's not *nothing*."

"No, it's not, I agree. It's more than I've known Rufus give any woman, and perhaps that means he will keep you for years. But in the past, his infatuations have been short-lived. At some point, all this may stop. You don't want to be in debt if that happens."

Amara's eyes have adjusted to the dark, and she can see the outline of the bench. She walks over to it and sits down. "I have to find some way to pay Felix back," she says. "And I can't ask Rufus."

Philos sits beside her, leaving a less obvious gap than usual. "Would Victoria sing at parties for you? The way you and Dido once did? That could earn you a fair amount."

"But it's not enough to send one woman on her own. Victoria needs an accompanist. And *I* can't do it – Rufus would never agree."

"Might Drusilla put up the money for a flautist?"

"I will ask her. But I don't know what she'll say when she realizes I've already bought a singer. Especially an old friend of mine. That's not what we discussed." Amara turns towards Philos. He is much shorter than Rufus, and their eyes are almost level. "You're right, this wasn't a clever thing to do, but I've done it, and now I have to make it work. I know you say I can't rely on Rufus, but it's Felix who worries me more. I have to pay him back. I *have* to." For a moment, she thinks Philos is going to put his arm round her, but instead, he shifts further away.

"You've outsmarted him before, and you will again," he says. "And of course, I will help you if I can." Amara does not reply. Instead, they sit together in silence. The space between them feels like a third, physical presence; she is acutely aware of how easy it would be to bridge it. She remembers the way Philos brushed her arm with his fingertips outside The Sparrow. A gesture so slight, it was almost imperceptible. She clasps her hands together, confused by the sudden, overwhelming impulse she feels to reach out and touch him. Philos gets to his feet. "Please forgive me if I said too much this evening. I hope I didn't upset you."

"You didn't upset me," Amara lies. "Goodnight."

His tread is so light she loses all sense of him almost as soon as he has walked away from the bench. She waits a moment longer in the garden. Her mind spins with images of Victoria laughing, Felix waiting in his study, Rufus turning his face away from her, cold, like the night Dido died. And the words Philos let slip, perhaps without realizing the implication. *Leaving you in that place was agony.*

8

In the estate of Julia Felix, daughter of Spurius
To Let
Elegant Venus Baths for respectable people, shops with upper
rooms, and apartments

Notice in Pompeii, on the praedia of Julia Felix

The harp arrives early the next morning. It is delivered along with a message for Amara inside Rufus's familiar wax booklet, its wooden case engraved with the figure of a swan. Amara reads the note at the door, before inscribing her reply and handing it back to his waiting slave. It is Vitalio who she knows never liked her much.

"He sends you gifts!" Victoria exclaims, hurrying after Amara as she carries the gilded instrument to her rooms. "Gifts for nothing! Just because he loves you?"

Amara is a little flustered. "It's not for nothing. He's inviting Helvius for dinner tomorrow night. He wants me to perform for them both."

"I can sing for you!" Victoria says, almost tripping Amara up in her eagerness to get close to her. "I can sing anything you like! Teach me anything!" Victoria has, in fact, been

81

singing for much of the morning, her sweet voice ringing out through every room in the house. Amara has never seen her look more beautiful. Victoria's body almost shimmers in her excitement at being free, like a flame dancing from a lamp full of oil. Even Philos was enchanted earlier, watching her in the garden. He looked foolish, gawping away, as if Victoria were performing for *him*. In contrast, he barely met Amara's eye. Their late-night conversation might never have happened.

"I need to invite Drusilla," Amara says. "Rufus will be expecting her to attend. I'm hoping we can all three perform together."

"Oh, I can't *wait* to meet her!" Victoria cries. "Shall we go now?"

Amara feels a pang, looking at Victoria's eager face. "I think I had better go alone," she says gently. "Just to tell her what's happened. Drusilla is much… grander than me. Then, when I've explained, I will bring her round to meet you."

"Of course," Victoria replies, still smiling, though Amara knows her well enough to understand she is disappointed. "She's your friend. Better you go on your own."

Amara climbs the steps to the Venus Baths' brightly painted portico, hoping Drusilla is not surrounded by too large a crowd. Julia, the owner, alternates the days the baths are open to the public between women and men. Drusilla is always here on a Wednesday, the regularity of her visits giving other courtesans a chance to pay their respects.

A slave girl greets Amara at the door, and Amara slips the entry fee into the girl's purse with practised discretion. Julia runs her baths for profit while maintaining the air that the service is only for friends. Amara steps into the small, square courtyard. The sense of privacy here is so different from the baths she used to visit near the brothel. There you had to queue out on the street, standing on display for any passing fool to catcall. Here, customers wait and drink wine together, sitting on benches shaded by a colonnade, a series of mythical landscapes painted above them on red panelled walls.

She spots Drusilla almost instantly, sitting in her usual spot underneath a scene of Theseus arriving in Crete, the hero's harbour looking suspiciously like modern Pompeii. Julia is with Drusilla, which Amara does not mind, but she is less pleased to see Fulvia there too. A waspish girl with a middling patron, Fulvia has been Drusilla's friend for far longer than Amara, but Fulvia's lover is no match for Rufus, and so, Amara has supplanted her in the courtesan hierarchy. Unsurprisingly, Fulvia is not delighted by this change in status. Amara watches her now, false blonde hair framing her face in a generous plait, no doubt sheared straight from a foreign slave girl's head. She is leaning towards Drusilla with an obsequious air, almost spilling her glass of wine on the bench.

"Amara!" Julia gestures at her to join them, fingers glinting with gold. "How lovely of you to come."

She smiles. Julia might put on a show for clients, but Amara has always sensed a seam of genuine kindness running through her professional patter. "Look at you three beauties!" Julia sighs, as Amara sits down beside her. "Oh, to be young again!" Julia cannot be much more than forty, and her handsome face is barely lined, but she knows how to lay on the flattery. "And how is *your* fine young man?"

"He sent me a harp this morning," Amara replies.

Drusilla gives a cry of triumph. "Perfect!" she declares. "I knew he would."

Fulvia's cheeks dimple as she smiles. "But I thought you couldn't play?"

"I'm learning."

"Young love," Julia says. "I'm sure *every* performance you give enchants Rufus, my darling, whatever the instrument. How could it not?" Amara catches the innuendo, the flash of mischief in Julia's eyes, and raises her eyebrows. It is almost a moment of intimacy, but then Julia's attention is caught by the arrival of other customers, spied over Amara's shoulder. "Oh, there's Sabina!" she exclaims, getting up from the bench. "Excuse me ladies, just for a moment."

Amara watches Julia greet Sabina, a respectable matron, and sees her manner change to suit the customer. She feels a sense of admiration, even envy, at the control Julia seems to exert over her life, shaping events by sheer force of will.

"Shall we go through to the baths?" Drusilla says, rising gracefully from the bench. "Unless you want a glass of wine first?" Amara knows Drusilla is only asking out of politeness and stands up, shaking her head. "Guess who called on me unexpectedly last night?" Drusilla murmurs, as the three of them walk through to the changing room.

"Quintus?" Fulvia asks.

Drusilla gives her a pitying look. "Lucius," she replies.

Amara pretends to be pleased, although she has never forgiven Lucius for failing to act as Dido's patron. "Will Quintus be *very* jealous?"

"He won't find out," Drusilla says, slipping off the outer layer of her clothes, and folding them carefully into a wooden locker. "Although perhaps a little *hint* isn't a bad idea, just to keep him keen. I had forgotten how very attentive Lucius can be." She smiles to herself, remembering the night before. "It's always better not to get too caught up in just *one* man. They grow too smug. Although I realize that's more difficult for both of you."

Fulvia and Amara, unlike Drusilla, own nothing other than what their patrons care to give them.

The three courtesans strip off. Another group of women have just finished bathing, leaving the small plunge pool empty by the window. Amara and Fulvia wait while Drusilla steps first into the freezing water. The pool is in an alcove overlooking Julia's enormous garden. Amara gazes out at the view. Leaves are just starting to bud on the fruit trees. In the summer, this place must be a haven from the hot, dusty city. Drusilla splashes herself in the pool, wincing at the cold, then steps briskly out. Fulvia goes next, jumping in before Amara has a chance.

By the time it is Amara's turn, she is already shivering before she slides into the water. "You're getting very thin," Drusilla says, laying a palm gently against Amara's ribs. The touch makes Amara flinch. Her skin is blue, reflecting the colour of the alcove walls. A shell mosaic of Venus sways through the ripples on the water. "Surely Rufus cannot like to see you like this."

Fulvia misses the concern in Drusilla's voice. "My mother always told me a well-born girl should be curved like Venus," she says, seizing the chance to put a rival down. "It's what men expect." She purses her lips, looking over Amara's body with satisfaction. "*Slaves* are thin."

Amara thinks of Philos sitting in the garden, holding his

arms to ward off the cold. *I am even thinner than he is,* she realizes. The memory of him from last night brings with it a rush of unexpected shame. Amara finds she cannot grasp the sharp retort that would usually come to her so readily.

"Your mother was clearly an even greater fool than you are," Drusilla says to Fulvia, her voice cold. "If such a thing is possible." Fulvia's mouth opens in surprise. She had perhaps forgotten that both Amara *and* Drusilla were once enslaved. Drusilla flicks her fingers in a sign of dismissal. "Leave us."

For a moment, Amara almost feels sorry for Fulvia standing naked in nothing but her borrowed hair, but then she is gone, flouncing back to the lockers, and Amara's shoulders sag with the relief of finally having Drusilla to herself.

"So what is it?" Drusilla asks, helping her out of the pool. "Why aren't you eating properly?"

"Rufus told me I was getting fat." She is conscious of the water sliding off her body, puddling onto the floor.

Drusilla touches the gold serpent curled around her upper arm, a gift from her late master, Veranius. Amara knows he left it to Drusilla in his will, along with her freedom. Drusilla murmurs her former lover's name, almost as if Amara were not there.

"Did Veranius like you slim too?" Amara asks. Drusilla stares, an unfamiliar darkness in her eyes. Amara thinks of her own unhappy past as an enslaved concubine in Greece, after her father died, and guesses the reason for her friend's silence. "I'm sorry," she says. "I should not have asked."

Drusilla does not reply. Instead, she leads Amara towards the warm room, as if she had not spoken. They strap on wooden shoes, left at the doorway to protect guests' feet from the hot floor, then walk through the arch to be embraced by tendrils of steam. The wall feels warm against Amara's back as they sit on a stone bench. Other bathers are similarly dotted about the room, and there is the murmur of women's voices, the hiss of water as it drips onto the burning tiles.

"Fulvia is a fool," Drusilla says, at last. "But what she says is true. Only a slave should be as thin as you are." Her gaze, when she turns to Amara, is sharp. "Are you absolutely certain Rufus wants you that way?"

Amara knows there is no sentimentality to Drusilla's view of men. Patrons are there to serve their purpose, to be indulged and, if possible, manipulated. "Yes," she replies. "I think it's what you once said to me. Rufus likes his women fragile." In spite of herself, Amara feels embarrassed, as if she somehow brought her lover's demands upon herself.

Drusilla strokes her hand. "Then there is no reason to be ashamed," she says. "You are wise enough to recognize his wishes and fulfil them. And next year, perhaps he will be aedile! A patron like that is worth the price of a few meals." She laces her fingers through Amara's. "Besides, understanding that he likes you to *appear* fragile does not mean you actually *are*."

"He has asked Helvius to dinner on Friday," Amara says. "He wants me to invite you and Quintus. For both of us to perform for him on the harp."

"But that's wonderful!" Drusilla says. "I'd be delighted. And Quintus will *love* to laugh at Helvius behind his back – he's always telling me how ridiculous the man is."

Drusilla's fingers are tight between hers. Amara knows

there will never be a better time to share difficult news. "I already bought a musician to accompany us," she says, trying to sound casual. "A singer."

"I thought we agreed on flautists," Drusilla says, surprised.

"You don't need to share the cost of this one," Amara says quickly. "In fact, she's..." Her voice trails off.

"She's what?"

"She's a former friend."

Drusilla withdraws her hand. "From the brothel?" Amara nods, and it is as if a veil has been drawn between them. "The coarse Italian girl or the foolish Egyptian?"

Amara wishes Drusilla did not have such a good memory and curses herself for gossiping about her friends. Surely, she never described Victoria and Beronice in such unkind terms? "The Italian," she replies.

Drusilla rests the back of her head against the wall and lets out a sigh. "I was worried you would do something like this." She closes her eyes, as if overcome by weariness. "I should have warned you."

"Warned me about what?" Amara asks, wondering if there are yet more unwelcome sides to Rufus.

"That it fades. The desire to free those from your past. It fades." Drusilla turns towards Amara again, a sheen of sweat on her face. "When Veranius died, all I could think about was how to buy Procris."

"But then you decided not to?"

"No, I tried many times. Veranius's widow would never sell her to me." Drusilla looks uncomfortable. She almost never speaks about Procris, the fellow slave who mothered her after Drusilla was brought to Pompeii from Ethiopia as a child, and who Drusilla later replaced in their master's affections. Amara knows that Procris once wore the golden serpent on *her* arm before Veranius took the charm and gave it to Drusilla, to show that he had chosen a new favourite concubine. "I cried for Procris every night for weeks," Drusilla says. "But now, sometimes, I am almost relieved. The life you share as slaves... it's different. You may find Victoria will not like to have you as a patron."

"I'm also her friend," Amara replies, stung.

"Yet you did not bring her here today. Why is that?" Drusilla nods when Amara does not answer. "Because you know she is not your equal. How can she be, when you bought her?"

"I insisted on her freedom. She's not my slave."

"Amara," Drusilla says. "Don't be an idiot. The only way you can keep her is as a musician to entertain *your* lover. What role does she have other than serving him, and through him, you?" Amara says nothing. Drusilla sighs again. "Well, I hope she *can* sing beautifully. She will certainly need to." They lapse back into silence. Amara knows now is not the time to ask for money to help buy the flautists, still less the moment to share her plan to rent Victoria out at parties, but she is encouraged that at least Drusilla is not angry. She even seems to sympathize. The hiss of dripping water, the ebb and flow of voices and gentle slap of wooden shoes on stone is so soothing – Amara soon starts to feel lulled back into a sense of intimacy.

"Thank you for understanding," she says, reaching over to squeeze Drusilla's hand.

Drusilla does not return the pressure of her fingers. "I forgive you this time," she says, her eyes still closed and her head tilted back, resting against the wall. "But not if you forget yourself again. The gods raised you to freedom. Treating slaves as equals only lowers you back to the gutter you came from."

9

She was welcomed by the kisses of the whores,
taught to wheedle, shown how to make all kinds
of movement with her body.
Seneca, Declamations 1.2

Amara stands in the doorway, watching Martha dress the dining room. It is hours until the men will arrive, but already, her nerves are stretched tighter than the strings of the harp she dreads playing. Martha is arranging armfuls of spring flowers, letting the blooms spill artfully from various vases. The air is heavy with their scent. Amara sent Britannica out at first light to buy all the stems she could carry. If Martha's frustrated efforts at fluffing them out are anything to go by, it seems several got crushed on the journey home. Amara knows Martha hates to be watched while she works, sees it in the irritated slope of the slave girl's shoulders, but she is so nervous she cannot help herself.

"Oh, leave her to get on with it!" Victoria exclaims, poking her head in. "Stop standing there like a twitchy old matron. We need to get ready. Drusilla will be here to practise soon."

Victoria is far more excited about the approaching evening than Amara, even though Amara felt obliged to warn her that Drusilla might not be entirely friendly. "She's not going to be my lover, is she?" Victoria had remarked. "So what does it matter?"

In Amara's private rooms, they help one another dress. Victoria is wearing a spare outfit of Assyrian silk, the soft lines of her body laid bare by its translucent folds. "I remember you and Dido wearing this," Victoria says, as she pins the dress at Amara's shoulder, helping the fabric fall in a generous fold to accentuate Amara's less obvious curves. "I always wondered what it was like."

Amara feels a tightness to her chest at the mention of their dead friend. "And how do you find it?"

Victoria laughs. "I'll tell you later, if Helvius likes it."

Upstairs they have prepared Victoria's bedroom, ready for her to entertain Helvius should he be persuaded to stay. There are yet more flowers to hide the lack of furniture and Amara has had Philos and Juventus carry up an expensive brass table from the tablinum, one she hopes Rufus will not miss. She has still not told her lover about Victoria or Britannica, gambling that she might better win him over by a successful evening than by sending a pleading note in advance.

"He's going to love everything," Victoria says, understanding her friend's silence. She cups Amara's face in her hands, so that their eyes meet. "You worry too much. How could he do anything but love you?"

Amara takes Victoria's hand in hers and kisses the palm. A shadow blots out the light from the doorway, and she turns round, thinking it is Philos. Instead, it is Britannica.

The Briton has slicked back her hair like a man – perhaps borrowing the oil, if not the style, from Juventus – and is dressed in a smartly fitted short tunic. They have decided Britannica should be the one to wait at the table – a titillating novelty that Amara has provided for Rufus by introducing an all-female ensemble to entertain him. Or that's how she intends to sell it. So far, Amara has struggled to persuade Britannica to lay the dishes gently on the table rather than thud them down like a challenge.

"Drusilla," Britannica announces, mangling the sibilant name with her harsh accent. "She is here."

Pompeii's foremost courtesan is standing in the atrium of Amara's home, dressed in a cascade of red and yellow silk. Her servant Thalia is beside her, carrying the harp she will play. "Shall we practise?" Drusilla asks, stretching out her arms to embrace Amara. She gives Victoria the barest nod, almost as if she were a second maid.

They sit together in the garden, Victoria placed a little at the edge of the gathering. But if Drusilla intends to snub Victoria by this arrangement, it only makes her voluptuous figure more eye-catching, especially when she starts to sway to the music. The only one to disgrace herself is Amara. The song is a hymn to Sappho that she has practised with Drusilla many times before, but this afternoon, her fingers seem to have been numbed by nerves, and she stumbles over the notes. After struggling on for an hour, Drusilla holds up her hand to call a halt. "You are not ready," she says.

"I practised all yesterday afternoon," Amara protests.

"It's not good enough. Better if you use the lyre tonight. You are a master of that instrument. Any man would be delighted to hear you play."

"But Rufus bought me the harp specially," Amara says, clutching it. "He sent it to me to play this evening! He will be so disappointed."

"He will be more disappointed if you show him up with a bad performance," Drusilla replies.

"What's all this fuss with the harp, anyway?" Victoria asks, hands on hips like a street seller. "She plays the lyre. Why does he even care? Men are such fucking idiots."

Drusilla stares into the middle distance as if Victoria has not spoken, but Amara sees her mouth tighten with displeasure. "The lyre please," she says again. "I cannot perform with you unless you agree to use it."

"Of course." Amara stands up. She avoids Victoria's eye as she hurries to her rooms to switch over the instruments. The lyre fits into her arms like a part of herself as she lifts it from the floor, the curve of it familiar against her hip. She isn't sure which emotion is stronger when she carries it back to the garden, fear or relief.

In the lamplight the dining room looks like a scene from the ancient myths, flames burnishing the skin of Jupiter's painted lovers, the flowers lending an air of modesty to their nakedness. The small space is filled with men's laughter. The real women are draped over the three couches, echoing the languid postures of the painted ones, and although she does not like to eat too freely in front of Rufus, wine is taking the edge off Amara's nerves.

Victoria is managing to vary her seduction routine, blunting its coarser edges and luring Helvius in with admiring glances rather than words. It is not only Helvius who is captivated by the fishing-net she's casting. Quintus is staring at Victoria with an intensity that tells Amara it is only a matter of time before he insists on enjoying her himself. Drusilla lies beside her disloyal lover, toying with the slender stem of her glass. She does not seem overly perturbed by his roving eye. But then Amara knows they have an unconventional love affair, that Drusilla has even been known to supply Quintus with other girls as a means of keeping his interest alive.

The only prickling of anxiety Amara feels is for Rufus. He is clearly pleased at impressing his friends, but she senses something about the evening is causing him disquiet. She notices it most acutely whenever Britannica appears; feels him tense up beside her on the couch. Perhaps it's nothing more than the startling way the Briton slams down the plates, but Amara starts to worry that perhaps Philos was right, that buying Britannica as well as Victoria was a step too far.

Quintus, on the other hand, finds the Briton highly amusing, smacking her on the backside whenever she leans over to set out the food. Eventually, Britannica whips round. For a terrible moment, Amara thinks she is going to throw a punch, but instead, Britannica bares her teeth and hisses. There is a shocked silence, before Quintus collapses with laughter.

"Rufus, it's too priceless!" Quintus declares, after Britannica has stalked from the room. "Look at you, keeping a house full of Amazons! A little empire of women. Or maybe nymphs," he adds, his gaze sliding towards Victoria's cleavage as he reaches for his wine. Victoria pouts and lowers her eyes, a coy gesture that jolts Amara back to the brothel. She remembers how her friend used to pick men up like that on the street, or in bars, or wherever else she could catch a punter's eye.

"An empire of women?" Helvius says, frowning. "That is *exactly* the sort of unnatural behaviour which makes the Taurian Games so necessary." He looks sternly at Amara. "What possessed you to dress that poor serving girl as a man?"

"She's not dressed as a man," Amara lies. "She's a savage from Britain. That's just what they all wear out there. They don't feel the cold."

"Barely better than animals," Drusilla agrees, effortlessly joining in. "You've done well to tame her."

Helvius does not seem entirely convinced. He looks round at the three courtesans, frowning at them as if they were wayward children. "Just because it's fitting for a savage, doesn't mean such behaviour should be encouraged here among *civilized* people. Still." He sniffs, nodding at Rufus. "Clearly, no harm was meant. And over-leniency with slaves is a natural, feminine trait. But women interfering in the running of the town, bribing men to get their way, that's something else. It's nothing less than an assault on the natural order."

"Do women really *do* such things?" Victoria asks. "Surely not!"

Victoria is gazing at Helvius with almost bovine adoration, reminding Amara of the painting of Io by the door. Everything about her looks soft and yielding, her body promising Helvius *she* would never be anything but the natural woman he requires. He flushes, laying a hand reassuringly on Victoria's wrist. "Not women like you, of course," he says. "Not women in their natural state."

Amara glances over at Drusilla. For the first time since she introduced her two friends, Drusilla is contemplating Victoria with something approaching respect, her eyebrows raised in two perfect crescents of surprise. *Maybe this is going to work,* Amara thinks.

"You can't still be sore about Julia Felix," Quintus snorts. "That was over five years ago! Let it rest now."

Amara is startled to hear the name of the owner of the Venus Baths. "What did Julia do?"

Rufus turns to her, perhaps wanting to forestall Amara from defending her friend. "A while back, Julia persuaded the council to close a public road to enlarge her apartment complex. Such a thing has never been done in Pompeii before. Many people were upset."

"She's not even married!" Helvius says. "Polluting her father's name. Disgraceful."

Quintus rolls his eyes at Drusilla whose mouth twitches with amusement. Amara has no idea who Julia's father is, but she knows now is not the time to ask.

"Pliny is fond of Julia," Rufus says mildly.

"The admiral is a well-known eccentric," Helvius replies. "He consorts with all types of people." Helvius seems annoyed at being contradicted. His face is shining from the wine, and it makes his eyes look more protuberant, like a hare. "If he cannot see the calamity such immoral behaviour risks in bringing down the vengeance of the gods, perhaps it is because he did not have to endure the Great Earthquake."

"You think we are in danger of another calamity?" Victoria gasps, pressing her body against Helvius, as if his bulk will protect her from the rage of the gods. The move looks completely spontaneous, but Amara knows Victoria will have been calculating it all night.

Helvius is caught off guard. He draws Victoria even closer towards himself, evidently seeing no hypocrisy in the prospect of enjoying a prostitute, even as he rails against the depravity of women. He caresses Victoria's waist with thick fingers. "Not if we propitiate the gods as we should," he says.

Quintus sighs heavily, perhaps irritated Helvius is getting to enjoy the newest woman at the party. "I thought you promised music?" he complains to Drusilla.

Rufus turns to Amara eagerly. "That's the moment I've been waiting for too, my love," he says, raising her hand to his lips and kissing it. "Why don't you lead the way?"

Amara wants to tell Rufus then, to warn him about the harp, but instead, she smiles with feigned delight. "Of course."

Afterwards, when they are alone together in her rooms, Rufus is uncharacteristically quiet. He sits on the couch, not looking at her, holding the unused harp on his lap. Amara knows she has seldom played better than she did that night. Philos had hung lamps from the two trees and trailed them around the fountain, and in the starlight, with the evening scent of narcissi, the garden had looked to Amara like a constellation borrowed from the heavens. Victoria had thrown her whole heart into the singing, while Amara and Drusilla played in harmony with one another in a faultless performance that almost brought tears to Amara's eyes. When they had finished, to delighted applause from the men, she had sought out Rufus, hoping to see his approval. He was smiling along with his friends, accepting their congratulations, but for the first time since the start of their affair, she had been unable to read the expression in his eyes.

"Helvius liked Victoria," she says pleasantly, sitting beside him, hoping to overcome his bad mood by ignoring it. "He's *still* enjoying her, hopefully," she adds, alluding to Helvius's decision to retire upstairs.

"Why did you humiliate me?"

Amara's mouth feels dry. "Humiliate you?" She pretends to laugh. "How difficult you men are! I did everything possible to please you!"

"Don't mock me, Amara," Rufus says.

"I don't understand, I—"

"The harp. The gaggle of women you decided to buy without telling me. That… creature you had serve us rather than the steward I left for you to use. What were you *thinking?*"

"I just wanted to make the evening special!"

"Don't lie to me!" Rufus says, raising his voice. "You never used to lie to me. What's happened to you?"

"How dare you!" Amara exclaims. "How *dare* you call me a liar." A display of anger has always tamed Rufus before, and she is about to flounce off to the bedroom, expecting him to follow, pleading apologies, but instead, he catches her by the wrist.

"You forget yourself." His voice is quiet, and she is about to argue, but something in his face stops her.

Instead of pulling her arm away, Amara presses herself against him, her expression beseeching. Rufus has never been able to resist an appeal to romantic drama. "Please," she begs. "Please, my love. I didn't want to upset you. I had to free Victoria; she would have died in the brothel, Britannica too. I had to save them, I really *had* to. And Victoria is such a talented musician! I thought you would enjoy her singing. I meant nothing bad by it. I promise you."

To her shock, Rufus is completely unmoved. "All this disorder you've brought to the house," he says, his voice hard. "It's like you're determined to drag the brothel back here with you."

Amara gazes up at him, this man whose love underpins the foundations of her life, and feels afraid. He looks like a stranger. In desperation she seizes his hand, holding it against her heart, wanting to bring back the man she knows. "How can you say that! How can you think it of me! Rufus, *please*."

"What were you *doing* going back to the brothel? Why couldn't you leave it alone?" He snatches his hand back like a petulant child. "I hate to think of you there, cheapening yourself. And getting Philos to help." Rufus disentangles himself from another attempted embrace, an impatient gesture that reminds her of his father. "Thanks to *you*, I'll have to have him flogged. And I absolutely loathe disciplining the slaves. But if I don't, they lose all respect. You've humiliated me in my own household."

The blood pounding in Amara's ears is like the roar of the sea. In her mind's eye she can see Philos, imagines the blows falling on his shoulders, flaying the clothes from his back, or worse, the skin. All because of her. "But it wasn't his fault!" she bursts out, unable to contain the anguish. "It wasn't his fault. I tricked him."

"What do you mean?"

"I told him that I had your permission to buy them," she falters, wringing her hands, unable to meet the disgust in Rufus's eyes. "Philos had no idea you didn't know. That's why he helped me. I told him it was on your orders."

"You mean you lied," Rufus says, taking her chin between his finger and thumb, making her look up at him. "You're a liar. You lied."

"I lied," Amara repeats, unable now to contradict him.

Rufus releases her. "I thought I'd never met a girl like you," he says, scooping the harp back into his arms and cradling it. "I couldn't *believe* how lucky I was. Even though I *knew* where you'd come from, I told myself it didn't matter. You were so sweet. So fearful and innocent. Just as you must have been in your father's house. The doctor's daughter. It was like the brothel never touched you."

"I'm not any different now!" Amara protests, unnerved by where the conversation is leading, by her lover's use of the past tense.

"But you're tainted by it," Rufus says. "It's *tainted* you. All the lies you learned there, all the wheedling, all the tricks." He sets down the harp. "Come here."

It's something in the way he places the instrument so carefully on the floor. Amara has experienced too much violence not to see how it sits in the tension of his shoulders, the slow deliberation of his movements. For a wild moment, she imagines disobeying him, pictures herself escaping, tearing out of the house into the night. But to where? Back to Felix? She has nowhere to go. She tells herself she is imagining things, reassures herself that this is *Rufus*. He would never hurt her; it's impossible. She forces herself to walk over. His fingers are careful as he takes the pin from her shoulder, removing the silk, undressing her. But even though his hands are gentle, her sense of physical danger is now so great she can hardly breathe. He turns her around, so she is facing away from him.

"You almost never let me have you like this," Rufus says softly. "Do you know that's how a man is meant to lie with his wife? Not all those brothel tricks you learned." Rufus's hand is resting on her neck. He is not applying any pressure, his touch is still gentle, but when she tries to turn around to face him, he holds her more tightly.

"Please," Amara says, putting her hand over his, trying to loosen his fingers, to appeal to the kindness she is so certain he possesses. "I don't like it."

"Why not?" Rufus asks.

Amara wants to tell him. She wants to explain that if she cannot see his face, if he is behind her, he will become Felix; he will become any of the men from the brothel, the past and the present will slide into each other, and the panic will blind her. But she knows that if she tells Rufus this, all he will hear is how many men she has slept with. All he will hear is that when she lies with him, she thinks of other lovers. Amara looks at the frieze of musical nymphs painted on the wall, and their figures blur into one another as her eyes fill with tears. "I just don't like it," she says. "Isn't that enough?"

Rufus does not release his grip. He kisses her lightly on the shoulder. "I'm just trying to help you be who you once were," he murmurs.

He does not hit her; she is not even sure whether he intends to threaten her by keeping his hand on her neck, although he never moves it. She has endured far worse violence from Felix and from men whose names and faces she does not even remember, but for Amara, the betrayal Rufus inflicts is a pain unlike any other, because she had believed he was different. He is not her safe haven, but yet another storm to weather.

Afterwards, he is tender and loving, kissing away the tears he caused, affectionate now he has succeeded in making her more like the fearful girl he wants her to be. He tells her that he will allow her to keep Victoria and Britannica if she promises never to lie again, and Amara cries with gratitude, loathing herself for feeling overwhelmed by relief. She tells Rufus that she loves him, letting him hold her, knowing that she has no alternative. When he falls asleep, she is left lying trapped in his arms, hating the touch of his skin on hers.

The next morning, everything seems to have slowed down, even the flow of water in the fountain is sluggish. Amara finds it hard to focus, still less to talk. She sits in the garden with her dearest friend who is now officially allowed to stay, while her patron rests his hand on her knee, occasionally lifting it to brush a strand of hair from her shoulder. It should be the happiest of moments, yet everything inside Amara feels numb, as if she has been hollowed out. Her two companions, on the other hand, are in great spirits. Victoria is excited about Helvius who did not stay the whole night but evidently still stayed long enough. Rufus is relaxed, sitting between the two women, behaving as if there was no argument the night before, even laughing with Victoria like an old acquaintance. Amara starts to doubt her senses, to wonder if everything really happened the way she remembers it. She can tell Rufus has succeeded in charming Victoria with his easy manners, just as he always used to charm her. Amara is not sure whether she has the energy left to hate him. After a short while, he leaves with Philos, promising Amara to return her steward to her after he has used him to carry out some business for his father.

As soon as Rufus has gone, Victoria is eager to recount the more lurid glories of her night with Helvius. Usually, Amara would want to laugh with her, to relish Victoria's outrageous storytelling, but instead, she pleads a headache.

"You don't look too well," Victoria agrees, peering at her. "I hope it's nothing serious." For a moment, Amara contemplates confiding in Victoria the way she would have done with Dido, but then she remembers how Victoria used to talk about Felix, the way she excused his violence. Amara can just imagine Victoria's reaction. "*So, he didn't slap you, or hit you, he just wanted you from behind? What do you think he pays you for!*"

"It's nothing." Amara smiles. "Too much wine, I think."

Victoria laughs and sprawls out across the bench. "Here's to too much wine!" she says. "And too much food, and too many men." She sighs in contentment, draping an arm over her face to shield her eyes, and Amara leaves her there, basking in the sun like a cat, luxuriating in her freedom to do nothing. Dido stands silent on the wall, and Amara's longing for her dead friend in that moment brings her dangerously close to resenting the one who is still alive.

Amara does not lie in bed but goes upstairs to the quiet of her study. It is too painful to imagine speaking with

Dido, so instead, she sits and thinks of Felix. His habits are still so familiar to her. She knows that at this hour her old master will be on the exercise track of the Palaestra, running as if all the hunting dogs of Diana were behind him. She wonders how Felix has survived so much violence, how he saw his mother die, yet decided to live, and wonders if she will manage to do the same, if she still has the stomach for it. Her money box rests on the table. Almost everything inside is destined for Felix. The first payment is due in days.

Hours pass, with Amara doing little other than stare at the wall, until a knock disturbs her. She calls for whoever it is to enter, expecting it to be Victoria, then realizes she must have locked the door and gets up to open it. It is Philos. She steps back to let him enter.

"You told Rufus that you lied to me," he says, looking agitated, pushing the door shut behind him. "That you tricked me into believing he had granted you permission to buy the other women."

Amara leans her back against the desk, not liking to remember her conversation with Rufus. "Yes."

"Why would you do that?" Philos exclaims, and Amara understands with a sense of surprise that he is not grateful but angry. "You made me look like some sort of idiot!"

"He was going to flog you."

"That's it?" Philos asks, throwing up his hands with exasperation. "You think I've never been beaten before? Didn't you realize that was *always* likely to happen after I helped you buy Victoria? What you've done is worse. I've spent years convincing Rufus to trust my judgment, eking out his respect, getting him to believe I have the intelligence to be left in charge of his affairs, and now you've let him think I'm the sort of fool who can be tricked by a..." He stops, flushing. The word *whore* hangs unsaid on the air.

"By a what?" Amara says quietly.

"A... courtesan," Philos replies, not meeting her eye. "I'm sorry, that's not how I think of you," he adds, looking even more embarrassed. "Really, it's not. That came out all wrong."

Somehow the apology makes it worse. Amara feels her whole body flush with shame. She remembers the way Rufus humiliated her, making her feel so small and worthless. All to protect a man who doesn't even care. Amara holds her arms around herself, as if that might dull the pain. She realizes Philos is staring, his grey eyes wide with dismay, and turns her face from him.

"Did he hurt you?"

The distress in his voice, and worse, the thought he might pity her, make Amara furious. "How dare you ask me such a question!" she shouts. "Get out!"

Instead of doing as she asks, Philos takes a step towards her. "I'm sorry, Amara. Please forgive me, I didn't realize..." She shrinks from the sudden onslaught of kindness. Philos is not going to see her cry. Instead, she thinks of Felix, remembering the coldness of his rage, the way it chilled anyone who dared come too close.

"*I said get out.*"

Philos stops as abruptly as if she had slapped him. The only sound is the click of the latch as he steps outside, leaving her alone. Amara stands rigid, her eyes filling with tears. She can still feel the pressure of Rufus's fingers on her neck, and the weight of him, almost as heavy as the knowledge she will never have the freedom to resist. Amara picks up a clay oil lamp from the desk and hurls it at the door. The shards explode outwards, skittering across the tiles, leaving a dark stain on the wood.

10

Give me the pimp's accounts: you will find the entries balance.
Seneca, Declamations 1.2

A light rain falls through the square in the ceiling onto the pool beneath. The atrium is damp, and the overcast sky makes it as dark as dusk, even though it is morning. Rainwater is seeping out over the sides of the pool, staining the terracotta shards that line it a darker shade of red. Amara stands with Victoria and Britannica, huddled by one of the four pillars surrounding the water.

"Are you sure you don't want me to come," Victoria asks. "Perhaps I can persuade him to be reasonable?"

"Better I go," Britannica says. "He not try anything with *me*. I protect you."

Amara looks at her two friends, at their earnest faces so full of concern. Their love goes some way to counterbalance the regret she feels, now that her first reckoning with Felix is finally due. "I think seeing you again might make him angrier," she says gently to Victoria. "And I will take both Juventus and Philos, I promise," she adds, pressing Britannica's arm.

"I better man than them," Britannica says, jerking her chin at the two waiting servants. "Give me knife, I prove you."

It occurs to Amara that both Victoria and Britannica have their own unfinished business with Felix, quite aside from any concern they feel for *her*. How gratified their old master would be to know the influence he still exerts over his women's lives. "I will be fine," Amara says. "He will never harm me, not now I have Rufus as a patron. And I will get Juventus to close the doors behind us so you can bolt them until our return."

Britannica shakes her head. "At least take knife."

Amara ignores the remark, embracing them both, before joining the two men. They pass through the narrow hallway, and when they have stepped out onto the street, Juventus closes the tall wooden doors. Amara can hear the scrape of the bolt from inside, and for one wild moment feels as if she has been locked out of her own house, that she will never get back in. She rests her hand on the brass studs that protrude from its surface, more grey than gold in today's dull light.

"Ready?" Philos asks. She knows he is trying to hold her gaze, to communicate with her beyond the words he says. Their relationship has been strained ever since he guessed that Rufus had hurt her. She accepted his apology shortly after their row but has avoided any private conversation since. His compassion embarrasses her. She doesn't like being reminded of her own weakness.

Amara nods at Philos then turns away from him. The three of them set off in single file, Philos in front, Amara in the middle and Juventus, as the most formidable figure, taking up the rear. It's a market day in the Forum, and by the time they reach the Via Veneria, the road is crammed with wagons and mules, the air thick with the shouting and ill temper of so many people trying to crush past at once. The pavements are packed too, a perfect environment for pickpockets. Amara can feel the leather purse sticking to her skin with sweat. Britannica insisted she hang it round her neck, hidden under her clothes. The money has been split between the three of them, in the hope that if robbers strike, they won't lose it all.

The faint drizzle is scarcely more than mist, but by the time they arrive at the Wolf Den it has coated their faces, and Amara knows it will have ruined her hair, seeping through the thin veil draped over her head and shoulders. She only hopes the kohl has not smudged around her eyes.

Juventus slams his fist on the wooden door, knocking so loudly that a couple of passers-by laugh, yelling a joke about being eager to get in the brothel. Paris opens the door then looks the burly porter up and down, his expression wary. "The men can wait outside," Paris says.

"Don't be an idiot," Amara hisses, her voice low to avoid their audience overhearing. "Do you think I carried all the money myself?"

Paris lets them in, grumbling as they troop up the stairs. "Well, I'm not having a bunch of thugs in the Master's room. You'll have to go in alone, and they can wait here." He chivvies them into the small chamber next to Felix's study. It's unpleasantly familiar, the walls with their dizzying, geometric design of black and white, the brazier on the floor with its faint heat. Amara's breathing is coming too quickly, panic pressing in on her the closer she gets to

confronting Felix. She is aware of Philos trying to catch
her eye, can sense his anxiety, but ignores him. He gives
up and mutters something to Juventus in their own dialect.
The porter starts fumbling under his cloak for the purse.
Juventus is the only one who looks unafraid. Instead, he
is gaping round, incredulous. If he hadn't known his new
mistress was a brothel whore before, he certainly does now.

Paris sticks his head round the door. "Move it!" he barks.

Amara's body obeys the old habit of jumping to Felix's
orders. She takes the rest of the money from Philos and
hurries into the corridor. She realizes too late she has not
removed her own purse, that she will have to fish it out
from between her breasts in front of Felix. Then she is
stepping over the familiar threshold into the red study next
door. Paris bangs the door shut behind her.

Felix and Amara stare at one another. It is the first time
they have been alone since she won her freedom. He is sitting
at his desk, the way she has imagined him a thousand times,
and she is standing in her old place by the door. Amara's
every nerve is taut, her whole being alive with readiness to
fight. She expects Felix to sneer, to threaten, maybe even
to grab her. Instead, he waves a hand towards a chair as
if she were an old friend. "Have some wine with me," he
says, pleasantly. "Zoskales claims it's his best, which means
it might almost be drinkable."

"You don't drink," Amara says, surprised into rudeness
as she sits down. "So why would I want to blunt my wits
while you keep yours?"

"Fine," Felix says, with a smirk. "I suppose you know
best. You've eavesdropped on me often enough." He nods
towards the place she used to sit doing his books.

"None of the new whores any good with accounts then?" she asks, glancing round and noticing the table is no longer stacked with tablets.

"No," he smiles. "You're irreplaceable."

"Are you trying to be *charming*?" Amara is amused in spite of herself. "Surely, you can't think I'm that easily fooled. I've had to sit here while you told me you had Drauca's eye cut out. I think it might be a little late for charm." She can see his smooth expression start to wrinkle, a curl of irritation forming at the edge of his mouth. Felix always did hate to be laughed at. "That's better," she says. "Why not get angry and call me a bitch? Then I'll start to feel at home."

"You *are* at home," Felix replies. "My favourite whore." Amara can see him absorb her discomfort, the smile on his face genuine this time. It has been so long since she was in his presence, she had forgotten how attractive he is. Victoria always used to say he looked like Apollo, with his sculpted physique, all hard edges and sharp lines. But thanks to Fabia, Amara knows Felix is all too mortal. *He was the most beautiful child. Those big brown eyes.*

"I don't believe a place can truly be your home," she says. "Unless you grew up there." From the way his smile tightens, Amara suspects her blow has landed.

"Perhaps you could get posh boy to take you back to Greece in that case," Felix says, his tone brisk. "Though not before you've paid me."

"Would you pursue me over the sea?"

"I would pursue you anywhere. When did I ever forget what I'm owed?"

"Then it's as well I have a rich patron to pay you off."

Amara shrugs, not wanting him to see that he has unsettled her. "Rufus says Victoria has a delightful singing voice. She performed for him and his friends at dinner the other night."

"Is that supposed to make me *jealous?*" Felix laughs. "You think I'm going to care if other men fuck a woman I rented out to all comers as a whore? They're welcome to her. Especially since I got twice what she's worth."

Amara thinks of Victoria breaking her heart over this man. If her own recklessness achieves nothing else, she will at least have spared Victoria from untold brutality. "You don't deserve her. You never did."

"I could say the same. Why posh boy decided to pay over the odds for *you*, I cannot imagine."

"It was the admiral who bought me," Amara says, answering too quickly and betraying more emotion than she intended.

Felix raises his eyebrows. "And then he left you here for another man. Or will Pliny be sending for you one day, to join him and the fleet in Misenum? No? I didn't think so." Amara says nothing. She has seen Felix with his clients, the way he unspools their lives, tugging at threads, groping his way to the weak points. No doubt he can sense her vulnerability now, even if the exact cause eludes him. "You told me posh boy was violent. What a little liar you are."

"Perhaps he is."

"He will be if he's wise. It's the only way to control a woman."

The hatred Amara feels is searing. "Rufus is not a man like you," she says, even though she is no longer sure if that is wholly true.

"Let's hope not," Felix replies. "And I don't begrudge

you keeping Victoria. I know she's not the one you really wanted."

Amara has been waiting for him to mention Dido, to strike where it hurts the most, and forces herself to stay calm. "Where did you bury her ashes?"

"What makes you think I buried her?"

"Because *even you* cannot have left her on the town rubbish dump. You can't have done. Not after what Pliny had just paid you for me."

"Whether I buried her or didn't bury her, you will never know." She opens her mouth, about to retaliate, but Felix cuts her off. "Enough now. Give me the money." Amara stares at him in impotent rage. She thinks of Dido painted on the wall, her hand raised in vengeance. Whatever this man did to her friend's beloved body, she hopes Dido's shade curses every remaining day of his life. Felix snaps his fingers, as if to break her from a trance. "Well? Where is it?" Amara stretches over the desk, placing the two purses from Juventus and Philos in front of him. Watching Felix count out the coins, grasping her hard-won fortune in his fingers, makes her feel nauseous. "That's not enough for a first payment," Felix says, looking up sharply. "Where's the rest of the fucking money?"

Amara rises and walks behind the desk towards him. Felix doesn't quite manage to hide his surprise at her uninvited approach. At the very last moment, he stands up. She has never willingly come this close to him before. His eyes do not leave hers, neither of them sure in this moment who is the predator or the prey. Amara reaches into her dress, drawing out the purse that is still warm from lying against her skin, pulls it over her head and drops it onto the desk.

Then she leans forwards and kisses Felix on the mouth, eyes open, staring into his. It is not a gesture of tenderness, still less of lust, though her hatred burns hotter than desire.

Felix does not close his eyes or move to touch her, but she can sense his breathing quicken. Fabia's words come back to her. *I always thought it was you he was sweet on.* An old woman's gossip is a faint hope to gamble upon.

Amara exhales as their lips part. "I missed you," she says.

Before Felix has a chance to reply, she turns and walks swiftly from the room.

FLORALIA

11

She stood naked on the shore to meet the buyers' sneers; every
part of her body was inspected – and handled.
Seneca, Declamations 1.2

The slave market at Pompeii is much smaller than the
giant harbour at Puteoli where Felix bought her and
Dido, but Amara can still feel her heart contract watching
the human cargo being unloaded onto the docks. Even at a
distance, the smell of so many sweating, unwashed bodies
almost overpowers the fresh breeze from the sea. It is a
brilliant day, the light on the water shines silver, almost too
bright to watch, before melting to blue in the distance. The
goddess of love rises from the heave and spray which gave
her birth, standing on a tall column in the centre of the
harbour, undisturbed by the waves breaking beneath her.
Venus Pompeiiana is guarding her town, her back turned
to the market behind her, blind to its ugliness. Perhaps it is
the noise which offends Aphrodite's ears: traders bellowing
their price, raucous laughter, angry haggling. Amara can feel
the tension building, like the smoke from newly lit wood
before it blazes into flame.

She glances at Drusilla whose brow is completely smooth, her beautiful face betraying no sign of discomfort. But then, Drusilla was last sold as a very small child. Perhaps she doesn't even remember. For Amara, the memory is so recent it makes the blood pound in her ears, the pain of it lodged deep in her chest. Drusilla turns to her and smiles. "I had Josephus ask for some to be set aside for us to view before all the pimps handled them," she says. "He will check their references."

Amara feels Britannica shift next to her. The Briton's face is red and sweating in the heat of the bright April sunshine, and she looks as on-edge as Amara feels. Perhaps it was a mistake to choose Britannica as a bodyguard over Philos. Amara stares straight ahead. Late arrivals are being shoved and mauled into lines in the swaying shadow of the nearest boat, some of the women openly weeping, one resisting as a blanket is stripped from her back. Sellers walk up and down, hanging placards over people's necks, that state their names, country of origin and history of enslavement. Buyers stand and gawp, or worse, maul the unresisting bodies of those on sale. Amara can feel her own skin crawl at the sight, and it brings back a buried memory. The way Dido – then a stranger – had reached over and taken her hand when they stood together in Puteoli's market.

Drusilla points out her steward Josephus gesturing at them from where he is standing beside a trader. He must have finished negotiations. "He's ready," Drusilla says, setting off towards them.

For a moment, Amara thinks she cannot follow, cannot take a step closer to the market. An irrational fear has seized her that if she reaches that line, one of the traders will rip away *her* cloak, and she will be forced to stand naked on the auction block, on sale again.

"I come with you." Britannica is squinting down at her, nose wrinkled as she faces the sun. "Come, Amara, come. I am here too."

Amara takes her arm, feeling both shame and gratitude, knowing she is free, and Britannica is not. "I promise I will *never* sell you," she says impetuously. "When I can legally free you, I will. I promise."

"I know this," Britannica says simply, as if any other action by her friend were unthinkable. Amara's sense of shame deepens.

Josephus is already haggling on Drusilla's behalf when they arrive. The trader nods at Amara to include her, but she cannot look at his face. Instead, her gaze slides down to his hands. They are tanned and leathery from being out in the sun, heavy with rings. Amara knows where those hands will have been, touching and pulling at the people he is selling, striking them, taking whatever pleasure he feels entitled to take. She grips Britannica's arm so hard it must hurt, but the Briton does not flinch.

"*Amara*," Drusilla is saying. "I said, which do you think?"

"Sorry, can you tell me again?"

"Two Greek flautists or a cithara player from Carthage. That's the best he has. Either could accompany Victoria, but flautists would be better, if they're worth the money."

"Either," Amara stammers. "I'm not sure."

Josephus exchanges more words with the trader who goes to fetch the women. They are not in the line, but huddled off to the side, along with a slim young man who makes Amara think painfully of Philos, although on second glance, she realizes he looks nothing like him. The three women line up in front of her and Drusilla. The cithara player stands a little apart. Her eyes are red and puffy, and she keeps trying to cover herself, the trader yanking her hands away from her body. Amara suspects she may have been kidnapped, like Dido.

The flautists standing beside her have the closed, blank expression Amara recognizes from her own time at the slave market. Most likely they have never known freedom.

"I think it has to be the pair, don't you?" Drusilla murmurs. "So graceful. As long as they can really play."

Amara looks at the flautists again, and this time, for a moment, she sees what Drusilla sees. She imagines them performing at one of their dinners, entertaining Rufus and Quintus, adding to the decoration and entertainment. Making money for her to pay back Felix. "Shouldn't we ask to hear them perform something?"

Drusilla nods. Josephus again speaks with the trader who goes off to retrieve the women's flutes. Amara realizes the cithara player is staring at them, her eyes round and desperate. "Maybe we should take all three?" Amara says, suddenly afraid of leaving her here.

"We can't possibly afford to," Drusilla replies in a low voice. It is true. Amara is already reliant on Drusilla to make the bulk of today's purchase. She has gifted Drusilla several pieces of jewellery instead of putting cash up for this, on the understanding that Drusilla will loan them back from time to time to avoid Rufus's suspicion.

The trader returns, handing the women their instruments, gesturing roughly at them to play. One of the flautists gives him a look of dislike, but only when he is not looking. They start piping together, their music cutting over the background swell of weeping and shouting, the ugly noise of the marketplace. It's only a simple melody, but enough to show that they are skilled at the flute and understand how to move. Set alongside Victoria, they would make an undeniably seductive trio. Amara wonders how much Egnatius might pay her if he saw these girls, remembering how he reacted when he first booked her and Dido to perform at last year's Floralia. Gradually, Amara starts to lose her shame, staring at the girls' bodies, calculating what they might be worth to her.

When the performance is finished, Drusilla beckons her over to discuss the sale out of the trader's earshot. "I think we should take them," she whispers.

Amara nods her agreement. "Have you already told Josephus what we can afford?"

"Of course. And if the man won't accept, we can come back another day. There will always be more."

They return to where Josephus and Britannica are standing. Drusilla's steward understands from the incline of his mistress's head that she would like to buy. Amara cannot take her eyes off the two flautists while the men haggle, wondering what they make of it all. Again, she remembers her own public sale, her foolish sense of relief that Felix seemed to have a pleasant face, that he had not groped at her roughly like some of the other customers. She had not understood then that his gentleness sprang from a desire to examine his goods as thoroughly as possible. Impossible to feel a woman's body when she's flinching. Neither flute player returns Amara's gaze, instead staring into the middle distance. For the first time, Amara reads the names on their placards. *Phoebe. Lais.*

"Whereabouts in Greece are you from?" she asks Lais, switching to her native language.

"Athens," Lais replies, with an insincere smile. The girl has a similar accent to Menander, the man Amara once loved, the one she abandoned for Rufus.

Amara is about to say that she too is from Attica, but the dead look in Lais's eyes stops her. As far as Lais knows, Amara might be just like Felix, an owner who will treat her with viciousness or indifference, not somebody she should trust. And it's true that Amara cannot answer for the behaviour of all the men Lais and Phoebe will be obliged to entertain. Perhaps she is not so different from her former master, after all. Before the unpleasant thought can take root, she forces herself to imagine Felix in the red study, waiting to call in his debts. *It's them or me*, she tells herself. *Anyone would do the same.*

Josephus and the trader agree on a sale of four thousand sesterces for the pair, less than the maximum amount Drusilla had bargained for, and significantly less than Amara paid Felix for her friends. Inexpert as she is in the sale of human beings, Amara still understands this is a good price. Josephus hands over a purse stuffed with coins as a deposit and signs an agreement to pay the rest on a set date. More arguing ensues over whether they can have the girls now or not. Josephus carries the argument by threatening to take the deposit back. Eventually, Amara and Drusilla take possession of Phoebe and Lais.

They head along the docks, back towards the town, Josephus and Britannica guarding the newly purchased women who have been bundled up in cloaks to spare them the humiliation of trudging semi-naked through the streets. Amara and Drusilla walk a little ahead. "You did well," Drusilla murmurs, so quietly that Amara almost misses what she says. "It gets easier." Amara darts a look at Drusilla's face. It is as smooth and inscrutable as before. "If it is the will of the gods, they shall find their freedom, as we did," Drusilla continues. "Those who are destined to rise, rise."

Light spray splashes onto Amara's face as a wave hits the harbour wall. The sea stretches out on her right, roiling and glittering in the sunlight, beautiful yet treacherous. Amara thinks of her friend Cressa, drowned in this harbour, choosing to end her own life rather than continue to live as Felix's slave, unable to bear the pain of losing the child she was carrying. It would be so easy for Amara to believe her own good fortune is fated, but she does not. "My freedom was partly your doing," Amara replies. "You gave me the confidence to ask Rufus to buy me."

Drusilla gives a small, gracious shrug. "You had already decided," she says. "I saw it in your face the first time we met. And I saw it in his. I had never known Rufus so enamoured of a woman before."

Amara thinks of all she has learned about her lover since that time and says nothing.

The walk across town is exhausting in the heat. Amara's house is at the opposite end of Pompeii from the harbour, and by the time they reach its golden door, she is sweating heavily. Even Drusilla looks a little flustered. They step into the cool darkness of the atrium. Amara blinks, adjusting to the dimmer light, and Victoria rushes through from the garden to meet them, embracing her.

"You found some!" she exclaims, looking curiously at Phoebe and Lais.

"Yes, there they are."

"Lovely!" Victoria says, smiling at the two newcomers. Amara is conscious of Drusilla watching and feels awkward. Victoria was not invited to the market, her status sitting somewhere uncomfortably between slave and freedwoman. Her lack of a patron, and the huge debt owing to Felix on her behalf, means she will have to go out and earn her keep with the flautists. It's unlikely the men using the three women will care much about the legal distinction between them.

Phoebe and Lais are huddled together by the pool, looking nervous now the shock of the sale is over. "You must be hungry," Amara says to them both.

They glance at one another, uncertain. Phoebe licks her lips. "Please, no trouble," she says in her heavily accented Latin. "Just water."

"Nonsense!" Victoria says warmly. "You must be *starving*. Come with me. Martha will get you something. Some bread maybe? And some cheese?"

Victoria leads the two flautists to the garden, smoothing over their fear with a flow of friendly chatter. Amara watches them go, touched by her friend's kindness.

"Good," Drusilla says, when the three women are out of earshot. "They will need to work together."

"Will you stay and have something?" Amara asks her.

Drusilla shakes her head. "I need to get home," she says. "I promised Primus I would spend the afternoon with him." She reaches for Amara, kissing her lightly on the cheek. "Let me know what it costs to feed and clothe them. Then we can set it against the lump sum of the sale. Make sure the balance between us is fair."

Amara nods. "Of course," she says. "Kiss your little boy for me."

Drusilla walks back across the atrium, joining Josephus who is waiting silently in the doorway beside Juventus. When she is gone, Amara is left with Britannica. "You must be hungry too," she says, embarrassed not to have thought of this before.

Britannica shrugs. "If you not need me now."

"Go and eat," Amara replies. "I will join you all in the garden in a moment, after I have spoken to Juventus."

The porter watches Amara as she approaches, his eyes lingering on her body. Ever since he went with her to the brothel, when he saw the low place she came from and heard the contemptuous way Paris spoke to her, Juventus has been more open in his leering, although never quite insolent enough for her to have to say anything. What could she say, in any case? A virtuous woman would surely not even recognize the sleazy look on his face. She stands a little apart from him, wishing now that they were not alone.

"When is Philos back?" she asks.

Juventus sucks his teeth. "He has business with the Master until the afternoon."

"When he returns, please tell him I need to see him."

Juventus stares until she is overwhelmingly aware, as he surely intends, that only a short while ago he would not have been limited to looking. He could have paid for her services himself. "Whatever you wish, mistress."

12

The body seeks that which the mind has wounded with love.
Lucretius, On the Nature of the Universe

Amara and Philos walk the back streets to get to Cornelius's house. Buildings are lit with the last orange glow before dusk falls. The air is cool. Some shopkeepers are already packing up, moving the overspill of baskets and jars from the pavement back into the store. The cook shop where Martha often collects their dinner is busy, customers crowded around the bright yellow counter, getting the last of the hot soup.

Philos looks tired. Amara had expected him to try to speak to her about Rufus again, but she has perhaps rebuffed him so many times, he has given up. She feels both relieved and disappointed.

"What did you think of Phoebe and Lais?" she asks, when they are further from the house and walking closer together on the pavement.

"I didn't see them for more than a moment. But I'm sure you and Drusilla chose wisely."

A street seller strung with clanking baskets of pots and

pans barges his way past, forcing them both to flatten against the wall. Philos puts his arm in front of Amara to prevent her being scraped or struck. She knows it is a gesture any slave is forced to use, obliged at all times to sacrifice his own comfort for others, but the way Philos turns to her afterwards is more like a friend.

"You didn't get hit, did you?" he asks.

Philos has lowered his arm, but they are still standing close together. Amara reaches instinctively for his hand, half-hidden by the folds of her cloak. "No," she says. "I didn't. Thank you."

Philos returns the pressure of her fingers, holding her hand so tightly that for a moment she thinks he is not going to let go. He runs his thumb over hers, slowly enough to be obvious it is not an accident. Then he releases her and steps away. They keep walking, not looking at one another or acknowledging the contact. He cannot have held her hand for more than a heartbeat, the street seller has barely passed them, but it feels to Amara as if time has jumped.

"It was strange seeing the slave market from the other side." Her heart is thumping so hard, she does not pause to think about what she's saying, or why she suddenly feels the need to share something so personal. "Although Felix bought me at Puteoli, not here, I still dream about it. The things people do when they know you don't matter. When they know you are nothing."

"It's not a rite of passage I've experienced," Philos replies. "I've only been sold once, and that was privately."

"It's brutal. And now I've done it to somebody else."

They have not been looking at one another, but at this, Philos glances at her. "We all do what we need to survive.

And you and Drusilla will not be cruel. If it hadn't been you, somebody else would have bought them."

"That's what I tell myself."

"It's true. Only fools think life is like a play, with any hope of holding on to your virtue." He smiles, as if the words are nothing more than a joke, but they both know who the target is: Rufus, his theatre-loving master.

Amara returns his smile but doesn't dare fully acknowledge the insult to her patron. "I suppose I am not asking more of Phoebe or Lais than I endured myself. And I never minded Egnatius, at least. He was almost a friend to Dido and me."

"How do you think you will feel, seeing him again?"

Amara pictures the last time she saw Egnatius, his heavily made-up face cracked from smiling, the way he fussed over Dido, dressing her hair with roses. Dido was always his favourite. The memory brings an undertow of sadness. "I don't know," she says.

The doorway to Cornelius's house is twice Amara's height and by far the grandest on the street. A sliver of light cuts through its half-open doors onto the darkening pavement. She and Philos do not go in that way, instead she guides him to a small door down a side alley, a less obtrusive way into the house. A porter lets them in, grease stains on his apron, leaving them to wait in a small, gloomy side room while he fetches Egnatius. Amara watches Philos as he stares round curiously at the paintings on the walls: nymphs pursued by centaurs. Nothing in Cornelius's house is very subtle.

"Darling!"

Egnatius, Cornelius's freedman, is in the doorway, arms thrown out in the theatrical expectation of an embrace. Amara runs over, kissing him on both cheeks. "And who's *this*?" Egnatius eyes Philos up and down, lips pursed, an unmistakable look of appraisal on his face.

Amara is embarrassed, fearful that Philos will be offended, but instead, he seems amused. "The steward," Philos replies. "Here to draw up the contract."

"Very pretty for a *steward*," Egnatius whispers to Amara with a wink. To her annoyance, rather than managing to think of a witty reply, she finds her cheeks growing hotter. Egnatius laughs. "Well, my fine pair, let's have some wine and talk about parties. And contracts," he adds, glancing back at Philos, one eyebrow raised.

They follow Egnatius into another slightly larger room, perhaps his own private chamber, with two couches and a small table, set with wine. The walls are painted a deep red, with images from the legend of Hercules. Iron lamps blaze in each corner, and a small brazier is lit. Amara has been to Cornelius's house many times, but always as a hired entertainer. She does not suppose the master of the house even knows she is here. The business of buying in women and performers is surely beneath him.

"Sit down, darlings, sit down," Egnatius exclaims, waving his hand. Amara and Philos cannot recline together so, instead, perch awkwardly on either end of one couch. Egnatius throws himself across the other with a sigh. "I'm so very sorry," he says. "Your little friend, my dear little lark. Such a loss."

Amara knows he means Dido. "Thank you," she replies. "What a voice she had! Did you ever hear her?" he asks Philos, who shakes his head. "Quite exquisite." For a moment, a look of genuine sadness crosses Egnatius's face. "May her shade find peace," he says, reaching over to pour the wine. "I'm glad you, at least, my love, escaped that *ghastly* master of yours."

"Do you still do business with Felix?"

"He has excellent stock." Egnatius shrugs. "One can't be too choosy about pimps. Not the most endearing breed." He smiles at Amara. "Present company excepted, of course."

"As I mentioned in my note, sadly I can no longer perform in public." Amara leans over to accept the wine Egnatius offers her. Philos, she notices, holds up his hand to decline. "My patron would be most upset by the idea."

"Of course!" Egnatius exclaims. "Young Rufus, isn't it? Or is it Admiral Pliny? Your new name leaves it a little unclear who you belong to." He takes a swig of wine and nods indulgently at Philos. "Not that there's any harm in a girl having *two* fine patrons, as I'm sure you would agree. We're none of us young forever."

"Rufus is my patron," Amara replies, not responding to the innuendo. "Although, I owe the admiral a debt beyond words."

"So what can you offer me?" Egnatius is swilling his glass, staring at the dregs dancing on the bottom. Light from the brazier shines through the wine, making it glow. "Cornelius doesn't accept boys, sadly. Although I've often suggested it."

"I have a very talented singer, with an exceptional figure," Amara says. "And two delightful flautists. The singer in particular is very skilled at pleasing a man, in whatever way he might wish."

"Where did you buy them?"

"The singer is my freedwoman," Amara says. "We used to…" She hesitates. There is no point being coy with Egnatius. "We used to work together. At the brothel. The flautists I bought with Drusilla, on her recommendation."

"Sounds delightful. I'd be happy to book them all for an evening to try them out. We can always make space at the Floralia. As I'm sure you remember."

"Given I am providing you with three women, I would expect the payment to be more than Felix received for Dido and me."

Egantius smiles, but without warmth. "If they pass the trial, we can discuss an increase in price." He glances over at Philos who has brought out the tablets and is balancing them on his knee. "Do you deal with all her affairs?"

"I am Rufus's steward," he replies. "I do whatever is required."

"You must have seen all these women. What would you advise me? Are they worth as much as she is?" Egnatius flicks his fingers playfully at Amara.

"Ignore his teasing," Amara says, irritated. "He's just being mischievous."

"How much did Rufus pay for her? Or was it the admiral? I can't keep track of all these wonderfully wealthy men!" There is an uncomfortable pause as Philos ignores the question. "You're the steward, aren't you?" Egnatius presses. "You must have drawn up that contract too?"

Philos is gripping the tablets so tightly Amara can see his knuckles are white. "Six thousand sesterces," he says. "Of which my master contributed a third."

"As much as *that*," Egnatius splutters, genuinely taken

aback. "*Darling*," he looks at Amara, impressed. "Six thousand sesterces? What on earth did you *do?*"

"Enough now," Amara says, uncertain what has upset Philos, but aware of his embarrassment. "Or I shall be offended you did not expect it to have been *eight* thousand, at least."

Egnatius laughs. "With you, nothing would surprise me." She laughs with him, more out of politeness than amusement. He looks at Philos's glum face and sighs. "Rather serious, isn't he? Never mind, I meant no slight to your master's judgment, boy, I assure you, or the admiral's either."

Philos makes an effort to smile. "Of course," he replies. "And I took none. Except, perhaps, at the idea you can put a price on perfection."

Philos's attempt at charm sounds strained to Amara, but Egnatius is mollified. They spend a little longer drinking and chatting, Philos finally accepting a glass which he barely touches. It reminds Amara of Felix, the way Philos always likes to keep his wits about him. She tries again to up the price and fails, but she does manage to persuade Egnatius to provide an escort home, for her women's safety, without having to pay for it.

When it is time for Amara and Philos to leave, Egnatius accompanies them to the door rather than calling the porter, helping Philos light the oil lamp for the journey home. He seems a little reluctant to let them go. Amara realizes that he might be lonely.

Saying goodbye, Egnatius embraces her, holding her by the upper arms as he kisses each cheek. "Rather thin," he says. "Be careful, darling. Your patron must want a little more flesh for his six thousand, surely."

"On the contrary," Amara says. "This is just what he likes."

Egnatius chuckles, mistaking her words for flirtation, not understanding that she means it literally. Amara steps onto the pavement with a last goodbye, and Egnatius shuts the door behind them. It is dusk. They will have to hurry to avoid being trapped out in the dark.

They walk along the narrow alleyway, Philos holding out the lamp, Amara with her hand against the wall to steady herself in the failing light. It doesn't prevent her from stumbling. "It would be safer if I held your arm," she says. Philos stops but does not reply. Even in the flicker of the lamplight, she can see he looks uncomfortable, just as he did when Egnatius asked him to recount her price. "Only if you don't mind," she adds, feeling embarrassed.

"I don't mind." Philos holds out his arm. She takes it, and he draws her close to him, much closer than she is expecting. The warmth of his body, the physical sensation of him, is a shock. They stare at each other. He is going to kiss her. Amara knows that she should step back, that the risk to them both far outweighs any attraction. Instead, she clasps his arm tighter, to let him understand she wants him.

But Philos does not kiss her. He turns his face back to the light, his expression drawn. "We should hurry," he says. They walk back to the house in silence.

13

Love and fear will not mix.

Seneca, Letters from a Stoic

The air smells fresh, the morning's rainfall still lingering in patches of shade on the pavement. Amara's spirit feels light as she weaves her way home from Drusilla's house. The pair of them had shared breakfast together in the atrium, cocooned by the soothing patter of the rain, its splash into the pool sending a gentle spray onto the tiles, while Primus pulled his wooden horse round and round, pretending to be a soldier. Drusilla insisted they celebrate Amara's success at booking Egnatius with sweet wine, and perhaps it is the wine that has made Amara feel light-headed, warming her from the inside. For the thousandth time, she draws last night's memory of Philos close to her, imagines he had kissed her, before letting the image go. *There is no harm in thinking it*, she tells herself. *As long as I never do it.*

She sees the crowd at the corner of her street before she reaches it. People have gathered around the shrine at the crossroads, and smoke is billowing from the small altar. Amara will have to wait with the rest; she cannot bring bad luck on her household by shoving past a ceremony for the local Lares. She stands at the very edge of the group, not wanting to give any man the chance to grope her under the cover of a crush. Time drags. Neighbourhood priests are always slaves and freedmen, and she knows they will be milking their rare moment of public importance. An acrid smell of burning feathers wafts towards her. They must have sacrificed a pigeon.

One of the priests is chanting, and she catches a glimpse of him through the sea of heads. He looks so young and earnest – he reminds her of Menander. The image of her first love cuts through Amara, swifter and more brutal than the sacrificial knife. Menander's face when the lamp smashed, when she dropped the gift he made for her with such love, at his feet. Pain swells in her chest, forcing her to catch her breath. She wonders what she would feel if *Philos* ever looked at her like that then realizes, with surprise, that she cannot picture it. Such a betrayal might not even shock him. Amara thinks of Philos's inscrutable expression whenever Rufus addresses him, the darker currents beneath his stillness, and feels a pull of recognition. *He is a slave*, she reminds herself, recalling Drusilla's warning. *And I left that gutter.*

The crowd starts to disperse. Amara quickens her pace, trying to keep her mind focused on Rufus as she skirts past the lines of fabric. There is no point imagining anyone else. Better make the most of the man she chose, rather than wish for one who would disgrace her.

At the doorway of her house, there is no porter to prevent her slipping into the shaded hallway. Juventus has his back to her, watching the atrium instead of the street. Beyond him, she can hear laughter and shouting. She brushes past Juventus's shoulder, making him jump.

"I was still on guard," he protests, looking back at the door.

Amara ignores him, uninterested in his oversight. A scuffle is going on beside the pool in the atrium. To her surprise, she sees Philos and Britannica are sparring, brandishing the wooden knives the Briton has been using to teach Amara how to defend herself. Britannica lunges forwards, and Philos scrambles out of the way, splashing through the shallow water to avoid a blow.

Britannica laughs. "You dead," she yells. "I kill you ten times already!"

"Still standing, aren't I?" Philos replies, darting behind a pillar while the Briton takes another swipe.

"You not even *try* to hit me," Britannica shouts, grabbing Philos from behind by the scruff of his tunic and holding the wooden blade to his neck. He holds his hands up in surrender, both of them laughing so hard it is infectious: Amara realizes she and Juventus are laughing too.

"What's this?" she says, stepping forwards. "More knife lessons?"

"Amara!" Britannica grins, exposing her knocked out front teeth. "Your man. He is useless!"

"I think that's a little harsh," Philos says, disentangling himself from Britannica's grip. Amara hears Juventus snort with amusement beside her. He yells something at Philos in their own dialect. Philos rolls his eyes, replying with a phrase Amara does not understand. Then he glances at Amara, as if not wanting to exclude her. "I said it's not like being beaten by an *ordinary* woman."

Britannica throws her knife at Amara who catches it, then grabs the other blade from Philos. "I show you, even *she* better killer than you."

"I don't doubt it," Philos says.

"Not now," Amara says, embarrassed by the thought of an audience.

"You not try, you never improve," Britannica says. "Now catch me with the sneak move, while I look away."

"Hang on," Philos protests. "There was none of that for me! I might have got somewhere."

"No sneaking for a man," Britannica scowls. "Cheating." She turns her face from Amara. "Now you try." Feeling foolish, Amara tries creeping up on Britannica a few times, each attempt more half-hearted than the last. She is conscious of Philos and Juventus watching, unimpressed. Britannica snorts with impatience. "You copy me," she declares, facing Amara. There is no longer any trace of laughter to her voice. Britannica uses a short swift upswing as if to stab Amara below the ribs. "Strike first," she says.

Amara copies the movement, her eyes not leaving Britannica's face. "*Strike first*," she repeats.

Britannica moves, as if withdrawing the blade from a wound in Amara's chest. "Always remove your weapon."

"*Always remove your weapon.*"

With a speed that takes Amara by surprise, even though she is expecting the blow, Britannica raises her arm in a lethal arc, bringing the point downwards to rest at her throat. "Second blow is hardest."

"*The second blow is the hardest*," Amara says, bringing her own knife to Britannica's throat.

Britannica falls against her, as if she has been fatally

wounded, forcing Amara to lower her to the ground. "But remember, him or you."

"*It's him or me.*" Amara pants, her arms trembling under the dead weight of her friend. She lies her flat on the tiled floor.

Britannica stares up at her. "And when you dead, you nothing."

"*When you are dead, you are nothing.*" The words bring with them a chill. Amara remembers Dido lying, wounded, in Britannica's arms.

Britannica jumps to her feet, a wolfish grin on her face. "You see, *boys,*" she calls to Philos and Juventus, who are watching in silence. "This is how *woman* kills a man." She stalks across the atrium to the stairwell, taking the wooden stairs two at a time with her long-legged stride. They hear the bang of the door to her room.

"I think you were lucky just to get splashed in the pool," Amara says to Philos. He does not reply, instead he and Juventus are staring at her. She realizes she is still clutching the wooden dagger in her hands, poised, as if it were a real weapon. She relaxes her arm. "Oh, come on," she says to them both. "It's just Britannica!"

"I'll have to remember that," Philos says. "If she ever decides to sneak up on me."

Amara glances upwards towards the balcony, where Britannica's door is still closed, with a slight sense of unease. She remembers Victoria's warning about the Briton. *Savage.* "Where are the others?" she asks, bending to pick up the second wooden dagger from the floor, well aware that this should have been Britannica's job. For a slave, she is not very diligent about household chores.

"Practising in the garden," Philos says, taking the wooden knives from her. "Where do these…?"

"If you wouldn't mind putting them in the chest in the tablinum," Amara replies, suddenly nervous of standing too close to him, embarrassed by the memory of all the imaginary kisses she has bestowed on him that morning. She walks outside, heading back into the sunshine. Victoria, Phoebe and Lais are sprawled over the bench, helping themselves to wine.

"Amara," Victoria cries, shading her eyes from the sun to look at her. "We're celebrating our new routine."

"Wonderful," Amara replies, remembering the hours she used to spend practising with Dido in the stuffy heat of Felix's flat. "Can I hear it?"

Victoria flicks her eyes towards the two flautists, eyebrows raised. "Of course. We'd *love* to."

Phoebe and Lais smirk. *Felix would never accept this sort of behaviour*, Amara thinks, then feels ashamed for making the comparison, even though she did not say it aloud.

"You sit here." Victoria gestures to the bench with a flourish. She saunters over to the fountain, a flautist on either side. The three of them sway slightly, bending like reeds in the wind. Phoebe and Lais begin to pipe. Amara recognizes the tune. It is one Victoria used to sing at the brothel, one she remembers her singing to Felix the first morning he asked her to stay upstairs, the day after Simo's murder.

Victoria adds her voice to the piping, and it is a haunting, unearthly sound, the folk lament of a woman abandoned by her lover. She dances, lowering her body almost to the floor, thighs quivering, before rising again. Phoebe and Lais move with her, and Amara finds herself swaying on the bench, remembering what it felt like to perform with Dido, although their routines were tame in comparison to this display. Victoria flings her head back, arm outstretched as if beckoning someone towards her. The gesture is so definite that Amara glances over her shoulder and, to her shock, sees Rufus, standing at the edge of the garden, a rapt expression on his face. She goes cold, realizing how close he came to walking in on an entirely different scene, the knife fighting in the hall. Rufus looks at her and smiles, then slips over to the bench, sitting beside her. They watch together until the song is finished.

"Wonderful!" Rufus exclaims. "These are Drusilla's girls?" He gestures at the flute players.

"Yes," Amara replies. "Though I hope it is still alright if they mainly stay here. I did want to help her out, as we also get the use of them. But only if you don't mind."

"Of course," Rufus replies, resting his hand on her knee. "Nervous little bird, I remember you asking my permission, don't fret." Amara can feel any trace of authority she held over Phoebe and Lais evaporating faster than the April rain, as they watch her cringe under her patron's touch. Rufus is kissing her neck. He has never been perturbed by an audience of slaves. When she used to visit him at his own house, he would start making love to her almost before Philos or Vitalio had had a chance to leave the room. Amara, on the other hand, has no desire to have the other women watch.

"Why don't we let the girls practise," she says, standing up.

"Whatever you want, my darling," he replies, taking her hand and letting her lead him from the garden.

As soon as they reach her private rooms, Amara begs him to wait outside her bedroom door, making the excuse that she wants to change into the transparent silk he likes.

Rufus sighs, but with indulgence. He never minds her fussing to please him. While he is outside, Amara swiftly undresses, throwing on the silk, and rifles through a cheap woven basket in her linen chest. It's full of dense, boiled lambswool: her contraceptive. She grabs a handful, and stuffs it up inside her body as high as she can, wincing. Then she hurries to open the door.

"Beautiful girl," Rufus says, kissing her. He leads her to the bed, not bothering to shut the door behind him.

Amara takes her time, running through the repertoire she knows he likes best. She has been with her patron numerous times since their argument on the night Helvius came to dinner, and since then, he has never been anything but loving. If anything, he has seemed even more devoted than before. Sometimes, she thinks she must have imagined what happened, that her memory has exaggerated the threat, that she misread his intentions, that *of course* Rufus did not force her, not really, but whatever lies she tells herself, her body remembers. Her heart beats painfully fast when he holds her, and a sick feeling churns her stomach. She fakes her sighs of desire, moving her body to excite him, and when he is lost to passion, breathing heavily in her ear, Amara stares wide-eyed up at the ceiling.

She tries to blot out the present, imagining herself somewhere else. She thinks of Philos, pictures him being chased by Britannica across the pool. His laughter. The way he held her hand, so briefly, in the street. The look in his eyes when she took his arm. "I love you," she murmurs, surprising herself.

"I love you too, darling," Rufus answers, although the words were not for him. He rolls off her body, kissing her tenderly. "Dear little bird."

Amara smiles. She has smiled at worse men, after all, and her comfortable life depends on his continued affection. Surely Rufus is an easier master to manage than Felix. *And he does not own me*, she reminds herself. She draws a finger gently over the outline of his face, as if it were the one she truly wanted to see. "I'm so happy for you that Helvius has been elected," she says. "You must be so pleased."

Rufus sighs with contentment. "Yes, it's a relief. My father had already sunk so much money in his campaign. And all that time in his pompous company!" He runs his hand down her flank, his fingers moving over her ribs into the hollow created by the jutting bone of her pelvis. "Such a *tiny* little thing, you are," Rufus says affectionately. "My little sparrow."

Amara thinks of the arc of her arm when she brings down the wooden knife, the deadly movement Britannica has taught her. *I am not so little*, she tells herself. But her heart still races at the pressure of his fingers gripping her waist. She has always known how much damage Rufus could do her, that he has the ability to destroy her life as well as save it. It is only recently that she has come to resent his power so bitterly. "What will happen now, at the Floralia?" she asks.

"Of course!" Rufus sits up in excitement. "That's what I came to tell you. Before you distracted me," he adds, taking her hand and kissing it. "I've arranged for you and Drusilla to be at the head of the procession to the theatre, the night of the performance."

"*Really?*" Amara asks, amazed. "Is that a public acknowledgement of..." She almost does not dare continue.

"Of your role in my life, yes," Rufus replies. "I will not be able to recognize you that night, my love. I will be with my family. But people will know who you are and why you are there." He bends to kiss her again. "They will know you are mine."

"Oh!" Amara exclaims, with genuine pleasure. She can already imagine herself, standing with Drusilla, the focus of so much envy and admiration, their path strewn with flowers. She kisses Rufus back, this time with more feeling. "How could I *ever* be anything but yours?"

He smiles at her, complacent in her adoration. Amara lays her head against his chest, in a false gesture of devotion, so that she does not have to look into his eyes.

14

I'm just a guest then, gazing at my darling
While at your touch another takes delight?

Ovid, Amores 1.4

Victoria catches Amara's eye, raising her eyebrows, but Amara ignores her. It's true that Drusilla's imperious tone is a little grating, but Amara has no intention of making faces behind her back. Victoria does not seem to grasp the hierarchy among courtesans, but instead, she is still stuck in the mentality of the brothel. Hot air from outside wafts into the dining room, spiced by the scent of mint which sits baking in the sun. Drusilla's garden is always fragrant with the flowers beloved by Venus: rose, mint and myrtle.

Drusilla fusses over Phoebe and Lais, instructing them where to stand. Her dining room is smaller than Amara's, but it opens directly onto the garden which is why they chose it for this evening. She also has more bedrooms, which may be important after the food is served.

"So, I'm with Quintus?" Victoria remarks, tapping her foot with boredom. "Even though he's *your* boyfriend?"

"He is my patron," Drusilla replies, not looking in

Victoria's direction, instead fussing over Lais's tunic, arranging it to her satisfaction. "I provide him with all manner of entertainments."

"Amara's with Rufus, the girls have to fuck those other two boys you've invited, and I'm with Quintus. That's all the men. What about you? Did nobody want you?" Victoria's voice is light, as if she is making a joke, but Amara cringes inwardly, fearing Drusilla will be offended.

"Me?" Drusilla raises her perfectly shaped eyebrows. Her cheeks dimple into a smile. "I'm the one who gets paid. The one who gets to *choose* her lovers. Not entertain a man on another woman's instruction."

Amara has never seen Victoria bested by a tongue sharper than her own. Victoria says nothing, only tosses her hair as if the words don't sting.

"I think Rufus will want to go home after the dinner," Amara says, changing the subject.

"I've had your old room dressed, just in case," Drusilla says. "I suspect the other three men will want to stay in here, on the couches, so they can share the women between them. That's after you and I have retired." Drusilla's deliberate elevation of them both makes Amara flush with embarrassment, even as she also feels pleased by her change in status.

"You won't mind that, will you?" Amara says to Victoria, feeling bad for her.

"Why should I mind?" Victoria gets up and stalks into the garden. Amara can see her stop at the fountain, keeping her back to them all. She wonders if she ought to go and join her, whether she owes Victoria that loyalty, but decides against it.

The garden is in shade and the air cooler, when Drusilla's guests arrive. Victoria and the flautists perform in the garden, outside the inner circle, while the four men greet one another, making themselves comfortable in the dining room. They are all a similar age, all the wealthy sons of powerful men, who have known one another since boyhood. Quintus is the most assertive among them, but Lucius is the most attractive; he has a sensual mouth, like a woman's, and his black hair shines with oil. Amara is reminded painfully of the times she used to attend Drusilla's dinners with Dido, when Lucius was Dido's lover. Now he is eyeing up Lais and Phoebe, no doubt deciding which he prefers.

"Your father is very insistent it has to be this year?" Quintus is saying to Marcus. "What's the bride like?"

Marcus knocks back the wine one of Drusilla's silent servants has handed him. "I've no idea," he says. "My mother chose her."

"Oh, bad luck!" Quintus laughs. "You'll get some fat little thing, devoted to Juno, weaving you lumpy-looking tunics."

"And she'll cry if you don't wear them." Lucius joins in the banter, without taking his eyes off Victoria and the flautists.

"Nothing wrong with a girl weaving her man clothes," Rufus says. He is reclining next to Amara, a sweaty arm draped over her.

"We all know what a tedious husband *you* will make," Quintus scoffs. "Horribly proper. But don't worry, darling," he adds, winking at Amara. "No doubt he'll be a screaming hypocrite too, so you're quite safe."

"Don't tease her like that," Rufus says, holding Amara closer. She is not sure whether the protective gesture is to reassure her of his constancy or to assuage his own guilt at the lack of it.

"Are you really going to talk about wives and weaving all night?" Drusilla wrinkles her nose. "I would have invited your fathers instead, if I'd known."

"I'm sure *Hortensius* would never turn you down," Quintus retorts, a sharpness to his voice. Amara remembers the greedy way Hortensius, Rufus's father, had looked at Drusilla when they met and is inclined to agree. Even Rufus does not leap to his father's defence, but laughs.

Drusilla smiles, laying a hand on Quintus's arm. "Then it's as well I'm always loyal to you." Lucius's mouth twitches slightly at this, and he flicks his eyes to Drusilla in a secret lover's gesture. Amara thinks Quintus will miss it, but he doesn't. His anger is plain, and Amara is momentarily fearful Quintus will be violent, but instead, he seizes hold of Drusilla and kisses her, running his hands over her body so aggressively it wipes the smirk from Lucius's face. Drusilla accepts the embrace then pushes him lightly away. Quintus obeys but keeps a hand clasped around her thigh, staring at her with an intensity that feels too private to watch.

Marcus, alone on a couch, and perhaps still brooding about his marriage, is restless. "Is that enough music now?" he says, refilling his wine glass. "Shall we ask the girls in to dinner?"

"Of course," Drusilla replies. She gestures at the musicians, a brusque command which Amara suspects will make Victoria furious, and they fall silent. Lucius takes hold of Phoebe's wrist as she passes, clearly having made his selection, while Lais sits beside Marcus. For one painful moment, Victoria is left standing, unclaimed, taken aback by the sight of Quintus pressed against Drusilla, his lust for his long-time girlfriend painfully evident.

"Room for you here!" Marcus cries, seizing the chance to be the man with two women. His eagerness makes the others laugh and goes some way to restoring Victoria's pride, or at least makes her smile.

It is not the most pleasant evening Amara has spent at Drusilla's house. Tension clings to everything like the transparent silk on her skin. The rivalry between Quintus and Lucius over Drusilla, although unspoken, still dominates, dampening the women's attempts to lighten the atmosphere. All the men drink too much. The only relief for Amara is watching Phoebe and Lais. Both are admirably professional: Lais does not vie with Victoria for Marcus's attention but instead fetches her flute to play to them all, while Phoebe gives no sign of being disconcerted by Lucius's bad temper. The flautists were a good investment, she decides.

"I think we should head home, little bird," Rufus says, rising from the couch, after yet another barbed exchange between Lucius and Quintus, "delightful though the gathering has been." He winks at her, and she smiles, enjoying his private joke.

"I will retire too." Drusilla stands at the same time as Amara.

"Let me join you," Quintus slurs, trying to push his hand inside her tunic.

Drusilla sidesteps him. "You made your choice for this evening. I'm sleeping alone."

"How do I know you won't have *him* upstairs?" Quintus

gestures at Lucius, his voice rising. "I saw you dabbling your fingers in the wine, scrawling little signs on the table. How do I know that wasn't some secret signal?"

"You are ridiculous." Drusilla's voice is ice.

"Just let me come upstairs, my darling," Quintus's tone is fawning, and he reaches out, trying to embrace her. "You know I don't want anyone else."

"You told me you wanted a whore this evening," Drusilla replies. "Here are some whores – go fuck one of them."

"If I find out you had him in your bed, I'll—"

"You'll what?" Drusilla does not even have to shout to silence him. She turns to Lucius who is sprawled on the couch with Phoebe, enjoying the row. His smile shrivels at Drusilla's look of contempt. She stands very still, even more beautiful in the coldness of her anger compared to the louche scene surrounding her. "Enjoy the rest of your evening, *gentlemen*." She sweeps from the room.

When she has left, Marcus bursts out laughing. "That's you two told." He guffaws, pulling Victoria against him.

"You do make a scene," Rufus mutters, clearly irritated, though it's not clear which of his friends he is addressing.

"We can't all use our father's money to set up some jumped-up little Greek tart like a fucking *wife*," Quintus snarls, still beside himself with anger at his lover's snub. "Why don't you go home and get her to weave some tunics for you?"

"You're drunk," Rufus replies. "You should do what Drusilla says: enjoy one of the girls and sleep it off." He takes Amara's hand and leads her from the room. She does not dare to look back, feeling guilty at leaving Victoria in such a poisonous atmosphere. She holds on tighter to Rufus, reminding herself that she is not making a profit from

Victoria's suffering: all the money Victoria earns tonight will go towards paying Felix for her freedom. "Quintus didn't mean what he said," Rufus mutters, mistaking the cause of her distress, and Amara squeezes his hand in answer.

In the atrium, Philos, Juventus and Drusilla's doorman are sitting on the floor, playing dice by the light of a single lamp. Philos jumps instantly to his feet at his master's approach. The anger Rufus suppressed at Quintus boils over at the easier target of his slaves. He berates them both for idling, especially his steward. "I would have thought better of *you*," he snaps, shoving Philos towards the door. Amara has seen other men treat their slaves much worse – and received worse herself – but this is the first time she has ever seen Rufus raise his hand against another. Any lingering affection she felt for him that evening is snuffed out by the sight of Philos stumbling.

They step onto the darkened street, Juventus walking ahead with a lamp, Philos following with another behind. For the entirety of their short journey, Amara wants to turn around, to look at Philos, to tell him with her eyes that she is sorry. But she does not dare.

They reach the tall, golden door of the rented house, its myriad metal studs shining in the moonlight. Juventus cannot find the keys and fumbles with the lock while Rufus swears under his breath, huffing with impatience. Amara turns to the side, as if glancing down the street, but instead, she looks at Philos. He stares back, and then, when she keeps holding his gaze, long past the point a woman should stare into a man's eyes, he smiles. Before Amara can answer with a smile of her own, Rufus tugs on her arm, pulling her into the darkened hallway of the house.

15

Even woods and the wilder aspects of Nature furnish
medicines, for there is no place where Nature has not
provided remedies for mankind – so that the desert
itself has become a chemist's shop.
Pliny the Elder, Natural History

Amara breathes in the scent of thyme and marigold.
Both take her back to her childhood. She remembers
gathering these herbs for her father, from their small garden
in Aphidnai. The leaves were so tempting to crush between
her fingers, releasing the sweetness of the thyme, the sharp,
peppery tang of the marigold. Her father, Timaios, could
have had a servant help him prepare his medicines, but he
preferred the company of his daughter. She would strip the
thyme carefully from its stems, chopping it finely while he
stood beside her and watched, explaining how a cough
syrup should be prepared. Sometimes, she struggles to recall
the exact cadence of his voice, but not the feeling it gave her.
The certainty of being loved. The impossibility that her life
could be anything but happy.

"Where do you want the marigolds, shall we plant them here? It will look nice when they flower in summer."

Philos is squatting beside her, the pair of them planning the garden. He has just cleared a space for the chamomile. The garden has too few beds to plant as many herbs as Amara would like, but she is determined to bring in a bit more variety, to make it more like her father's house. Rufus was delighted by the idea, urging her to buy the plants when she mentioned it. Any reminder of her respectable past pleases him.

"Yes," she replies. "We can put the yellows together, good idea."

She hands Philos the plant, and he starts to dig it in. Above them, the sky is fading from pink to blue, and the air is loud with birdsong. Martha is busy sweeping the atrium, but nobody else is around. Britannica always slips out before dawn to go running by the arena, and Phoebe, Lais and Victoria are still at Drusilla's after spending the night entertaining her guests. Juventus is out too, keen to leave his dreary role as doorman, even if it's just running errands at the bakery. Amara could almost pretend she and Philos lived here alone, that their relationship were something different. She remembers how it felt to take his arm when he pulled her in close, and warmth spreads through her body.

"So did your father teach you much about medicine?" Philos is intent on his planting. She has been telling him about her father Timaios, about her childhood.

"I suppose so. He certainly taught me everything he knew about herbs, their properties, how to prepare various draughts and lotions. When I was a child, I thought he wanted me to be a doctor, like him. Until I realized that wasn't possible." She can still remember her father's amusement at the idea. *You can be a good doctor to your family, when you run a household of your own.* "He would have liked this garden," she says, looking round at the space. "He believed plants were good for our health, that even spending time contemplating them grow could have benefits."

Philos starts to make room for a marshmallow plant. "I'm sure your father would be proud to see you honouring his memory."

Amara thinks of the future her father imagined for her, the one he failed to protect, and cannot keep the bitterness from her voice. "You are kind. But we both know my father would not see any *honour* in the life I lead now."

"Most doctors I've encountered are pragmatists," Philos replies. "So perhaps you are mistaken."

"And your father?" Amara asks. "What sort of man was he?"

There is a silence while Philos continues to handle the mallow, carefully teasing out the roots without breaking them. He sets it in the soil. Nobody born into slavery can lay claim to a father, Amara knows this, and yet, she also knows that slaves love their parents the same as anyone else. Philos is quiet for so long she thinks he is going to ignore the question. She is about to change the subject to save them both embarrassment, when he speaks. "It depends which father," he says, sitting back on his haunches, so that he can look at her better. "You asked me once how I learned Homer, how I had any education, when I have never been free. That was the gift of the Master, the man who sired me, though I never think of him as my father."

Amara knows this type of parentage is common for

slaves but is still embarrassed. "Was he..." She falters. "Was he a good man?"

"My mother neither liked nor desired him. But she had no choice in the matter. Any more than any other slave, ever has," Philos is still looking at her, and Amara feels her face burn. "After the Master got my mother pregnant, my parents were obliged to raise me as if I were wholly theirs. But my father always treated me with kindness, even though he knew I was not his son."

"Is that certain?" she asks, as if she has the power to change the past by wishing it away. "Might you not be his son, if your parents were together?"

"I looked more like the Master than *any* of his legitimate children. And I heard later, from the cook, that his pursuit of my mother was relentless when she was young. He never gave her any peace." Amara can sense the anger in Philos, even though his voice is calm.

"But he educated you?"

"Yes. And for that, I owe him. For all the hours I spent reading at his house." Philos turns back to his planting, digging into the earth as he speaks, spilling it on the stone. "Not that he acted out of affection, although I was once stupid enough to hope that might be why. It was a joke of his, played against his heirs. The idea I might be cleverer than they were. A point of pride for him, the mark he left of himself, even on a slave."

Amara feels her own anger tighten like a knot in her chest. "But your true parents loved you."

"I often think of my father," Philos says, with a slight smile. "He was the kindest man. He never added to my mother's suffering by blaming her, or me, for what nobody could help. And of course, my parents imagined the Master would leave me my freedom in his will. It was what everyone expected, after he died." Amara says nothing, dreading the next part of the story, knowing who Philos was sold to. "Those who are born free," he says, "they talk in front of slaves as if we have no ears, as if we are fools. But we hear everything, we see everything, and we remember. I could tell you the intimate secrets of half the great families of Pompeii, if either of us wanted to waste our time that way. My parents knew *exactly* what awaited their seventeen-year-old son when they learned I had been sold to Terentius. And in the worst moments, after I left my family, when I thought I could no longer bear my life, I would remember the last thing my father said to me. *Whatever happens to you, in my eyes you are always a man.*"

Philos avoids looking at her while he speaks of Terentius. She understands the shame he risks by telling her this, a humiliation so profound she has seen it warp other men, driving them to violence. But when Philos turns to face her, he does not look ashamed. "And that is why I believe your father would understand. He would not judge you for the choices life has forced you to make, any more than I do."

For a while Amara does not speak. She stares past Philos at the fountain, watching the water splash downwards. "I'm glad they're dead," she manages at last. "Both your old masters. Or I might have to tell Britannica to kill them."

"I'm sure she would be delighted to be asked," Philos says. They smile at one another, allowing their shared amusement to lighten the weight of all he has told her.

"Thank you for what you said about my father."

"It's true," Philos replies, turning back to the mallows, patting down the earth to hold them steady.

She can tell the moment of intimacy between them has passed, that he has already given her as much of himself as he can, but she finds she doesn't want to let go. "Do you miss reading books? It was one of the things I missed most at the Wolf Den."

"Yes, I miss it." He picks up a crumpled hyssop plant from the ground and starts to dig that in too. "On the whole, contracts aren't very entertaining to read."

"Any time you like, whenever you aren't working for Rufus, you can go to my private study and read. You don't need to ask me. I trust you. I don't really have anything exciting." She stumbles on, unnerved by his silence. "No Homer. Just a medical text Pliny gave me, in Greek. But you're welcome to share it, if you want to."

Whatever Philos might have replied, he does not get the chance.

"What are you two doing digging up the garden?" Victoria is standing in the corridor from the atrium, leaning against the wall, her hair tousled.

"You're back!" Amara exclaims, wondering how much Victoria just heard of her offer to Philos. She gestures at the garden. "I'm planting some herbs. Like my father used to grow."

"So *that's* why Juventus came home with half a meadow yesterday morning. I always forget you're a doctor's daughter." Victoria yawns, heading over to the bench. "I suppose the house you grew up in might have been even grander than this one!"

"No," Amara says, not wanting to move away from

Philos but feeling obliged to join her friend on the bench. "It was much smaller. But the garden here reminds me of home."

"I cannot imagine growing up *owning* a garden, can you, Philos?" Victoria says, kissing Amara playfully on the cheek. "I started out on the town dump!"

Amara knows Victoria's life story, how she was abandoned on a rubbish heap at a few months old, as so many unwanted babies are, then picked up to be raised as a slave. She has always admired Victoria for her will to survive, but today there is an unpleasant edge to her voice.

"And now you can share Amara's garden," Philos says, as he digs in the last plant.

"I remember *somebody* once telling me she didn't own it." Victoria's hostility is unmistakable this time.

"Rufus is very generous," Amara says, embarrassed. "The garden belongs to all of us, thanks to him."

Philos has finished the planting and is scraping all the spilled earth back into the beds. The noise of iron on stone grates across Amara's nerves, making her shudder. He stands up. "Do you need anything else?"

"No, thank you," Victoria replies, even though his question was not for her. Philos bows his head, a more formal gesture than he has used to either of them before, and leaves.

"Why were you so rude?" Amara hisses, as soon as he is out of earshot.

"I don't trust him," Victoria replies. "The man creeps about like a cat – I never even know when he's there! And the way he looks at everything! As if *he's* better than everyone, even though he's just a fucking slave."

"That's unfair!" Amara exclaims, surprised that Victoria has noticed so much about Philos, yet somehow managed to mistake his self-containment for arrogance.

"I'm sorry," Victoria says, not sounding sorry at all. "But I can't forget the way he spoke to you, when you first brought me here. Bragging that *you* weren't the mistress of the house! To your face! As if *he* were the one in charge. I still don't know why you put up with it."

Amara is about to defend Philos, to explain that he was trying to protect her, not insult her. But she stops, realizing she may end up betraying feelings she cannot even admit to herself. "Well," she says, as if wavering. "Rufus chose him. It's not my place to say anything about who he has in the house."

Victoria links her arm through Amara's, giving it a squeeze. "Just don't take any shit," she says. "Promise me."

Amara and Victoria have bread and dried fruit together after Juventus returns from the bakery. Victoria is reluctant to talk about the night before, dismissing Amara's anxious questions about Quintus, which makes her suspect the evening was far from pleasant. Instead, they discuss the performance Victoria has planned with Phoebe and Lais for the Floralia. Amara knows she needs to buy Victoria and the two flautists better outfits to perform at Cornelius's house, but is also aware that if she trails round the shops with all three of them, she will unavoidably look like what she is: a pimp. Instead, Amara suggests to Victoria that they go alone, after she has received the client she is expecting that morning. Victoria's delight at the idea assuages some of Amara's guilt at what happened the night before.

In the tablinum, Amara sits waiting for the debtor who promised to call on her. Myrtale is a fellow courtesan, a woman on the very edge of Drusilla's circle, who Amara met at the baths. Myrtale must be in her thirties, and although she is still beautiful, Amara has noticed the envious way she looks at the younger women's bodies, especially Drusilla with her dark, ageless skin. It is always uncomfortable thinking about getting older. There are times Amara suspects one of the reasons Rufus likes her so thin is to starve away the weight of her twenties, to make her look like the young brides men of his class marry.

There is a faint knock at the half-opened door, and Philos shows Myrtale inside. He slips in after her and stands like a shadow under the window to Amara's bedchamber, holding the wax tablets. Amara always does business in Philos's presence now, just as she always discusses her rates and strategies with him.

She rises to greet Myrtale, kissing the air near the other woman's overly rouged cheeks. "So delighted you could call on me."

"What a place this is!" Myrtale says, gawping around at the yellow walls and their finely painted birds. She has a similar accent to Philos and Juventus, which Amara is beginning to understand marks a lower class in Pompeii, the Latin coarsened by the pungent flavour of the local Campanian dialect. She is well aware her own Greek accent is also deemed lower-class, though at least it carries a hint of the exotic.

"I'm very lucky to have such a generous patron."

"Aren't you just!" Myrtale lets out a nervous laugh then clamps her hand to her mouth. It is perhaps intended to be a coy gesture, but only highlights her vulnerability. Amara thinks of Felix, how he would probe this woman's weaknesses, eviscerating her, forcing her to take on debts she could never repay. *But I am not Felix*, she tells herself.

"I cannot remember your patron's name?"

"Oh." Myrtale looks embarrassed. "I have a couple of callers. One is very loyal, but he's been sick lately. Which is why I need the loan."

"I'm glad to hear the man is loyal."

"Well, not *that* loyal." Myrtale huffs. "He's promised for years to marry me. But don't they all? Still, I'm grateful for what he does. Better than nothing."

Amara cannot help feeling exasperated at the woman for exposing herself. "How much do you want?" she asks, more curtly than she intends. She realizes she is looking in the drawer, rooting about, just as Felix does when he is irritated. Amara slams the drawer shut, making Myrtale jump.

"Five denarii." Myrtale lowers her voice, perhaps alarmed by the idea her creditor finds her annoying.

"My rate is five per cent." Amara is about to explain that after three months the interest rises, but she sees the alarm on the other woman's face. Even five per cent is going to be a struggle. She decides to waive the higher rate. "If you are happy with that, my steward will draw up the contract. Though you also need to give me some surety."

"I was wondering," Myrtale says, "given this is between friends, could we do without that part?"

Amara is conscious of Philos staring at her, but whereas

he usually gives some indication of his opinion, his face is completely blank. "No," Amara says. "But I can see a lovely ring on your right hand. That will do very well."

Myrtale hides the ring, clasping it inside her fingers. "That was a gift from my first patron," she says. "It's worth more than five denarii."

"If you don't pay me, I will refund you the difference." Myrtale still looks uncertain, so Amara holds out her hand to press home her demand. "If you want the loan, give it to me, please." Myrtale pulls the ring from her finger, gets up, places it on the desk, then sits back down again. Amara can see tears in her eyes. "I've no doubt you will be able to pay me," she says, tucking the ring into a string purse. "And then you can have it back. Now, if you would like to sign, my steward has the contract."

While Philos is in the process of scratching out the higher rate of interest and getting both women's signatures, Martha sticks her head around the door. "Master wants him," she says, nodding at her fellow slave.

Philos hands Amara the tablets, after Myrtale has signed. "If you will excuse me," he murmurs.

"That's a lot of servants you have," Myrtale says, when Martha and Philos have left.

"They are my patron's servants."

Myrtale nods. "It all goes very fast, you know," she says, her voice bitter. "I was like you once."

The make-up on Myrtale's face has cracked, and tears have smudged the kohl, so it cakes in the creases around her eyes, making her appear even older than she is. It reminds Amara of Cressa at the Wolf Den, that look of a woman on the slow downward slide, or worse, of Fabia, the abject destitution of old age. It is a terrifying thought, and her fear curdles into cruelty. "I very much doubt you were ever like me," she says, walking to the door and opening it in a sign of dismissal.

Philos has already left by the time Victoria and Amara set off on their shopping trip. No doubt he was summoned, as usual, to help Rufus or Hortensius in the administration of the family business. Amara thinks of the gem-cutting workshops and jewellery stores that line the outside of Rufus's house. They have been a source of gifts for her, and a source of curiosity too whenever she dares pass by, but for Philos, every room, every item, must be familiar. Not to mention his knowledge of the accounts. It gives her a strange feeling, imagining all the many things she does not know about his life.

"Where shall we go?" Victoria is asking, bouncing on the balls of her feet with excitement. "Here on your street? Or somewhere new?" Her face shines bright as Amara's silver mirror when it catches the light.

"I thought we could go to the Via Veneria. Try one of the bigger shops. The one near Julia's place has so many Assyrian silks – we'll be there for hours."

Victoria seizes Amara's hand. "Perfect!"

Amara is aware of the sidelong glances they attract, walking along the pavement together, but Victoria does not care. She never seems to have learned that there is no need to fish for male attention anymore, or perhaps she wants to make up for the slight Quintus paid her yesterday. Her eyes are everywhere, hungry for admiration. Amara is not sure whether to be amused or exasperated.

"We'll never get to the shop at this rate," she says, after

Victoria's passing causes a row between an outraged woman and her leering husband.

"Think of the tips I'll make at the Floralia," Victoria replies, tossing her head. "This is just practice."

The fabric shop is one of the prettiest on the Via Veneria. Above the open front, paintings from the legends of Venus look down. The goddess of love receives offerings from her servants, a serpent coiled at her feet for good fortune. Unlike Virgula's place, very few fabrics have been hung out on the street, perhaps too precious to be left to chance. Amara has a sudden misgiving about the price.

Victoria darts in before Amara can voice her anxiety, heading to the counter with the confidence of a woman who has imagined herself doing this for years. "Assyrian silk," Amara hears her say to the serving girl. "We'd like to see everything you have."

The girl glances from one woman to the other, sizing them up. Her eyes come to rest on the silver pendant at Amara's neck, with its perfect amber drop. The first present Rufus ever gave her, the one that still retains the sheen in Amara's memory of something close to love. "At the back, ladies," she says, with an obsequious smile.

Amara follows the girl, Victoria tripping eagerly ahead. It is impossible not to picture Dido's slighter form replacing Victoria's voluptuous one. Only a year ago, Amara and Dido visited a clothes shop in Pompeii for the first time. She remembers Dido's amazement at the transparent silver silk. *It's like wearing a cobweb.*

The girl leads them both to a small, white room, decorated with a series of painted cupids. An interior window high up on the wall must open onto the atrium of the grand house that owns the shop space, although Amara cannot see anything through it but the rafters. She finds herself thinking of Philos again, wonders if right now he is working in a room like this.

Victoria stands hovering near the shop assistant. The girl is leafing through a wooden frame that looks like a book of giant wax tablets, only silk has replaced the dull yellow of the pages. "They vary in price," she says. "Cheapest at the front. The best at the back."

"We'll see your cheapest material for two dresses and a range of silks for a third. But nothing too pricey." Amara glances at Victoria who nods in agreement. They have already discussed the money. Every penny Victoria makes will help pay the debt to Felix. Only when that is finally cleared will she keep her own earnings, with a small cut to Amara as rent. For now, her choice of clothes is limited.

Amara quickly chooses some silk for Phoebe and Lais, the cheapest on offer, and two of the plainest pins. Victoria, however, is in no mood to rush. The shop girl has brought her five different silks and she savours each one in turn, touching the fabric with the reverence of a priest handling offerings at sacrifice. Victoria lifts her arms and the material clings to her body, revealing and burnishing her nakedness. Amara smiles. She knows how much Victoria loves clothes, remembers the hours Victoria spent at the brothel regaling everyone with tales of the finery she would buy if she were rich. But when Victoria tries on the last, a translucent, shimmering green, Amara realizes with surprise that Victoria's eyes are shining with unshed tears.

"What is it?" she whispers, pulling her aside, so that the curious shop girl cannot hear.

"It's so beautiful," Victoria whispers, her voice trembling. "And he'll never get to see me this way or tell me how lovely I look." She scrunches up her face, reminding Amara of Drusilla's son Primus when he is trying not to cry. "I miss him so much. Sometimes, I just can't *believe* I'll never see him again."

Amara puts an arm around her. "You'll find somebody else," she murmurs, her cheek pressed to Victoria's. "I promise you."

"He's the only man I've ever loved," Victoria says. "There's nobody else like him."

Bitterness wells up in Amara's heart, like sap from a hemlock stem. *That's true enough*, she thinks. "I promise it will pass," she repeats. "I promise you'll forget him."

"Could I come with you tomorrow?" Victoria asks. "When you go to pay him? Just to explain that I forgive him. And say that I hope... I hope he forgives me, too."

Amara thinks of Felix, his utter lack of concern for Victoria, his endless brutality, and cannot help but feel irritated by her friend's lack of sense. "I don't think that's a good idea," she says. "But I can tell him for you if you like."

Victoria looks up at Amara, her expression uncharacteristically vulnerable. "Would you? You promise me?"

Amara smooths the tears from Victoria's cheeks, cupping her face in her hands. "Of course I will," she lies. "I promise."

16

Now that I know you, you're much cheaper, lighter,
And yet desire in me flares even brighter.

Catullus, Poem 72

"**Y**ou want go in *here?*"
 Britannica is looking doubtfully at Amara, the
pair of them loitering by the doorway of a tavern. Asellina's
bar is on the busiest stretch of the Via Veneria, and even in
the middle of the day, the noise inside is raucous, hot air
billowing from the door.

"It's the only place Fabia would agree to meet," Amara
says. "And besides, we can see Nicandrus again." Britannica
scowls, unsentimental about the idea of meeting old friends.
"I need to know what Felix is up to before I see him,"
Amara adds, exasperated at having to coax her own slave
into doing as she asks.

Britannica shrugs, a gesture of half-hearted agreement.
They scan the street, making one last check that nobody
they know is in sight, then duck to enter, trying to avoid the
metal phallus hanging over the door. The Briton is so tall
she still manages to hit it. The chimes clank out a warning,

bells quivering. Heads turn. Some drinkers only glance over, curious, before returning to their own business, but a number laugh and whistle.

"Here to slum it ladies?" one shouts. "Want the taste of a real man?"

"Fuck off," Britannica says. "*You* no man."

The drinker hesitates, torn between wanting to defend his honour and alarm at the speed with which Britannica's hand has slid inside her cloak, reaching for her knife.

"You're an ugly bitch anyway," he mutters, slouching down lower in his chair.

"*None of that, thank you.*"

A woman is standing by Amara's elbow. She must have crossed over from behind the counter. Her face is shining from the heat of the oven, and she has an unfriendly expression.

"We didn't mean any trouble," Amara says in a low voice. "Are you Asellina? We're here to see Fabia, a friend of Nicandrus."

"*That* old bag of bones," Asellina replies. "She's over there, by the stairwell. Claims friends are buying her lunch."

Amara looks across the small fuggy room in the direction of Asellina's gaze. Fabia is waving a scrawny arm from where she sits at a table in the corner, half-hidden in the shadows. "That's her," Amara says, nodding. "And yes, I will be buying stew for the three of us. Please can you make sure it is Nicandrus who serves. I should like to see him again."

The landlady raises her eyebrows, taking in Amara's fine cloak and her eccentric-looking slave. "As you wish," she says.

Amara and Britannica weave their way through the tables to the back, avoiding their earlier tormentor, although the man now seems equally keen to ignore them. "What the fuck were you thinking?" Amara says to Fabia as she sits down, her tone slipping to fit the surroundings. "How is this more private than meeting at my place?"

"I can't have Victoria seeing me," Fabia replies, unperturbed by the rude greeting. "Don't trust her not to tell Felix."

Britannica nods. "Is best," she says. "He still own her."

"He does *not* still own her," Amara replies, but before she can get into another fruitless argument with Britannica, Nicandrus appears, ducking under the stairwell with a tray of dishes.

"Amara!" he exclaims.

She looks at him, and in that moment, she is back at The Sparrow, back with Dido, Nicandrus hovering beside them, his love for Dido as evident as if he had painted it in red graffiti across his tunic. "Oh," she says, clamping a hand to her mouth, tears springing to her eyes.

"Amara," Nicandrus repeats, setting down the tray. She can see he is similarly affected. It is all she can do not to embrace him.

"It's so good to see you," she says. "Can't you sit with us?"

"I'm needed at the shop," he replies, looking embarrassed. "Asellina told me I can only stay if you pay her a tip for my time. And even then, not for long." Nicandrus looks grubbier and skinnier than Amara remembers. She suspects his new boss is less amiable than Zoskales.

"Of course I'll pay," she says.

Nicandrus pulls a stool over and sits at the edge of the table, glancing over his shoulder. He looks nervous. Amara pushes two asses towards him for Asellina, which he pockets, and then offers him her stew. He shakes his head. Fabia is already slurping noisily, spoon scraping against the sides of her bowl.

"How are you?" Amara asks.

Nicandrus flicks his eyes back towards the kitchen, a gesture to show he cannot talk freely. "My mistress is generous," he says. They stare at one another, and the weight of Dido's unspoken absence grows more painful, the longer she is left unmentioned. "Not that it matters," he adds. "Nothing has mattered since that night."

"I'm sorry."

"You loved her too. You understand how special she was."

"Did he bury her?" Amara knows it's a cruel question to ask, but she cannot stop herself. The need to know burns through, like embers wrapped in parchment.

"I don't know," Nicandrus says, his face contorted with grief. "I begged him to tell me. I even…" He hesitates, swallowing. "I threatened him. So Zoskales sold me."

"*You* threatened Felix?"

"I loved her. She was everything to me."

Nicandrus always made an unlikely romantic hero, with his scrawny frame and hopeless, largely silent devotion. Amara used to think her friend had deserved better, but now realizes how profoundly she underestimated him. "Dido loved you too," she says, reaching across the table to take his hand. "I don't know if she ever told you, because she didn't want to suffer more by loving someone she could not have. But I promise you, you were the only man she ever cared for, the only one she considered to be truly kind. You were a light in her life."

Nicandrus cries silently while she speaks. Then he takes his hand back, pressing both palms to his eyes with a ferocity that leaves smears of dirt on his face. When he has wiped away all trace of tears, he stands up. "I have to go."

Amara watches his thin figure slip between the tables, until he has stepped behind the counter, disappearing into the adjoining shop. The shapes of the other drinkers and diners waver and blur as she stares, unable to call him back.

Fabia taps her spoon against Amara's bowl. "You going to eat that, or can I have it?"

"Don't you have any fucking feelings?" Amara snaps.

"Feeling sorry for Nicandrus and Dido won't keep the stew warm," Fabia retorts. "And I haven't eaten in two days."

Britannica has started to eat too, leaving Amara the only one staring at her untouched food. She pushes the bowl towards Fabia. "Have it."

The hubbub of the tavern is loud around them. She watches the old woman polish off the second bowl, licking around the edges to pick up every last smudge of sauce. Amara can hear two men haggling over the sale of a mule at the table behind, their tone increasingly heated. She looks away from Fabia to the wall. There's a small, peeling painting of a waitress handing out flagons of wine, a caption running above her head: *Everyone wants a kiss.* Underneath, somebody else has scratched a reply: *Fat chance with this landlady.*

"So what do you want to know?" Fabia's stew is finished.

"Has he said anything about me?" Amara does not use Felix's name, but there's no need. They all know who she means.

"Been in a much better mood since your last visit. Beronice caught him *whistling* the other day. Whistling!" Fabia shakes her head. "Otherwise, the same old bastard."

Britannica, who is still eating, snarls something in her own language. Amara does not have to understand the words to catch the murderous intention. She ignores the outburst. "Has he spoken about Victoria?"

"Won't let us mention her," Fabia says, lowering her voice. "Not that anyone would dare. Though he doesn't exactly seem heartbroken. Has the new girl upstairs a fair bit. Nothing like the time he used to spend with *you*, of course." She darts a sly glance at Amara, as if she might be flattered by the information.

"And Beronice?"

"Still lovesick for Gallus. Surprised by how long that's lasted. I thought he'd have dropped her by now." Fabia has her arms folded, and her eyes have drifted to the door. The old woman is obviously nervous staying here, now her stew is gone. *She's not the only one*, Amara thinks. Then Fabia suddenly leans over the table, and Amara does the same, so their heads are close together, almost touching. "The real news is, he's branching out," she whispers. "He's renting a small bar outside the baths. Gallus and Thraso are both desperate to run it. But the boss is stringing them along, not decided yet." In spite of herself, Amara feels a flicker of admiration. If she were Felix, the brothel would not be enough for her either. Fabia straightens up. "And that's about it."

"Thank you," Amara says, though she is not sure, on balance, that the risk of discovery was worth the information. "I don't think I can do this again, Fabia. It's too much, coming to a tavern right on the Via Veneria. Rufus might find out."

Fabia nods. "It doesn't feel safe."

"And you really won't come to the house? I *promise* you Victoria would never tell." There is no hesitation to Fabia's shake of the head. Her fear of Felix is greater even than the risk of starvation. "Then I will leave a tab at the counter for you," Amara says. "Enough for ten meals. If you come twice a week that's five weeks. After that I will send Britannica back to renew it."

"Why?" Fabia asks, frowning. "I can't give you any more information that way."

"But you can," Amara says. "You can leave messages with Nicandrus if there's anything you think I should know. Britannica will come by each week to collect them for me. That's if you think it's a fair exchange."

Whether she is enthusiastic about this idea or not, Fabia is not fool enough to turn down free food. "Of course. A small price to pay for such generosity." The two women smile at one another – the beautiful courtesan, and the shadow of what she fears to become.

Amara does not take Britannica with her to see Felix. She returns home to collect Philos and Juventus, to share out the money between them for the walk over. At the brothel, they wait upstairs in the black-and-white painted room. Amara remembers the comfort she used to feel hearing

Philos call for her when she lived here, knowing it signalled her escape for a few hours to be with Rufus. She takes no comfort looking at Philos now. His head is bowed, his arms tense as he grips the bench. Juventus, sitting between them, looks more at home. He has spread himself out so much, Amara has to shift over to avoid his thigh touching hers. He turns to Philos, grinning, and says something in their dialect. From the slight hesitation before Philos replies, and the sudden surliness of Juventus's expression, Amara guesses they were talking about her.

She cannot name the feeling she has, getting up when Paris calls her, or fully explain the anticipation she feels stepping into the study. Felix is seated at his desk. Amara wills herself to look at him as if he were any other man, to study him, to see his weaknesses and not her own fear. She breathes in, noticing the smell of fresh oil. His hair is slicked back, his face smooth. He must have shaved that morning.

"I want the money first this time," he says curtly, gesturing at the empty seat. She crosses over, dropping the leather purses on the desk, standing as she watches him count out the coins. He glances up, aware of her looming over him. "*Sit.*" Amara does as he asks. "That's fine," Felix says, shoving the empty purses at her, then scraping the money noisily over the side of the desk into a box. "It's very trusting of posh boy, letting you come here to see me. I'm surprised he allows it."

Amara calculates the value of lying, before deciding on the truth. "He doesn't know."

"And is Victoria compensating you for taking such a risk?" Felix never bothers to ask about Britannica.

"I believe she will," Amara replies. "Now that I have other girls to sell alongside her."

She cannot read the emotion behind Felix's stare, only sense its intensity. "You're a pimp now?"

Amara shrugs. "Of course. I know a little about the business. We all have to make money."

"Perhaps I should up your interest."

"You can't. Philos wrote that into the contract." She knows Felix already knew this, that he was testing how far he could frighten her. He smiles, and Amara catches the scent of his carefully oiled hair. Somehow, she knows then, that he dressed it for her. The thought makes her bold. "You never made the best use of me," she says.

"What's that supposed to mean?"

"I could have made us five times as much." Felix does not pick her up on her use of the plural, though she knows he has heard it. "For a man who likes making money, I never understood why you didn't pursue your own interests better."

"You think you'd have made a good business partner?"

"You know I would. You just couldn't bear to admit we're the same."

Felix laughs. "That's what you think?" Amusement lights up his eyes, so easy to mistake for affection. "And tell me" – he leans his head on his hands, a pose of false intimacy she remembers from her life as his slave – "if *you* had been me, how welcoming might you have been, if you saw yourself in another?" Amara hesitates. She had not considered this, had not seriously imagined that Felix had, in fact, understood her. "Exactly," he says, his voice dry. Felix opens a drawer in his desk and reaches inside without looking down, taking out an object whose place must be so familiar he can find it by touch alone. It is the statue of the hunter goddess Diana which she sent him after she gained her freedom. Her promise of revenge. He sets it gently on the desk. "You cannot fool me, Amara. I know what hatred looks like. And I know how my father died."

Amara stares at the small figure. Diana with her bow, poised to strike. She flicks through her memories of Fabia, gossip stacked like a linen chest, the words she thought less important, shoved to the back. *The old Master died in a street brawl. Enough men wanted him dead, didn't they? All that money he was owed.* Amara thinks of Drauca, of Simo, of all those Felix has killed without wielding the knife himself. And she understands. Felix avenged his mother's death, after all.

She does not dare return his gaze. "You're wrong about this," Amara says, picking up the statue and turning the roughly hewn god over in her fingers. "I wasn't wishing you ill. You told me once that I reminded you of Diana when you bought me. What woman is not touched by being compared to a goddess?" Felix has narrowed his eyes, and she knows he is not convinced. She will have to give him something more, something that is closer to the truth. Amara reaches for the shame she carries in the darkest part of herself, letting it spill out between them. "I am like you Felix, but not you. If you could have brought yourself to acknowledge me, instead of humiliating me, nobody would have been more loyal."

Amara's cheeks are flaming, her emotion unfeigned. "So that's what you wanted," he sneers, as if cruelty can hide the answering flush on his own face. "Just like any other fucking woman. For a man to pretend he loves you. You're no better than Victoria."

"It's not about *love*!" Amara shouts, unable to contain herself. "Do you think I ever gave a shit about that?" She stands up, and Felix scrapes back his own chair, mirroring her movement so they are facing each other across the desk. Amara leans over it, her palms pressed flat to its surface. "I could have made us rich," she says. "I could *still* make us rich."

Amara's arms tremble from the pressure of so much pent-up hatred. Felix reaches for her, but she pushes him away. "No," she says, stepping back. "I'm not a slave anymore. *Earn it.*"

He is cold in his anger. "You think I won't just take it?"

She holds up her hands, turning them, her fingers playing over the rings Rufus has given her. The symbol of her patron's ownership and his power. Amara smiles at her old master, enjoying his impotence. "I think you wouldn't dare."

17

It's because they're smitten by our looks that our lovers worship us; when our looks have faded they take their fancy elsewhere; if we haven't made some provision in the meantime, we find ourselves abandoned.

Bacchis speaking in Terence's play "The Self Tormentor"

The weight of the hair being pinned to Drusilla's head must make her neck ache, but she gives no sign of discomfort. Thalia, her maid, is winding plaits into an intricate design, pausing now and then to fix them in place. Drusilla stares calmly ahead, facing the window to her garden. It is late afternoon and a shaft of sunlight cuts through the room, catching the dust motes as they dance.

Amara's hair has already been dressed, pins digging painfully into her scalp to keep the false tresses in place. It had been Rufus who suggested that she allow Drusilla to dress her, anxious that she make the right impression at the Floralia, which is also her public appearance as his lover. Rufus also wanted the afternoon's events to be a surprise for her, telling her nothing of what would be happening in the planned procession, but Drusilla, fortunately, believes surprises are only for children.

"You've seen the carriage?" Amara asks.

"I've ridden in it once before," Drusilla replies. "Last year. It belongs to Quintus's family. Did you not see the procession?"

Amara shakes her head. Last year, she was performing at Cornelius's house with Dido, the same place she has sent Victoria and the flautists to perform tonight. Victoria had been disappointed to miss the theatre, but Amara is secretly relieved. She is not sure how Victoria might have reacted to the sight of her carried in triumph through the streets. "I've never ridden in a carriage," she says. "I can't imagine it."

Thalia has finally finished Drusilla's hair and hands her mistress the mirror. Drusilla checks the maid's work then nods to dismiss her. "There's nothing like it," Drusilla says, when they are alone. "You will feel like a god."

Both women stand, helping one another with last-minute adjustments to their clothes. Drusilla's fingers are gentle as she fixes the line of Amara's red silk at the shoulder. Amara had been surprised by the robes Rufus gave her. The silk is not transparent, but still more revealing than she would have expected, the folds clinging to her body. She had insisted upon wearing the silver necklace with the amber pendant, his first gift to her, and the sentimentality of the gesture pleased him, though he has made sure more of his wealth is pinned to her body in other ways: pearl drop earrings loaned from his family business, silver bracelets, and glittering pins that stud her tightly coiled hair.

For all this, Amara knows that Drusilla still outshines her. Pompeii's foremost courtesan is swathed in yellow silk and decked in gold, the gilding she has painted around her eyes glowing bright against her dark brown skin. The knowledge gives Amara a pang, not so much of jealousy, more bitterness towards her lover. *If I were not so thin*, she thinks, *we would be more evenly matched.*

The sound of trumpets, carried on the warm afternoon air, alerts them both to the approaching procession. They hurry downstairs to the atrium, standing to wait near the door. Amara's heart flutters with anticipation as the noise grows louder, not just trumpets but singing and shouting. It reaches a crescendo: the parade must have stopped right outside Drusilla's door. To her surprise, Drusilla reaches over and grasps her hand. "Don't be nervous," she says, although Amara is not sure, from the uncharacteristically wide-eyed look on Drusilla's face, whether the command is as much to herself.

There is a lull in the noise, followed by two trumpet blasts. Drusilla's steward Josephus opens the door. Standing on the road outside is an enormous, crimson carriage, its four gilded wheels almost the same height as Amara. Two bay horses are harnessed to it, their sides flecked with froth and their nostrils wide. One of them is pawing at the paving stones, shaking its head in a way Amara finds alarming. Perhaps it is agitated by all the commotion.

She steps onto the pavement to meet the waiting crowd, and her fear is drowned by a surge of excitement. The scene reminds her of the Vinalia, the huge gaggle of women flooding the street. The ones at the front are finely dressed, draped in garlands of flowers, mingling with the musicians; she sees one throw back her head and laugh, throat flashing white in the sun. Behind the carriage, a long trail of rougher-looking women snakes down the road. Some are staring at the wealthy courtesans; others talk and laugh among themselves. Amara knows they are prostitutes: the Floralia is one of the only times whores get to be celebrated in public. The stench of sweat, covered by cheap perfume, is overpowering. Amara looks over the sea of faces, thinking of Dido, until it occurs to her that her abandoned friend, Beronice, might be somewhere in the crowd, and quickly turns away.

Drusilla is the first to be handed into the carriage. Amara waits, her eye caught by the painted metal medallions on the back of the seat. It is a writhing fretwork of naked bodies – satyrs embracing nymphs, the women's forms contorted in their attempts to get away. For a moment Amara feels unsteady, unwelcome memories pressing against the edges of her mind. She sways, and the attendant holds out his hand to steady her. Amara grips it as he helps her up onto the seat beside Drusilla. She forces the brothel from her imagination. The Floralia celebrates sexual pleasure; the women are here to be enjoyed. It's what the guests at Cornelius's house will expect from Victoria, Phoebe and Lais later; it's why Amara sent them. It's the unspoken bargain she made with Rufus too, the reason she is being celebrated.

The movement of the horses startles her, even though she is anticipating it. Amara holds the seat of the carriage, looking about in amazement. They are so high up she is seeing the passing street from a totally different perspective, almost level with the upper windows of the houses. She glimpses a young boy's face, peeking between shutters, before he ducks out of sight. The rumble of the wheels, the noise of the trumpets and the singing makes it almost impossible to speak, but Amara turns to Drusilla and smiles, seeing the same excitement on her friend's face. Drusilla is clutching the sheaves of wheat and roses they were handed, and Amara remembers her own flowers just in time, grabbing the stems before they spill from her lap to the floor.

The late afternoon sun beats down on them as they make their slow progress along the Via Veneria. The carriage jolts, even though it is slow moving, the wheels finding their way into the ruts on the road. Amara and Drusilla look down on the people who have crowded out of the buildings to watch them. The men stare, no doubt eyeing up the goods richer men get to enjoy, but it's the gaze of the women that Amara savours. It is a new sensation to be the subject of so much envy, a reminder of how far she has come, of all Rufus has given her. She thinks of how he was when they first met, his joy at giving her the necklace she is now wearing, and wishes she could still see him that way, as a more innocent man than he really is.

Amara is faint from the heat by the time the procession reaches the theatre but still steps down from the carriage with reluctance. She and Drusilla are absorbed into the crowd of women and musicians, their loss of height suddenly lowering their status. She watches the carriage leave with regret, jostled by the crush. The Floralia is never a festival for restraint, and squashed beside her, a woman from the procession is already kissing one of the musicians, the flowers in her hair crumpled in disarray. Not everyone in Pompeii is invited to the free performance at the theatre, most will be making do with celebrations outside in the square. Drusilla takes Amara's hand, and the pair of them push their way towards the theatre's entrance. Drusilla's height is imposing, and enough memory of their arrival in the carriage lingers for people to let them pass.

There is very little queue in the corridor, or up the stairs; most of the other spectators have already been seated – all except Rufus and the most important men in attendance. Drusilla and Amara make their entrance high up in the auditorium, which should provide them with a more discreet arrival, but Amara is aware of murmuring, of eyes on her body. The great curve of the theatre confronts her, a wall of faces, watching. She feels the heat flood to her cheeks. It is many years since she was respectable, but the shame still lingers: she knows notoriety is frowned on in a woman. The honour Rufus pays her is double-edged, possible only because she has no real honour to lose. Amara feels a flash of anger. She thinks of Britannica, the way she stands, the challenge in her eyes, and stares back. *Let them look.*

"Don't enjoy the attention too much," Drusilla murmurs, amusement in her voice.

They pick their way carefully down the stone steps nearest to the empty box of honour, which sits beside the stage. It is difficult to walk modestly in her silk dress, and Amara is conscious of how much of her body must be showing as she moves. Drusilla, who chose her own clothes, has an easier time, stepping gracefully, the yellow folds of material exposing less. Eventually, they reach the space which has been reserved for them both. Rufus explained they will sit behind the wall separating the ordinary spectators from those in the box. He will be on the other side of it – close but totally unreachable.

Amara is grateful for the cushions on the hard stone. She is making herself comfortable, smoothing out the silk, beginning to feel her excitement rise again, when applause breaks out. Rufus, Helvius and their supporters have entered the auditorium. Everyone knows it is Rufus who paid for the entertainment. Amara may no longer be sure how much affection she has for her lover, but the pride she feels is undeniable. She sits upright, trying to get a better view, and feels Drusilla's fingers rest on her arm. "I suspect you never felt happier to see him," Drusilla whispers.

Rufus is climbing the stairs to the box, and Amara tries to catch his eye, but he does not look at her. Hortensius, his father, is beside him, and it is the older man whose gaze flicks towards the two courtesans. He ignores Amara, instead acknowledging Drusilla with a slight smile. Then both he and Rufus disappear from view.

"Hortensius always seems very taken with you," Amara says, covering her hurt at the lack of Rufus's attention.

Drusilla purses her lips. "He'd have to bring a city of gold for me to tolerate *that* temper."

"Is he a violent man?"

Drusilla shrugs. "Not so much as his own father, by all accounts. You are lucky Rufus is sweeter natured than either."

"Do you mean *Terentius*?" Amara says, her voice rising louder than she intends, shocked that Drusilla might have known the man who caused Philos so much pain.

"Not now." Drusilla casts her eyes to the side to indicate the possibility they might be overheard.

Amara can see the musicians taking their place on the stage, stepping through the brightly painted doorways. Rufus already explained the series of entertainments to her: a short mime for Flora, then his chosen play before another, longer, mime. She settles back, trying to lose herself in the show, to let go of her own life for a while. Movement and colour pass across the stage in a river, the performers indistinct. Amara finds her thoughts wandering, taking her back to Cornelius's house at last year's Floralia, her own performance with Dido by the fountain with the gilded nymphs, the rapt look on Dido's face when she sang. Amara closes her eyes, remembering.

A familiar word jolts her back into the present. *Chremes.* Even with an Italian accent mauling her native Greek, the name hits Amara with unpleasant force. It is her first master, the man her mother sold her to in Aphidnai, who used her as a concubine before allowing her to be sold on as a whore. Except here, on the stage, he is a different Chremes: an old man troubled by his son's relationship with a prostitute. Amara tries to concentrate, her palms sweating. Rufus does not know what the name might mean to her; she has never spoken of Chremes to him.

Bacchis the courtesan enters the stage to whistles and laughter. The actress's mannerisms are exaggerated, and she is swathed in bright green robes, beads hanging from her wrists. A troupe of dancing girls follows her. From so far away, Amara cannot catch all the words, but she hears enough. The woman is obsessed with amassing money, terrified of her looks fading, playing a part for as long as she can. Amara looks at Drusilla, but her friend appears undisturbed, smiling as the indignities of their lives are laid bare. Amara turns back to stare at Bacchis, mesmerized by this unkind version of herself, appalled that this might be how Rufus sees her.

A more innocent girl on the stage professes her love

for a single client, hands pressed to her heart in sincerity. Amara feels a rush of relief. In Rufus's imagination, surely *this* fragile creature is her, not Bacchis. The story settles back into the familiar tale she has heard from her lover a thousand times before, as well-worn as cart grooves in the road: the virtuous girl, snatched into prostitution, freed by her generous patron who marries her when the reality of her high birth is revealed. Amara has never found it comforting, having no high birth to fall back upon, and now it reassures her even less.

Amara finds herself thinking of what Philos said to her. *Only fools think life is like a play, with any hope of holding on to your virtue.* Philos is a very different man from Felix, but both, she realizes, are more like she is than Rufus will ever be. It is not difficult to imagine her old master's scorn at the tale being performed on the stage. Her cheeks burn as she remembers their last meeting, the suggestions she made. There are times she cannot believe the game she is playing with Felix. That she would even contemplate doing business with him seems like madness, even if she is in his debt. And yet, Felix knows how to protect himself. He will never be like Myrtale, or worse, like Fabia. And should Rufus drop her, Amara may have little choice over who she associates with. Better to be Felix, or his ally, than to starve.

She glances over at the box where her patron is sitting, as if she might seek his reassurance, even though she cannot see him. The blank wall brings her no comfort. Rufus has placed her here, dressed in scarlet, borrowed jewels pinned to her body, and even if he does not understand the truth today, he will eventually: she is Bacchis. Amara thinks back

to the night he revealed his anger, remembering his words
– *it's tainted you.* She closes her eyes, imagining herself
at home, safe in her private study, not sat here, on public
display, smiling through her fear.

18

First Writer: Lovers, like bees, live a honeyed life.
Second Writer: I wish.
Pompeii graffiti exchange

A mara is carried back from the theatre in a litter. Evening is only just falling, but she cannot join Drusilla for dinner without Rufus present, not when there are men attending, and her patron is with his family tonight. Inside the litter, it is dark, the curtains cocooning her, screening her from passers-by but also shutting her in. She tries to enjoy the luxury of being carried, but it makes her nervous to think of her weight bearing down on the shoulders of the men outside, the poles bruising their flesh. The disorientation of not seeing where she is going means it is both a relief and a surprise when the litter comes to a stop. The bearers lower her to the ground, and she steps out onto the pavement. Amara knocks on the tall front door, the men who have carried her a shadow at her back. The heavy wood creaks open, and she slips inside.

Juventus does not immediately step back when she enters.

Amara tries to move out of the way, but he leans across her to bolt the door, forcing her to squeeze past or be trapped. She hurries out of the corridor while he is busy locking up, swiftly crossing the atrium to her room, pretending to herself that she is not afraid of him.

Light flickers over the dancing nymphs painted on the walls of her room, giving the illusion of movement. Martha has left a lamp burning for her on the table by the couch. Beside it is a glass of wine – perhaps the maid imagined her mistress might want to indulge in some solitary celebrations for the Floralia. Amara thinks of Dido and, not for the first time since Rufus freed her, wonders if she would trade everything she has, even endure being in the Wolf Den, to have Dido back again.

There is a noise from the atrium, no doubt Juventus checking over the house before settling down to sleep. Amara resists the urge to take both wine and lamp and lock herself in her bedroom. It's not as if she is totally alone in the house with the doorman. Philos, Martha and Britannica must be somewhere around too.

Instead of hiding herself, Amara sits down at her dressing table. The studs Rufus loaned her are tightly fastened in her hair, and she removes them carefully, counting them out twice, laying them with the priceless pearl earrings in a box. The wine is overly sweet, but she keeps sipping it, until she can feel its warmth spread through her limbs, loosening them. She picks up the silver mirror, trying to see her face, but the reflection is distorted by shadows: it could almost belong to anyone. Amara half expects to see Bacchis, the prostitute from the play, staring back at her. She spends her life pretending, and without Dido, without anyone to trust completely, Amara is afraid she might be forgetting what it means to be herself.

The glass is empty now, but Dido's absence is not dulled by the wine. Amara's longing to see her friend, to talk to her, makes her fingers shake as she unpins her hair. Dido is dead, and without her, grief and loneliness swallow the unspent love in Amara's heart. She thinks of the money box in her private study, and the need to touch it, to reassure herself it is still there, becomes overwhelming.

The lamp in her hand throws its beams across the atrium, and her shadow is a wavering dark line, as she creeps over the cold tiles and up the stairs. Amara pushes open the study door. The first thing that surprises her is that another lamp is already burning on the desk, the second that Philos is sitting behind it. Pliny's scroll is rolled out in front of him.

"What are you doing in here?"

"I didn't mean to surprise you." Philos rises from the chair. "You told me to come any time I wasn't working. I didn't expect you this evening."

"Of course," Amara says, flustered. "I don't mind at all." She steps over the threshold, letting the door close, shutting them both in. Philos watches her, keeping very still. Silence builds like smoke, filling the room, making it harder to breathe.

"The text is more difficult than I expected," Philos says, at last. "The scribe's hand is very cramped, and my Greek perhaps not as good as I thought."

"Which part are you reading?"

"Have a look, if you like." He lifts the scroll slightly from the desk.

She walks over, the wine still hot in her veins, and

stands beside him. Spread out below is a familiar diagram. Herophilus's explanation for the circulation of the blood. Amara stares at it. She has read the words many times before, but in this moment, she cannot process any of them. All she can see is Philos's hand resting on the parchment. She lays her own over it and turns to face him. He is gazing at her, as if waiting to see what she does. It reminds her of Felix, both of them standing at the desk, and the thought makes her feel suddenly uncertain.

Philos takes her free hand, laying it over his heart. "Do you want me to leave?" His voice is so quiet it is almost a whisper, even though there is nobody to overhear.

Amara leans forwards, closing her eyes as their lips touch. She feels the thud of his heartbeat under her palm, then he is kissing her back, the pair of them almost stumbling over in mutual eagerness. Philos has clasped hold of her, his hands running over her shoulders, over the red silk Rufus bought, and she is leaning against the desk, pulling his body against hers, blinded by desire. Then just as suddenly, she realizes he is pushing her away, trying to disentangle himself. She lets go immediately.

"I'm sorry." He is breathing hard. "I'm so sorry." Philos puts a hand to his mouth. "I should never have touched you."

"You have nothing to be sorry for," she says, reaching out to reassure him. "It was my choice. You didn't do anything wrong, I promise. I wanted you to touch me."

He does not take her outstretched hand. "But you wouldn't if you knew."

"I don't understand."

"I've not been honest with you."

"About what?"

"About you."

"*Me?*" Amara repeats, thoroughly confused.

Philos looks agitated. "I drew up the contract," he says. "When Rufus took over as your patron from Pliny. I didn't have any choice. Rufus didn't want you to know about it." He starts pacing in the small space of the study, and Amara watches in bewilderment. "I always meant to tell you, to warn you, but when you arrived here you were so upset about Dido, I couldn't bear to hurt you even more. And then I thought perhaps it was better if you never knew."

Amara sits down against the desk, alarmed now as well as confused. "What's there to know? The contract just transfers patronage from one man to the other."

Philos looks miserable. "No, not entirely. The admiral freed you without condition. Rufus's patronage is conditional." He stops close beside her and reaches for her hand, but this time it is Amara who draws away. "It's a common clause in a freedwoman's contract when she is released to serve as a concubine. Any other man but Pliny would have demanded it from the start."

"Stop frightening me! Just tell me what the contract says."

Even now, Amara can see Philos does not want to tell her, but he has left himself no choice. "If you are unfaithful to Rufus, you automatically revert to enslaved status."

The sense of unease Amara has felt since she came to this house grows heavier, solidifying into understanding. It is not shock she feels, but recognition. *Rufus owns her.* "Why didn't you tell me this before?"

"I thought it would be easier for you not to know." Philos

is looking at her anxiously. "That you might even be able to love Rufus if you believed he had truly freed you. And then, when I realized you didn't love him, I thought you would be safe as long as you didn't care for anyone else…"

"Apart from *you*," Amara bursts out. Philos says nothing, his silence an admission that makes her even angrier. "So what happened just now, between us, here – that would be enough to make me revert back to…?" She cannot say the word.

"The contract is to prevent you betraying Rufus with another patron," Philos says, avoiding her question. "There wasn't any need to protect himself from a servant. He has always had the right to kill either of us."

"But at least I wouldn't die a *slave*," Amara retorts, spitting out the word with all the hate and disgust she feels for her own past.

"Like I am." An angry flush is spreading across Philos's cheeks, and she knows he has misunderstood the cause of her revulsion.

"That's not what I meant."

"I think I know *exactly* what you meant."

Amara covers her face with her hands, unsure who she is more frustrated with, herself or Philos. "You are mistaken," she says, trying to control her temper. "And clearly an *idiot* if you think I would risk my life for someone I didn't love!"

Amara's outburst takes them both by surprise. Philos says nothing, his expression telling her even less. She turns and walks to the door, fumbling with the handle in her haste to get out, desperate to escape from the humiliation of her own confession.

19

I've never been so foolish in my young life, I swear,
Or done one thing that I've regretted more,
Than going from you last night and leaving you alone,
Trying to hide how desperately I love you.

Sulpicia, Roman woman poet

Victoria's laughter rings out in the garden. She is sitting on the bench with Phoebe and Lais, the three of them draped over one another. Amara is sitting a little apart on a stool, while Britannica stands beside her, rigid as a Praetorian guard.

"Can you believe the amount?" Victoria exclaims. "Did you ever *see* so many tips? We'll have paid Felix off in no time!"

Victoria's haul is undeniably impressive. Amara and Dido never came close to making such a generous profit. "And it wasn't too upsetting for any of you?" Amara says, looking nervously at the flautists, the women who won't see the benefit of any of the money.

"Oh, I explained it all to the girls," Victoria says. "You still have to fuck for a living too, even if it's only one man."

She laughs. "Though I think that's pretty obvious anyway! Rufus isn't very subtle, is he? And I told them once the debt's paid, we can up their cut."

"Very generous mistress, thank you," Phoebe says, looking a little nervous at Victoria's disrespectful tone.

"I'm so glad you got Egnatius to introduce me to Fuscus," Victoria continues. "That man can tip! But what a sad little cock he has! Such a chore. What did *you* used to do to keep it up for long enough?"

A growl comes from Britannica, startling them all. Amara glances up at her and is alarmed to see her staring at Victoria, lip curled, hand resting on the hilt of her knife. She touches Britannica on the arm in warning. "You must realize I cannot talk about the past like that," Amara says to Victoria. "It dishonours my patron."

"Is she Rufus's personal guard dog now?" Victoria says angrily, jerking her chin at Britannica. "And he's not even here!"

"A man like Rufus expects absolute loyalty," Amara says, the memory of last night bringing its own bitter aftertaste. "No less in his absence than when he is present."

"Oh, fine then!" Victoria says in exasperation. "We're not even allowed to laugh now. And it's not like you ever showed that sort of loyalty to Felix."

"Felix wasn't my *patron*," Amara snaps. "He's a fucking *pimp*!"

Victoria looks unruffled by the outburst. If anything, there is satisfaction on her face at hearing Amara swear. "What did he say about me anyway? You never told me."

"What?"

"When you passed on my message." Victoria is staring at her. "The one you *promised* to give him."

In that moment, her heart still full of rage at Rufus's deception, Amara feels nothing but cruelty. "He said he doesn't give a fuck about you," she replies, her voice taking on Felix's characteristic coldness. "Why would he care what happens to a woman he used to sell to all comers as a whore." The moment she has said it, Amara is back in Felix's study, back when she saw him humiliate Victoria so viciously. She feels sick with self-loathing. "I'm sorry," she stammers. "I should not have..."

Victoria does not answer. She gets up from the bench, walking from the garden. Phoebe and Lais are left behind, looking awkward, unsure what to do. "You can go and get some rest too," Amara says, not wanting to look at either of them, unable to bear her role as pimp, her hideous resemblance to Felix. She is aware of them hurrying away.

Britannica sniffs loudly. "She deserve it. She is idiot."

"Don't," Amara says. "Please."

"Felix still own her," Britannica continues, ignoring her plea.

"Why don't we practise," Amara says wearily, changing the subject. "Can you get the knives please?"

* * *

The air is hot, and the red silk sticks to her body. Amara is playing the harp Rufus bought her, plucking the same refrains over and over, trying to perfect them. Two glasses of wine wait on the table. Rufus promised to come to her this afternoon, and he is late. She is aware that the last man to touch her in this dress was Philos and feels a shiver of fear, as if Rufus will be able to see the imprint of another man's hands on the fabric. Her breath quickens when she remembers what it felt like to hold Philos, to *want* a man that much, rather than just tolerate his embraces. Then she remembers Philos's face when she left, and she is torn between frustration at his deception and remorse for what she said. She plucks the wrong note on the harp, and sighs, closing her eyes for a moment, before starting the refrain again, from the beginning.

"Little bird?"

Rufus is standing in the doorway, a sentimental look on his face. Her body stiffens. Did he smile like that when he dictated the terms of the contract? She can picture him poring over it, his nod of satisfaction to Philos, knowing he had claimed total possession. Amara's tightening grip on the harp is the only sign of the rage she cannot express. "My darling," she says, her voice soft. "I have been *longing* for you all day."

"Look at you," Rufus murmurs, joining her on the couch. He eases his hand up her leg, a gesture she remembers from their first evening together. "I can never resist you."

Amara lays aside the harp and kisses him with a false show of delight, unable now to imagine how indulging Rufus ever felt close to love. He is nearly on top of her, but she is skilled at manoeuvring a customer, knows how to make a switch in position look like an excess of passion. In truth, she cannot bear to lie beneath him, wanting to escape his weight, not to have his face so close to hers.

When Rufus has finished, they recline together, drinking the wine, and he recounts all his triumphs from the night before. Amara exclaims encouragingly, her lines of devotion well-rehearsed. It is only when he asks her about the carriage, wanting to know how she felt, whether she was excited to see how much he loves her, that she falters. "You have done so much for me," she says, knowing it is true. "I don't think I will ever know how to thank you."

Rufus smiles, pleased to see her emotional, mistaking it for humility. "Your love is enough thanks," he says, lifting her hand to his lips.

Night has fallen, but Amara cannot sleep. She sits in the garden. Dido is a faint outline, the moon illuminating her in her guise as Diana. The hairs on Amara's arms stand up in the cold, but she cannot bring herself to move inside yet. The fountain murmurs, louder now it does not have to compete with the hubbub of the day. She can still picture the moment she saw Philos here, at night, when she began to understand what she felt for him. She tells herself that she has waited long enough, that she was a fool to imagine Philos would come looking for her after Rufus left, but as she shifts, getting ready to rise, she becomes aware she is not alone.

"Why don't you join me," she says, her voice so quiet she is not even sure he will hear.

Philos sits beside her. Her hand is resting on the bench, and she feels the warmth of his fingers brush hers, a gesture so slight, she understands he is giving her the choice to ignore it. Amara remembers how it felt when she belonged to Felix, all the times she gambled her life on the faintest hope of freedom, the exhilaration and the terror, and knows she will choose the same again. She touches Philos's hand, and he responds, their fingers interlacing.

Amara's heart is beating so hard she cannot move. Rufus owns her, believes she is his to dispose of as much as every other object in the house, including the man holding her hand. Nothing is worth taking this risk, and yet the thought of *choosing* a lover, of finally acting on her own desires, is intoxicating. She cannot let go. "Every night, when I go to bed, I lock my door," she whispers, still not looking at Philos. "But this evening, I won't." She stands up, feels his fingers slip from hers, and leaves the garden before she has a chance to change her mind.

In her bedroom, Amara moves methodically, opening the linen chest, taking out the contraceptive, undoing the pins in her hair, running her fingers through the curls to loosen them. The waiting is agony, and she does not know which is worse: the idea that Philos will come to her or that he won't. She stands staring at the door she left ajar, until the shape of it no longer makes sense. Then he is pushing it open.

Philos stands half-inside the doorway, as if unsure, even now, whether he is really invited. "Shall I lock it?"

The practicality of the question surprises her. Amara nods. Philos closes the door behind him, bolting it, then turns back to face her. They stare at one another, and she understands that he is not going to move towards her, that he is even more afraid than she is.

"I've often imagined you here," she says.

"Have you?"

Amara nods. "Have you thought of me…?" She does not finish the sentence, unsure what she wants to ask.

"Every night."

"And now you're here."

"Now I'm here," he repeats, taking her outstretched hand.

Unlike the night before in the study, they are both clumsy and nervous as they kiss, until their fear kindles into desire. Amara tells herself that they can always stop, that they can turn back, that they have not yet done enough to risk everything. She tells herself this again as they sit down on the bed together, when Philos pushes the dress away from her shoulders, even when she is naked. She tries to remove his tunic, but he gently pushes her hands away.

"I want to see you too."

There is no mistaking the shame in his eyes. "I don't want to disgust you."

"That's not possible," she says. "Please."

Philos pulls the tunic over his head, and Amara immediately understands what he meant. The left-hand side of his chest is not only branded but disfigured. Whoever marked him must have botched the job, or perhaps Philos resisted, as the words are blurred, run over by scar tissue, though she can still make out what it says. *Non Subdito.* Disobedient.

Amara knows she only has the briefest moment to act before Philos mistakes her shock for something else. He flinches as she lays her palm over the scars but does not push her away. She moves closer, bending her head to kiss him on the part of himself he was so afraid of revealing, then looks up. "Nobody in the brothel was branded," she says. "It would have reduced our value. But sometimes, I think there is not a piece of my skin that was left unmarked."

This time when Philos kisses her, Amara does not tell herself there is a way back.

Afterwards, when they are tangled up together, Philos keeps murmuring apologies into her hair, promising that he will last longer next time, but Amara cannot reply because she does not want him to know she is crying. Tears start to pool onto his shoulder, and he sits up in alarm.

"Did I hurt you?"

"You didn't hurt me," she says, crying even harder. "It just felt different. It made me realize…" Amara cannot continue, cannot even put into words the sense of loss she feels.

"I understand," Philos says, drawing her closer. "It's alright." Amara holds onto him tightly, her distress gradually subsiding as he strokes her shoulders. "I know it can get you that way," he says. "If it's any consolation, the first time I was with a girl after Terentius, I bawled my eyes out."

"*You* did?"

"It was terrible. I was so embarrassed."

"What did she say? Did you see her again after that?"

She senses the hesitation in his body even before he refuses to answer her question. "Maybe that's a story for another time," he says. "But you must know all this already, from your affair with that boy with the lamp. I knew when I saw you together that you loved him."

"Menander?" Amara asks, unnerved by his perception. "I did love him, yes. But he was never my lover. We never had the chance."

"Am I your *first* then?" Philos sounds both delighted and surprised. The question is so ridiculous that Amara has to stifle a laugh. "I'm serious! If you didn't choose, it didn't count."

"Philos," Amara says, amused, "I must have slept with

literally hundreds of men. I worked in a *brothel*. I can't even begin to keep track."

"None of it counts, though," he says, his voice even more earnest. "Not if you didn't choose."

She is about to argue then realizes from the intense look on his face that perhaps he is thinking of his own life rather than hers. "In that case, yes. You are my first lover." In spite of her good intentions, Amara is unable to finish the sentence without snorting.

"You might laugh," he says, kissing her. "But I just brought you to tears."

"Is that something to *boast* of now? Making girls cry with your love-making?" They both laugh so hard they shake uncontrollably from the effort of keeping quiet, and every time Amara thinks she has recovered herself, Philos catches her eye, making her laugh again.

Slowly, their amusement ebbs, and Philos props himself up on one elbow, so he is looking down on her. Amara notices he instinctively moves his other arm to cover the scar. "So can I come back and make you cry again tomorrow night?"

"Yes," Amara says. "Though I'm not sure how I can be without you between now and tomorrow."

Her answer brings a darkness into the room. In the lamplight, with Philos so close, bathed in its glow, she feels completely safe, and yet, she is aware that neither of them has ever been more at risk. "If we are going to meet like this," he says, "we have to protect one another. That means, in the daytime, we don't acknowledge each other *at all*. No secret gestures, no stolen glances. You just ignore me. If Rufus ever punishes me, you let him. And if he hurts you, I cannot intervene." Philos pauses, obviously uncomfortable. "Does he ever... I mean, has he ever hurt you?"

"No," Amara says, but Philos is looking at her, waiting to see if she is going to tell him more, and suddenly, she doesn't want to lie. "Well, he did once, so I know it's possible. But he hasn't done it again since." The anger in his face is so unfamiliar, it alarms her. She reaches out to touch his arm. "I should not have told you."

"No, you should. We need to share it all, so we know how to act. One evening, I will tell you everything I know about him, but I don't think I can bear to, not now."

"Not after making me cry," Amara jokes, trying to bring back the laughter from before.

Philos smiles, though she can still sense his sadness. "I love you," he says.

Amara stares at him, realizing that, for the first time since Dido's death, she does not feel alone. She takes hold of his hand, the one shielding his chest, drawing him back down to her. "I love you too."

LEMURIA

20

For this reason too, if proverbs interest you,
folk say bad women marry in May.

Ovid, Fasti: On the Rites of the Lemuria

The five women sit in the dining room, both slave and free, drinking together in honour of the Lemuria. It is a festival which has always disturbed Amara – the night the unburied and the murdered come back to haunt their kin, when the vengeful dead must be appeased. And yet, even on such a dark evening as this, she finds it difficult to feel anything but happy, knowing that soon she will be with Philos. He has been to visit her almost every night since they first lay together, both of them talking endlessly of the risks, yet seeming unable to keep apart.

Amara is not the only one in high spirits. Phoebe and Lais are starting to enjoy themselves, encouraged by Victoria who plies them with wine and compliments, the food long since eaten. For the first time since they came to the house, Amara forces herself to acknowledge the flautists, to imagine how she might have felt if she had met them at the Wolf Den. They are sitting close together on the couch, the lazy curve of Lais's arm as she rests it on Phoebe's knee recalling the white flash of limbs from one of Zeus's lovers on the wall. Amara is not certain she likes Lais. There is a hardness to her face, a ruthlessness. Felix's voice comes into her head. *If you had been me, how welcoming might you have been, if you saw yourself in another?*

Amara laughs at a joke, lifting her wine, sipping it slowly to give herself the excuse to keep looking. Phoebe is different. Watchful, but without the coldness. She has been witty this evening, her observations of the men she serves making everyone laugh. At the Wolf Den, Amara suspects they would have been friends. She does not delude herself that this is possible now.

"You're very quiet. Thinking of your love?"

Victoria's question catches Amara by surprise. "Well of course," she says. "I'm *always* thinking of Rufus."

"I didn't mean *Rufus*," Victoria replies, causing the colour to drain from Amara's face. Victoria gestures at the paintings surrounding them. "I think we all know that if Jupiter offered himself to you as the king of the gods or as a pile of gold, the gold would win."

Amara laughs, as much in relief as amusement. Seeing their mistress's reaction, the flautists laugh too, knowing it is safe to join in. She can feel Britannica shift beside her and does not have to look to know how stony the Briton's expression will be.

"Mistress is right," says Lais obsequiously. "Money is important."

"Did you two train together?" Amara asks. "In Attica?"

Phoebe and Lais look at one another. "No," Lais replies. "We meet in Baiae. We work there together."

"Where in Attica are you from, mistress?" Phoebe says to Amara, her tone more polite than curious.

"Aphidnai," Amara replies.

"You train as a courtesan there?" Lais asks.

"In a manner of speaking."

"Hardly!" Victoria snorts. "Amara was a *doctor's* daughter."

"Yes." Amara smiles. "And then a concubine. And then a whore. And now a courtesan."

Lais nods vigorously. "Courtesan is good," she says. "*Hetaira.*"

Lais's whole face changes with just one word of her native language. Amara cannot resist switching to Greek too, to see who Lais becomes. "*Fortune was kind to me with my beloved patron Rufus,*" Amara says to her. "*Perhaps life will grant you a similar opportunity to rise. You are both quite skilled enough to take it.*"

"*You are generous, mistress,*" Lais replies, her voice deepening. "*I pray, by the will of Aphrodite, that I find myself a patron as gracious as yours. One who can pay you and Mistress Drusilla a suitable price, of course. So that everyone benefits.*"

"*Nothing would please me more. A woman's cunning lasts longer than her looks.*"

"*And both last longer than her virtue,*" Phoebe adds. It is a commonplace remark, but the three of them still laugh.

"What you saying?" Britannica is irritated. "Latin bad enough. Greek, impossible."

"Sorry," Amara replies. "I said I hoped the girls would do well in life, because they certainly have the talent."

"Shame there's nobody here to speak *your* language Britannica," Victoria says. "It's so melodious."

"You also train as a concubine, Britannica?" Phoebe asks, before a row can start. The question almost causes Victoria to spit out her wine with mirth.

"Fighter," Britannica says, ignoring Victoria, striking her heart hard with her right hand.

"How are you here?" Lais says, and Amara realizes with a sense of shame that she has never, in all the time she has known her, asked Britannica this question.

"They raid us," Britannica says, her face expressionless. "Kill men. Burn everything. Take women, children. My family, all dead. I see them die." Even Victoria cannot reply in the dark silence that follows. Britannica looks round, absorbing their discomfort. She smiles her gap-toothed grin, the one Amara recognizes as having no warmth to it. "You all pray tonight for spirits to stay away. I say, come! Come for vengeance!" She glances at Amara and the flautists. "No quarrel with Greeks. Italians only."

Victoria, the only Italian present, is not oblivious to the insult. "Then you should stay away," she hisses. "Don't dare bring your dead here!"

Britannica rises from the couch, and they all jump back. Amara holds out her arm, unsure if she needs to restrain the Briton from violence, but Britannica only nods at her. "I have had enough, Amara. I go to bed." She strides from the room.

"Why didn't you stop her telling that story!" Victoria exclaims, looking at Amara. "Tonight of all nights! We don't need a hoard of savage spirits turning up!"

"I didn't think," Amara replies, unable to admit that she

didn't know about Britannica's past. "I'll ask Philos about it."

"I can't believe it's fucking Philos that Rufus nominated as head of the household!" Victoria says, still agitated. "At least Juventus is bigger. How's Philos going to scare the spirits off? Being *sneakier* than they are?"

"Rufus knows what he is doing. He's assured me Philos will have the authority to protect us," Amara replies, getting up from the couch to go and sit next to Victoria. She puts an arm round her, knowing how much Victoria has been dreading this night. Britannica's angry tribe are not the only ghosts to fear. Even more worrying is the man Victoria killed, whose shade will be waiting to revenge himself on the murderer who left his corpse, unburied, in the hidden alleys of the Necropolis. "Nothing's going to hurt you," Amara says. "I promise." Victoria leans on her, but the words don't seem to bring her any comfort, perhaps because Amara herself is afraid. Amara wishes Philos were here now – his presence never fails to reassure her. But the pair of them decided last night it was safer to split the household, for him to eat as usual with Martha and Juventus in the small storeroom off the kitchen. They have both been scrupulously ignoring one another, yet both felt the risk of eating together and letting some familiarity slip was just too high.

"We'll just have to beat the pots louder," Victoria says, pulling herself together. "We should go get them. It must be time soon."

They line their sandals against the atrium wall and stand in a huddle, clutching sticks and pans from the kitchen. The hall could almost be a tomb, darkness filling every crevice like black soil, the small square onto the night sky their last link to the living world. The dread is suffocating. Amara can hear Victoria's breathing coming too fast beside her and strokes her arm. Victoria isn't alone in wishing she had not just learned Britannica's entire family were massacred.

"What if she's up there, speaking to them?" Victoria whispers. "Sending them down here for revenge?"

Amara does not get the chance to reply. It is midnight. Philos leaves the group, holding an oil lamp in his left hand, and walks silently in his bare feet to the centre of the hall. He stops in a dull patch of moonlight, a slight figure to set against the forces of darkness.

"Ghosts of my fathers and ancestors," he calls in a clear voice. "Be gone and do not linger here." He starts to walk around the hall, reaching into a bag tied at his waist and throwing black beans over his shoulder. The sound of them falling on the tiles is like the patter of rain. Light flickers over his face from the lamp, its glow barely enough to illuminate the space ahead as he walks. Philos never looks back – to do so would be to invite the dead to take him.

"I send these," he says, passing them so close Amara might touch him if she stretched out her arm. "With these beans, I redeem me and mine."

Amara watches Philos, knowing the shades of the dead will be curling around his ankles like smoke, scenting blood, but contenting themselves with the offering instead. Or at least she hopes so. Juventus starts to strike his pot, and they all follow suit, Victoria most lustily of all. "Ghosts of my fathers and ancestors," they yell. "Be gone!"

All down the street, others are doing the same,

everyone's timing out of rhythm, so that their neighbours' clanging drifts over the night air, while Philos repeats the incantation. The more chaos the better, to set the spirits in confusion. Philos walks around the house, casting the beans, and they accompany him, clashing away any shades who dare to linger. Amara's voice grows hoarse from shouting. She remembers performing this rite at home, her father in Philos's place. Back then, the thought of having unburied kin was unthinkable, the threat less tangible. She tries not to count up all the unhappy dead she knows now. Her mother, surely, would not have left Attica. Her father would have found some way to claim his wife, to take her with him to the underworld. She glances at Victoria, who is pale beside her, and knows what she is thinking. Amara tries to shut out the memory of the way the murdered man fell, blood spilling from his neck, his life cut short by a shard of broken pottery. And then there is Cressa, unburied, her bones rotting in Pompeii's harbour. Would she envy her two old friends from the brothel their good fortune?

The ritual is almost finished. Philos returns to do a final circuit of the atrium, his face calm, letting the dark hail fall behind him. *Not Dido*, Amara thinks, shutting out the image of her crawling after the black beans, a hideous, shapeless form. *He buried her. Felix buried her.*

Amara sits on the edge of the bed, wide awake, waiting. She wonders if Philos will be too afraid to come tonight, whether he will baulk at creeping alone across the hall, where the dead might still be scavenging. Not that he seemed concerned earlier. She strains to hear him, but there is only silence. He is always so quiet; by the time she is aware of his presence, it is usually because he is already in the room. She is just wondering whether she's brave enough to sneak to the atrium to look for him, when he finally slips inside the doorway and makes her jump.

"I'm sorry," he whispers, bolting the door. "I had to be sure Juventus was asleep." He turns to her, his diffidence entirely at odds with the authority he held earlier. "You're not too tired, are you? I don't have to stay, if you don't want me to."

"I'm not too tired!" Amara says, sounding more eager than she intends. "I'm *never* too tired for you."

"That's a relief." Philos sits down beside her, looking amused now, rather than nervous.

"No need to be so smug." Amara tries not to laugh, any lingering fear of the dead dispelled by his presence. She pulls off her robe, impatience preventing her from making a performance of it, and pushes him back on the bed.

It is not difficult to give Philos pleasure. Amara is always delighted by how easily she can make him lose his self-control, even if she suspects his years of loneliness might play as much a part as her skill. But after their first few frantic nights together, he is starting to resist, wanting to give her pleasure in return. This is less easy to manage. Amara would never have survived the brothel if she had not learned to sever herself from her body, and now, when she wants to feel everything, the habit is hard to unlearn. She tries to tell him that it is enough for her to enjoy his enjoyment, but he is not satisfied, refusing to kiss her until she tells him something she likes. Amara is tempted to lie, to make the moment pass, but he is gazing at her so earnestly she surprises herself with the truth: that she needs him to look in her eyes. Almost instantly, she regrets it, certain he will understand the reason why. But Philos only kisses her and moves his body to make it easier to do what she's asked.

"I was worried you might think it bad luck on the Lemuria," he says, afterwards. His voice is a whisper – everything they do has to be in near silence – and he is lying facing her, their noses almost touching. It has become a familiar posture. The easiest way to hear and hold one another.

"You're not allowed to *marry* on the Lemuria; there's no rule about making love," she whispers back. "Although if we had the chance to marry, I'd take the risk, even on the unluckiest night of the year." Philos smiles but only squeezes her shoulder in answer, and Amara feels mortified at exposing her infatuation. She sounds worse than Beronice. All her experience as a prostitute, all the false protestations she's made, yet with this man, she seems incapable of keeping her feelings to herself. She turns away from him to look at the ceiling, at the ripple of light and shadow from the oil lamp.

"I didn't mean to be cold," Philos says, and she can feel the back of his fingers brush her cheek. "I just don't think it will make us happier wanting things we can't have."

"That sounds very defeatist."

"It's realistic." When Amara does not answer, but stays staring upwards, he leans over to kiss her on the forehead. "Don't be upset, my love, I didn't mean it that way."

Amara is unable to resist and turns back towards him.

He takes her hand, laying it over his heart, caressing her fingers. The gesture reminds her of Britannica when she declared herself a fighter.

"Britannica spoke about her family tonight," she says.

"Did she?" Philos says. "I thought of them during the ritual. It's very sad. She tried so hard to protect her younger brother. I hope one day she can forgive herself."

"When did she tell you about him?" Amara feels even guiltier at all the questions she has never thought to ask.

"A while ago. I asked how she came here, where her people are from. A lot of the tribes in Britain have women warriors. I was curious." Philos has his grey eyes on her, so open and kind, Amara never wants him to look away. "But then, nobody's journey to enslavement is a happy one. Even if you are born into it. I know yours wasn't, either."

"If I had never been enslaved, do you think you could still have loved me?"

"I wouldn't have had the chance. You would never have looked at me. Or at least, not as a man."

Philos is still gently stroking her fingers. Memories, like the black beans he threw for the shades, cascade through Amara's mind. Chremes, Felix, the brothel, even Rufus. All the men she wishes she had never been forced to endure. She takes back her hand, covering her face, as if that will blot it out. "I wish you really *were* the only lover I had ever known."

"You can't be worrying about lost virtue, can you?" Philos says, his tone light. He puts his arms round her. "I don't have any of that myself."

"That's not what I meant."

"I know," Philos murmurs, stroking her back, a gesture

he has used a number of times when the darkness of her past seeps between them.

The rhythm of his hand against her skin is as soothing as the thud of his heartbeat. Amara's breathing eases. She imagines what it would feel like if Philos were her family, if he belonged to her. "Do you *never* think about how we might be together?"

"I try not to, honestly."

Amara pushes herself away from him, so she can see his face. "But why?"

"*Amara.*" He sighs, with a hint of exasperation. "It's not about how much I love you. Think of how little control either of us has. One day, if we're not caught, Rufus will lose interest in you or move me. It's inevitable. And I can either drive myself mad thinking of all that pain on the horizon or be grateful for whatever days of happiness Fortune grants us. It's useless planning a future you don't own."

"I'm not *grateful*," Amara says, surprised by the strength of her own anger. "You can't sit by hoping Fortune will turn her wheel for you! What sort of excuse is that? You have to seize it and force her." Philos is amused by her passionate outburst, but Amara is not interested now in his indulgence or attempted kisses. "I mean it!" she says, almost forgetting herself and raising her voice. "You're smarter than Rufus, *I'm* smarter than Rufus. Why shouldn't we think of a way to free you?"

"You say that because you were born free. I cannot imagine what it feels like."

"You *can* imagine. You *know* what it feels like. When you recited Homer in the garden, and the other children hated you because you were cleverer. You felt you had the right then, didn't you, to what they had? And what are we even asking of the Fates? That you have a little more control over your life. I'm not suggesting you aim to be Emperor."

Philos looks taken aback by the ferocity of her speech. "You want to marry me that much?"

Amara tries not to laugh. "Don't worry, it's not about that. If you gained your freedom and left me, so be it." She pauses, the noble sentiment heavy in the air. "Though I'm not saying I wouldn't be annoyed."

They both laugh this time, or at least, the silent shake of the shoulders that passes for laughter between them. Amara can feel her willpower slipping again, and she twines herself round him so that barely any scrap of her skin is not touching his. Even that is not close enough. She can feel the ridges of the scarring on his chest press into her cheek.

"You really love me." It is hard to tell, with a whisper, if he is asking a question or stating the obvious.

"No," Amara replies, holding him even tighter. "I can't stand you."

21

*See to it, slave boy, that water washes feet and a serviette wipes
away the drops; and that our linen covers the couch.*
Motto from a Pompeii dining room

Amara spends her morning at the Venus Baths. It is
not a day to see Drusilla, rather a chance to meet
more clients. Since her appearance in the chariot at the
Floralia, Amara's status – as well as her notoriety – has
risen considerably. She may never be respectable, but her
public display has certainly lent her an aura of wealth.
Julia has become increasingly friendly and acts as a useful
go-between, introducing her to women who might need
financial assistance, giving the lie of a social occasion.

When their business is done, Amara and Julia sit together,
sipping watered-down wine in the courtyard. The May
heat is oppressive, even this early in the day, and Amara is
grateful for the shaded colonnade.

"Sweet girl," Julia says, of the young wife who has just
left them. "A shame she is such a magpie. Though not a
shame for you."

"I'm grateful you introduced us."

Julia waves her hand, gold rings shining. "Looks only last so long, lovers are just as bad. But a closet full of coin never made any woman cry. That's what my dear mother used to say. She would certainly have approved of *you*. I'm delighted you are a sensible girl. Don't *ever* let some man tell you money is unromantic."

Amara smiles, thinking of her reckless assignations with Philos – behaviour Julia would surely despise. "*Hail Profit.* That was written on the doorway of a house on the last street where I lived," she says, daring to make an oblique reference to the brothel. "I took the lesson to heart."

Julia laughs. "Hail Rufus, in your case," she says, eyes sparkling with mischief. Amara cannot help laughing back. Julia has the gift of disarming anyone she speaks to, making them feel like the most important person in the room. She would have made an exceptional courtesan, though as far as Amara knows, Julia has no interest in men at all. "You certainly glow with it," Julia says, gazing into her eyes. Amara stares back, curious. Julia raises her eyebrows and smiles, perhaps amused that Amara does not look away. "I cannot believe you have not yet called on me at home," she says. "I live with my nephew's widow, Livia. I'm sure you would like each other."

"I didn't know you had a niece," Amara says. "I would be honoured to meet her."

"Come then," Julia rises, resting her hand briefly on Amara's shoulder as she stands to leave. "I will introduce you."

It is the first time Amara has been invited to the private section of Julia's estate, and she understands the honour her hostess is paying her. She follows at a respectful distance, breathing in the scent of lavender bushes whose sprigs, she knows, are used to perfume the waters of the baths. Julia's garden, which she has only glimpsed from the baths' windows, is even more luxurious than she imagined. A long canal runs down the centre, shaded by trees, and she can see eels beneath the surface of the water, their bodies writhing silver and grey.

"Livia, darling, look who I've brought."

Amara had been expecting a younger woman, perhaps even a girl, but instead, the figure who rises from a bench on the shaded colonnade looks, if anything, even more formidable than her aunt. "Who's that?" the woman declares, her tone imperious, shading her eyes as she steps into the sun.

"The admiral's freedwoman, Amara. The girl I told you about."

"Pliny's little Greek girl? Oh, how delightful!" Livia beams at Amara, her gaze both curious and amused. "I almost died laughing when Julia told me about you. How on *earth* did you catch his attention? I never thought Pliny had his nose out of a scroll long enough to notice a woman."

Amara flushes slightly, unsure how to answer without insulting her patron. "I read to him."

Livia throws her head back and roars with laughter, the way a man might, utterly unconcerned by her appearance. "You wicked creature." She takes Amara's arm and gives it a squeeze. "I *insist* you tell me all about it." She pulls Amara over to the bench, waving impatiently at Julia. "Didn't you think to send for wine, for Venus's sake?" Julia raises her eyebrows, but to Amara's surprise, she gestures at one of the lurking servants, complying with Livia's peremptory demand. "I can't believe Julia's been hiding you away all this time," Livia continues, regarding Amara with appreciation, before glancing sidelong at her aunt-by-marriage, eyebrows raised. "Or perhaps I can believe it."

Julia laughs. "I've brought her now, darling, so you can't be too angry."

"Do you both know Pliny well?" Amara asks, a little disconcerted by the teasing, unsure who might be the target.

"He's a great friend of Julia's," Livia replies. "And I'm very fond of the old man too. So don't worry yourself, my love! We're not mocking him. But in any case" – she lowers her voice to a conspiratorial whisper – "I never gossip. You are perfectly safe, whatever you say."

It is such an unlikely claim that Amara finds herself laughing.

"I thought you pair would get on well," Julia says, with a smile.

Amara spends at least an hour answering all Livia's impertinent questions, and when she arrives back at the house, a little flushed from the wine, Rufus is waiting for her. He stands by the pool, Philos and another of his servants, Vitalio, beside him. Vitalio is clutching a large basket, nobody having instructed him to set it down.

"I wasn't expecting you today, my love," Amara exclaims, running to greet him. Rufus kisses her and lifts her off her feet in an exuberant embrace. She is conscious of Philos close by, even though she cannot see him. Rufus sets her down but does not remove his hands from her waist.

"Aren't I allowed to surprise you?" Rufus stares down at her, the lines from his smile crinkling around his eyes.

"Always," she says, smiling back.

"I'm going to take you to someone very dear to me." Rufus draws her arm into his, walking towards the door. "A visit outside the city walls."

Philos and Vitalio follow silently behind. Juventus steps back to let them through, no danger of him leering at her in the master's presence, his eyes look to the floor. Outside on the street, Virgula bows as they pass, Rufus acknowledging her with a gracious tilt of his head. Philos slips ahead of them, and to her dismay, Amara realizes that wherever they are going, Philos must have been ordered to walk in front while Vitalio is behind. She will have no option but to stare at her lover for the duration of the journey.

Rufus and Amara attract respectful glances as they pass, people giving them space on the pavement. She is aware this is for Rufus, not her, but the shine of his status casts a wide protective glow. Nobody gives space to Philos. His sole purpose is to alert others to get out of his master's way. In the harsh glare of the sun, his tunic looks even poorer than it does at home. The dark material is wearing thin at the shoulders; there is a small rip he must have carefully repaired at the back. His stance is always upright – Philos does not stoop like so many slaves – but without wealth and its attendant power, even his good looks give him no authority. If she did not already love him, Amara realizes, with a sense of shame, that she would barely notice him.

They walk through town to the Vesuvian gate, the blue mountain rising slowly above the rooftops as they approach. It is not the main trading route into town, and the street has space for them to walk comfortably. Beyond the walls, Amara knows there are vineyards and villas, a wealthy enclave outside Pompeii.

"Who are we going to visit?" she asks, trying to infuse her voice with excitement, hoping that wherever they are destined to be, Philos will melt into the background, that the day will not be overshadowed by the many shades of guilt she feels towards both men.

"I'm not spoiling the surprise just yet," Rufus replies. "You'll have to be patient."

They draw closer to the edge of town, and the street grows more congested, people queuing outside the cook shops that cluster the gate. Many are chatting together in small groups, some carrying baskets like Vitalio. Amara and Rufus find themselves squashed between the loiterers and a gaggle of small children who are perched on the edge of the pavement, throwing stones at a dog on the opposite side of the road. Before Philos can clear them a path, a man barges over, shouting, smacking one boy round the ear and dragging him back into the line. The other children scatter.

"Is it a day for visiting the dead?" Amara asks, looking uneasily at all the queuing families. Rufus squeezes her hand but says nothing.

The archway provides a moment's welcome shade, before they pass through onto the wider stretch of road. It is lined with enormous graves and monuments, their solemnity undermined by the picnicking families dotted around them. A few are making offerings of food and wine to their dead relatives, but most are chatting and eating. Amara and Rufus follow Philos to a family tomb within sight of the town walls. It is tall and square, face open to the street, its inside hollowed out with a circular bench, while a domed ceiling keeps off the sun. Small, painted statues of the dead stand in niches in the wall. Rufus stops, pointing up at a couple. "My grandparents."

Philos and Vitalio are standing behind them. She is grateful Philos cannot see her face, or her look of feigned delight at meeting Terentius. "How lovely of you to bring me here," she exclaims. "I hope they won't mind me visiting."

"Grandfather would have *adored* you," Rufus says, leading her to sit on the shaded bench inside the tomb. Vitalio leaves the basket beside her, then he and Philos retreat, to stand outside in the heat. "He was such a character." Rufus reaches across Amara's lap, drawing out a small bottle of wine. "This is for him, before we leave," he says, setting it on the stone floor, before gesturing at her for the basket. She hands it to him. It is packed with bread, olives, even some dried figs wrapped in a cloth. Not unlike the supplies she would have taken to share with her parents at their own ancestors' more modest graves.

Amara's stomach is too knotted to eat. Philos has his back to her, facing the road, his skin no doubt burning as he stands in the sun. "You must have been very fond of your grandparents," she says to Rufus. "What an honour this is."

"I'm coming again with the rest of the family tomorrow," he replies, tucking into the olives. "But I suddenly wanted you to see them too."

"Thank you," Amara says, touched, in spite of herself, by his affection.

"Grandfather is the one who got the family into politics," Rufus continues, looking round at the glittering walls, spitting a stone into his hand. The tomb is painted with symbols of wealth, silver work and jewellery heaped on imaginary shelves. "He was duumvir at one time. People still talk about the games he put on at the arena." Rufus reaches for a vial of watered-down wine, offering it to Amara first. She takes a sip. "He could be quite a difficult man, but he meant well. He told the most wonderful stories. I used to love to listen to him as a boy, the way he would describe Icarus falling from the sky! I felt I had wings myself, hearing him describe it all. And he adored the theatre. Father never cared for it much, so Grandfather would take me."

Philos is standing beside Vitalio, entirely still. Amara knows he can hear every word. "And your grandmother?" she says, hoping to steer Rufus off the topic of Terentius.

"Oh, she was very grand," Rufus says. "From a much older family. If she hadn't been, I suspect Grandfather wouldn't have listened to her half as much as he did. He became a little... eccentric as he got older. I used to feel a bit sorry for the slaves who got in his way. One time, he was hitting some poor boy round the head with his sandal in the garden, and Grandmother came rushing out yelling at him, so he stopped. I thought she was annoyed at the punishment, but it was the *sandal* that upset her. So the boy got hit twice – once with the sandal, and then again with the whip." Rufus gives a rueful laugh, inviting her to smile with him at his grandparents' foibles. "The older generation." He shrugs. "They're all a bit strict like that."

Amara is grasping her bread so hard it has partly disintegrated between her fingers. She remembers what it felt like when Felix slapped her, or Thraso. The rage at being unable to retaliate, forbidden from defending a body which is not even yours. Terentius must have hit Philos like that.

Perhaps Philos was the boy in the garden, with the sandal. He is still standing beside Vitalio, both of them unmoving at the edge of the tomb.

"Are you alright, little bird?" Rufus asks. "You look upset."

At that, Philos does move. Amara sees him shift slightly on his feet, as if resisting the urge to turn around. "Oh," she exclaims, swiftly thinking up a lie. "I was just remembering my own grandfather. How sad I am you will never meet any of my family."

"Dear girl," Rufus says, kissing her forehead. "Why don't you tell me about him?"

Amara hesitates. She never knew any of her grandparents. Her mother came from a much poorer family than her father, so they were subsequently avoided, while her father's parents died before she could remember them. "My grandfather was a doctor, like my father," she begins, truthfully enough. "He used to like me reading to him. He would make me recite all the different herbs and their properties. I don't think there was a plant he had not encountered. After all, his own father was a chemist. He was the kindest man," she adds, warming to this imaginary forebear who is, in fact, another version of her father.

"What a clever child you must have been," Rufus says. "I can just imagine you, a solemn, pretty little thing, all big eyes and curls. I'm afraid I was much slower at my own learning. My poetry recitations certainly never gave Grandfather any joy. Though he always had a favourite slave boy on hand for all that. Another annoyance for poor Grandmother." Rufus strokes a ringlet of hair behind her shoulder. "It's why I know he would have approved of you, though. He always put a high value on romantic love. *Why not satisfy your desires*, he used to say. *Enough time for denial when you're dead.*"

Amara does not dare look over to where Philos is standing this time. She takes Rufus's hand and lays it against her cheek, masking her inability to speak with a gesture of affection. Above them, Terentius and his wife stare out from their alcoves with sightless, painted faces.

That night, Amara is certain Philos will not come, that his humiliation will make him hate her. She keeps seeing him as he appeared on the street, when she was embarrassed by his poverty, and the guilt is smothering. When he eventually slips through the door, she feels ashamed all over again.

"I had no idea Rufus was taking me there," she says, as he sits beside her. "I'm so sorry I didn't stop him; I'm sorry he said those things, I wish—"

Philos lays a finger on her lips. "Do you mind if we don't talk about it?"

"No," she replies. "I don't mind."

They lie beside one another on the bed. Philos does not try to undress her as he usually would. Nothing about his body language suggests he is in the mood. Amara moves closer to him, aware of how much she hates to be pitied, how it only makes her feel smaller. "Will you hold me?" she murmurs, as if asking for comfort rather than offering it.

The familiar warmth of his body is soothing. She presses close to him, tucking her head under his chin, and he responds by caressing her back. Slowly, Amara feels him relax against her. His breathing deepens, and as the silence stretches on, she starts to worry they might both fall asleep.

"Rufus was modest about his childhood today," Philos says, his hand still lightly stroking her shoulders. "He was the most endearing boy. I've often wondered who he might have become, if he had been born to a different family."

It is the first time Philos has spoken of the man who owns him in such an intimate way. Amara is surprised but does not show it. "How old was he when you first met him?"

"He must have been about seven. I used to help him with his studies. He's right that he wasn't any good at reciting. The *hours* it would take him to learn just a few lines of verse. Enough to make you despair." Philos sighs. "Love warps people's memories. Or maybe he didn't want to tell you about all the times his grandfather hit him when he read badly. That was why I used to help. He was only a child. I hated seeing him cry."

"You love him," Amara says, her shock making it sound like an accusation.

"No," Philos replies. "I *loved* him. There's a difference."

"When did you stop?"

"It happened very gradually. You can't just name a day with these things, can you? Children start to learn who matters. Over time, I stopped being the older boy who helped him to read and became another object owned by his family. The sort of object you might see being beaten round the head by a sandal, and turn away in embarrassment."

"That was you? He *knew* and told that story in front of you?"

"Even I don't know if it was me. It was a very violent

house, Amara. It could have been any of us. I don't recall every beating." Philos is no longer caressing her back; he is holding her tightly, and she can feel the tension returning to his body. "Perhaps it was after Faustilla that I started to despise him. When I could no longer pretend he was the child I had known."

"Vitalio's daughter?" Amara asks, perplexed. "The serving girl he had an affair with?"

"An affair isn't the way I would describe it."

"You told me she was in love with him."

"No, you assumed that. And I let you."

Amara remembers Rufus setting down the harp on the night of Helvius's dinner, the suppressed violence in the way he carried himself, her own confusion, the feeling of his fingers at her neck. And she understands what happened to Faustilla. What Rufus must have done. "No," she says, gripping hold of Philos, not wanting to hear it.

"I made so many excuses for him," Philos replies. "I told myself he was no different from any other man of his class, they *all* use their slaves that way, and nobody thinks anything of it. Perhaps they don't even know what they're doing. Except that's a lie, isn't it?" Philos gently disentangles himself, so they are facing one another. "Because in the end, it's two people in bed together. And when you are this close" – he grasps her by the shoulders – "it's impossible not to notice another's distress. It's not a difficult thing to see. He *cannot* have been unaware. But hurting a slave is meaningless to him, just as it was to his grandfather. They're no different from one another."

"But your relationship to them both is different," she says, suspecting Philos is more conflicted about his master than he is able to admit. "And Rufus is a hard man to hate. I don't always manage it, in spite of everything. You mustn't blame yourself if you can't, if you still love him sometimes."

"I don't find it hard to hate him," Philos replies, his voice cold. "He's not a child anymore. He's a man, like his father and grandfather. One who would kill me for touching a woman who belongs to him."

"But I don't belong to him now," she replies, kissing him. "Not when I'm with you."

After a moment's hesitation, he kisses her back, and Amara is relieved to end the conversation. They lie for a while, caressing one another, lazily at first, then with more urgency, until he moves his body over hers. She tries to pull him closer, wanting to feel the weight of him, to blot out the sense of shame, the memory of the tomb, the thought of Faustilla. But he resists, kissing her neck rather than look her in the eyes. "You always belong to him," Philos says, his voice a whisper by her ear. "I should know. He made me draw up the contract."

Amara pushes herself upright, angry and disorientated. "*What* did you say to me?"

Philos sits up too, not attempting to keep hold of her. "Is it easier for you to hate him now?"

She recognizes the passion in his face. It is as familiar to her as her own heartbeat, the all-consuming hatred of another, as tormenting as desire. Amara understands, seeing him then, that it is not only tenderness that leads Philos to visit her every night. Perhaps she should be repelled, imagining her body absorbing his loathing for Rufus as well as his love for her. But that is not what she feels. Instead,

Amara thinks of the brothel, remembering the times she deceived Felix, how it gave her a pleasure so intense, it made her risk everything she had.

"Show me how much you hate him," she says.

22

*The praetor should not endure the slave of yesterday, who is
today free, to complain that his master has spoken abusively to
him, or struck him lightly.*

Ulpian, Roman jurist

"Is this supposed to impress me?" Felix is holding up
the purse, an overpayment on what she is due, with a
look of distaste.

"What makes you think I'd want to impress *you?*"
Amara leans back in the chair, as if it were her study rather
than his, smiling to belie the coldness of her words. A trick
she learned from him. Felix does not smile back, which only
amuses her more.

"Ipstilla told me Victoria had been to Cornelius's house."

"Of course," she says. "Why wouldn't I use my old
contacts? The benefit of having a patron, and not being
stuck in a cell, is that I can make even more. Just think,"
she says, an unpleasant edge to her voice, "you could have
shared all that with me."

The air in the study is close, and her clothes stick to her

skin. Felix no longer offers wine when she visits. But his hair, she notices, is still slicked back, his skin smooth from a shave. And is that *pomade* she can smell? Her mouth twitches in the effort of suppressing her amusement. She looks at him through narrowed eyes, observing. He stares back, unfriendly. "If you want to sit there and brag, I have other business."

"The new bar?"

"You're very observant."

"I thought it was a good way to expand your profits. Makes sense."

"Glad I *impressed* you," he replies, voice heavy with sarcasm. She laughs, this time, and is gratified to see him smile back. It transforms his face, giving the illusion of warmth. He leans over the desk, resting his chin on his hands. "Each time we meet, you speak like a woman with a proposal, yet you never make it. What is it you want from me?"

Philos is next door, Amara thinks, and the knowledge gives her a savage sense of satisfaction. She suspects Felix would be no less furious than Rufus at her deception, at the possibility that she is laughing at his efforts to charm her. The euphoria of love and risk, which she lives with daily, is starting to lend a recklessness to everything she does. And yet, it is not only her affair making her bold. This is an old, familiar feeling: the intoxication of holding the Master's attention, the possibility of manipulating him. It's unwise to tell Felix too much, she knows this, yet she cannot resist leading him on a little further. "Patrons don't last forever," she says.

"Unless they marry you," Felix replies, and Amara knows

then, from the look on his face, that she has miscalculated. "Or isn't posh boy romantic?"

She tries to shrug him off. "You know men of his class don't marry whores."

Felix smiles, and the switch in power between them is so sudden Amara's stomach lurches like a cart hitting a rock on the road. "You want to do business with me when posh boy leaves. That's what all this is about, isn't it?"

"Perhaps."

Felix lifts the purse again, contemplating it. "You certainly have a talent for making money. I won't deny it. But doing business with a woman is senseless." He drops the coins which land on his desk with a clink. "What happens when you get married? All my investment in you, any cut you give me, *gone*." He snaps his fingers. "You belong to someone else, and so do your earnings."

The effort Felix has made with his appearance, the smell of the pomade, no longer feels like a joke. Instead, it adds to her unease. "Maybe I'm not interested in marriage."

"So my profit relies on the prospect of you remaining a cold-hearted bitch for the rest of your life?"

"It's been good enough for you."

"The only way to own a freedwoman's assets is to marry her. Is that what you're offering me?"

On the red wall behind him, she can see the black plinths, the bulls' skulls at the top, the empty eye sockets. It was madness to imagine she could ever claim this space from him. "No," she says, standing up.

Felix is too fast. He crosses in front of her, blocking her way to the door. "Do you think I'm a fool? That I'm one of your fucking customers you can string along with hints?"

His face is contorted with anger. Amara is desperate to get away from him and tries to push past. "Don't you *dare* walk away from me." He seizes her wrist.

"Philos and Juventus are next door," she says, raising her voice to mask her fear. "They will hear me if I call."

Felix does not release her, but he does not pull her any closer either. "You shouldn't offer what you're not prepared to give."

"I didn't offer you *anything*," she says, her own anger rising.

"No?" Felix raises his eyebrows. "Too bad for you, then. The more I think about it, the more your little hints make sense. One day, Rufus will leave you." He stresses the words with relish. "And then who will you belong to? Another patron? Perhaps. Or perhaps you will be alone and in need of protection." Felix tightens his grip on her wrist. "That's what you've been after, isn't it? To talk me into doing business with you, to use me but keep me at a distance. Even though you know my protection always has a price."

Now, when it is too late, Amara understands the magnitude of her mistake. All that time she wasted as a slave fearing Felix's indifference, when it was his desire that was far more dangerous. Only, this isn't love, or even lust, which she might be able to manipulate. It's *owning* her that Felix enjoys. Her eyes flick to the door. Impossible to fight him off and reach it. And in spite of her threat, the last thing she wants to do is draw Philos into a scuffle where Felix will almost certainly be armed. "What are you proposing?"

"When Rufus leaves, I have you. You're free to make as much money as you like, however you like, as long as you make it for me."

"You seem very confident I won't find a better patron before that."

"You might." Felix shrugs. "And I might find a woman who will make me more money."

"I'll think about it," Amara says, attempting to smile.

"I know you're trying to get rid of me." Felix smiles back, as if they were friends sharing a joke. "Perhaps proposal was the wrong word. A promise might be better." He pulls her a little closer, growing more confident when she does not try to resist him. His body is so close she can feel the heat of him. "You are a whore who caught the eye of a rich man, who has *nothing* of her own. And you owe your former master several thousand sesterces. I don't think you are in a position to turn down anyone's generosity, especially not mine." Felix is staring into her eyes, and Amara has no choice but to stare back, not wanting to provoke him by looking away. "We're the same, you and I. And I know you see it." He pulls her so close, the smell of his pomade, shot through with sweat, is overpowering. "That's why I'm not going to fuck you yet, even though we both know you wouldn't fight me off – you'd just let me take whatever I wanted. Because that would be safer than explaining all those bruises to posh boy."

Rage finally overpowers Amara's fear, and she tears her arm from Felix's grasp. "Am I supposed to *thank* you for that?"

"Yes," Felix says, finally stepping out of her way. "You are." He laughs, waving his hand in a gesture of dismissal. "Let's just add it to your account, for when the final payment is due."

★ ★ ★

Amara knows, the moment she steps into the small waiting room where Juventus and Philos are waiting, that Philos has noticed her agitation. His eyes widen, full of unasked questions, and she can do nothing but turn her face aside.

They leave the flat, walking down Felix's narrow staircase, heading back onto the street. Still Amara and Philos can say nothing to one another, the tension from her silence growing between them, but when they reach the Via Veneria, Philos turns suddenly to address Juventus in dialect. Amara waits, perplexed, unable to understand a word. The doorman nods then slopes off towards the Forum, the opposite direction to home.

"What did you say to him?" she asks, shocked by the unexpected dismissal.

Philos has already started walking again, forcing her to keep pace. "Rufus wanted me to run an errand for him," he says. "Something to take back for the gem cutters. I just sent Juventus instead." They pause to let a group of chattering women pass, obviously on their way to an afternoon's hot soak at the baths. "Don't look at me, Amara," Philos says, lowering his voice. "But please tell me he didn't hurt you."

"He didn't hurt me."

"What's wrong then?" And in spite of his order not to look, he glances at her.

Amara stares ahead as they walk. "I just don't like being near him, that's all. It brings back too many old memories."

"I don't believe you. Something happened."

"He wants to marry me." Saying the words out loud sounds so preposterous, it almost makes her want to laugh. "He didn't ask. He told me that's what will happen when

Rufus leaves." Amara doesn't need to see Philos's face to read his shock from the silence that follows.

"You need to pay him back. *Immediately*. Ask Drusilla, ask Julia. Even Rufus. Be in debt to anyone rather than him. We cannot live with that sort of threat."

Amara does not like Philos's peremptory tone. "You think I can just ask for that much money?" She darts an angry look at him from the corner of her eye. "Drusilla has a child to support, and my whole business with Julia depends on her thinking I have spare cash to lend! And you *know* how furious Rufus would be if I asked him." Philos mutters something explosive-sounding in his own language. "Anyway, it's just Felix making threats. It means nothing."

"Nothing!" Philos swears in dialect again, kicking his feet against the pavement. "What did you do to make him suggest it in the first place?"

"Are you blaming *me* for this?" Amara's voice rises with anger and a passer-by stares. She looks back at the ground, quickening her pace. Never has the pressure of having a secret lover felt worse than now, when she wants to shout at him in the street.

"I heard you once," Philos says, his voice low. "You yelled at him, *It's not about love*. What did that mean?" Amara feels the shame wash over her, and she puts a hand over her mouth. "I'm not angry," Philos speaks even more quietly. "Please, just tell me."

"I don't know," Amara says. "I don't know what I've done."

"Do you love him?"

"No!" Philos shoots her a warning look for her raised voice. "Of course I fucking don't. Fabia told me he liked me, and I was stupid enough to think I could manipulate him. And now I've paid for it."

"Please borrow the money to pay him," Philos says, and she can hear the desperation in his voice. "Please ask Drusilla. I'm frightened he's going to hurt you."

Amara understands what Philos means by *hurt*. "I would call for you before he did anything like that," she lies. "I promise you. And this is Felix we're talking about. He won't have meant what he said. He just loves to play games. I can handle him. Trust me, I've had plenty of practice."

They have reached the turning to their own street. Back at the house, Amara knows Victoria is waiting for her. Egnatius has recommended them to another client, and she and Victoria are due to visit the client's steward to discuss the terms and confirm the booking. It will be impossible to talk to Philos in private.

"You promise you would call for me if he threatened you?"

Amara looks at Philos, who she knows would willingly die at Felix's hand if she asked him to protect her. She will never allow that to happen. "I promise."

23

*If anyone wishes to have a slave – male or female – punished
privately, he who wishes to have the punishment inflicted shall
do as follows. If he wants to put the slave on the cross or fork,
the contractor must supply the posts, chains, ropes for floggers
and the floggers themselves.*

Inscription at Puteoli, Roman city near Pompeii

Egnatius's private room seems seedier in daylight. Even the lavish paintings of Hercules look grubby, smuts from the constantly burning oil lamps dimming the hero's exploits. Amara reclines beside Egnatius on the couch, breathing in his familiar scent of acacia oil. There is a slim, but deliberate gap between their bodies, though his proximity still makes her sweat. Not from fear of her long-term client, who she is well aware has no sexual interest in her, but rather from imagining how her patron might react if he saw her like this. So far, Rufus has asked very few questions about her business dealings, perhaps preferring to believe her claim that she has an artistic interest in the music, rather than face her insatiable need to make money.

On the opposite couch, Victoria is sprawled against their newest client, Castrensis. He is a small, wiry man who looks like he has drawn on his thin beard with one of the kohl pencils Amara uses for her eyes. His hand is currently lurking somewhere up Victoria's thigh, hidden by the folds of her tunic. Victoria gives a theatrical sigh, as if she finds the man's attentions irresistible.

"I take it you will make the booking," Amara says. "Given your enthusiasm for handling the goods."

She can hear a huff of amusement from Egnatius behind her. He rests his fingers lightly on her upper arm. "Castrensis knows your girls come with the highest possible recommendation, my darling," Egnatius says. "I've never disappointed him in the past."

"I should hope not at this price," Castrensis says.

Amara glowers, but Victoria leans back even harder against him. "I've a *feeling* you're more interested than you seem," she says. Victoria exchanges a glance with Amara who takes the hint and rises. They have rehearsed this routine many times.

"If you are not buying, we are leaving." Amara motions Victoria to join her. Castrensis grips Victoria more tightly, face flushed.

"I didn't say I wasn't buying. Perhaps you could leave me alone with your friend for a moment, then I will give my decision."

"Sign the contract first, and then you may have more than a *moment*."

Victoria swivels her body round to face him. "Say yes to her," she says, gripping him by the waist, pulling him even closer. "Please."

"Very well," Castrensis replies, looking flustered. Amara is beside him with the wax tablets before he has a chance to reconsider, handing him the stylus to sign.

"I think we should witness this outside," Amara says to Egnatius, gesturing at the contract. Egnatius rolls his eyes, annoyed at being asked to move, but he does as she asks.

"When did you become so fastidious?" Egnatius drawls when they are standing in the corridor. He signs the contract with a flourish before snapping the tablet shut and handing it back to her. "Castrensis was more than capable of performing with an audience. And I can assure you it really *won't* be more than a moment."

"I didn't want to look at his ugly face for longer than was absolutely necessary."

"He's not as pretty as your steward, it's true. I cannot *believe* you've never brought lovely Philos back to visit me again." Egnatius pouts. "Wasn't he one of Terentius's boys?"

Amara shrugs. "I don't know that much about his past – he's Rufus's man."

"Such gorgeous eyes. And those cheekbones!" Egnatius looks sidelong at her, smirking. "I hope he's not competition for you, with Rufus."

Amara slaps his arm, a playful gesture, but one hard enough to sting. "Hardly." Egnatius laughs and swats back at her, and the absurdity of their scuffling together, like children, almost makes Amara laugh too. She pauses, wondering how much interest in Philos she can afford to show. "Did you know Rufus's grandfather, then?"

"Only by reputation." Egnatius shudders. "Men like Terentius are the reason you and I should thank the gods every day for being granted our freedom."

Victoria interrupts Amara from discovering further details, opening the door abruptly onto the corridor. She turns to look back into the room she has just left, suggestively wiping her mouth with the back of her hand, a gesture Amara remembers from the brothel. It is a mercy Castrensis's response is hidden from view.

"So we're all friends," Egnatius says brightly, kissing first Victoria and then Amara as a sign of dismissal. "Just don't forget the cut you owe me for the introduction, darling," he murmurs into Amara's ear. "I know what a shocking hoarder you are."

Out on the street, Victoria takes Amara's hand. They walk close together on the pavement, passing the same spot where Philos once offered Amara his arm. "No tip!" Victoria grumbles. "What a tight little shit. I've known penniless laundrymen more generous than *that*."

"I'm sorry. I wish you didn't have to do this." There is a tremor in Amara's voice. "I wanted to take you away from Felix, not end up like him."

"Don't be ridiculous!" Victoria exclaims, turning to look at her. She sees Amara's expression and gapes in surprise. "What's wrong?"

"We owe Felix so much money." Amara bites her lip to stop herself crying. "And he threatened me today. I don't know what I'll do if he really tries anything; I can hardly fight him off and go home looking a mess. What would Rufus say?" Somehow, it's easier to confess her vulnerability to Victoria than to Philos; she knows Victoria will understand. "I was such an idiot for thinking I could ever get the better of him."

Victoria stops before they reach the busier main road and

puts an arm around Amara's shoulders. "I wish you'd let me talk to him. I really think I might be able to help."

"It's too dangerous."

"But why should you take all the risks? And it's hardly the same problem for Rufus if Felix gives *me* a black eye, is it?"

Amara is too touched by Victoria's generosity to admit that the danger she fears most is Felix's power to manipulate his former lover, not that he will hurt her. "You don't have to do that. And anyway, he'd only find some other way to come after me. We just need to pay him back as quickly as possible. The more parties we can fix up, the better."

"I'm *trying*. Believe me, I never stop. I couldn't work the room any harder, when we go out, than I already do."

"I know you're trying, I know." Amara squeezes her arm. This is not what she imagined freedom to feel like when she bought Victoria. The pair of them still scrabbling around desperately for money to pay their old master. They set off again, walking close together, but saying little.

It is a surprise, when they reach the house, to find the large golden doors shut against them. The metal studs glint in the afternoon light, as if the house were wearing armour. Amara feels confusion, followed by a cold rush of fear. She glances swiftly up and down the street, checking to see whether Virgula or the other neighbours are watching. She raps against the wood, not too loudly, hoping not to draw attention to herself. There is no answer. She tries again, and again, each time becoming more flustered, until she and Victoria are both hammering on its unyielding surface.

At last, the door opens a crack. It is not Juventus who looks out, but Vitalio. Amara stares at him in astonishment.

"What are you doing?" she hisses. "Let us in!" Vitalio opens the door wider, and Amara and Victoria bundle inside. "What the fuck was that about?" Amara snarls, when the door is safely closed to the street. "Where is Juventus? And Philos?"

"Called back to the house."

Amara grips hold of Victoria to steady herself. "Why? How long for?"

Vitalio shrugs. Amara tries to stay calm. She knows Vitalio has always hated her, but she also knows he loves Philos, that the two are friends. Surely, the man would not be so cold if someone he cared about were in danger? "You must have *some* idea," she says, trying and failing to keep her voice steady.

"They've gone for questioning."

"Questioning?" Amara can no longer control her shaking. "But *why*?"

Vitalio's expression twists in a sneer. "Got a guilty conscience, have we?"

"You shut your mouth!" Victoria explodes. "Who are *you* to talk to her like that? What is it with the rude fucking slaves in this house?"

"You know all about manners, do you?" Vitalio shouts back. "Service here not up to the usual standards of *fine ladies* like yourselves?"

"There is problem?" Britannica's presence makes them all jump. She must have crept, panther-like, down the stairs at the sound of raised voices. She looms over Vitalio, smiling slightly to reveal her knocked out front teeth. "You have problem with us?"

Vitalio takes in the three former brothel whores, ranged

together in a rare show of unity. "No," he says to Britannica. "I meant no offence."

"Why are they being questioned?" Amara asks again. "Please, you're a good friend to Philos, you *must* know." She can see the flicker of surprise in Vitalio's eyes but is too desperate to hide her anxiety.

"I have no idea," Vitalio says, stiffly, his attention still drawn to Britannica. "Believe me. I would tell you if I did."

The effort of hiding her anxiety is becoming unbearable; Amara knows she has to get away before the others grow too curious. She nods at Vitalio then turns her back on her friends. "I'm tired," she says in a low voice. "If Rufus calls, I'm resting in my room."

As soon as she is in the seclusion of her own chambers, a sob escapes her. Amara clamps a hand to her mouth. Even here, she does not dare cry. Instead, she climbs onto the bed she has shared so many times with Philos, and lies rigid, fingers pressed to her face, covering her eyes. Pain lodges in her chest as she breathes in, then out, trying to expel images of her lover being beaten into confessing their affair. Amara is used to thinking on her feet, to facing down danger, but somehow, when confronted with the possibility of Philos suffering, she finds herself paralysed. "It's not true," she murmurs to herself, rehearsing the words she might speak to Rufus. "It's not true, my love, I promise you."

Amara keeps her door wide open, straining to hear any sound from the atrium, her panic rising as time passes. When she finally hears Juventus and Philos's voices, speaking dialect with Vitalio, at first, she cannot move. Then she scrambles from the bed, creeping to the edge of her second chamber to eavesdrop. With a sense of shock, she hears Juventus laugh. Philos's reply, though curt, does not sound distressed and is followed by Vitalio's voice, speaking in a low monotone. Clearly, whatever happened at the house, she and Philos have not been discovered. Amara presses her forehead against the cool of the painted wall, biting her lip to stop herself weeping with relief.

She has to wait until after nightfall to hear the truth of what happened. The story is so banal, Amara feels even more ashamed of the panic she suffered, and worse, her near inability to hide her emotions. Philos explains that a slave girl at the gem cutters was suspected of stealing, leading Rufus to call in him and Juventus to ask their opinion of the girl's character. In the end, the missing items were discovered, and nobody needed to be punished. Amara can see Philos is unsettled after she confesses how she reacted.

"But even if I *were* questioned about us, you can't go to pieces," he whispers, arms tight around her. "Please, my darling. If something happens to me, it won't be your fault. I chose to take this risk. And you must know I would never betray you, whatever they do to me. But if you get upset, you'll only give yourself away, and that would ruin everything."

"But why wouldn't Vitalio tell me what had happened? I *begged* him, and he just shrugged it off."

"He didn't know what it was about, that's all."

"But he saw I was upset! He could at least have explained

that you weren't in danger. Instead, he insinuated I might have a guilty conscience."

"I'm sorry Vitalio was rude to you," Philos says. "But he wasn't trying to be cruel. He has no idea how you feel about me, or about our affair. Which is exactly how it should be."

"What did he say to you about me, afterwards?"

"He told me to watch you, as you seemed agitated. I reassured him that I do, relentlessly, and that you are nothing but loyal to Rufus." Philos kisses her on the forehead. "I don't want you to live in fear like this, my love. Being with me is meant to make you happier, not more miserable. Perhaps I shouldn't visit so often."

"No," Amara says, holding him closer. "Don't say that." She can feel the heat of embarrassment creep over her skin, but still presses on. "I couldn't bear it if you stopped coming. Sometimes, it feels like my whole life exists in the moments I'm with you. The rest is just waiting. Don't you ever feel that?"

"Yes, but that's what worries me."

"You don't want to love me?"

"I don't want to lose you. And perhaps..." He hesitates, as if thinking better of whatever he was going to say, before seeing the expectant look on Amara's face and realizing he has to finish. "If I'm honest, I didn't expect to love you *this* much."

It is a relief for Amara to laugh. "Well, that's flattering. So you thought I'd just be a pleasant diversion?"

"No," he replies, laughing too. "You know that's not what I meant."

In a swift movement, Amara pushes herself upwards, so

that she is no longer curled up in his arms but sitting astride him. She sees his lips part in surprise. "Are you sure *this* isn't what you wanted?"

The look of lust in Philos's eyes is familiar – she has seen desire in so many men. But the tenderness with which he draws her closer, is unlike any other she has known. "Always," he says.

24

Crescens, the Netter of young girls by night
Pompeii graffiti

The heat of the sun under the awning is making her sweat. Amara sits between Victoria and Britannica in the arena, high up in the back rows reserved for women. There is room to stretch out, at least. Today's entertainment has an entrance fee, thinning the crowds to those who can afford to buy their way in. The Fishermen's Games in June do not have the draw of larger public entertainments, though Amara suspects many will still be cramming the harbour right now, grateful for some time off work, even if it's only to watch the day's haul of fish being sacrificed to Vulcan, an offering to pray that the sea continues to be fruitful.

"I wonder if Celadus will remember me," Victoria says, fanning herself to create a breeze. Amara thinks back to last year, when the gladiator singled Victoria out from the crowd, lifting her off her feet to kiss her, murmuring a secret message in her ear, before continuing on his procession into the arena. It was the same day Amara met with Menander, the only afternoon they ever spent together. Dido was here then too, and Cressa. The sense of loss is heavy, as oppressive as the heat.

"You never told us what Celadus said to you," Amara says.

Victoria smiles at the memory but doesn't answer Amara's question.

"The fighters," Britannica says, impatient at this distraction from the real point of interest. "Who are they? Why they here?"

"Well, what do *you* think?" Victoria says, pursing her lips. "It's mainly net men fighting today, obviously."

"What is netmen?"

"Gladiators who are styled as fishermen," Amara says. "They have a net to catch their opponent, and they fight with a big trident, which is a sort of spear with three prongs. And a dagger too, in case the trident gets lost or broken."

"If *I* have trident, I kill too quickly," Britannica says, though she looks more interested than Amara has ever seen her before, sitting up as tall as possible, craning to see into the ring.

"*Amara! Victoria!*"

The voice is a familiar one. Amara turns to Victoria, sees the same look of disbelief on her face.

"Beronice!" Amara shouts, standing up. She stares around the arena, trying to spot her friend.

"There she is!" Victoria yells, waving frantically. "Over here! *Beronice!*"

Beronice is struggling to make her way along the row, other women having to squash aside to let her pass. Amara and Victoria watch her slow, painful progress, until with a last undignified shove past some bad-tempered-looking matrons, Beronice reaches them. Felix's three women fall on each other, shrieking and laughing, unable to believe they are together again.

"Look at you!" Amara exclaims, astonished by Beronice's appearance. "Just look! What happened?"

Beronice is not in the gaudy yellow toga she was obliged to wear to mark herself out as a prostitute. She is dressed like a respectable married woman in a long tunic and shawl, her hair covered by a thin veil. "He married me!" Beronice shouts, wild with happiness. "I'm married!"

Neither Amara nor Victoria need to ask who the man is. It can only be Gallus. "Felix let him *marry* you?" Victoria is so shocked she is clutching her chest as if Beronice just dealt her a physical blow.

Beronice pulls them both down onto the bench, so that they are sitting together in a huddle. "Felix has a bar now. He put Gallus in charge of running it!" she exclaims. "And Gallus, *my* Gallus, persuaded him it would be better for business if he had a wife to help!"

"So you're *free*?" Amara asks, almost speechless that the dim-witted Beronice, who never put in a day's scheming for her liberty, might have stumbled upon it simply by winning the heart of the brothel's equally dim doorman.

"No," Beronice says. "But it doesn't matter. I belong to Gallus now, and he's married me. He's even taken a cut in his wages to pay Felix off," she adds, in the tone of a woman recounting an act of untold generosity.

"I thought he always promised to free you as well?" Victoria says, sharply. "That's why you used to pay him *all* your tips!"

"It hardly matters," Beronice says, too happy to be perturbed by Victoria's question. "I don't mind him owning me. It's not like I'd ever leave him, is it?"

Victoria and Amara exchange an anxious look, united by their scepticism over Gallus's good intentions. Beronice does not notice. Instead, she finally sees Britannica. "You're here too!"

Britannica nods. "I am happy for your fortune," she replies.

Before Beronice can start exclaiming over Britannica's ability to speak, they are loudly shushed by the women sitting behind. Trumpets ring out, signalling that the games are about to start. Amara strains to hear the announcement, the man's shouting largely lost this far back. It is moments like this she is very conscious Latin is not her native language. "What did he say?" she whispers to Victoria.

"It's a public punishment," Victoria replies. "Before the duels. It will be runaway slaves, thieves, criminals, that sort of thing. They set the beasts on them."

The arena is humming, spectators murmuring to one another in excited anticipation. Then there is shouting. Amara cranes to see what is happening. A group of men are being driven into the arena. They are unarmed, dressed in shabby tunics. Some carry spears to defer death and prolong the entertainment, but none have any real protection. Amara is too far away to see their faces; she cannot even hear if they are shouting or weeping, the jeering of the crowd is too loud. One stumbles. She grips the seat. In her mind's eye she can see Philos – how slim and insubstantial he looked walking to Terentius's tomb. *He would kill me for touching a woman who belongs to him.*

Fear of punishment has haunted Amara ever since her scare over Philos being called for questioning a few weeks ago. When she is with her lover, she refuses to dwell on the horror, telling herself they will never be caught. But now, like a child who has climbed up into the highest branches of a forbidden tree, she cannot help but look down. The drop is terrifying. What would Rufus *do* to Philos for such an act of betrayal? Not shame himself by having a slave slaughtered publicly for adultery, surely, but there are many other accusations a master might make. Rufus could easily invent a less embarrassing crime. Philos would have no defence – he is already branded, an indelible mark against his character seared into his skin.

A bear is released into the arena, and the prisoners scatter. Spectators start to scream with excitement, eager to see the first kill. Amara stands up. "I don't want to watch," she says, turning her back on the scene. "I don't want to see it."

Her three friends look up in surprise. Amara tries to force her way along the row to the exit, but panic has made her light-headed. Beronice stands, catching hold of her arm.

"Here," she says. "I'll go with you. I don't mind missing a beast hunt. The duels are much better."

The pair of them shuffle along to exclamations of irritation whenever they block the view, eventually reaching the stairs. Amara feels better almost as soon as she's in the open air, out of the heat of the arena. She continues to clutch Beronice's arm, growing steadier as they make their way down the long flight of steps. "Thank you," she says, when they reach the bottom.

"That's alright, I'd rather chat anyway. I've so much more to tell you! Let's go sit over there." Beronice points at a shady spot under the plane trees, not far from where Amara once sat with Menander. They weave their way through the market stalls of food and souvenirs. It is almost more crowded out here than it was in the arena. A lamp seller tries to press his wares on them, bumping the tray into Beronice, but they swat him away, intent on reaching their space before anyone else grabs it. When they get to the shade, Amara flops down on the grass. The feel of it under her hands as she leans back, her fingers digging into the soil, is reassuringly solid.

"It's so good to see you," she says to Beronice, looking at her with affection. "I want to know everything."

"So much has happened, I hardly know where to start," Beronice exclaims. "Gallus came into the brothel one morning and just announced in front of everyone that we were getting married! I thought he was joking, but then he grabbed me, and we went up to see Felix, and it was all agreed. Felix signed me over to him! I *never* have to work there again." She sighs, tilting back her head to gaze at the sun glinting white through the dark of the branches. "I know you and Victoria used to laugh; I know you always thought I was an idiot. But the first time Gallus and I were alone together in our *own* room above the bar, I thought I'd die of happiness."

It has always been impossible for Amara to fathom Beronice's devotion to Gallus who, at best, she found to be an oafish annoyance and, at worst, a devious thug, but hearing Beronice talk, Amara has no urge to ridicule her. After all, what might Beronice think of Philos? "It's wonderful," she says. "I hope he always deserves you."

"I'm sure he will. And you should see him at the bar! It's

like he's born to sell wine! It's not all that big – there's not much more than standing room, really – but we've been bringing in such a profit for Felix." Beronice fusses slightly with her hair under the veil, patting it at the back, a gesture Amara remembers from the brothel. "He does still get a bit jealous, if I'm honest. It puts him in a bad mood if the customers are too friendly. He wanted to rename me, you know – now that he owns me he can do that. That way, he told me, if another man said my new name, I'd always remember who gave it to me and who I belong to. But then we worried Felix wouldn't like it."

"Probably for the best," Amara says, finding this account of Gallus's possessiveness less than endearing. It reminds her of Rufus, with his contract. "Did Felix say anything to you, when he sold you to Gallus?"

Beronice shakes her head. "Felix never found me very interesting. Thankfully."

Amara thinks of the last time she saw Beronice, when she failed to save her, and reaches over to take her hand. "I'm so happy you're safe now. And I wish I'd had the money to get you out before this. It was never because I loved Victoria more, I hope you know that. But I owed her."

"And you knew what Gallus had promised me," Beronice says, without a trace of resentment. "That's what I told myself afterwards. You must have guessed he would manage it." She beams. "And he did!" Roaring erupts from the arena – perhaps another beast has been released on the prisoners. Amara sits forwards, clasping her knees. "I should have asked you about Rufus, though," Beronice says, mistaking the reason for her change in mood. "How lucky that you found love too, and with someone so rich!" There is no envy to her voice, and Amara knows Beronice would not trade Gallus and their tiny, smoky bar for the wealthiest patron in Pompeii.

"I'm very lucky."

"And you love him?"

For a moment, Amara wants to tell her. She imagines the relief it would give to talk about Philos, to enumerate all his charms, to explain that she too understands what it feels like to love someone that much. But it is unthinkable to risk his life, or her freedom, for a moment's gossip. "Of course," she replies. "Rufus is a generous patron to me, more than I could ever have hoped."

"Has Victoria found another man?" Amara shakes her head, and Beronice pulls a face. "I still can't believe what a shit Felix was to her, or why she *ever* put up with it."

"Felix has another side; he's capable of being very charming. I think he used that against her."

"Well, I never saw any fucking charm," Beronice replies, with a shudder. "Gallus told me, if it hadn't made the boss feel bigger to say he had a *freedman*, Felix would never have let him go."

"Does Gallus not like him then?"

Beronice looks nervous. "I didn't say that. Gallus works very hard for him. We both do."

Amara thinks of how hard Philos works for Rufus, and she knows this means nothing. "Shall we get some wine, while we wait for the fighting?"

They wander over to one of the stalls, Amara paying for both drinks. The wine is bitter and watered-down, but it loosens Beronice's tongue still further. Delighted to have the chance to talk about Gallus without ridicule, she barely draws breath. Amara feels her attention drift as Beronice chatters on about his gift for sharp selling, his desire for sons, his miraculous stamina in bed. She no longer has any desire to share her feelings for Philos. Instead, she has an unpleasant sense that perhaps even *Beronice* would judge her. Amara has chosen a lover whose status is so low, so utterly degraded, he cannot even be classed as a man. He is, legally, a non-person. All the qualities she loves about him, which make him superior to Gallus in every respect, become meaningless in a slave. It hurts thinking about the gulf between what she feels and what others see. The only person Amara knows would have completely understood her love for Philos, is Dido.

"It must have been very difficult back at the brothel after Dido died," Amara says, when Beronice has finally run out of praise for her tedious husband. "I know you loved her." The grief on Beronice's face almost brings Amara some comfort – at least it proves how much Dido is missed.

"It was the worst time. She was the kindest person I ever met."

They are both silent for a moment, before Amara asks the question she has been waiting to raise all afternoon. "Nobody seems to know what Felix did with her body. Have you ever asked Gallus where he buried her ashes?"

Beronice looks embarrassed. "The second time I asked, he threatened to slap me," she replies. "And Gallus only does that if he's really, *really* angry, so I can't ask again."

"Felix *must* have buried her though, mustn't he?" Amara says, not liking to think of Gallus bullying Beronice. "Even *he* can't have left her at the dump."

"No!" Beronice exclaims, shaking her head. "Definitely

not. Even Felix wouldn't do that. He's just being a shit by refusing to tell." They both sit contemplating the man who has caused them so much pain. Amara thinks of his recent promise to claim her, and all the effort it is going to take to evade him.

"Do you want to go back in?" Amara asks. "The beast hunt must have finished by now."

"Only if you're sure." Beronice jumps up eagerly. "I'd better not miss it all, Gallus will be wanting to talk about the fights later. It annoys him if I can't follow what he says."

The duelling has already started by the time they are back inside. Their shuffle along the row is greeted with even less tolerance this time; one angry woman throws olive stones at them, the pits stinging as they hit Amara's hands. They dodge the worst of the hail and squash in next to Victoria and Britannica who, Amara notices, have left a large gap rather than sit side by side. She had hoped after the row with Vitalio, that her two friends might grow closer, but it seems their mutual dislike is too ingrained.

"Amara," Britannica says, gripping her arm. "How you miss this?" Britannica's face is flushed, one hand clutching the gladiatorial amulet she always wears. "It is *real* fighting."

In the arena, two men are circling one another. The net man is easy to spot, bare-headed and bare-chested, only his trident keeping the heavily armed chaser at bay. The chaser barely looks human, his face obscured, his torso shining metal. He lifts his shield to fend off jabs from the trident, trying to come close enough to strike a blow on his opponent's unprotected flesh. The net man responds by flinging out his fishing-net, flicking it at the chaser's legs to make him stumble. There are screams from the crowd as the chaser only just manages to leap out of the way of the lethal, jabbing prongs.

"Too heavy," Britannica says. "He will tire."

Amara does not need to ask which man she means. Inside his armour, the chaser must be sweltering, his entire head encased in a metal ball which blazes silver in the sun. The net man, in contrast, is light on his feet, his tanned skin shining with sweat. There is something familiar about the way he moves, taunting the chaser, body rippling with muscle. Amara thinks of the Palaestra, of the time she went to find Felix, the way he out-paced the other men sprinting round the circuit. She steals a glance at Victoria who is gazing at the net man with a rapturous expression. "Do you know what his name is?" Amara asks.

"Crescens," Victoria breathes, not even turning to look at her.

Amara turns back to Britannica, whose attention is no less rapt than Victoria's, the two women united in their interest. The same cannot be said for all the other spectators. Many women are chatting, enjoying the chance to gossip while they watch the two men fight to the death. Gladiator duels don't have the unpredictability of beast hunts – there's more skill and less savagery, and so perhaps less excitement. Amara herself feels nothing but dread as she watches the chaser tire, the net man constantly baiting him, exhausting him, until he is finally too slow to evade the jabs of the trident and has the shield knocked from his grasp.

"Now, netman will finish him," Britannica says, with satisfaction.

The kill when it comes is neither glorious nor swift, but Victoria and Britannica still leap to their feet, screaming.

Amara rises with them, watching as Crescens lifts his arms, shaking them in victory, while his opponent – and perhaps former friend – lies dying at his feet. The sound is deafening, the roaring of the arena pounding in her skull, but Amara can still hear Britannica shouting, close to her ear.

"I do this when you free me! One day, I am gladiator!"

Amara turns to look at her in surprise, even amusement, but Britannica's eyes are fixed on Crescens. The look of ferocity on her face is frightening.

25

Oh, if only I could hold your sweet arms around my neck
In an embrace and place kisses on your tender lips
Pompeii graffiti

A mara had agreed with Rufus to leave the ?mes early,
but it is impossible to persuade Victori? ? Britannica
to accompany her. Instead, she leaves th? ?with Beronice
and makes her way to the exit at the ?? time, knowing
Philos will be ?? ?ottom of the arena
?? as a trusted go-between,
just as he did when she lived at the brothel.

When Amara catches sight of Philos, it is clear he had
already spotted her. From the top of the arena steps, he
is a slight figure far below, but his presence, even at this
distance, has an immediate impact. Every reservation
she has felt about their affair vanishes. They smile at one
another, an open expression of affection neither would
permit themselves at the house, but here, the significance is
lost in the anonymity of the crowd.

The closer she gets, the more reserved Amara is obliged

to become. Standing beside Philos, she wants to take his arm, but instead stands slightly apart.

"Were the games good?" he asks.

"Not really," she says as they set off, walking through the bustle of the marketplace. "But we saw Beronice. Gallus has married her."

"He's *married* her?" Philos is as astonished as Amara was at hearing the news. "While Felix still owns her?"

"No, Felix sold her to him."

Philos is silent, and she suspects that he is thinking, just as she did earlier, that Beronice has managed to achieve something that they cannot. "I'm very pleased for her," is all he says. "I hope Gallus will treat her kindly."

"He won't. Or not as kindly as she deserves. But he is a much better man than Felix." The crowds are starting to thin, and soon they will be back on the pavement, where there is even less privacy. "When Beronice talked about love," she says impulsively, "I wanted to tell her."

"But you didn't?" His tone is sharp.

"Of course not!" She is hurt he would think her so careless. "I only told her I was lucky to have such a generous patron."

"Of course. I'm sorry." It's unclear to Amara whether Philos is apologizing for his momentary distrust or their unsatisfactory situation. They have reached the walled vineyard at the end of the marketplace and turn left towards the street. The games are always a good time for prostitutes to pick up business, and Amara is sure many of the women currently embracing lovers against the wall are drawn there by money rather than lust. One man leers at her when she passes, mistaking her interest in the scene. She moves a little closer to Philos, wishing he could make some gesture to claim her. The ownership of one man is always helpful in deterring the attention of another.

"We'll be back in town soon." Philos glances at her. "Maybe walk on my other side." He holds out his arm to shepherd her over, brushing her lightly on the shoulder as she passes. It looks like an innocent mistake, but Amara knows it is deliberate. Her heart beats faster. She thinks of the evening, when they will finally be able to touch one another and speak freely. "Rufus will be joining you later than planned," Philos says. "He is bringing a friend to dinner. I expect he intends to stay the night."

"Oh," Amara says, unable to hide her disappointment. "Did he say which friend?"

"It's a surprise. He didn't even want to tell *me*, though he did say you would be pleased. I know it cannot be Quintus and Drusilla – she has Phoebe and Lais with her this evening." They have reached the street, and Amara will need to walk ahead of him. "It's only one night," Philos murmurs, his voice so low she can barely hear. Amara steals a glance at him, but he does not return it.

At the dressing table, Martha pulls at Amara's hair, her fingers unkind. Amara wonders how her maid might react if she learned her brothel-raised mistress is cheating the Master. Philos has assured her that neither Martha nor Juventus suspect anything, and Amara is obliged to believe him. Her lover shifts between the worlds of slave and free, wearing a different mask for every role. His conversations in dialect with the porter are as unknowable to Amara as is the precise nature of the work he does for Rufus in the family business.

An especially hard twist with the comb makes Amara wince. "Careful, please."

"Sorry, mistress," Martha says, not sounding remotely contrite but easing off on the styling.

Amara sighs and closes her eyes. She prefers Martha's hands, however rough, to entertaining Rufus. Anticipation makes her nauseous. It is impossible to be intimate with Philos, to try and allow herself to feel, only to be confronted by Rufus and turn her body back to stone. Perhaps it would be different if her patron simply took what he wanted, without needing her to love him too. Her bedroom is now a place she associates so completely with Philos that Rufus's presence there feels like an obscenity. And yet, Rufus is the one who owns the house, owns her, owns her lover, and grants her every privilege she has. Even her relationship with Philos depends on his continued affection.

Martha has finished with her hair, and Amara dismisses her to finish preparing the dinner. Amara changes her earrings, and once she is satisfied with her appearance, she sits on the couch, reaching for the harp to squeeze in some more practice, in case Rufus demands to hear her play.

"Rufus is coming?" It is Britannica, standing in the doorway.

"Yes," Amara says, pleased to see Britannica looking more like her usual surly self, no longer frenzied by the prospect of violence. "I'm happy you and Victoria made it back without killing each other."

"She still there."

Amara frowns, confused by the Briton's poor Latin. "What do you mean, *still there*."

"She stay to fuck Crescens. Not for me to tell her no."

"She did *what*?" Amara's voice is a shriek.

"She stay to fuck Crescens," Britannica repeats slowly, as if her accent were the trouble, though Amara can see from the malice in her eyes that Britannica knows perfectly well her message was understood.

"She can't have done!" Amara leaps to her feet, still shouting from the shock. Her voice has brought Philos to the door. "What were you *thinking*, letting her do something like that?"

"She is whore. Is what she does."

"She could be killed!" Amara yells at Britannica. "I told you to bring her back!"

"Amara," Philos is beside her. "Rufus will be here soon. Calm yourself."

"Victoria has gone off to fuck a gladiator," she says, turning on him. "And now she will have to get across town on her own, in the dark. That's if she even leaves the barracks alive!"

"Victoria knows how to look after herself. Think of the life she used to lead. Please stay calm. You cannot be in a state when Rufus arrives."

It is fortunate for Philos and Amara that nobody but Britannica is present to witness their conversation, because in the heat of her emotion, Amara reaches out to touch his arm for reassurance, and Philos, unthinking, lays his hand over hers. "You're right," she says.

"She is whore," Britannica repeats. "What you expect?"

"That's enough," Philos says, before Amara can begin shouting again. "Enough, Britannica, please."

The Briton shrugs. "I only say truth," she replies, turning on her heel and striding out.

When they are alone, Amara realizes their posture and swiftly removes her hand as if Philos's skin had burned her. "Did she...?"

He looks equally shaken. "No." He clasps his hands together as if that might erase their touch. "She won't have noticed. Just make sure you're calmer when Rufus arrives."

Philos walks from the room, and Amara sinks back down onto the couch.

Victoria is still missing when Amara hears Rufus's voice from the atrium. She gets up, walking slowly, a gracious smile on her face, ready to welcome whoever he has brought to meet her. Her patron is standing by the pool, blocking his guest from view, but Amara sees the guest's servant standing next to Philos, watching her. It is Secundus, Pliny's steward.

She runs across the atrium with a cry, any pretence of composure gone. Pliny turns towards her as she throws herself at his feet.

"It's you!" she cries, clasping the hem of his cloak and pressing it to her heart, so amazed she does not even manage to greet him properly. "You came back for me!"

"Of course I came to see you," Pliny replies, embarrassed, trying to raise her from her knees. "Or do you think I'm in the habit of writing nonsense?"

"How can I ever thank you for what you've done." Amara is still clutching his hem, barely resisting the urge to seize his hand and kiss it. "Nothing I do will ever be enough. You've given me *everything*. I can never repay your kindness, never."

"Come now." Pliny hauls her to her feet. "You wrote very prettily already, and Rufus must have read you my reply. I told you, there's no need for any more thanks."

Amara glances at Rufus, whose existence she had briefly forgotten. Only then does it dawn on her that Rufus never told her Pliny had responded to her message of gratitude, which she wrote as a coda in his own letter to the admiral. Nor has he ever passed on a message that Pliny planned to visit her. Rufus gives a strained smile. "I knew you would be pleased."

She flings her arms around her patron, kissing him. "How good you are to me!" she cries, hoping her feigned gratitude will be as convincing as the genuine emotion she just displayed.

"Let's not overwhelm the admiral with hysterics." Rufus disentangles himself, though he looks better pleased by her show of affection. "I told him to expect dinner, not weeping."

They head to the dining room, Pliny remarking politely on the paintings, though Amara knows they are far inferior to anything he must own himself. She is conscious of how small the room must look to him, nothing like the grand home where they first met. All three couches have been dressed, as she was not sure of the exact number of guests. Pliny and Rufus recline opposite one another and as Rufus makes himself comfortable, Amara knows he will expect her to lie next to him, the way she always does. She hesitates. As soon as she joins him, Rufus will drape an arm over her and she will be no more than an object, her status demeaned in the admiral's eyes. The prospect is uninviting. Instead, she takes the empty couch, reclining between the two men, not daring to look at Rufus.

"I'm delighted to see you so well settled," Pliny says to her. He is propped up on his elbow, without appearing remotely relaxed. She remembers this look of his, the distracted air of a man who would prefer to be working than socializing. "And Rufus tells me you have been continuing your interest in medicinal herbs which is excellent. I must send you a recent text I found, from Greece. I believe it would interest you."

"That's very generous, thank you," Amara says. "Rufus has kindly encouraged me to plant a herb garden, and I would love to add to it. I do hope your research is proving as fruitful as ever."

Pliny waves a hand. "I have very little opportunity for research these days. The fleet takes up almost every moment of my time, save what I can spare at night. Though as you know, I care very little for sleep."

"I remember," Amara says, with a smile. Pliny also smiles, in a rare expression of affection, perhaps remembering, as she is, the long hours she would read to him, late into the night.

"The admiral is in Pompeii as part of his campaign against piracy," Rufus interrupts.

"Will you be here long?" Amara asks. Martha has come in with the roasted pigeon and serves them while Pliny talks.

"Only one night," he says. "I have been overseeing the defences of towns across the bay. Tomorrow I must be back in Misenum." He dips his bread into Martha's offering of crushed chickpea, and tastes it, nodding in appreciation.

"But I hope you will both join me for a short visit. I've invited a number of friends to the villa, so you will be well entertained in the day, while I work."

"You are too generous," Rufus replies. "But sadly, my father's business will keep me in town."

"I'm sorry to hear that. But perhaps you can spare Amara for a few days." Pliny gestures vaguely at her. "If it's not too much for a man to ask to borrow his own freedwoman?"

Pliny chuckles, meaning it as a joke, not dreaming of giving offence, but Rufus flushes red to his hairline. "Of course. No doubt Amara will be *thrilled* to accompany you."

"Do you still call her Amara?" Pliny continues eating his pigeon, oblivious to the tension. "I would have thought you might use the name her father gave her, not some title the pimp invented." He turns to her. "Wouldn't you prefer that?"

The name her father gave her. A name Rufus has never even asked. She stares at Pliny, wishing she could convey her real feelings, to tell him that, yes, she would like to be Timarete again, but she cannot risk making Rufus even angrier. "I prefer Amara now," she says. "Because it is the name Rufus has given me, and he takes the place of both father and husband in my life."

Pliny raises his eyebrows. "Well, as you prefer. It just seems rather irregular."

Amara looks at Rufus, hoping her declaration of total self-effacement might have been enough to placate him, but he turns away, not meeting her eyes.

26

Next comes the well-known fertile region of Campania. In its hollows begin the vine-bearing hills and the celebrated effects of the juice of the vine, famous the world over, and, as writers of old have said, the venue of the greatest competition between Bacchus and Ceres.

Pliny the Elder, Natural History

The happiness Amara feels at spending the night with Philos is darkened by their mutual unease at Rufus's decision not to stay over. They whisper together, Amara relaying the dinner, the many times Pliny offended Rufus without even realizing, while Philos holds her, his hand warm at the small of her back. He winces when she repeats the admiral's request to 'borrow' his own freedwoman.

"I wish you had found some way to refuse the invitation. I can't see any good coming of making Rufus jealous like this."

"It's Pliny! Why be jealous of the man who helped him to buy me?"

"I imagine that's exactly why he *is* jealous. He understands the hold the admiral might have on you."

"But he knows there was never anything like that," Amara says, wondering if Philos might also be feeling possessive. "Pliny never used me that way. He was kind and respectful, nothing more."

Philos draws her closer, kissing her, until she feels the warmth spread through her body like wine, prompting her to pin him underneath her on the bed. "It wasn't my business," Philos says, looking up at her. "But it's a relief to know Pliny never hurt you."

"Not a relief from jealousy?" Amara teases.

"I've told you so many times," he says, cupping her face in his hands, her hair spilling over his fingers. "The only lovers that matter are the ones we choose."

In the morning, Victoria is finally home, just as Philos predicted she would be. She is already in the garden when Amara wakes, her singing filling the house. Any anger Amara feels as she heads out to confront her wayward friend is disarmed by the sight of Victoria kneeling by the fountain, head thrown back to greet the sunlight. She looks so full of joy it is impossible not to smile.

"I take it Crescens wasn't a disappointment?"

Victoria turns to her. "You have *no* fucking idea."

Amara laughs. "Aren't you going to fill me in?"

Victoria heads to the bench, and Amara joins her, touched when Victoria puts an arm around her. "It's not a pleasure you can describe," she says, although this has never stopped her in the past. "He's just... perfect! And his body! Like holding Apollo." She sighs, a sound dangerously close to the sort of moan Amara remembers her making at the brothel.

"Don't go too wild, will you? I can't have you inviting half the barracks back here. Rufus will have us all thrown out."

"I love him!" Victoria says, indignant. "I'm not interested in the others! It's not like I fucked anyone else last night."

"Love already? That was quick."

Victoria sighs. "It's definitely love," she says. "But quick is *not* the word I'd use." They both laugh then, the sort of unrestrained cackling that would no doubt appal Rufus, and Amara feels lighter than she has in weeks.

"I hope I am not disturbing you?" It is Secundus, Pliny's steward, standing at the edge of the garden.

"No." Amara rises to her feet, embarrassed at being caught lolling around like a slave at the Saturnalia. "Of course not. Though I wasn't expecting you until this afternoon."

"The admiral sent me to collect you. His business at Misenum cannot wait, and he sets sail within the hour."

"Oh." Amara is thrown by having less time than she'd hoped to prepare, and worse, no chance to speak to Philos in private before she leaves. "I was just expecting..." She stops herself, but Secundus is staring, eyebrows raised, waiting for her to finish. "I was expecting to leave instructions to my... to the steward."

"If that's the capable young man I met last night," Secundus speaks slowly, his eyes fixed on hers, "I'm sure he will have no difficulty in anticipating your every wish. But in any case, you have time to instruct him. We do not have to leave on the instant."

"You are right, of course," she replies, turning from him. "Thank you."

★ ★ ★

In her own chambers, Amara finds Martha has already packed for her, leaving everything she might need on the couch. She rifles through the bag, making sure her maid has included the gowns Pliny gave her. Not that she expects the admiral to notice, but she prefers to be prepared. Refolding the dresses, she hears Philos's characteristic light tread, and is both touched and alarmed he would risk coming to say goodbye. "My darling," she says softly. "You should not be here..." She turns to face her lover, eyes full of affection, and the words die on her lips. Secundus is standing in the doorway, his face silhouetted by the light behind. "You should not be here," she repeats, more firmly, trying to pretend she always knew who it was. "This is my private chamber." Secundus bows, without speaking, and leaves the room.

Secundus gives no sign that he suspects her as they walk through the streets to the harbour. He carries her luggage without complaint, smiling blandly whenever she asks questions about the week ahead. His manner goes some way to soothing her fears, though Amara knows the admiral's steward is surely too astute to have missed the endearment she spoke so foolishly. She can only hope he decides to keep any suspicions to himself. After all, Secundus owes Rufus nothing.

Outside the town walls, as the road dips down towards the sea, Amara sees the vessel waiting for them. It dwarfs the others at the dock. The glare of the sun on its massive sails is blinding, the ship's body painted red. "How big is the fleet the admiral commands?" she asks Secundus.

"Fifty ships," he replies, with pride in his voice. "The largest fleet in the Empire. You will see many of them when we arrive at the harbour in Misenum."

Amara says nothing, overawed by the prospect of the next few days. The only people she knows in Misenum are the fleet's commander, who will surely be too busy to pay her much attention, and Secundus, whose company makes her deeply uneasy. She almost wishes Rufus were here.

At the dock, the quadrireme has attracted a small crowd of curious onlookers and, beside them, two familiar figures. Julia and Livia are waiting with an attendant laden with bags. Amara greets them both with a cry of relief.

"How wonderful," Julia exclaims, embracing her. "I did *insist* Pliny invite you, though I hope you won't miss Rufus too much." From the mischievous look in her eye, Amara suspects Julia knows this is unlikely.

"I should think not," Livia says, nose wrinkled in distaste. "Tediousness over a boyfriend is quite insufferable. A woman should always relish her moments of freedom. Not pine for confinement."

It is perhaps an inappropriate remark for a widow, but Julia only laughs. "I should think the villa at Misenum will provide enough distraction," she says. "It truly is extraordinary. I'm afraid you will be quite spoiled for Pompeii afterwards."

"If you are ready to come on board, please, ladies." It is not Pliny, but one of his sailors. The man is nothing like the ragged crew on the trading vessel that brought Amara from Piraeus to Puteoli. Instead, he is dressed in the uniform of the Emperor's personal guard.

"Thank you," Julia says, while Amara can only stare at him.

The walk up the wooden gangplank brings back unpleasant memories, but once she is safely on the spacious, gleaming deck, any similarity to the experience of travelling as cargo vanishes. "It's beautiful," she breathes. The sailor who has helped her aboard, laughs.

"Not what Rome's enemies say when she's bearing down on them with the speed of an eagle," he replies, walking off to join Pliny, who she sees now is at the prow of the ship, speaking to another sailor. Even from this distance, he looks very different from the distracted scholar she is used to seeing. For the first time, Amara is able to picture what he must have looked like as a young man, during his long years of military service in Germania.

"Travelling by sea always makes me think of my father, may his shade be granted peace," Julia sighs, leaning against the wooden railings. Livia joins her aunt-by-marriage, resting a hand on her shoulders, caressing her. It is a surprisingly intimate gesture, reminding Amara of the way Philos touches her.

"Was your father also in the Emperor's service?" Amara asks.

"His last post was with Pliny, in Spain, when Pliny held the Procuratorship there," Julia replies. "My father had great experience in financial affairs – it was how he earned his freedom at the Imperial court, many years before I was born of course." Amara knows from the inscription on the Venus Baths, describing her friend as the *daughter of Spurius*, that Julia is illegitimate, her mother perhaps a concubine like Amara herself. "I was a child of his winter years," Julia says. "I am grateful he lived to so great an age."

Amara grasps the railing as the oars rise from the water. She can hear shouting but cannot make out the command. The quadrireme makes its way slowly out of the port, skirting the column of Venus at the mouth of the harbour. The goddess is even more enormous this close, and as Amara looks up, she has an irrational fear Aphrodite might reach out a giant hand to crush her like an ant.

As soon as they reach the open water, there are further shouted commands, and the oars rise and fall in rapid succession, the ship swiftly reaching an astonishing speed. Wind tears Amara's hair from her face as she clings to the railing.

"It takes a little getting used to," Livia remarks.

Amara stays crouched over the bar, too fearful to stand any straighter, as Pliny advances on them. He moves with ease on deck, undeterred by the motion of the water. Amara forces herself to stand upright, not wanting him to think her feeble.

Pliny does not waste time with greetings but points straight towards the coastline. "You get an unrivalled view of Campania from the water," he declares, urging them to look in the direction he is pointing. Amara gazes out over the brilliant blue they are scudding over at such terrifying speed, to study the coastline as he commands. The land is moving past at a less dizzying pace, though Pompeii is already in the distance, the Venus of her harbour shrinking. "Those darker hollows on Vesuvius that you can see," Pliny informs her, "are some of the finest vineyards in Italy. People there train the vines to poplar trees, and the plants climb to the highest branches, which makes them extremely difficult to harvest. I've even heard," he adds, with a smile, so that Amara is unsure if he is joking, "that those harvesting the grapes make a point of arranging for a pyre and a grave in their terms of employment."

"I doubt any experienced vintner would fall from a poplar tree unless he had sampled too much of *last* year's wine," Julia remarks, making Pliny laugh.

"Back that way is Surrentum," he continues. "You should be able to see the promontory of Minerva, over there, look, where the Sirens once lived."

"The Sirens were *here*, on the Italian coast?" Amara asks.

"Well, if you believe the legends," Pliny replies, amused.

The hours of their journey across the Bay of Naples are some of the swiftest moving in Amara's life. She listens with rapt attention as Pliny describes not only the physical features of the landscape, the hot springs, the towns, the rivers, but also the legends behind them, the animals that live in each region, even the plants and their properties. Occasionally, Amara catches Julia looking at her, unable to hide her mirth at the picture of wide-eyed adoration she is presenting to the admiral. Even Pliny, whose interest in Amara has never been obviously sexual, does not seem entirely immune to the compliment.

The ship starts to lose speed as they approach Misenum, and Pliny excuses himself to join his crew. "He does love an audience," Julia murmurs affectionately, as she watches him speaking to the captain at the prow of the ship. "No wonder he made you his freedwoman."

"It's astonishing," Amara says. "He must remember

everything he's ever read. There cannot be another man like him, anywhere in the world!"

"Amara, *please*," Julia says, as Livia snorts with laughter. "I have to insist you don't treat Pliny like a god for the next few days – you'll make him quite insufferable."

The quadrireme slows on the approach into Misenum, and as it turns, Amara sees the inner harbour clearly for the first time. A floating forest lies in the basin, its thicket of masts as dense as the trees she has just seen crowding along stretches of the coastline. Men are working on many of the decks, cleaning and repairing the ships, some hanging on ropes off the sides, close to the water. Their own vessel, which is larger than many of those moored, edges past the rows of warships to dock by the naval barracks, a process that takes some time.

It is Secundus who helps Amara onto land, and she clutches his arm, still unsteady even though the ground is no longer moving under their feet. Pliny does not come ashore, and as Secundus leads them away, Amara realizes with disappointment that he must still have business with the fleet. They head in the opposite direction to the town – a distant jumble of colourful buildings clinging like molluscs to the edge of the harbour – and cross a wooden bridge that spans a wide canal. Looking along it, Amara sees that it leads to an even bigger enclosed harbour. The huge thicket of masts she saw on her arrival is only a fraction of the fleet.

The road climbs steeply uphill, the harbour dropping below them, the vast blue of the bay becoming more visible the higher they rise. When they reach the summit, the admiral's private carriage is waiting for them. Amara climbs inside, sitting beside Julia and Livia on the cushioned benches. Secundus piles in their luggage then climbs in too, keeping a discreet distance away. Amara can see the back of the driver as he steers the horses along the path, the motion causing her to tip slightly into Livia. The journey is a brief one, and when they come to a stop, and the women are helped out, blinking, into the sunlight, Amara realizes they have driven right into the heart of Pliny's magnificent estate. It is enclosed by high walls, and perched on the edge of the hillside is the villa, a vast terrace sweeping around it, facing the bay and the towering peak of Vesuvius.

"I will tell Plinia you are here," Secundus says, leading them onto the terrace. Amara can hear the swell of the waves below, the cry of gulls and the distant murmur of sailors calling to one another. It feels very different here, to Pompeii.

"Who is Plinia?" she asks in a whisper, even though there is nobody to overhear.

"The admiral's sister," Julia replies.

Secundus returns, and they follow him into the house, through a bewildering series of painted corridors and courtyards, until they reach a beautiful garden with an ornamental pond. Two men and a woman sit on benches under the shade of the colonnade, the sound of the fountains covering the murmur of their voices.

The woman stands to greet them, and Amara immediately sees the family resemblance. Plinia has her brother's square jaw, even more pronounced on a stout woman in her forties. She embraces Julia and Livia affectionately and greets Amara politely. "The freedwoman." She nods. "Delightful."

Plinia introduces them to the other guests: Alexios, a scholar from Greece, and Demetrius, an Imperial official. It seems Julia and Demetrius are old friends, embracing one another warmly, and Amara joins them both, while Livia and Plinia talk to the scholar.

"Why are you not hard at work in Rome?" Julia asks. "I hardly expected to find you sunning yourself in a garden at this time of year."

"I'm retired," Demetrius declares, smiling at her.

"Nonsense! You're like my father. You'll never retire."

Demetrius looks some years older than the admiral, deep lines fanning out from his eyes, marking the grooves around his mouth. From his accent, he is clearly Greek, like Amara and Alexios, and when he looks at her, she is aware it is not a casual glance but an appraisal. "Perhaps retire is an exaggeration," he says, agreeing with Julia. "But the Emperor is generous in allowing me time to visit my estates in Campania."

Julia, noticing his interest in Amara, draws her into the conversation. "This is dear little Amara's first time visiting Misenum. She takes her role as the admiral's freedwoman *very* seriously. I'm afraid she's likely to scold us all if he's treated with anything but the utmost reverence."

Amara is irritated by the teasing, but Demetrius only smiles. "A freedwoman's loyalty to her patron is entirely proper," he replies. "For what service did he free you, girl?" His dark eyes are not unfriendly, but it is still uncomfortable to be the subject of his scrutiny.

"You would need to ask the admiral to know the reasons for his exceptional kindness," Amara replies, thinking carefully about how to disclose her status as another man's concubine. "But I believe it was for the service I gave him in his research, and as an act of generosity towards a young man, the nephew of Julius Placidus, who wished to become my patron."

"It was indeed extremely generous to bestow such a gift on another," Demetrius replies. "But then the admiral is a remarkable man."

"I owe him everything," Amara says, not looking down demurely in response to his compliment as modesty required, but meeting his gaze directly. They smile at one another, before Demetrius turns back to Julia to talk about her father.

The late afternoon passes in a luxurious haze. There is no need to move from the garden – a constant stream of refreshment is brought to them by Pliny's slaves. Amara cannot help but think of her offer to Pliny to serve out the rest of her life as one of their number, never imagining she might come here as a guest instead. Conscious of her low status compared to the others, she is largely silent, listening to Demetrius speak about his work at the Imperial court, grateful to Julia for her friendliness and the effortless way she keeps including her as one of the party.

By the time the admiral joins his guests, dusk is falling, and they have already moved to the outdoor dining room. The back wall is carved to resemble a rock face, and water tumbles down it into a pool, a mosaic of marine life rippling under its surface. Lamps are scattered over the table and set in niches on the walls. Amara realizes the pattern of lights mirrors several of the constellations her father once taught her.

Pliny greets the arrival of a young boy, his nephew, with much affection. The child must be about twelve, and the admiral pays him a great deal of attention, asking him to recount what he has learned that day, and persuading Alexios to test the boy on his Greek. It reminds her of Pliny's eagerness to press scrolls upon her when she stayed with him, the questions he would ask to see if she had read them all.

Among the guests, it is Demetrius of whom Pliny seems fondest, and watching the two men together, Amara is relieved she answered the questions about her history as honestly as possible. Demetrius is a man who would likely make his own enquiries on any subject. Attendants lay out the dinner while the guests speak: boiled eggs, then a seasoned broth of sea urchins caught in the bay, and platters of expensive fruit, grown out of season. Everything is so delicious, Amara is unable to restrain herself from eating properly, resigned to annoying Rufus by putting on weight. After the meal, she can tell Pliny is distracted, and remembers his remark about only having time to work at night. His eyes come to rest on her.

"Amara," he says. "I wonder if you might delight everyone with your reading, while I make some notes. The texts I am thinking of are in Greek, not Latin, so should be easy for you to manage. You have such a musical voice – I'm sure the others would enjoy hearing you."

"Nothing would make me happier," she replies, pleased to have some means of repaying him. She waits while two slaves bring out the scrolls and Pliny's writing materials, along with a small table. He fusses a little when she sits beside him, making sure she has the correct section of text, but when she bends to read it, he rests his hand briefly on top of her head, a gesture she remembers from her father, and one she saw Pliny use earlier in the evening towards his nephew.

The text, by the philosopher Democritus, is written in a

clear hand, but is the strangest Amara has ever encountered. She reads it slowly while Pliny scribbles notes. The other guests linger for a while then start to retire. Plinia is the first to leave, shepherding her son to bed. Julia, Livia and Alexios slip away a little later. Nobody bids Pliny good night, evidently judging he would be irritated to have his train of thought broken. Eventually, only Demetrius remains. Amara cannot see him, but is aware of his presence, and the strong scent of lavender from the pipe he is smoking. Then he too leaves, and there is only Pliny. The garden has fallen into total darkness, the void filled with the whisper of crickets and the splash of invisible fountains. The only reason Amara can still see to read is thanks to the exhausted slaves who keep returning to replenish the oil lamps.

It is deep into the night, and her voice is growing hoarse, by the time Pliny finally allows her to stop. "What did you think of it?" he asks.

It is some hours since Amara has been able to concentrate fully on the sense of the text. "I had not heard this idea before. That we are made of indivisible atoms, that even the soul within us is material and cannot be destroyed."

"And does it seem likely to you?"

"I don't know," she says truthfully.

"It is nonsense. The idea death leads to a second life is a childish fantasy, nothing more." He reaches over and takes her hand, turning it over, pressing his fingers into her palm. "This is your body, Amara, so where is your soul? Why can't I see it, or touch it? Because it does not exist." Pliny does not let go of her, but continues holding her hand tightly in his. "Neither body nor mind has any more sensation after death than it had before birth. That is my view."

Amara thinks of Dido, of all those she has lost. "I'm not sure I can bear to believe that."

"Why?" Pliny asks, turning to her, frowning in surprise. "Death is Nature's gift. It's better to know that suffering ends. Once we accept this life is all we have, we can make better use of it."

Amara does not feel able to reply. The idea Philos might never know freedom, even after his death, is inexpressively painful. She thinks of him alone in his cell, at the house in Pompeii, and longs to hold him, to stop the passing of the hours and days that will lead to their inevitable, agonizing separation. Instead, she sits beside Pliny. He seems to have forgotten her and stares out into the black of the unseen garden, showing no signs of dismissing her for bed. She shifts on the couch to remind him of her presence, and he releases her hand.

"You must be tired. An attendant will show you to your room." Without needing to be asked, one of the men who has been keeping the lights burning, steps forwards from the shadows, holding a lamp. Amara rises, bids Pliny good night, and follows the stranger into the darkness.

27

*He always said there was no book so bad that some good could
not be got out of it.*

Pliny the younger, on his uncle, Pliny the Elder

The days at Misenum pass with the same soothing, sensual
rhythm as the waves which Amara hears breaking
beneath the villa. She wakes every morning in the beautiful
guest-room Plinia assigned her, a much bigger, airier space
than her bedroom in Pompeii. It is covered in exquisite
frescoes of the myth of Daphne and Apollo. She spends
hours gazing at the paintings: the expression of ecstasy on
Apollo's face as he is struck by Cupid's vengeful arrow of
lust, Daphne's terror as she flees from the maddened god,
and the nymph's transformation into a laurel tree, her arms
tapering into delicate branches. The image is so realistic
Amara feels she could almost pluck the leaves from the wall.

Each day, after breakfast, she joins Julia and Livia in the
private bath suite, to have her body pummelled and plucked
by silent attendants, every knot of tension released by the
luxuriant heat of the steam. Her afternoons are spent in
the gardens or sitting on the terrace. Pliny has continued

his habit of lending her scrolls, and she reclines for hours in the shade, poring over them. Demetrius often joins her, ostensibly to ask what she is reading or discuss the texts with her. The older man's interest both flatters Amara and makes her nervous. It is hard to know how to respond. He seems especially amused by her nightly reading to Pliny. Since her arrival at his villa, the admiral has dispensed with his other secretaries, declaring that Amara's voice has exactly the right cadence for particular writers.

"You are only encouraging Pliny's tyranny by doting on him," Demetrius remarks one afternoon, on the second week of her visit. "The man burns through books and will wear out your voice in the process."

They are sitting alone together on the terrace, Julia and Livia having found some excuse to leave soon after Demetrius arrived. Amara has noticed that the pair increasingly make themselves scarce when Demetrius joins them, almost as if by request. "Reading to the man who freed me hardly begins to repay the debt I owe him," she says. "And besides, I enjoy it very much."

Demetrius raises his eyebrows. "Either you are sincere in your dedication or a supremely talented actress. I'm not sure which is a more desirable quality in a woman." He leans forwards to adjust the shawl that has slipped from her shoulder, as if protecting her from the sea breeze. It is a fleeting gesture, but an uncomfortably proprietorial one. Amara has noticed that Demetrius increasingly finds excuses to touch her.

"In this case sincere," she says, and he smiles, understanding she has left open the possibility of possessing both talents. They contemplate one another, until his obvious desire makes her feel uncomfortable. "Perhaps I can convince you, by granting you the same favour? If it would please you to be read to."

"It would please me."

She unravels the scroll of Hesiod's *Theogony* and starts to read, aware that Demetrius is still staring at her. Her heart beats faster. Amara has lived by the use of her wits and her body for too long not to comprehend that if she did not love Philos, or have to endure Rufus's contract, Demetrius would represent an opportunity. Julia has told her intriguing details about his life; that Demetrius is a freedman, that he is high in the Emperor's favour, and above all, that he is astoundingly rich. He is not, unlike Philos, a man she could ever imagine desiring, even with his aura of power – he is too old. But he does not repel her either. Julia has left many sly hints about the querulous concubine her old friend keeps in Rome, and her suspicion that he means to replace her. The thought that Julia might be angling for an alliance makes Amara uneasy.

She has only just started to relax into the text and forget that she is being gazed at when a shadow crosses the parchment in front of her. Demetrius is leaning towards her. She hesitates, unsure whether to carry on reading, then he takes her chin between his finger and thumb, pressing down on her bottom lip. It is unlike all the other times he has touched her. Amara's reaction is visceral. She pulls away, her body instinctively withdrawing from a man she does not love or trust. A man who is not Philos.

"Are you so very besotted with your young patron?" Demetrius asks, not looking offended by her reaction but not moving further off either.

"I am loyal to him," she replies. Still Demetrius does not move, clearly not finding this a compelling answer. She looks at him, this powerful man who was himself once enslaved, and understands what will convince him. "There is also a contract."

"Ah." He sits back, his whole manner changed. "Now that *is* a pity." He turns from her and stares out to sea, at the endless expanse of blue and the mountain beyond. "I'm sorry to have interrupted you, please continue."

Amara does as he asks. Time passes, the shadows lengthen, and in spite of his protestations about protecting her voice, Demetrius does not move, until finally, Alexios the visiting Greek scholar joins them. He interrupts Amara's reading, keen to speak to his fellow guest. She takes the hint and excuses herself.

In her room, she sits down on the bed. It is eight days since she left Pompeii. She pulls her legs up onto the mattress and holds her arms around herself, wishing Philos were holding her instead. There are times, in this house, when Philos does not feel real. The thought that they might ever build a life together seems so preposterous while she's in Misenum – it may as well be a dream. A knock at the door startles her.

"Who is it?" she calls, worried Demetrius might have changed his mind and come to hunt her down.

"Julia."

"Come in."

"You look a bit peaky." Julia plumps herself down beside her on the bed. "I hope Demetrius didn't upset you?"

Julia's gaze is shrewd, and Amara understands that she must have known of his intentions. "Not at all, he paid me an unimaginable compliment."

"One I hope you accepted?" Julia looks delighted.

"One I was unable to accept."

Julia clicks her tongue. "My dear girl, I hope you aren't harbouring some foolish notion of remaining faithful to Rufus. My mother was a concubine, and let me tell you, fidelity wins you no favours *at all.*"

"I'm under contract. If I betray Rufus, I lose my freedom."

"How very tiresome of him!" Julia exclaims. "And after Pliny paid for you! I wouldn't have thought Rufus was such a schemer. Men really can be utter *shits.*" Julia looks so thoroughly put out that Amara laughs, but Julia shakes her head. "It's not amusing. A concubine has a handful of years to make her fortune and the rest of her life to live off what she's earned. Unless Rufus has also agreed to pay you a pension, as my father did for my mother, then he is being appallingly selfish."

"I don't believe he has."

"Then I hope you weren't too firm in rejecting Demetrius. He might be persuaded to keep his current woman a little longer, until you are free. You know with all these contracts, a patron's hold over his concubine is automatically ended if *he* leaves *her.*"

"But Rufus has only had me a few months!" Amara protests, thinking not of her patron but of Philos.

"Rufus imagines himself in love with you, and believe me, that sort of arrangement burns itself out very quickly," Julia says. "A man like Demetrius, on the other hand, will have more sensible expectations. You didn't *spurn* him, did you? I do hope you weren't rude."

"Of course not," Amara replies. "I would hardly dare. I simply told him there was a contract."

"Well," Julia says, her good temper returning. "He won't be under any illusions you're a naïve little innocent after *that*. But perhaps not a bad thing. He does hate hysterics. Let's hope you've made enough of an impression that he's prepared to wait a while."

There seems to be no possibility in Julia's mind that Amara might decline Demetrius, that she might have any other hopes for her life. The thought makes her uncomfortable. "It's very kind of you to take such an interest in me," Amara says. "I'm not sure what I've ever done to deserve it."

"Ridiculous girl." Julia reaches over to squeeze her knee. "It's because I like you. Why else?"

Amara is touched by her affection. "Thank you."

"And besides, you intrigue me. A prostitute who persuaded Pliny – of all people! – to free her, who seems quite unmoved by an offer from one of the richest men in Campania. I'd like to know what your secret is."

Amara is well aware that Julia would be horrified to know her real secret, but she hides her fear, as always, and smiles. "What makes you think I have a secret?"

"Everyone does." The look in Julia's eyes is no longer playful, and Amara understands. Julia is not prying – she's talking of herself.

"I rather envy you and Livia," Amara says carefully. "To have the solace of sharing so much with one another. Men rarely understand such things."

Julia rises, kissing Amara gently on the top of her head. "There's my clever girl," she murmurs.

★★★

The following day, Demetrius does not trouble Amara or seek her out. She is relieved and, although it shames her to admit it, also a little disappointed. Pliny has offered to send her home, expressing a half-hearted concern that Rufus might be missing her, and Amara had felt duty-bound to agree. She has no doubt that Julia must have suggested the idea to him, realizing the danger of making Rufus too jealous. Amara's feelings about returning are more complicated than she cares to admit. The last time she stayed with Pliny, she had imagined life in one of Pompeii's grander homes represented a height of indulgence that could never be surpassed, but the villa at Misenum has shown her that wealth, and its pleasures, are limitless.

She is deep in her reading when she becomes aware of someone standing near her. Amara looks up, expecting it to be Demetrius, but instead, it is Secundus. She glances round the garden, wondering who sent him, and realizes they are completely alone.

"You startled me," she says.

"Forgive me." He sits beside her. "I heard you were leaving."

"Tomorrow. I'm very sorry to go, but Rufus will be missing me. And I have duties to my household."

"Of course," Secundus agrees. "Though I'm sure your patron's steward is taking good care of it all for you. What was his name again? The handsome young man who was kind enough to keep me company while the admiral dined with you. He had the most unusual grey eyes."

Already wary, Amara's anxiety increases. "Philos," she says, putting no emotion into the name.

"*Beloved*," Secundus says, nodding. "How could I forget. That's what Philos means in Greek, isn't it?"

"Yes."

"He seems a capable boy," Secundus says, his tone light. "Impeccably discreet on the habits of his master, as I would expect. Discreet about his master's concubine too, though surprisingly well-informed." Amara says nothing, not wanting to arouse suspicion by begging to know what he means. "It just so happened," Secundus continues, "that Pliny had asked Rufus a number of questions about you when we walked to your house. About your hometown, your father and so on. Rufus hardly knew any of the answers. Whereas your 'Beloved' knew them all."

"I'm sure he's not the first steward to have a better memory than his master."

Secundus smiles. "True. A steward's first role is to protect his master. I am always careful to protect the admiral's reputation. A responsibility you share with me, given Pliny granted you the extraordinary honour of his name."

"I would rather die than dishonour the admiral."

Secundus nods as if he believes her, though his eyes are cold. "No doubt Philos is keen to protect his *own* master's reputation. Perhaps he does not approve of you. Perhaps that is the reason he turned his face to the side when Rufus kissed you. It was such a slight gesture; I would never have noticed it, if I had not been looking straight at him at the time."

"Perhaps," Amara says. "I'm aware not everyone approves of my change in station."

"It is quite an astonishing change. And Rufus's patronage raises you still further." Secundus leans towards her, a more aggressive posture than she has ever known him adopt. "A woman's status is only as high as that of the man she allows to master her. Or if you allow me to put it more crudely, her body only holds the value of the man who uses it."

"That *is* a little crude." Amara wrinkles her nose. "For you."

"I saw you," Secundus says, lowering his voice. "The look on your face, when you thought I was him. That would have been enough to tell me what he is, even without the lover's language. Rufus may have forgotten that a slave is also a man, but I never do."

"You insult me." They stare at one another, their hostility now open. Amara is expecting Secundus to go on, but instead, he is silent, waiting, and she knows that she cannot leave the conversation on such a knife-edge. "When the admiral hired me for a week," she says, trying to ignore her sweating palms, the frightened thumping of her heart, "I remember you telling me you wagered him a denarius I would beg and wheedle for gifts, but I did not. So perhaps you will believe me now when I tell you no man's reputation is more precious to me than his. I *swear* to you, I will never bring Pliny dishonour."

Secundus blinks, and Amara sees, at last, the emotion he has been struggling to hide. It is fear. "I truly hope you mean that."

28

*I want a girl who's easy, who goes around in a coat and nothing
else. I want a girl who's already given it up to my slave.*

Martial's epigrams 9.32

When she returns to the house, Philos is absent. It is
Victoria who greets her, embracing her in the atrium.
Amara can tell instantly that something is wrong.

"What is it?" she asks, thinking of Secundus's suspicions,
frightened he must have warned Rufus about Philos.

"Why don't we go to your rooms?" Victoria says, leading
her out of earshot of Juventus. They hurry to her first
chamber and sit down together on the couch. Victoria takes
her hand, which only makes Amara more afraid. "Rufus
isn't very happy," she says quietly. "He's jealous. He's even
been asking *me* questions."

"Why?" Amara asks, clutching her. "About what?"

"Pliny of course!" Victoria says. "And I'm not surprised.
Why on earth did you decide to go on a jaunt with a former
lover?"

"The admiral was never my lover!"

"Oh, save it for Rufus." Victoria sighs. "I was *there*,

Amara. I remember when you came back to the brothel, all lovesick for the old man. You even told me the pair of you slept together! Though of course, I swore blind to Rufus you never did."

"But it's true," Amara protests. "We didn't have sex; we just slept in the same bed. I didn't want to tell you at the time, in case you laughed at him." She is telling the truth, but even to her own ears, the claim sounds ludicrous.

"You know it's only Rufus you have to lie to," Victoria retorts. "I don't see why you can't be honest with *me*."

"But it's true – I swear it!"

"Fine," Victoria says, obviously annoyed by what she perceives as Amara's lack of trust. "You didn't fuck him. The man hired a prostitute for a week and lay in bed with her and only wanted her to read him books, which any other slave could have done for him. There you were, completely naked, and he never touched you." She stands up. "Maybe invent something more plausible for Rufus. And please remember it's not just *your* future on the line. If you can't convince Rufus, I've nowhere to go either."

Amara watches Victoria leave, unable to suppress her bitterness. "Dido would have believed me."

Victoria stops. Amara waits for the explosion, but Victoria does not turn around. "Maybe if you treated me the way you treated her, I would believe you too."

There is no sign that Amara suspects anything is amiss in the note she sends Rufus, informing him of her return and declaring herself impatient to see him. After it is sent, she sits in the garden practising the harp, trying to steady her nerves with a distraction. By the time Rufus arrives, she is considerably calmer, so it is a shock to hear him shouting for her in the atrium as if she were a runaway slave. She leaves the harp and hurries to meet him.

"My love," she starts, ignoring the thunderous look on his face. "How wonderful to see you, I've been—"

Rufus interrupts her. "*Ten days?* You spend ten days with another man and expect me to believe you're longing to see me?" Amara shrinks from his shouting, but it only encourages him to advance on her. "You must take me for a fool. I suppose I should be grateful you finally managed to tear yourself away from the admiral's bed?"

He is unrecognizable with rage. Drawn by the noise, the entire household has gathered to see her humiliation. Amara can see Victoria with the flautists, clutching each other by the stairs, Britannica standing beside them with clenched fists. Juventus and Martha are gaping at her from the doorway, but worst is Philos, who must have arrived with Rufus. He is standing by his master's shoulder, staring at the floor, not daring to look at her.

"Rufus, please," Amara says soothingly. "You know I would never betray you. Can we not discuss this in my rooms? I will have some wine sent in for us to enjoy, and then I can answer any questions you have, in private."

"So you want to get me drunk and seduce me like a whore? You think you can fool me that way?"

"No," she says, barely managing to keep her voice calm. "Nothing happened with Pliny. Please, my love, you *must* believe me. Nothing has ever happened between us; Pliny has only ever shown me the greatest respect."

"Of all the men you could have chosen, you humiliate

me with one I can *never* confront." Rufus looms over her, yelling in her face. "It's always been him, right from the beginning – I know it has! How you must have laughed at me, thinking I'd never dare complain, thinking you could just fuck him and come back to me."

"You're being ridiculous," Amara shouts back, no longer able to contain her anger. "Listen to yourself! If you have no respect for me, at least show some for the admiral."

"You can't even hide it! How much you prefer him to me."

His face is screwed up with self-pity, like a child. It takes everything Amara has not to retaliate with all the scorn she feels. "My dearest love," she says, her voice breaking under the strain of suppressing her contempt. "How can you imagine I care for anyone but you?"

Rufus seizes her by the upper arms, his grip so tight it hurts. "Look at me." She looks up, but evidently not in the way he wants because he pulls her head back by the hair. Amara stares at him, eyes wide. "If I ever find out you did betray me with another man, *even the admiral*, I will kill you."

"I would never betray you," Amara replies, her voice a whisper. Rufus stares at her, then still holding her by the hair, he bends to kiss her. Amara is too shaken to respond properly, but this does not seem to deter him; it only adds to his passion. Rufus scoops her up, holding her in his arms as if he were her rescuer, not her tormentor.

"It's only love that makes me so jealous," he says, more gently. "No need to be upset. I believe you." He carries her off to her rooms, and Amara hides her face in his shoulder, hating herself for feeling afraid.

★ ★ ★

After Rufus has gone, Amara does not leave her bedroom. There is nobody in the house she wants to see, not wishing to confront either their pity or scorn. It feels as if her patron still has his hand in her hair, and she cannot stop reliving it – the way he pulled so hard she was terrified he might break her neck. She is not sure how she will face Phoebe and Lais again, or Juventus, not now they've seen her humiliated in public. Nobody dares to bring her food or undress her hair for bed, though Victoria, at least, tries to reach her, calling softly from the door. Amara ignores her entreaties then listens to the sounds of the household retiring for the night, the room growing darker. She tries to remember how she endured Felix, how she would force her fear underground, and be left with only the anger. But she is so very tired.

When Philos finally visits, she is still scrunched up in a ball, lying under the covers. He doesn't say anything but gets into the bed, curling himself around her body and holding her.

"I'm sorry," he whispers. "I'm so sorry." They lie like that, with Philos apologizing over and over for the harm another man has caused her, until she turns around and cries into his tunic, the way she used to with Dido when they comforted one another at the brothel. He does not stop her but waits until her emotion is spent. "I didn't think he would be like that," he says. "I always told myself that if he found out, Rufus would hurt me and not you. And now I can see what a self-serving lie that was. I should never have put you at risk."

"It wasn't up to you. It was my choice."

"Nothing is worth the risk of him harming you."

"So you are capable of making a decision about your life, but I'm not?"

"Amara," he says, stroking her hair. "I don't think I can live with the strain, knowing you might lose everything because of me."

"I'm not going to lose everything, and neither are you, because we won't get caught," she replies, more like her usual, forceful self. "If you no longer love me, then say so. But if you've only just realized the danger, and you want to abandon me to handle Rufus on my own, that's something else."

"But I can't protect you from him; I will *never* be able to protect you. All I'm doing is putting you at risk."

"You think that's all you do?" She leans back, exhausted, her face blotched and swollen from tears. "I was never able to protect Dido from a single customer, even though I knew how much she suffered. All I could do was love her, just as she did me. And she was always there. Her love is the reason I survived that place." Amara takes his hand. "Do I need to beg you to stay?"

"No." He gathers her close to stop her saying more. "Please don't. You never have to do that." He does not loosen his grip, and the longer he holds her, the more Amara starts to relax, knowing he is not going to leave. "But you have to promise me something. I know you say we won't be caught, but if we were, I need to know you would tell Rufus I raped you, that I blackmailed you into having an affair."

Amara struggles out of his grasp. "I can't!"

"You can, and I need you to promise that you would. There is no way I would survive if we are discovered – it's impossible. But you might just have a chance, more than a chance, if I confessed to forcing you."

"No." She covers her face, not wanting to think about it.

"Please." Philos moves her hands away, so he can look at her. "You're right. We won't get caught; we'll be even more careful than before. But I can't live with the guilt unless you promise me this."

Promises are easy to make, Amara thinks. She has already discarded so many. Even lying here with Philos is a broken promise to Rufus. Yet, she also knows how strong her will is to survive, how she dropped Menander, without hesitation, to gain her freedom. Philos is giving her permission to live, even at the cost of abandoning him in the worst possible way. She nods, unable to say the words aloud.

The Venus in Drusilla's garden shines white in the sun. The marble goddess stoops at the edge of the water, her breasts half-hidden by one arm, a sly smile on her face, almost as if she were listening to the conversation between her two disciples. Amara is recounting her trip to Misenum, while she and Drusilla sit together by the fountain. Primus and his nurse have been banished to another part of the house, leaving the women to enjoy the morning's sunshine, when the heat is more bearable.

Amara does not mention Demetrius, even though she would like to boast a little to Drusilla, to make her envious. Julia warned her in the strongest terms to say nothing. "Rufus was very jealous when I returned," Amara says, when she has finally recounted the voyage home.

"But that's excellent," Drusilla declares. "There's nothing

that makes a man keener or more devoted than sensing he might have a rival."

"I'm not sure," Amara says, wondering how much she can confide in her friend. "He was extremely angry."

Drusilla laughs. "I'm sorry, but the thought of *Rufus* angry is a little ridiculous." Her smile fades as she sees Amara's expression. "He was violent?"

"He was... not very gentle." Amara struggles to find the words to describe the line Rufus walks between violence and the threat of it. "But it's not as simple as that. I think he likes me to know he is stronger. That he could hurt me if he wanted to."

"Rufus likes his women fragile," Drusilla says, her tone more dismissive than Amara had hoped. "You've always known this. It's what he enjoys."

"But he used to like it when I stood up to him, made demands on him even! I thought *that* was what he wanted from me, rather than wanting to make me smaller."

"You were a slave at the start of your affair and quite small enough already. I'm sure being told off by a woman held a novelty for him back then. It's different now. Look, forgive me if I sound harsh," Drusilla says, "but you speak as if you expect a real relationship from Rufus. You will be so much happier if you only consider how best to manipulate him, nothing more. Unless you really do love him?"

"No," Amara admits, looking round, as if even here she risks being overheard.

"Well then. You've always known he likes to think of you as a delicate creature; you're discovering now that he occasionally likes to frighten you. Just prepare yourself for those unpleasant times and try simpering over him a bit more in between." Drusilla shrugs. "You're an intelligent woman – I can't believe I need to explain it."

Amara feels resentment, thinking of the house Drusilla owns, the shop she rents out, all the security she has to fall back upon if her lovers disappoint her. "How are things with Quintus?" she asks, changing the subject.

"Oh." Drusilla shrugs. "I think that's run its course. It's only a matter of time before I leave him – it would be fatal to my reputation if he dropped me first. Fortunately, I've found another lover who is more than accommodating."

"Tell me," Amara says, rather enjoying the idea of the arrogant Quintus being dropped.

"Ampliatus," Drusilla replies, drawing out the name. "He owns half the warehouses at the port. It's true he's not from such a well-connected family as Quintus or Rufus, but you simply cannot *believe* how rich he is. And I'm finding it rather refreshing to be with an older man. They can be so grateful in bed and a good deal less exhausting to entertain."

"And he's kind?"

In reply, Drusilla raises her wrist in a languid fashion, so that Amara can see the new bracelet shining red and silver against her skin. Amara gasps. "I told you he was rich," Drusilla replies, with satisfaction. "He's generous too. I'm thinking of inviting him to dine with me privately. And to stay the night, of course. That's the sort of public insult Quintus will be unable to ignore. There'll be a scene, and then it will be over."

"Is Ampliatus attractive?" Amara asks, wondering just how much older the merchant might be, whether he's the same age as Demetrius.

"Is the admiral?" Drusilla replies, raising her eyebrows.

She laughs at Amara's look of annoyance. "My darling, I've always known you preferred him. It's horribly obvious every time you open your mouth to deliver a breathless remark about how generous or intelligent the man is. And I'm quite sure the villa at Misenum only made him even more appealing. Rufus isn't a complete fool – he knows you'd drop him for Pliny in a heartbeat. Who wouldn't?"

"I am grateful to the admiral, and I respect him, but I don't think of him that way. As a lover, I mean."

Drusilla rolls her eyes. "What does that even mean, *as a lover*? You know he is rich and powerful. Even if he weren't as intelligent as you insist, surely that would be quite enough."

It is impossible to judge Drusilla, not when her remarks are so similar to Amara's own private calculations. But Amara also knows this is not all she wants, that it's not enough. Instead, she thinks of the man she loves, who at this moment is dressed in a shabby tunic, hard at work in a shop whose profits he will never own, taking orders from a man who will never pay him. Shame burns in her chest, knowing how much she would hate her love to be exposed to Drusilla, yet at the same time, loving Philos so deeply she wants to defend him, even if it's only to herself. "You are always right," Amara says, with a cold smile. "There is nothing else a woman could possibly want from a man."

The house is almost empty when she returns. Victoria, Lais and Phoebe are at the baths, and Juventus is unable to tell her where Britannica might be. The Briton never bothers to report her movements. Amara heads upstairs to her study.

The conversation with Drusilla has made her eager to go over her accounts, to see whether she might be able to make more money renting out her women, or how much she can afford to lend to new clients. If she is not going to rely on a wealthy patron, if instead, she might manage to find a way of freeing Philos, she needs to earn as much as possible.

It is not a surprise when Philos himself visits her a little later, since he often helps plan her financial affairs, but she is startled when he shuts the door behind him and locks it.

Amara stands up. "What are you doing?" They have an agreement never to risk being intimate in the day. Philos puts his finger to his lips. He looks agitated, in a way she cannot place. He walks over to her, so they are standing close together by the desk.

"He wants me to spy on you."

"Rufus?"

Philos nods. "He's convinced you might be plotting to leave him for Pliny, or if not Pliny, then for some other wealthy man you met at Misenum. I've been ordered to trail your every move, note down who calls on you and who you see, and to stay here at the house more often."

"You don't think he suspects us?" Amara is unable to believe that her patron is colluding in his own betrayal. "We should be careful in case he wants to turn up and catch us out."

"I've known Rufus a long time," Philos replies. "I promise you, there is absolutely no possibility he suspects me."

Relief makes her giddy. She puts her hand to her mouth to suppress a laugh. "Then we're safe?"

"For now." Amara anticipates his kiss, pushing herself up onto the desk so she can wrap herself around him, but even though lust is at risk of drowning out all her other senses, she can tell he is holding back.

"What?" She places her hand flat on his chest.

"It was the way he spoke about you."

"What did he say?"

Philos lays his hand over hers, pressing it against his heart, as if that will stop the words from hurting. "He ranted on about how much he loved you then called you an ungrateful whore. A woman *any* man might seduce, because so many men must have used you. That, however innocent you were once, you are irredeemably tarnished now. I don't really want to repeat it all."

"That's not what you think though, is it?" Amara says, wondering why Philos looks so upset.

"Of course not! But for him to say all those terrible things, I don't know how much longer he will want to keep you, what he might do."

"I'm sure we can set his mind at rest. Given you're the one who will be telling him what I'm up to." Philos doesn't look entirely reassured, and so she kisses him again, hoping to distract him that way instead.

"Doesn't it bother you." He stops her from drawing him even closer. "That I'm reporting to him about you?"

Amara understands the question he is asking. Whether she minds the power he holds over her life. She runs her fingers through his hair, leaning closer, removing the space between them so that he instinctively tightens his grip on her waist. "No, it doesn't bother me," she says, her forehead resting against his. "Because I trust you."

It feels very different being intimate in the daylight, while the house is awake, even though Amara has often imagined how it might be. Outside the semi-darkness of the bedroom, Philos looks more real, and somehow more vulnerable. She breaks off from kissing him, so she can see him better, stroking his face. He leans his cheek into her caress. "I suppose it's fortunate he doesn't consider me a man," he says. "Otherwise, he'd never risk leaving me here with you." He means it as a joke, but Amara can hear the anger in his words, and worse, the shame.

"I know you are a man," she says. They look at one another. He kisses her again, gently, because he is always careful how he touches her, and Amara knows without question that whatever she did, even if she betrayed him, Philos would never use his body to hurt her. She wants to tell him all that he means to her, but she cannot find the words. Instead, she wrestles her tunic up her thighs, forcing him to move from where he is leaning on it, and pulls the garment over her head. He looks shocked by her sudden nakedness.

"We said not in the day," he whispers, although he already has his hands on her body, touching her bare skin.

"I changed my mind," Amara replies.

Every time she is with Philos, pleasure edges a little closer, but this is still not how she imagined her body would finally grant her release, in a frantic, rushed encounter, crammed together against a desk. When Philos realizes what is happening, he slows down, holding her tightly while she clutches him, trying not to cry out. Afterwards, she does not want to move apart, enjoying the warm glow of tenderness, all their murmured protestations of love, until realization hits. She has not used her contraceptive.

29

*Seen in a dream, the butchers who cut up meat and sell it in the
marketplace signify dangers.*
Artemidorus, The Interpretation of Dreams

The old man sits underneath the shrine to Venus on the
street corner. The sharp tang from the fullers next door
makes it an unpleasant spot for lingering, yet he still seems
to have drawn a crowd. Fortune-tellers are always popular
at the Fors Fortuna, the festival in late June to honour the
goddess of good luck.

Amara and Victoria join the onlookers. They have earned
the right to dawdle. Victoria just persuaded the unsavoury
pimp, Castrensis, to pay them more, as he has very particular
demands for the performance Victoria and the flautists will
give that night. Amara cranes past the crowd to see what is
happening. The fortune-teller is running through his patter,
offering to throw his dice to predict the future, or interpret
dreams. Victoria nudges her in the ribs as a slave boy pays
up then relates a long tedious dream, clearly hoping it will
predict his freedom.

"Are you Greek?" the old man croaks. The boy shakes

his head. "Pity." The fortune-teller sniffs. "Wearing white in a dream signifies freedom for a Greek slave, death for any other.".

The boy's face falls. "Are you sure?"

The fortune-teller raises his hands to the heavens. "Fors Fortuna never lies!"

Before Amara can stop her, Victoria has grabbed her hand and barged them both to the front. She chucks a coin at the man's feet. "Throw the dice for us, father," she says.

The old man looks up at Victoria, taking in the seductive way she stands, tunic slipping from her shoulder. "Very well, *daughter*."

He throws his dice then leers at them both. "You will meet a man on a street corner, who is the best lover you've ever encountered."

The crowd laughs. Even Victoria is amused, though she pretends to pout with annoyance. "Come *on*," Amara says, trying to drag her away, irritated to be the centre of so much lascivious attention.

"Don't you want to hear *your* fortune, daughter," the old man says, pointing at Amara, raising his voice to be heard over the guffaws.

Amara has no desire to hear the old man's seedy predictions but knows it is bad luck to decline. "Very well."

The old man throws his dice again, leaving a long theatrical pause afterwards as he stares at the battered cubes lying in the dust. "You will profit from pain," he intones.

"What's that supposed to mean?"

The fortune-teller looks up at her, his eyes sly. "Costs extra to interpret."

"No, thanks," Amara draws back. An eager slave

immediately jostles in to take her place, no doubt also longing to hear predictions of freedom.

"It was only a penny!" Victoria says, as Amara hustles her away.

"After the prediction you had? Why would I pay for that!"

"You have no sense of fun sometimes. And I'm earning you *loads*. We're working almost every week! Surely, you will have paid Felix off soon?"

"No," Amara replies, not pleased to be reminded she has to visit their old master in the afternoon. Philos has been fretting over it for days, bringing them dangerously close to another row. "We're not even close to clearing the debt."

Amara watches him pore over the wax tablet on the desk. The movement of his body is so familiar, all that tension, the pent-up energy straining for release, never far from explosion. His face in profile reminds her of the trickster god, Hermes, the one whose statue she used to stare at in the Forum of her hometown. He is at his most attractive like this, absorbed in something other than her, when she might forget what sort of man he is. Felix looks up. "Aren't you interested?"

Amara shrugs. The nicer he is, the warier she feels.

"I'm not going to trespass on your virtue," he sneers. "You needn't worry."

She has no intention of getting any closer, so she kneels on the chair and leans over the desk to see.

"Fine," he snaps, getting up and walking round, slamming

the tablet down in front of her. "Those are the takings from the bar. Look. That's the rental on the other place. What do you think?"

"Why are you asking *me*?"

"You're good with figures. I'm interested to hear if your calculations match mine."

Amara frowns at him but takes the tablet, unable to resist the temptation of having a closer look. She pores over the numbers: the expenditure, the takings, the possible risks. "I'd say it's worth it, but you'll be close to the margin. Probably better to wait another month to see if Beronice and Gallus keep up this level of profit."

Felix grunts, taking the tablet back. "The other place could be gone by then."

"There will be another." She shrugs. "Not worth the risk."

"More cautious advice than I was expecting."

"It's your money. Just telling you what I'd do if it were mine."

Felix is still standing next to her, and she wishes he would move, but then, her old master has never done what she wanted. "Another overpayment," he says. "What am I to make of you throwing all this money at me?"

"I don't like being in debt to you," she replies, folding her arms, trying to hide the fact his close proximity frightens her. He takes a step closer. "Don't." She doesn't dare raise her voice. The thought of Philos next door, ready to spring to her defence, sets her even more on-edge. To her amazement, Felix stops where he is. The expression on his face, if she did not know him so well, might be mistaken for embarrassment.

"I didn't mean to threaten you last time."

For a moment, Amara can only gape at him. "What?"

"For fuck's sake, I'm not going to apologize. *I didn't mean to threaten you.*" Felix smacks his palm down on the desk, making her jump. "It's not fucking hard to understand what I'm saying."

"You've never done anything *but* threaten me," Amara says, still incredulous. "Right from the first day I met you."

"What if I said I wouldn't anymore?"

"You'd be lying."

Felix runs a hand through his carefully slicked-back hair, another wholly unfamiliar gesture. It makes him look insecure. "You think I'm such a fucking monster."

"You *are* a fucking monster," she retorts, finding his contrition unexpectedly painful. "You've never given a shit about hurting me, or anyone else. There have been times I thought you might even kill me."

"I'd *never* have done that."

"No, because it would have cost you too much fucking money!" Amara shouts. To her dismay, she is dangerously close to tears. Felix reaches out to touch her, and she flinches away. "Don't!"

Felix clenches his fists, and she can see he is struggling to control his temper. "You've always known how to provoke me."

"Breathing provokes you. You've never needed an excuse to hit anyone."

"You act like I did nothing but hurt you. What about all the times you worked up here on my accounts, when I helped you start lending money? What about that night you stayed with me? For a whore, you were always terrible at sex, completely unable to pretend you liked it, so I can't believe you suddenly acquired the ability to smile like that at a man if you *hated* him."

Amara knows exactly which night he is referring to, and even worse, the crushing shame of the morning after. It was when she had decided to feel nothing but loathing for Felix, because loving him would destroy her. "It's too late for this."

"Why should it be too late?" he says, seizing on the fact she has not entirely contradicted his version of their encounter. "You're not denying how it was. What if I hadn't hurt you so much; what if I'd been kinder to you? You might have seen me differently."

"But you *weren't* kinder."

Felix sits down heavily on the edge of the desk. "The way you look at me," he says; "it's the way I remember looking at my father when I was willing the bastard to die. And don't tell me I'm like him, because I fucking know I am."

"You chose to be like him," she says, devoid of sympathy.

"You're such a heartless bitch," he says, and she realizes that his shoulders are shaking with laughter. "No other woman dares say this shit to me. And even when I owned you, when you kept your mouth shut, I could still see you thinking it. It's why I've always liked you."

If Amara did not know Felix so well, or if she did not love another man, perhaps his flattery might reach her. But she understands how mercurial his moods are, and has seen the way he treated Victoria, with his constant, terrifying switches between tenderness and cruelty. "You can't expect me to trust you all at once." She softens her voice and tries to force a smile. "If you manage not to threaten me over the next few months, perhaps I might believe you."

"That sounds very fucking convenient for *you*," Felix

retorts, eyes narrowed with distrust. "How am I to know you aren't stringing me along?"

Amara's smile is genuine this time. She prefers Felix's suspicion to all his attempts to charm her. At least she knows it's real. "You don't." She leans closer, feeling the familiar burn of hatred in her heart. "I might be playing you, and you might be playing me. We'll have to wait and see how the game ends."

NEMORALIA

30

Nothing can last for all time:
When the sun has shone brightly it returns to the Ocean;
The moon wanes, which recently was full.
Even so the fierceness of Venus often becomes a puff of wind

Pompeii graffiti

The scent of late flowering jasmine from the garden infuses the whole house. Its sweetness takes Amara back to the first days of her courtship with Rufus, except now it is not her patron holding her hand, but Britannica, trying to teach her how to land a more forceful blow. They stand barefoot in the atrium, the mosaic of stars pleasantly cool on a hot August morning.

"For you, important to be quick," Britannica explains. "Not strong enough for a long fight. Try again."

Amara lunges, one of the many moves her friend has taught her. Britannica blocks her easily, but she nods in approval. "Better," she says.

From the garden, Amara can hear singing and laughter. Victoria and the flautists are practising their routines for an upcoming dinner. They have managed to win two bookings in one week, largely thanks to Victoria's hustling. Amara is grateful for the way Victoria has taken to that side of the business, often attending meetings with their fellow pimps on her own, sparing Amara the embarrassment. Those evenings when she does not work, Victoria is often absent, her affair with Crescens showing no signs of cooling. Amara had worried that Victoria might find it difficult to continue servicing clients now she is in love, but Victoria only laughed, saying Crescens is not a jealous man.

"How old were you when you first learned to fight?" Amara watches Britannica's manoeuvres with the wooden knife, her footsteps light, almost as if she were dancing.

"We learn as children," Britannica replies. "All my people do this. Better that way."

"I'm sorry about what happened to your family."

Britannica keeps moving, gestures Amara remembers from the brothel when the Briton would enact imaginary fights in her cell, keeping up her strength. "Death is no dishonour. They die as they live, as fighters," she replies. "Dishonour is mine."

"Not now," Amara says, thinking she means her time as a prostitute. "That's over."

Britannica stops, slowly lowering her arm. "Always dishonour. It never leave me."

"Your brother?"

"Philos tell you." Britannica's eyes are shrewd. Not for the first time, Amara wonders how much she knows. "My brother was not man, not child." Britannica's expression darkens. "My family tell me to hide him, protect him. I am not quick enough."

"But there was only one of you, and there must have been so many soldiers."

"I am not quick enough," Britannica repeats. "Not for Dido, either."

"That wasn't your fault!" Amara exclaims, shocked that Britannica might blame herself for Dido's death. She is so used to seeing Britannica's strength, her daunting height and increasingly muscular physique, that she has almost forgotten the Briton as she first saw her. Angry, but also traumatized, unable to fight off the men at the brothel, even though she nearly died trying. "It was not your fault." Amara's gaze is fierce. "It was *Felix*."

Britannica nods. "One day I kill him," she says, her voice calm. "The first time he touch me, I promise myself this. But first, I regain my honour."

Amara is unsurprised by the Briton's vow of vengeance, more puzzled by her desire to postpone the bloodshed. "How?"

"When I am gladiator," Britannica says. "Win or die. *This* is honour."

"Gladiators are slaves. It might look glorious in the arena, but it's a hard, brutal life. I wouldn't want to see you die that way."

Britannica laughs. "I not intend to die." She whips round, bringing the blunt point of the knife to rest at Amara's throat. "You see," she says. "They not catch me."

The restaurant is one Amara remembers well. She smiles at Rufus, pleased he would think to bring her here, the place they visited before their first night together. The roof terrace is just as lovely as she remembers, shaded by its trellis of creeping vines, the view looking out over the rooftops to the deep blue of Vesuvius as dusk falls. It is partly guilt, she suspects, that has led Rufus to choose this place. Amara knows that he has slept with Victoria.

She reaches for her wine, and he catches her hand, kissing it. Amara tilts her head affectionately, as if charmed by the gesture, then raises her glass to drink. "You're so beautiful," Rufus murmurs.

Amara wonders if he says that to Victoria too. It has only happened a few times, and afterwards, Victoria tells her, Rufus is full of remorse, swearing her to secrecy lest they break Amara's heart. Poor Rufus has no idea the two women have set him up.

"You're so good to me," Amara replies, looking at him from lowered eyelashes.

Rufus accepts the compliment without a hint of discomfort. *Not that guilty then*, she thinks. It had been Amara who first noticed her patron's attention starting to stray to her friend's voluptuous figure every time Victoria performed for them in the garden. The glazed look in his eyes. After that, she mentioned the idea to Victoria and found her surprisingly happy to help. Amara left them alone together at every opportunity then dropped hints to Rufus about a whole day she intended to spend with Drusilla. Sure enough, Rufus called at the house when she was out.

"I don't know why he's always moaning about you eating," Victoria had mused afterwards, while she and Amara gossiped together in her rooms. "He didn't seem to mind *my* curves at all."

It made Amara uncomfortable then, thinking of her patron and Victoria together, but she had still managed to laugh. Let Victoria crow a little. Amara would, after all, prefer not to sleep with Rufus herself, so why should it matter? Drusilla has always held on to a patron's interest through a variety of women. And this is one way of ensuring she does not lose Philos.

"Don't you think that's enough, little bird?" Rufus asks, interrupting her thoughts. He is looking pointedly at the chunk of sea urchin she is in the process of lifting out of the bowl that sits between them.

"I don't really think I'm fat, my love," she replies, continuing to spoon the seafood onto her plate.

"Of course not," Rufus exclaims, eyes widening as if horrified by the idea. "I just think you're perfect exactly as you are."

"This is such a treat for me," she adds. "We do try to be sensible with meals back at the house. And I have such happy memories of this place."

"You remember then?" The way Rufus looks at her seems so guileless. She remembers how he used to charm her like that, how his innocence touched her, how he appeared so different from other men. The thought of what he is really like makes her sad rather than angry. After all, she is not his little bird either.

"I remember," she says, meeting his eyes and smiling.

"Drusilla and Quintus were just over there." He gestures at the best table in the corner, where some other wealthy young man and his courtesan are now seated under a fresco of Venus. "A bit much, the way she went off with that wine merchant or whoever he is. Did you know he's a freedman?

His former master adopted him as his heir, but he swans around referring to the man as his *father*."

"I think he loves her though." Amara knows this is a delicate topic, given Rufus's friendship with Quintus and her own with Drusilla.

"I doubt that." Rufus laughs. "I suppose she's told you *all* about him. How rich he is. Dropping jewels in her lap. Poor Quintus."

Amara feels oddly offended by his mockery, even though it is directed at Drusilla not her. "I think she truly loves him. She says he's very kind."

"You can be such an innocent sometimes." Rufus looks at her indulgently. "It's why I liked you. That first evening you came to my house, after the theatre, you were so terrified."

"I wasn't terrified," Amara says, annoyed by his inability to remember. "I was angry."

"I know I'm an idiot," Rufus replies, with the easy self-deprecation she used to like so much, but which now rings false. "But even *I* know when a girl is frightened. You were bluffing. And that absurd ultimatum you gave me! About winning your heart first. It was both the most outrageous and most adorable thing a woman has ever said to me." Amara knows he is not thinking of declarations made by respectable women of his own class, still less, the young girls he might marry one day. It's the most adorable thing a whore has ever said to him. Rufus sees her expression and sighs. "There's no need to sulk. I was paying you a compliment! Anyone would think you're *still* a doctor's daughter when you get huffy like that."

Amara cares so little for Rufus now it amazes her that

he has any ability to hurt her. "I will always be a doctor's daughter," she says quietly.

Rufus flushes, and she knows he is embarrassed. "I'm sorry, that was uncalled for. Forgive me."

"Of course," she says, and perhaps she means it. In spite of all he has done to her, all she suspects he might be capable of doing, it is impossible not to remember that if it were not for Rufus, she would still be in the brothel. She reaches across the table impulsively and takes his hand. "Let's just enjoy the evening. Maybe I *was* a little nervous that night."

"I wasn't saying it like it was a bad thing," Rufus replies, giving her hand an answering squeeze. "You've always been such a perplexing girl. Sometimes, it feels like I really did meet you at your father's house. I remember that very first time I saw you..." He trails off, no doubt thinking of Amara sitting modestly in the garden beside Pliny who introduced them.

"I promise you there was nothing between us," she says, knowing what he's imagining.

"Even if there were," Rufus says, with a tight smile. "If he was paying, who am I to complain? My father tells me I'm absurdly sensitive over it. It's not like I didn't know where you came from."

The thought of Rufus being advised by his father Hortensius – with his hard, grasping hands and harder eyes – is not one that brings Amara much comfort. "There was nothing," she repeats.

"Little bird," Rufus says, affecting a knowing demeanour that does not yet suit him. "I walked past the place once. I know *exactly* where you used to live."

"You walked past it? When?"

"When I first started seeing you." He shudders. "I came home afterwards and resolved never to send for you again, but then I kept imagining your funny, hopeful little face. How disappointed you might be."

"You knew what the place was like," Amara repeats stupidly, still unable to imagine how Rufus left her to suffer in the brothel for so many months after he had seen it.

He mistakes the cause of her confusion, and his face grows colder. "I've always known," he says. "Did you think I wouldn't be curious, after you went to such pains to hide where you lived? But I told myself the place hadn't touched you. Which I now understand was too much to expect."

It is, perhaps, the politest way a man has ever called a woman a whore. The waiter arrives before Amara has the chance to think of a reply. The man fusses, laying down more food, collecting dishes, but she is aware of Rufus's eyes on her, not distracted by the movement going on between them. His judgment makes her angry. She imagines his reaction if she stood up and declared her love for Philos, if she told Rufus his slave is a hundred times more of a man than he will ever be. The words can never be said aloud, but even thinking them makes her feel better.

The waiter leaves, and Amara smiles at Rufus who is still staring at her. "I don't think you hate everything I learned there," she says softly, slipping her shoes off under the table then lifting her leg to touch him, caressing his thigh with her foot.

She feels relief when his lips part, the coldness of his expression replaced by desire. For now, at least, he still wants her. But Amara also knows that, for Rufus, lust is a weak tie in comparison to love. She has no doubt that they are on the downward descent, and the fall, when it comes, could be rapid.

31

Whoever loves, let him flourish
Let him perish who knows not love
Let him perish twice over whoever forbids love
Pompeii graffiti

The heat of the baths soothes every sinew, loosening the tension in her body, and rivulets of condensation slide over her skin in a soft-fingered caress. Steam rises from Amara's hands as she holds them out in front of her. She turns the palms upwards, interlacing her fingers, then parting them. Her hands belong to her; her body belongs to her. After the horror of being owned, this will never feel anything other than remarkable. She closes her eyes and leans back, feeling the hot tiles press against her spine, and thinks about Philos, remembering the last night they spent together. It seems impossible, now, that there was ever a time her body did not grant her pleasure, instead only giving it to those who used her.

She breathes in the steam, taking the hot air deep into her lungs. Every detail of Philos is clear in her mind: his movements, his gestures as he talks, the way he laughs or looks at her. How expressive he is in private, so different from the total self-effacement he is obliged to show as a slave. And everything she now knows about his life, all the memories they have exchanged: the fables his mother told him as a child, his long friendship with Vitalio, her father's compassion for the sick, the way Dido sang. He has become more precious to her than any other living being. Amara feels the tension returning, knotted like a serpent in her chest, coiled around her heart. It is unbearable to know Philos is enslaved. That he has no control over his life.

There were times at the start of their affair when she resented his fatalism, his seeming acceptance that their love would be brief. Now she misses it – his pain is so much worse. She can sense it in the way he looks at her, committing every detail of her face to memory in case she is taken from him. Or the times he holds her too tightly, and she can feel his heart racing. Worst is when they part at night, when he has to return to his cell, and she knows both of them are thinking about when the last time might be, whether they will even have the chance to say goodbye.

Amara opens her eyes and sits up, on the verge of panic. The shakier her relationship with Rufus becomes, the more desperate she is to free Philos. They have both schemed over it so many times, whether she might ask Rufus if she can buy him, what the best timing would be, even how much to offer, but none of the possibilities are convincing. Before Rufus ends his patronage, there would be no rational explanation for her desire to buy Philos, any more than she might suddenly demand to buy one of the tables. It would only cause suspicion. That leaves the possibility of waiting until Rufus has announced his intention to take Philos back, when perhaps his feelings for Amara will be at their lowest ebb.

Amara clasps her hands to her waist, as if that might keep the anxiety inside. There is another possibility, one she has set in motion without telling Philos, knowing how dangerous it might prove to be. She stands up, condensation damp on her skin, light-headed from heat and fear. Fortuna only turns her wheel for those who dare to ride it.

Victoria is breathless when she arrives at the courtyard for the baths, just as Amara is leaving.

"I'm sorry I'm late," she says, face flushed and hair damp with sweat from the sweltering August heat. "Rufus called."

Amara takes Victoria's arm, hurrying her back down the steps onto the street, not wanting her friend's loud voice carrying to anyone else at Julia's establishment. "Never mind," Amara says. "Sorry he sprang that on you."

"Oh, it's fine," Victoria says, generously. "He didn't demand a full fuck or anything. Though he seems to be feeling less guilty afterwards. And I think you might need to put in a bit more effort. He says you're much more inhibited than I am."

"What a shit," Amara says, stung. "If I go too wild, he broods about the brothel. Now he's moaning I'm not wild enough. He's impossible!"

They head together towards the marketplace by the arena; it's closer than the Forum, even though there are fewer stalls. Already, the cool of the plunge pool is wearing off, and Amara feels uncomfortable in the sun. She gestures at the stepping-stones, and they pick their way carefully over the road to walk on the shady side of the street.

"You do seem to have gone off him a bit though," Victoria says, taking Amara's arm again. "Is there any reason?"

"You saw how he was when I returned from Misenum."

"He got jealous," Victoria replies. "But nothing so awful, unless he was violent afterwards. I did wonder, but you wouldn't let me in."

Amara knows Victoria's tolerance for brutality is very different from her own. Twice, Rufus has used his physical strength to frighten and overwhelm her, and that is more than enough to lose Amara's loyalty. But it is impossible to explain this to a woman who once loved a man as violent as Felix, whose current lover kills for entertainment. "I don't want to talk about it," she says.

Victoria rolls her eyes. "Fine. We'll just have to make sure that, between us, we get him to keep paying the rent."

The marketplace is busy, travelling traders sitting or standing by their temporary stalls – some no more than a rug spread on the ground. A man selling pans is clashing them and bellowing right by the roadside, reminding Amara of the Lemuria. They try so hard to skirt out of his way that Victoria nearly trips over an old woman selling small clay statuettes of Venus and Cupid. "Bring you luck in love, girls!" she cries, trying to foist a cherub on Amara. They make their excuses and hurry off.

The flower seller is a permanent feature on the edge of the square, a garrulous man who always greets Victoria and Amara like long-lost daughters, with cries of rapture. His theatrical style is at least memorable, and perhaps effective, since they now buy all their garlands from him for Victoria's entertaining.

"My girls!" he shouts, as they approach. "Look at my beautiful girls!" He pinches Victoria's cheek, knowing better than to try and touch Amara. "You want something for the Nemoralia, yes?"

"You always know what we're after, Hermeros," Victoria says, batting her eyelashes and playing up to his flirting.

"Six garlands," Amara says. "Perhaps you could do us a price on that?"

"Six! Oh! You have even more beautiful friends! When are you going to bring all these other girls to meet me?"

"Maybe soon, if you do a great price," Amara says.

"I *always* do my favourite girls a good price," he replies, with a wink.

They carry on with the banter, back and forth, putting in the order and arranging to collect it. Hermeros manages to persuade them to part with even more money, insisting they try some of the honey-glazed pastries a passing trader offers on a tray: *Even better than my mother used to make!* Amara suspects the two men have an agreement to bring each other business. The order of garlands agreed, their goodbyes are not lingering, the flower seller is already eyeing up his next customers. Victoria and Amara amble to the side of the square with their pastries, and sit on a stone bench in the shade by the vineyard wall.

"When am I going to meet Crescens?" Amara asks, brushing the last crumbs from her fingers. She is ravenous and bitterly resents the thought of Rufus sighing over Victoria's breasts while denying her food.

"It's so hard for him to leave the barracks! And I don't think you'd like the bar where we meet. Rufus would have a fit if you started hanging out there."

"As long as you're happy," Amara says. "And staying safe."

Victoria is distracted, staring at someone. "Isn't that the potter's boy? Look! Over there."

Amara looks. Menander is standing at the edge of the crowd, watching them. When Amara's eyes meet his, he turns away. Without thinking of the consequences, she leaps up, desperate to catch him. He turns back again, and she knows he has seen her moving towards him. There is a brief moment when she thinks he might hurry off to avoid her, but instead, he waits.

The closer she gets, the more she is aware of how great the distance is between their past intimacy and now. Then she is standing in front of him, and his dark eyes are on her, no longer looking at her with the warmth she remembers. It brings back all the horror of the Saturnalia. "I didn't mean to drop the lamp," she blurts out, unable even to say hello. "I promise you. It was an accident."

"I realized," he says, obviously embarrassed. "Not at the time. But afterwards, I realized."

"It was so beautiful. And I'm so sorry. For everything."

"Nicandrus told me that he freed you, that night. Your patron." Menander can barely meet her eyes. She had never imagined he could look this stiff and uncomfortable. "And he told me that... He told me what happened to Dido. I'm truly sorry. She was a lovely person."

"Thank you. I miss her." Amara presses a hand to her mouth, not wanting to cry. She breathes in deeply, controlling herself. "I hope that you are doing well." She tries to sound brighter, to look him in the face.

He nods. "I am, thank you. But I have to go now, Amara." His use of her slave name, rather than her real name Timarete, the one he always used to call her by, hurts more than anything else he could have said. "I'm sorry. I wish you well." He turns his back and hurries away, not even waiting to hear her goodbye.

Victoria, who had kept a tactful distance, hurries over and takes Amara's arm. "Don't cry," she says quietly, moving her out of the flow of people. "Not here." They make their way back to the bench, and Victoria holds Amara while she sobs. "It's alright," she soothes. "It's alright."

"I'm sorry." Amara wipes her face, embarrassed when the rush of grief has passed.

"It's alright," Victoria says again. "I know you cared about him."

"I don't now," Amara says. "Or not like that. I just never wanted to hurt him."

"I always thought he was a bit of a selfish prick, not taking the lamp back straightaway when he saw Rufus." Victoria fusses over Amara's hair, trying to make her look less rumpled after her cry. "I'm sorry – he might have made you a nice lamp and everything, but it wasn't worth losing a fucking patron over." Amara starts to laugh, Victoria's caustic attitude making her feel better in a way sympathy never could. "And besides," Victoria sniffs. "He's a *slave*. You can do better than that now."

"I don't think being enslaved makes him less attractive," Amara says, unable to stop herself from defending Philos, even though he was not the target. "What about Crescens?"

Victoria stands up, helping Amara to her feet. "Crescens is a *gladiator*," she says, her expression haughty. "It's not the same at all. And besides, Crescens is better looking."

They both smile then walk back to the house, Victoria holding tightly to Amara's arm.

32

Amara knows, as soon as she walks into his study, that Felix has changed. The cold way he looks at her is a shock. Over the past two months, as the days slid into the heat of summer, she has slowly grown used to seeing his more amiable side, almost starting to wonder whether he might be sincere in his remorse. Or at the very least, she had begun to believe she might be able to exercise some control over his moods, to keep his violence at bay. But then, Victoria must once have been lulled into thinking this too.

Felix does not answer Amara's greeting or her half-hearted attempt at a smile. Instead, he walks towards her, holding out his hand for the money. She drops the three purses into his palm, and he turns around, spilling the coins over the desk. The hard clank of falling metal jars on her nerves. He counts it by scraping each penny over the wooden surface, not remarking on the fact she has given him yet another overpayment. His total silence makes her nervous, as he no doubt intends.

"If you don't want to chat today, I'll be leaving."

Felix speaks to stop her moving, as she knew he would. "I don't like the rules of your game."

"What game is that?"

"How many clients do you have now?" He jabs his finger at her to emphasize his words. "How much money is Victoria bringing you in each month?"

"Why should I tell you anything about my business?"

"You were keen enough to brag before. She's obviously worth more than we agreed. I'm not sure six thousand sesterces was enough for her."

"Well, that's too bad for you," Amara says, growing angry. "Because that's what we signed in the contract."

"You're not leaving." It is a command, not a question.

"You don't own me anymore. I've paid you more than this month's instalment. You have no reason to keep me here."

"There are many reasons." He tilts his head and smiles, so that she almost hopes his mood might be shifting, until she sees the cruelty in his eyes. "Posh boy doesn't know you are here. That's a reason. You don't want him to find out. There's another reason. Don't you think?"

"I thought you weren't going to threaten me anymore?"

"That was last month," Felix says, with his most charming grin.

"I'm not here on my own. I can call for the men I brought with me."

"Yes, your two hard men next door." He nods, as if seriously considering her threat. "The smart one who's almost skinnier than you are, and the brawny one without any brains. I'm fucking *terrified* by the thought of either of them taking me on."

"What do you want?"

Felix puts his hands on her waist, cautiously, as if testing what she might do. She grips his wrists, making it clear she will resist him. "I don't care what the contract says. I think you need to pay me more, the way you've always paid me."

"No."

"I've waited long enough for you. I want proof you're not stringing me along."

"What about winning my trust?"

"Fuck your trust. Who do you think you are?" He lets go of her waist and starts to circle her, so that she's forced to keep turning to watch what he's doing. "Let me tell you again. I expect you to pay. Either you agree, and I won't hurt you. Or you don't agree, and posh boy wonders where all the bruises came from. I imagine he might not be too thrilled to know another man has fucked you. How are things between you both these days? He's had you a long time now. Would he even believe you, I wonder, if you cried rape?"

Felix comes to a stop in front of her. Amara is dizzy from all his turning, though she knows exactly what is happening. Every conversation they have had, since she placed herself in his debt, has only delayed this moment, the payment she owes for saving Victoria and Britannica. Perhaps she has always known what Felix would do, and yet, she kept coming here, hoping it would be different. She wishes, more than anything, that Philos were not next door. It makes everything so much harder.

Amara tries to imagine Felix as he must have been as a child – the frightened boy who loved his mother, who suffered as she has suffered – and wills herself to believe she can reach him. It is the only throw of the dice that remains. He glances down in surprise as she takes his hand in hers. "I don't believe you want to do this. You are not your father, Felix. I don't believe this is who you really are."

His expression, when he looks up, reminds her of the tigers in the arena: the savagery the condemned men must see before they die, the face of a creature incapable of compassion. He grips her fingers so hard it hurts. "Then say yes to me."

When Felix takes hold of her, Amara is taken back to the days after he bought her, when she first understood the cruelty he was capable of inflicting. She thinks of Philos and tries not to panic, tries to stop herself from crying out when Felix pushes her against the desk, knowing what is about to happen. There is only one thing she could take from this that might be worth the pain.

She grips Felix's face in her hands, making him look at her. "I want something from you first."

"What?" He is startled enough to pause. "You want me to take something off the debt? Is that it?"

Amara stares into his eyes, knowing she cannot miss anything, that she will not have a second chance. "I want you to tell me where you buried her." The briefest flicker crosses his face. On another man, it would look like shame. Felix tries to push her hands away, to stop her looking at him, but she only grips hold of him more tightly. "No," she says, still staring into his eyes, wanting to see a different answer. "Not Dido. Not even *you* could have done that. You can't have done. Not on the rubbish dump." Amara is willing Felix to deny the accusation, yet still he does not. "You *must* have buried her," she repeats, her voice rising with hysteria. She lets go and shoves him hard in the chest. "Tell me you didn't leave her there!"

"So I was supposed to do you a favour, was I? Straight after you screamed to the world that you wanted me dead?" Felix grabs her by the shoulders. "You expected me to pay to cremate the body of a slave, just because *you* cared for her? Why the fuck should I?"

Amara looks at his hard, unrepentant face, and all the grief and rage she has suppressed for so long erupts, obliterating any semblance of self-control. She screams at Felix, pushing him away from her, cursing his name, demanding the gods erase him from the face of the earth. He stares, uncomprehending, and she realizes that she is shouting her tirade in Greek, that in this moment, she cannot find the words in any other language. She seizes the chair, the nearest object to hand, and when he darts out of her way, she smashes it into the shelves behind him. Jars splinter, money cascading out onto the floor. Her violence builds momentum, driven by the fury in her heart. More jars are hit, this time exploding over her head. Amara swings again, smashing straight into the wall so that the chair legs splinter.

The door bursts open, and Philos is in the doorway, a look of terror on his face. "*Get back!*" She screams at him, spinning round. "*Get back!*"

Philos stays where he is, Juventus behind him. He holds his hands up. "Amara, it's me," he says in Greek. "It's me."

She starts to become more aware of her surroundings, that she is no longer shouting, but crying, her chest heaving, holding out the ruined chair in front of her like a weapon or a shield. Felix is near her, his knife drawn.

"Put down the fucking chair," he says. Amara does not reply. He takes a step closer, gesturing with the blade. "If you put it down, I won't hold this against you. I know you are upset." Felix has never spoken to her like this, placatory, almost as if he is afraid of her. She does not let go. He takes another step towards her, his eyes on hers, speaking quietly. "If you put it down, Amara, I promise to forgive you for what you've just done."

It is his offer of forgiveness that tips her over the edge. She throws the chair at him, so that he ducks. When he straightens up, she spits in his face. "I would see you dead first," she says. "You son of a whore."

Felix wipes his cheek, hand shaking with anger. "If you leave me now, I swear by all the gods I will destroy you."

Amara does not reply. She turns her back on him and walks to where Philos is standing, appalled, in the doorway.

33

How soft is violence?
Herculaneum graffiti

R age carries Amara on her walk back from the brothel. It is not until she sees the door of her own house, half ajar to the street, that she feels the first stirring of fear. Felix, who runs a protection racket and thinks nothing of murder, has just vowed to bring down her household. Her sense of misgiving grows as she walks into the atrium and hears the sound of Victoria singing, the high pitch of the girls' flute playing. It is not just her own life that she has put in danger.

"Lock the door," she says to Juventus, who nods and hurries to do as she has asked. Amara looks up at Philos. "I have to tell Victoria."

In the garden, the afternoon sunshine falls on the fresco of Dido, and the sight of her immortalized at her most beautiful only makes it worse to think of what Felix did to her body. In her guise as the huntress Diana, Dido is twice as tall as the women singing beneath her, and for the first time, Amara feels guilty at caring less for her living friend than the dead one. She should have paid Victoria more attention.

Victoria sees her watching and smiles, but she does not stop her singing. Amara waits until they have finished. "Egnatius will be thrilled," she says. "You get better all the time."

Victoria looks pleased by the compliment. "Let's hope the guests are all in the mood to tip."

Amara joins the three of them by the bench and takes Victoria's hand. "I have something to tell you," she says. "It's about Felix."

Victoria looks terrified. "What's happened? What has he said to you?"

The flautists exchange glances. They have never met Felix, but Amara has already warned them about the potential violence from her former pimp, describing him in case they are ever followed. "I discovered what happened to Dido," Amara says slowly, wanting to prepare Victoria for the shock. "He dumped her body outside the town walls. She was never cremated. When Felix told me—"

"You didn't threaten him," Victoria says. "Please tell me you didn't threaten him."

Amara thinks of the total destruction she wreaked on Felix's study. The broken jars, the smashed chair. The embers of her rage flare back into life. "I called him a son of a whore, and I prayed for his death."

Lais claps a hand over her mouth to stifle a nervous laugh, but Victoria is furious. "You did *what*?"

"He left Dido to rot," Amara says, starting to feel angry at Victoria. "Do you understand? Her shade will never know peace. She will never join her ancestors. She is trapped now, between this world and the next. He did that to *Dido*."

Victoria gestures at the wall. "Then maybe you should

have left the vengeance to her shade. And not brought his rage down on the rest of us!"

Amara knows Victoria is right, but it only makes her angrier. "You always fucking excuse him, whatever he does."

"It's *me* he's likely to take this out on," Victoria shouts. "Or one of the girls! When Simo crossed him, it was Drauca he killed. He can't strike at you, not without angering Rufus, so who does that leave? From now on, I want Juventus to come with us whenever we entertain. We need all the protection we can get."

"Of course you must take Juventus," Amara says, feeling more contrite. "And I'm sorry this has put you at risk, truly I am, but I didn't have a choice."

"You've always done whatever you fucking wanted, Amara. Today is no different." Victoria storms out of the garden, leaving the flautists behind.

"Your old master," Phoebe says nervously, in Greek. "Is he a *very* bad man?"

Amara thinks of all the violence she has known Felix commit – against her, against so many others – his total lack of compassion and his tenacity for holding a grudge. "The worst man you can imagine," she says.

Victoria does not talk to Amara for the rest of the afternoon, and Britannica, when she is told, immediately offers to murder Felix: *strike first*. Confronted by her two friends' extreme reactions, Amara's unease only grows. By the time Philos finally arrives in her bedroom, she has had hours for the anger to drain away, leaving behind its dark sediment of fear.

"What have I done?" she whispers, as he sits beside her. "What have I done?"

The answering anxiety she can see in his face is not reassuring. "It will be alright," he says. "We'll think of something."

"He left Dido's body on the rubbish heap. He left her there like nobody loved her, like she was nothing. I couldn't bear it."

"I know." Philos hugs her, and she leans into him. "I don't blame you. It's not your fault."

"Of course it's my fault!"

"No, it's not. Sometimes, a person can be pushed beyond endurance."

"You would never have lost control of yourself like that, I know you wouldn't."

Philos gently separates himself, taking her arms from around his neck and holding both her hands. "But I have," he says. "I *have* lost control like that."

Amara removes her right hand from his and touches his tunic, where she knows the branding lies on his skin. In all the time they have been together, she has never dared ask him how it happened. "Is that why they marked you?"

Philos moves her fingers from his chest, as if the scar still hurts. "Do you remember, when we were first together, I told you that I once embarrassed myself by crying over a girl?" Amara nods. "I did see her again. I loved her very much." He stops, and Amara is about to tell him he doesn't need to share this story, that he doesn't have to tell her everything, but he continues. "We were married."

"*Married?*"

"I know slaves' marriages aren't recognized," Philos

replies, as if this were the reason for her surprise. "But that doesn't mean it never happens." He pauses. "Her name was Restituta." The reality of Philos's wife rests in the air between them for a moment, like a shadow passing. "After Terentius lost interest in me, it was almost worse than enduring him. I had no sense of myself. I hated what he had made me; it felt as if he had destroyed everything. And Restituta was so kind – I cannot even begin to explain how kind she was."

"Like you are to me," Amara says, realizing then that perhaps Philos was not always this gentle, but instead learned from the love another woman showed him.

"When you marry a slave in the same household, you always know it's possible you might be separated, but you just hope it won't happen. I don't even know why the family decided to sell her. When I found out, we were both distraught, and I promised to go to Terentius; I promised her I could persuade him." He stops, and Amara feels as if she cannot breathe, understanding how desperate Philos and Restituta must have been. "I begged him. I cried. I got on my knees. And when he refused me…" Philos trails off. "I don't even remember what happened. I know I broke things, screamed and raged. Whatever I did meant a flogging wasn't sufficient punishment. But the branding wasn't the worst part. They never let me say goodbye. I never saw her again." Amara grips his hand, unable to find any words of comfort. Whatever she had imagined lying behind the mark, it had not been this much pain. "We managed to exchange a few messages after she left. Through the slave network, which is slow, relying on porters and good memories. Then two years ago, I learned she had died in childbirth." He breaks off, turning his face away. "I hope she was carrying the child of a man who loved her."

"I'm so sorry, Philos," Amara says, taking him in her arms. They hold one another for a long time, not speaking.

"I'm not such a kind person as you think," he says, at last, his voice still unsteady. "When Rufus told me I was to run a household for his concubine, the girl I had been escorting from the brothel, I wanted to seduce you to spite him. But then, when you came here, I fell in love with you."

"I've done worse than contemplate seducing someone out of revenge," Amara says, touched Philos would feel guilt for an act he didn't even commit. "Believe me."

She lies back on the bed, pulling him down beside her, so that they can hold one another more easily. They rest their foreheads together, and she can feel the palm of his hand on the back of her neck.

"I'm very sorry I didn't tell you about Restituta before. But now that I have, do you think you might be able to tell me about Felix?"

"I did tell you."

"I didn't mean about today."

It hurts to think of Felix, and Amara knows it will hurt even more if Philos starts probing at the parts of herself which bring her so much shame. "I don't know what you mean."

"You told me once you didn't love him, but I've always felt that wasn't true." Philos keeps hold of her as she tries to pull away. "Please, my love, I'm not jealous. I just want to understand."

In her mind's eye, Amara can see Felix at the slave

market at Puteoli. The way he stood, slightly apart from those surrounding him, in the full glare of the sun. The most beautiful man she had ever seen. And when he approached, when he smiled at her and Dido, she had felt relief. Because she was foolish enough to believe he would be kind. "I don't want to think about him," she says, her voice breaking. "Don't make me do this."

"It's alright if you loved him. It's not your fault. You know that, don't you?"

"Were you stupid enough to love Terentius? After all he did to you?"

"Not Terentius, no. But I loved my first master very much. I spent years wanting him to notice me, wanting to impress him, to be as important to him as he was to me. It's so common. I don't want you to feel guilty about it."

"How can I not feel guilty? I hate Felix so much. I have wished him dead a thousand times, and yet, when I thought he really *was* going to die, when Balbus came at him with the knife, I prayed for Felix to move out of the way." Amara pauses to control herself, not wanting to cry. "And then the knife hit Dido instead."

She almost expects Philos to let go of her, that he will feel the disgust she feels, but he does not. "Just because you wanted Felix to live doesn't mean you wanted Dido to die. It wasn't your fault."

"Maybe," Amara says, and allowing herself to say the word aloud is like setting down a weight. "Maybe it wasn't. But today was my fault."

"Do you blame me for what happened with Restituta?" She shakes her head. "Then why would I blame you for what you did? You're not made of stone. I just wish I had asked you about Felix before. I should have realized it was too much for anyone to deal with."

"I'm not sure it would have made any difference," Amara replies, trying to make her voice lighter. "I wouldn't have listened to you anyway."

Philos smiles. "Well, that's true. But I hope you listen to me now. We really do need to pay him back the money, all of it. Can't you take out a loan from Drusilla, now she's got that new man?"

"Three thousand sesterces is still far too much to ask!"

"I think you're going to have to. Better to upset Drusilla than keep going back to Felix." Amara sighs, knowing he's right. He kisses her, his lips at the very edge of her mouth. "But that's for tomorrow. I should leave you to rest now."

"I'm not tired yet," Amara says, holding on to him, not wanting to let go. "Not unless you are."

In answer, Philos shifts his body further towards her so that no space remains between them, and all she can feel is the warmth of him.

34

Hail Profit

Mosaic in a Pompeiian house

It is one of the most ostentatious villas she has encountered in Pompeii. Amara steps through the giant doorway, Philos beside her, an octopus unfurled in an elaborate mosaic beneath their feet. Woven between the creature's tentacles is the motto, *Profit is Joy*. Ampliatus clearly makes no secret of the gods worshipped in his house. The porter who greets them both is dressed in a scarlet tunic, his sandals so well-oiled they shine.

"My master is expecting you?" His expression makes it clear he finds this doubtful.

"We are here to call on Drusilla," Amara replies. "Her steward Josephus told me she is receiving visitors here. I am Amara, concubine of Placidus Rufus."

The name of her patron gains her admittance, though the porter cannot bring himself to look pleased by an uninvited visit. He calls over a slave girl who, like him, is dressed in scarlet. "Your boy must wait here with me. The girl will show you to Drusilla."

Amara leaves Philos with the bad-tempered porter, smarting at the insulting use of the word *boy* to describe her lover, who is at least ten years older than she is, and walks through the giant atrium, following the maid. The red walls create an optical illusion, a glorious painted cityscape she imagines must be based on Rome. She can feel a light spray from the central fountain as she passes, the marble dolphin sending its jet of water high into the air, before it tumbles down in a noisy cascade.

The garden is full of roses, swathed in thick bands of trellising around the walls and sprawling beside the enormous fishpond, their heavy scent mingling with the smell of the sea. Drusilla is sitting in a shady alcove, and to Amara's astonishment, she is engaged in needlework. Another maid, who Amara does not recognize, is sitting beside her.

"Amara!" Drusilla stands up in delighted surprise. "How wonderful to see you here."

"What a beautiful garden this is," Amara says, joining her friend on the amply cushioned marble. Drusilla reverently lays aside the tunic she is working on, smoothing it out to avoid creasing. "Is that for Ampliatus?" Amara asks, amused at the thought of such a wifely occupation.

"He likes to be fussed over. And I like to fuss over him."

The affectionate look on Drusilla's face seems genuine enough, though she has always been a formidable actress, and Amara is conscious of the presence of the eavesdropping servant, no doubt owned by the man in question. Drusilla sees the direction of Amara's gaze. "Fetch us some refreshments," Drusilla says to the maid. "And when you return, please wait there, by the fountain, until I call for you."

ELODIE HARPER

"This place is extraordinary!" Amara exclaims as soon as the girl is out of earshot.

"I told you." Drusilla is smug.

"And what's with the tunic? I didn't even know you could sew!"

"Of course I can sew," Drusilla retorts crossly. "He likes wearing things I've made; he says it means I'm always near his heart."

"You *like* him!" Amara has never, in all the time she's known Drusilla, heard her repeat a patron's flattery with fondness.

Drusilla purses her lips. "Why shouldn't I like him? Who doesn't enjoy being doted on?" She lowers her voice. "It's better than a man like Quintus who takes and takes and makes you feel like a whore every time he gives you a present."

"I'm glad to hear Ampliatus treats you well."

"More than that, he's kind to Primus," Drusilla whispers. "He's taken him all round his warehouses in the port, making a fuss of him. None of the others had any interest in my boy – they just found him a nuisance. Ampliatus even tells him stories. Primus *adores* him."

Amara is so used to seeing Drusilla's public face – the hard, glittering front she shows to the world – she has not imagined her ever looking this vulnerable. She supposes it makes sense, that the way to win Drusilla's heart would not be sex or flattery or even wealth, but kindness towards her child. "He sounds like a good man," Amara says.

"As much as any of them are." Drusilla tosses her head, clearly not wanting to appear too sentimental. "How is

Rufus? I hope he is planning to spend some of the Nemoralia with you."

"I'm spending it with Julia," Amara replies. "Rufus says he has to spend the festival with his parents."

"His *parents*?" Drusilla raises her eyebrows.

"That's what I thought," Amara says.

Drusilla is silent for a while. The maid has returned with the tray of refreshments and is standing at the opposite side of the garden, but Drusilla does not call her over. "Have you thought more about what we discussed?"

"Yes, and I've stopped."

"Stopped completely?"

"Completely. For many weeks now." The two women stare at one another, both aware of the implications. It is such an unusual moment of intimacy between them that Amara hates the thought of ruining it by begging for money, but she has to get the loan. "Drusilla." She takes her friend's hand. "There's something I need to ask you and which I hope you will be able to forgive. It is the reason I have called on you."

Drusilla is wary. "What is it?"

"I am still in debt to Felix for Victoria, and I cannot be left vulnerable to him if Rufus leaves me. This is too much to ask, and I know it, but please, I am begging you, as your friend, to lend me the money. I swear to repay you, at whatever rate you choose, and relinquish any claim on my investment in Phoebe or Lais."

"How much?"

"Three thousand sesterces."

Drusilla breathes in sharply. "How will you ever repay this if Rufus abandons you?"

It is a brutal question, but no more than Amara expects. "I am not completely friendless," she says. "The admiral still has some loyalty to me as his freedwoman, and Julia has already made me aware of other possibilities."

They are so close to the sea that, in the silence that follows, Amara is conscious of the sounds of the port, ships unloading, the cry of gulls. Drusilla is making her wait, and for that, Amara cannot help but hate her friend a little. "I will lend it to you," Drusilla says, and Amara clutches the bench with relief. "Without interest. But this is the last favour you may ask of me until it is repaid. And I must warn you that, if Rufus leaves you, I *cannot* have you stay at my house." She sees Amara's hurt expression, and softens her voice. "I'm sorry, I wasn't going to tell you when things are so unstable with your patron, but Ampliatus has asked me to marry him. I intend to rent the place in town and live here."

"You are more than generous. Truly, I cannot tell you how grateful I am." Amara places her hands over her heart in a formal gesture of sincerity. "And many congratulations on your marriage – this is wonderful news."

"Neither of us intend to make a fuss over the arrangement," Drusilla says, looking embarrassed. "I'm hardly a young virgin, and as a freedman, Ampliatus cannot hope to make some illustrious match with a freeborn woman. His wife died two years ago, and he's lonely. As for me, well, you know how precarious the life can be. This suits us both very well." She gestures at the maid to come over, signalling the end of their private conversation. "Send Philos to see Josephus with a contract this afternoon. I will make sure he has the money."

★ ★ ★

The porter looks in better spirits when Amara returns to the atrium. He is standing, chest thrust out, recounting some anecdote to Philos who is listening politely, no doubt having worked hard to win the man's trust. The pride Amara always feels in Philos, for his ability to dissemble his feelings, is somewhat undercut by the knowledge Drusilla has managed to snare a man who owns half the port, while hers doesn't even own his tunic. She crushes the thought, ashamed, when Philos turns to her and smiles.

"Your mistress is here," says the porter, looking aggrieved to be cut short.

"So she is," Philos replies to him, with a bow. "Thank you for your hospitality."

The porter nods, pleased that Philos treats him as if *he* were the person important enough to be called upon, not his master or future mistress.

"She said yes," Amara whispers, as soon as they have stepped out onto the street.

"Thank fuck for that." Philos breathes out with relief.

They both stand for a moment, the busy life of the port unfolding before them. "I don't want to go back yet. Do you think we could walk along the waterfront?" Amara asks. "Or would it look suspicious?"

"I could tell Rufus you wanted some air, if anyone sees," Philos says. "It's not as if I've let you go wandering off on your own."

They skirt round Ampliatus's enormous villa, walking towards one of the colonnades that frames the harbour. Small fishing boats bob against the sea wall as they pass, men dragging their nets onto the stone. Amara sidesteps to avoid being splashed as the fish jump and writhe by her feet. Past the noisy hustle of boats in the harbour, the blue of the bay stretches out, its horizon limitless. The gap between her and Philos as they walk feels almost as large. She wonders if he is thinking of Restituta, whether his wife's absence is an ache as constant for him as Dido's loss is for her.

"How far do you want to go?" he asks.

"Maybe we should just keep on and never stop," she jokes, before she sees from his face that she has pained rather than amused him. They reach the colonnade, and the space is less crowded. She remembers sitting here with Victoria and the others, dangling their legs over the wall. There is no way she and Philos could do anything so brazen. "Josephus will have the money for you this afternoon, when you go round with the contract. Has Rufus said anything to you about staying away during the Nemoralia? Drusilla thought it odd he was seeing his parents."

"He is not. Or not only his parents."

"Do you think he has another lover?" It almost makes Amara want to laugh at the dread she feels, when she cares so little for Rufus.

Philos stops, so that they can stand side by side, looking out at the water. "I'm rarely with him now. Any time I'm at the house, I work on the business, not his personal affairs. But I don't think it's a lover. I think his family expect him to get married. That is what Vitalio has heard." Amara puts out her hand to touch the column, wanting to feel something solid. The marble is warm under her fingers from the sun. "I'm sorry. There was no good time to tell you. But it's another reason I wanted you to get that money from Drusilla."

"He's not going to want to keep renting a house with a concubine in it, is he?"

"I don't think so."

"I'll speak to Julia; I know she has some apartments to let. It might be cramped with Victoria and the other women, but we'll manage. Rufus must owe me something; as a patron it would look bad if he threw me out on the street, and if I involve Julia, that will make it even harder for him. It's all I'm going to ask: rent to Julia, and letting me keep you. Surely, he can't say no to that?"

She is looking at Philos, but he is staring out at the water, the light of the waves reflecting onto his face. "I hope not," he says.

35

I see you hurrying in excitement with a burning torch
To the grove of Nemi where you
Bear light in honour of the goddess Diana.

Propertius, Poems

The garden is filled with the sound of laughter. All the women of the household are gathered together, even Martha, and they splash one another as they wash their hair. The water is cold when Victoria pours a jug over Amara's head, making her shudder, but the heat of the sun is so intense the water dries on her skin almost as fast as it falls.

Amara takes another jug and pours it over Britannica, who shakes her hair like a dog, spraying the water everywhere, making Phoebe shriek. Martha yelps and darts out of the way as Victoria tries to fling water at her too. Amara realizes it is the first time she has ever seen her maid smile.

"Careful!" Amara laughs, as Martha nearly crashes into the carefully planted herbs in a vain attempt to dodge the spray. Victoria tips the last of the water into the flowerbed, and Martha flops down on the hot paving stones, stretching out her legs. The Nemoralia is the goddess Diana's festival for women and slaves, and they have nothing to do today but wash their hair and dress themselves in garlands of flowers, ready for the evening's torch-lit procession to the River Sarnus. Philos and Juventus have been banished to the atrium where they are lounging about playing backgammon, though occasionally, the sound of their laughter drifts as far as the garden. Amara allows the holiday atmosphere to beguile her too. She tells herself she will worry about Felix and Rufus when the festival is over.

Victoria sits at the edge of the fountain, trailing her hand in the water. "I know what I'm going to ask Diana this evening," she says.

"Endless victory for Crescens?" Amara suggests.

Victoria purses her lips, not telling. "You can't ask Artemis for gifts in *love*," Lais says, fluffing out her hair to help it dry. "She has many faces, but she's still the virgin goddess."

"So you won't ask for help to snare Juventus's heart?" Victoria asks.

Lais rolls her eyes. "One time I said he is not too ugly, and you *never* let me forget about it."

"I don't imagine Juventus would take much hunting," Amara says, thinking of the way he leers at them all. "He's not exactly playing hard to get." They laugh, and Amara feels a little uncomfortable, hoping the porter does not overhear their mockery.

"Rather him than Philos though," Victoria says with a shudder. "Can you imagine Philos trying to fight anyone?"

There is less laughter this time. Amara bends her head, letting the hair fall to hide her face, raking her fingers through the curls. Philos's body is as dear to her as it is familiar, and over the course of their affair, he has become increasingly confident, no longer inhibited by the need to cover up his scar. She doesn't like to hear him belittled.

"Philos has a *really* lovely face though," Phoebe says.

"A lovely face?" Victoria repeats, amused. "You can't *fancy* him?"

The guilty flush on Phoebe's cheeks is answer enough. "I didn't say that," she protests, looking round at the others for support. "Just because you notice a man looks nice, doesn't mean you want to bed him."

"Nice face," Britannica agrees, picking at the gap between her teeth. The declaration is so startling it makes everyone laugh. Britannica shrugs, unconcerned by the mockery, though she glances at Amara, holding her gaze for a moment, before looking away.

"Sounds like you've got competition for him, Phoebe." Victoria has a needling edge to her voice.

Amara remembers Victoria's incessant taunting of Beronice at the brothel and knows she could keep this up for hours if nobody intervenes. She picks up a half-empty jug of water and flings it at Victoria. "And *you* are a tease!"

Victoria shrieks, splashing Amara with water from the fountain in revenge, and the gathering degenerates into more yelling and leaping to escape the spray. After they have exhausted themselves, Amara goes to the kitchen to fetch the food for lunch, making several journeys. As the mistress, she is expected to wait on the others. The kitchen is tiny, little more than a hole with a ledge for broiling meat or heating up pans. A shelved storeroom opens onto it and, beyond that, the latrine. The lingering smell of wood smoke, stale roasted fish and excrement makes Amara feel nauseous. She is unsurprised neither Martha nor Juventus have much enthusiasm for cooking in here.

When she has served the women, Amara takes food out to the men in the atrium, water dripping from her hair as she walks. Juventus stares at her body where the wet material clings, but she barely notices – she is too busy enjoying the way Philos smiles at her.

"You're winning!" she says, looking at his side of the board as she sets down the plate. Philos is so close to her, and there is such affection in his eyes, it is an effort to stop herself from kissing him.

"The game's not over yet." Juventus scowls.

Philos replies to him in dialect, something that makes Juventus look less sour. As she walks away, Juventus makes an expressive-sounding comment, rounded off by a filthy laugh. Amara has worked long enough as a prostitute to recognize sexually charged remarks, whatever the language. She cannot read anything into the tone of Philos's reply, but she is not entirely pleased that whatever he has said makes the porter laugh even harder.

"You can have Juventus whenever you like," Amara says to Lais in Greek, sitting beside her. "Maybe the man would be less insufferable if he had a lover."

Lais raises her eyebrows. "If you paid me, I'd be happy enough." Amara thinks she is joking, then realizes from the sharpness of Lais's expression that she is keen to make money. It reminds Amara of how she used to be at the Wolf Den.

"If that's what you want."

"You could charge him too," Lais suggests. "And then perhaps we can split what he gives you?"

"No, you keep what I charge him. You're the one earning it. Though we don't need to tell Juventus that."

From the smirk on Lais's face, Amara suspects Lais had calculated that would be her mistress's reply. *I am not like Felix*, Amara tells herself, *or she would not even dare to ask me*. The fear Amara has been trying to suppress rises again. She looks over at Britannica, reassuringly large and muscular, standing by the fountain. Men are not allowed to accompany them for this evening's ritual, but should Felix try his luck on the way home, Britannica will be armed.

The August evening begins to cool, and Victoria goes to fetch the garlands from the atrium. They dress each other's hair, the two freedwomen waiting on the slaves. Victoria helps the flautists while Amara weaves flowers into Martha's thick black curls and tries to persuade Britannica to wear a garland of red Amaranthus.

"The goddess will be more likely to listen to your request if you dress to please her," Amara says, as Britannica flinches away.

"Not too much," Britannica mutters, finally letting Amara fix it in place. With the Briton's bright-red hair, the garland looks like a halo of flame. She tilts her chin up at Amara. "You think hunter goddess will hear me?"

Amara lays her hand to her heart. "I hope so." They turn towards the wall where Dido is painted, a version of Diana who is sacred to them both.

"I ask for revenge." Britannica speaks as if she is addressing Dido.

"Do you even know how to write?" Victoria says. She is busy scrawling on a ribbon with charcoal, one of the five they will leave at the shrine. Martha, who is Jewish, won't be praying to the goddess and declined the offer of a ribbon. Amara was surprised her maid even agreed to join the procession.

"I can write Britannica's prayer," Amara replies. She lays out two strips of white ribbons on the marble bench, writes *vengeance* on the first for Britannica, and *deliverance* on the second for herself. Britannica squints uncomprehendingly at the Greek letters.

At the approach of dusk, they agree to prepare the lights. Amara goes to the storeroom, holding her breath to avoid the smell, and gathers up the small terracotta torches that she and Victoria bought from the Forum. When she comes back out, Philos is waiting with an oil lamp. The women illuminate their torches from it, one after the other. Watching them, Amara wonders how long they will all be together in a household like this, and it is not only the habitual fear of being separated from Philos that makes her chest tighten. She has grown used to this place, to the strange almost-family of women she has collected.

Amara lights her own flame last. She does not dare look in Philos's face, but deliberately touches his hand as she reaches out to hold the lamp steady, forming an unspoken connection between them. She glances round to make sure everyone else's light is still burning, then leads the women through the darkened atrium. Juventus lets them out onto the street.

Other women are already walking along the pavements, holding up torches or candles. Those furthest away glimmer like a scattering of stars in the dusk. Men and children watch from windows and doorways as they pass, and neighbours call to one another, the air warm with good humour and the last lingering heat of the sun. Lais and Phoebe hold hands, and Amara remembers how she used to walk like that with Dido. She hopes the flautists are not separated whenever she and Drusilla sell them.

It becomes darker as they leave the town, walking out of the Theatre Gate towards the river. A narrow path off the main road has been set with flaming lamps to guide them. They pass villas and vineyards, the trailing lights of their torches illuminating everything they touch. Some of the women in the procession sing snatches of song, and Victoria joins them, her sweet voice ringing out loudly. The words are unfamiliar to Amara.

They reach the small shrine to Diana that sits at a curve in the river, planted round with Cyprus trees. It is surrounded by women and dancing flame. In spite of the crowd, the air is much cooler here near the rushing black water, and Amara is grateful for her cloak. There is no formal ritual or priest, and so Amara and the others wait until it is their turn to tie the prayer ribbons to the Cyprus trees. Britannica knots hers to a high branch where it hangs, alone, above the rest.

"Did anyone bring an offering?" Amara asks. The others shake their heads. She turns to Britannica. "Will you come with me, while I leave mine?"

The Briton nods, and from the savage expression on her face, made even more sinister by the glow of the flame she is holding, Amara guesses Britannica is eager to see some token of violence left at the hunter's shrine. They walk side by side to the heap of offerings.

A small marble statue of Diana watches over her worshippers, and Amara stares at it while they wait. The goddess of the moon will always make her think of Felix. Amara remembers when he compared her to Diana for her savagery and pride, and it was Diana the huntress she once sent him as a token of her undying hatred. But it is not a clay stag or hunting dog that Amara has brought tonight. When she finally reaches the shrine, she hands her torch to Britannica and kneels down to lay a small clay figure of a mother and child at the edge of the heap. Then she rises, and takes back the flame, without looking in Britannica's eyes.

36

Resitutus has often deceived many girls
Pompeii graffiti

The water that bubbles over the stone steps seems to keep pace with Julia's laughter. Amara has never been inside Julia's garden dining room before – it is reserved for invited guests and tenants. She cannot imagine a more relaxing space to celebrate the second day of the Nemoralia. The place is painted deep blue, with scenes from the Egyptian Nile, and the goddess Isis looks over them. Wine and figs are set out on a bronze table, its legs shaped into the forms of three lustful satyrs.

The festival, with its upending of hierarchies, means that Britannica has also joined them as a guest. To Amara's surprise, both Julia and Livia have been very welcoming towards the taciturn Briton, admiring her strength and encouraging her to demonstrate her skills with the knife.

"It's as if she is dancing," Livia says, watching Britannica's cat-like moves in the shaded walkway beside the long pool. "She really is very clever."

"She is loyal," Amara says, pleased that, finally, somebody

other than Philos can understand why she loves Britannica. "I value her highly."

"I cannot believe you've been getting her to teach you how to use a blade," Julia says. "What a mysterious girl you are." She sips her wine. "It is a shame Rufus could not spend some of the festival with you."

Amara knows Julia well enough by now to understand this is not an idle remark. "His parents were insistent he spend the time at home," she says. "He has not mentioned it to me, but I believe he is considering getting married."

"I wondered if you had heard the rumours," Julia says. "Unsurprising, given he is standing for election next year."

"I've never cared much for Rufus," Livia says, her eyes still following Britannica's every move. "Rather spoiled, I think."

"All men are spoiled," Julia declares. "Though some grow kinder as they age. Like dear old Pliny. Or my friend Demetrius."

"Rufus never gives me news of the admiral," Amara says, ignoring Julia's mention of the Imperial freedman. "I do hope he is well."

"Both of them are well. I have been trying to persuade Demetrius to visit me here, when he next tours his estates. I'm sure, if I have a beautiful new tenant, it won't be very difficult to persuade him."

"You really think I could stay here with you?"

"Of course," Livia answers, for her aunt. "Even if she didn't like you, she's desperate to rent that apartment. Nobody else wanted it."

"Don't be awful." Julia swats affectionately at Livia, who is now reclining against her, then turns to Amara. "It's true though, darling. The place is very small compared to where you live now, and rather dark, but you would be most welcome to use the garden."

Amara's eyes burn with unshed tears of relief. "Thank you so much," she says, her voice sounding more steady than she feels. "I cannot tell you how grateful I am."

"Think nothing of it." Julia waves a hand. "Now, do you think your girl would like something to eat? Perhaps you should call her over. I'm longing to ask her what Britain is like – my father was always curious about the place."

Amara had intended to stay at Julia's until late but finds she is exhausted and, with the constant soothing murmur of the water, fears she might even be in danger of falling asleep. It is not yet dusk when she sets out for home with Britannica. The streets are less busy than usual, with most businesses closed for the holiday.

To her surprise, Amara can hear voices from the dining room door as soon as she steps into the atrium. She was expecting the house to be empty: Rufus sent for Philos in the afternoon, the flautists are entertaining Drusilla and Ampliatus at the port, and Victoria was due to meet Crescens. Instead, Victoria's laughter carries on the late afternoon air. It is hours earlier than Amara expected to be home.

"Is it the Master?" Amara whispers to Juventus, mortified by the prospect of catching Rufus with her friend.

Juventus looks down. "Crescens," he says. "The gladiator."

"She brought a *gladiator* to the house?"

"He was wearing a cloak," Juventus protests. "Even I couldn't see him properly, and I was only a few paces away."

"But that's worse! What if the neighbours tell Rufus we've been smuggling muffled-up men in here?"

Juventus gives an angry shrug. "What if he sees us all go to the brothel?" he retorts. "It's hardly a house of vestal virgins."

Amara knows, looking at his mutinous expression, that any trace of authority she once held has gone. If it weren't for Britannica standing beside her, she suspects Juventus would be even less civil. "Fine," she snaps. "I'll deal with it."

She walks across the atrium, Britannica beside her. At the threshold of the dining room, she pauses. The voices have gone ominously quiet. For a moment, she wonders if it's better to wait until they have finished, but the anger and curiosity are too much, and she pushes the door open. Victoria and her gladiator are sprawled over a couch. Amara can see the muscles on the man's bare back, the tension of his shoulders as he moves. She gasps. Then Victoria sees her and scrambles up, yanking her dress back over her breasts. "Amara!"

The man does not rush himself. He picks up his own tunic, pulling it over his head before he turns to face her.

"Felix." The shock of him standing in her home is so great Amara cannot say anything other than his name.

"Only command me," Britannica says, her knife drawn. "And I kill him."

Felix has his hand on the hilt of his own weapon. "That declaration seems a little over-confident." He turns to Amara with a mocking bow. "Are you in the habit of threatening to murder your guests? I imagine a dead pimp might not be such a welcome scandal for posh boy at the start of his political career."

"Get out."

"Not even a tour of the place?" Felix saunters towards her, although she notices he keeps his eyes trained on Britannica's weapon. "Very thoughtful of your lover to choose musical nymphs to decorate your rooms. A happy reminder of when you whored yourself out for me."

"*I said get out!*"

"Then tell the bitch to put down her knife," he says, no longer bothering to affect a casual tone. "Unless you want me to open her fucking throat in your boyfriend's dining room."

Amara turns to Britannica. "Make sure he leaves, but don't touch him. Then come back here."

Britannica lowers her arm with reluctance. "You try anything," she hisses at Felix. "You a dead man."

Amara does not look at Felix as he passes, but he stops, forcing her to acknowledge him. "I always keep my promises," he says. They stare at one another, then he turns away, walking beside Britannica to the door.

"How could you do this?" Amara can hardly bear to look at Victoria standing quivering by the couch. "How could you bring him into my house?"

"I'm sorry."

"*Sorry?* Is that all you can fucking say? Did you ever even have an affair with Crescens, or has it always been Felix?" Victoria is silent, and Amara guesses the answer. "I don't believe this. You lying, cheating whore!"

"Please," Victoria says, clasping her hands to her chest. "I never wanted to hurt you; I didn't want to lie. I thought

I could persuade him to ease off on the debt. That's why I agreed to see him at the games. But when we met, he told me how much he missed me, how it was killing him to be without me, and he meant it, Amara, I swear he meant it." Victoria starts to cry. "I love him. You've always known I love him. It was too much not to see him anymore. I couldn't bear it."

Britannica returns to the room, quietly closing the door behind her. Amara barely notices. "How can you be such a fool?" she shouts at Victoria. "Felix doesn't love you! He's only using you to get back at me, and you're stupid enough to fall for it. I cannot *believe* you let him into my house! How often has he been here? Was today the first time?" Victoria shakes her head, too choked by sobs to speak. "Which rooms has he seen?" Still Victoria doesn't reply, and Amara grabs her by the shoulder. "Answer me!"

Victoria cringes from her. "He wanted to see all of the rooms. This is the second time he's been."

"So he knows the entire layout of my house." Amara releases Victoria, pressing her hands to her own eyes, trying to take in the magnitude of the betrayal. "Tell me you didn't let him go through the accounts."

"No! Of course not!"

"Why 'of course'? You've had him in my bedroom. You were fucking him in *here*, just moments ago." The image rises up again in Amara's mind, and with it, a rage so blinding there is no room for any other feeling. "You really are trash, Victoria," she says, her voice as cold as Felix at his cruellest. "No wonder your parents left you to die in the rubbish. It's where you've always belonged."

The two women stare at one another, the full ugliness of

what Amara has said hanging between them, dark as smoke from the guttering lamps. "I've defended you to Felix so many times," Victoria says. "Whenever he told me how little you cared, how you were just using me to make money. I defended you to Felix even after you asked me to fuck Rufus, because I was so grateful to you, because I *loved* you. And all that time, you were nothing more than the spoiled little doctor's daughter, just like Felix always said you were, looking down your fucking nose at me." Victoria's anger builds as she speaks, leaving her too distracted to notice the object Britannica places on the table behind her. "The only person you *ever* thought was good enough for you was Dido, wasn't it? The pair of you at the brothel, sneering at everyone, thinking you were above us all. And I *know*, I've *always known*, that you would have exchanged Dido for me in a fucking heartbeat."

Blood pounds in Amara's head. She can no longer see Victoria clearly, instead she is back at the Forum, the night of the Saturnalia. Dido is lying wounded at her feet, and there is nothing Amara can do, except watch her die. "It should have been *you* that night," she screams. "If you love Felix so much, why didn't you take the knife that was meant for him? Why was it Dido? She was worth a thousand of you."

"Perhaps she was." Victoria flings her arms out in a gesture of defiance. "But look who ended up on the rubbish heap. It wasn't me, was it?"

The words break like glass in Amara's heart, shattering the remains of her self-control. She seizes Britannica's knife from the table, and with a move so swift Victoria has no time to react, she grabs her by the hair and brings the point to Victoria's throat. "Did you *know*? Did he tell you what he did to Dido's body?" Victoria stares at her, eyes wide with shock. "Did he?"

"No," Victoria gasps.

"Amara." Britannica lays a hand gently on her arm to avoid startling her into a sudden movement. "Be calm." Victoria swivels her eyes to look at the woman she has hated so long, who appears, inconceivably, to be coming to her aid.

"I am calm," Amara says, though her trembling arm betrays her.

"You must kill her now," Britannica says.

"No!" Victoria cries. "*Please*!"

Britannica grips Amara's shoulder, holding her steady. "Think of what she may *know*. What she may tell Felix. About your life, your secrets." Britannica squeezes her even harder. "Listen to me. I tell Rufus she try to kill you first, that I defend you. We both say I killed her."

"Amara, you can't listen to her," Victoria begs, gazing at her desperately. "I would never tell Felix anything to hurt you, I swear it. Please, I'm begging you, please don't do this. *Please*."

Amara's gaze slides from Victoria's face to her throat, and she starts, as if the sight of her own hand holding the knife shocks her. She lets the blade fall, clattering, onto the tiles. Victoria collapses against the couch, holding her fingers to her neck, gasping for air like a woman who has been held underwater.

Britannica hisses through her teeth. She seizes the knife, stowing it at her belt. "This is mistake," she says.

Amara ignores Britannica, still looking at the crumpled

form on the couch, the friend she nearly murdered. "I am thousands of sesterces in debt because of you," she says to Victoria. "I risked my life to save you; I gave you everything, and you repaid me by bringing Felix into my house."

"And you nearly killed me," Victoria looks up, some of her old spark returning. "I think we're fucking even."

"I *never* want to see you again. Do you understand? You will leave this house immediately."

Victoria gets unsteadily to her feet. "I never wanted to choose between you both." She reaches out to Amara. "I didn't want to choose Felix over you."

"But you did." Amara steps away from her. The two women look at one another, and there is no trust left in the ashes of their friendship, only regret.

Victoria takes a step backwards, retreating slowly, eyes darting between Britannica and Amara, as if even now, she fears one of them will try to kill her. Then she turns her back on them both to open the door and runs across the atrium, barging past Juventus and hurtling onto the street where Felix is no doubt waiting. Amara sits down heavily on the couch.

"This is mistake," Britannica says again. "She will betray you."

"What more can she do now?" Amara says wearily. "She's already shown Felix the house. There's nothing more for him to see."

Britannica moves, leaning in so close that her breath is warm on Amara's cheek. "Philos." The word is only a whisper, but Amara is instantly alive to the meaning behind it. She looks up at Britannica, and seeing her expression, wastes no time pretending not to understand.

"Victoria doesn't know," she murmurs. "She *can't* do."

"Yet, I know."

"How? When did you guess?"

"You are alike," Britannica says simply. "You are like him. Victoria would also see this."

Amara looks over towards the door which Victoria left ajar, the door through which she just allowed her to escape. "Even if she does know, I couldn't *kill* her," she says, putting her head in her hands. "What sort of monster do you think I am?"

"You regret this one day. Trust me."

Amara glances up at Britannica who is still staring at the door with a look of murderous ferocity. "You always hated her," she mutters.

"That is nothing." Britannica raises her eyebrows, a flicker of amusement on her face. "I hate most people."

37

I bought my wife's freedom so nobody could wipe his dirty hands on her hair.

Petronius, The Satyricon

When Amara wakes the next morning, only a brief moment passes before the memory of Victoria's betrayal hits her. She lies rigid in the bed, not wanting to move. High up on the wall, the early morning light filters through from the window into the tablinum. She closes her eyes, but when she does, she can still see the movement of Felix's back, Victoria underneath him. The way Felix turned to face her. And worse, the memory of her own anger, the knife she held to Victoria's throat. The sound, as the metal hit the tiles.

Nausea grips her, and Amara sits up, trying not to retch. She crouches over her knees, shuddering, until the urge to be sick has passed, her forehead damp with sweat. Then she forces herself to get up. At the bottom of the bed, Amara opens the chest to take out her clothes. The woven basket of boiled lambswool, her contraceptive, sits in the corner, and she moves it underneath some linen, so she doesn't have to look at it.

The lid is heavy as she lowers it. She leans forwards, resting her weight on its wooden surface, the carved design of grapes and vines imprinting onto her palms. The pain of Victoria's betrayal has not yet fully sunk in. Felix has been in her private rooms, rifling through her belongings, laughing at her. Perhaps he lay here, in this bed, with Victoria. Just as Amara lies with Philos.

Philos himself had been surprisingly calm when she broke the news last night. He will be the one who tells Rufus about Victoria today, destroying her reputation as effectively as possible. It was Philos who had the idea of suggesting they not only claim Victoria risked disgrace by inviting a pimp to the house, but also slandered Rufus. They hope, by playing upon his guilt, that Rufus might be less inclined to take his anger out on Amara for having Victoria in the house in the first place.

Amara opens her bedroom door. Martha is already waiting by the dressing table. The maid's face is as blank as wax, no imprint left of last night's events. Though she must surely have heard the shouting and be aware, by now, that Victoria has gone.

Amara walks over to sit for Martha, and is met by the same quiet greeting her maid gives every morning. It is impossible for Amara to read anything into the way Martha styles her hair either. Martha has always been silent, her hands unkind. The only sound is the sigh of the comb, scraping against her scalp. Amara knows as little of Martha now, as she did the day she first came to this house. She thinks of the unexpected way Martha smiled at the Nemoralia, of how lonely her life must be, the losses of her past, and knows she should have made more effort to earn her maid's trust. Perhaps then, Martha might have told Amara if she had any suspicions about Victoria, or about the man Victoria had brought to the house.

Amara only speaks once Martha has finished the rituals of dressing her hair and face. "Could you send Britannica to me, please?"

Martha bows her head in acknowledgement and leaves the room. The sight of the Briton a few moments later, silhouetted in the doorway, gives Amara the first sense of hope she has felt all morning. Britannica is not fond of embraces, but she joins Amara on the couch and pats her shoulder. "Fabia also betray you."

"What?"

"All these months I go to the bar – she leave no message to warn you about Victoria."

"Perhaps she didn't realize."

Britannica gives her a pitying look. "She must know."

Anger makes Amara feel more like herself. "If she wants to continue eating, she had better start talking."

"Come," Britannica stands, holding her hand out. "We go to the bar." She hauls Amara to her feet then looks down, her expression a perplexing mixture of savagery and tenderness.

The two women go through the farce of asking Philos's permission to visit the temple for the Nemoralia, as if he were still reporting on Amara for Rufus, rather than the three of them united in deception. It is impossible to know whether Juventus is fooled, but he lets them out without comment.

The streets are quieter than usual, Pompeii's more generous masters granting their women and slaves a respite from work on the final day of the festival. Virgula's shop is shut, as is the grocer on the corner. A dog trots past them on the pavement, its neck wound round with battered-looking flowers in tribute to Diana. Britannica stares, muttering something in her own language. They stop and watch it jump onto a paving stone, back legs scrabbling.

"Victoria go to Felix," Britannica says, as they observe the dog's progress across the road.

"I suppose you think I'm a fool for ever trusting her."

"No." Britannica starts walking again. "Even I not see this. Though I know she is bad."

There are no stepping-stones to cross the language barrier that sits between Amara and Britannica. All the shades of meaning that could lie within the word *bad*, reduced like everything else Britannica says into blunt, unsophisticated phrases, even though Amara has long suspected she is anything but. "Why did you always think badly of Victoria? Is it because she called you savage?"

"I watch her eyes. Even before I understand all the words, what she say is different to what she think. When you, Amara, go out at the brothel, she is different; when you return, she is different again."

"When *I* went out, she was different?" Amara says, struggling to follow.

"You are strongest. She know this; she not like it." Britannica looks at Amara, resentment plain in her face. "I try to warn you many times. Always, I am warning you."

"I thought you just didn't like her."

Britannica shakes her head. "You want ask me about Philos? What I see?"

"You've watched him?"

"Always watch him, after I understand what he is to you."

"And what did you learn?" In spite of herself, Amara is almost afraid to hear the answer.

"He *never* protect you. Felix kill him quickly, more than quickly. But I watch his eyes. He is good." She places a hand to her heart. "I trust him. Better man for you than others." Britannica's words affect Amara in ways she had not thought possible. Not having to face another's judgment, when she has been burdened with the fear of punishment and disgrace for so long, makes her want to weep. "No," Britannica warns, seeing her emotion. "Don't."

They have reached Asellina's bar. The reek of stew, smoke and alcohol wafts onto the street, along with the hubbub of voices. It seems the hard-faced landlady has not chosen to give *her* slaves a day off. Amara puts a hand over her mouth to stop herself retching from the stench. Britannica looks at her with apprehension. "I go in for you?"

"No." Amara shakes her head. "I should speak to Nicandrus myself."

They enter through the shop, rather than the bar. Nicandrus is serving, looking even skinnier and grubbier than the last time Amara saw him. The place is sweltering. A vat of water is boiling over the fire at the side of the counter, steam billowing from it, making Nicandrus drip with sweat, hair matted to his forehead. Amara and Britannica join the queue. Nicandrus spots Amara, long before he is due to serve them, and she is grateful to see him shout over his shoulder for assistance.

Even with another slave at the counter to help serve, they have only the briefest time for a conversation. "When does Fabia come in?" Amara asks. "Does she have regular times?"

"Every Friday," he replies. "Usually early."

Amara nods. "Don't tell her to expect us." For a moment, she wonders if she should share what she knows about Dido, then decides against it. Better let Nicandrus believe his love is at peace. "Thank you," she says. "And stay well."

Nicandrus nods, distracted, already being hassled by other customers who are displeased that he is daring to snatch a few moments to chat rather than serve. Some believe, it seems, the only rest a slave should enjoy is in death. Amara and Britannica abandon him and make their way back onto the street. Breathing in the cooler air is a relief. "Nicandrus wouldn't be stuck here if it weren't for Felix," Amara says. "I can't believe Zoskales sold him to such a bitch."

"No good masters." Britannica glances at Amara, both of them conscious of their own relationship. "One day, you free me. It is different."

They continue walking up the main road towards the Forum. Every street corner in this part of town is somewhere Amara once loitered with Dido, but today, as well as the sense of loss, she feels an unusually strong pull of solidarity towards Britannica. When they reach the turning to the brothel, neither speaks but both quicken their pace, passing it as swiftly as possible.

In the Forum, the stone ribcage of the buildings traps

the heat reflecting off the white marble. Voices rise like the incense outside Jupiter's temple, in a murmur that is almost musical. There are no hawkers to interrupt with screeching cries, only a few stalls selling the last drooping flowers for offerings to Diana. Amara chooses two stems of gladioli which look slightly less crumpled than the rest.

"We cannot go inside the temple precincts," she says to Britannica. "We'll have to leave these at the door."

They join a small queue of women and slaves who are waiting by the entrance to Apollo's temple, where the god's sister Diana is also worshipped. The woman in front of Amara is heavily pregnant, stroking her belly gently with the sprig of flowers she has brought for the goddess.

"The hunter is also for childbirth?" Britannica asks.

"Yes," Amara says. For a moment, she thinks Britannica is going to say something more, but she does not.

At the doorway, a dour attendant waits with a basket in which worshippers silently lay their offerings. He does not look especially pleased by the sight of Britannica who peers straight over his head to catch a glimpse of the temple precincts. He shoos her away. Britannica does not hurry herself to obey, and Amara has to tug her arm to get her to move. "Always the hunter is your chosen goddess?" Britannica says, as they walk back towards the Forum.

"No. My parents worshipped the goddess Pallas-Athene, above all others."

"But now you give to the hunter twice." Amara does not reply, and Britannica nods as if this is answer enough. "Philos knows?"

Britannica is striding through the crowd, confident Amara will keep up with her. Nothing about the way the Briton carries herself suggests she is asking a question that might be too personal. *Knows what?* Amara nearly says. It is the answer she would have given Victoria. But it is impossible to dissemble with Britannica. She will only spell out her meaning more clearly, and with absolutely no shame, until she gets a reply. "No," Amara says. "Not yet."

Phoebe and Lais are back from the port when they return, huddled in the atrium beside Juventus and Philos, all of them whispering together. With Victoria gone, everyone in the household, but Amara, is enslaved.

"We knew nothing, mistress," Phoebe says in Greek, as soon as she sees Amara. "I promise you."

"I know where she hid all the tips," Lais adds. "I can show you, when you clear her room."

Victoria's room. Amara had not even thought about going through her friend's belongings yet. "Show me now," she says to Lais who hurries up the stairs, only too eager to pull apart Victoria's bedroom along with what remains of her reputation.

The moment she steps inside, Amara is returned to the first day Victoria came to the house, with all its joy and excitement. Grief swells in her chest. Lais is rifling through Victoria's clothes, piled neatly on a stool in the corner. "There!" she cries, holding up a purse. Amara takes it from Lais's outstretched hand. "I think she used to give gifts to Crescens," Lais says, nodding. "Or the man we *thought* was Crescens." Amara tips the coins onto her palm. It is only a few pennies. She can picture Felix taking Victoria's stolen tips, praising her, rewarding her with a show of tenderness.

Perhaps that is how he is treating her now. Or perhaps he is angry she did not bring him more – an anger Victoria will seek to assuage with yet more information about Amara.

"You can share everything between you," Amara says to Lais and Phoebe who is now standing in the doorway. "All her clothes, the money. They are all yours."

She walks out onto the balcony. Down below, Philos and Juventus are still standing close together by the door. "Philos," she calls, leaning over the railing. "I want to know what the Master said." He turns to look up, but she backs away, heading to her study, not waiting to watch him come up.

The moment Philos has closed the door, she drops her show of coldness and embraces him. "There are too many people in the house," he murmurs, loosening the grip of her arms, pulling himself away. "I've told Rufus. He was angry, but no more than I expected."

"What did he say?"

"He was more concerned about the damage Victoria might do to his own reputation than the fact she had a lover visit the house."

"Does he still care so much about what I think?" Amara asks in surprise. "Perhaps he's not planning to get rid of me, after all."

Philos leans against the door jam, scuffing his heel against the skirting, not looking her in the face. "I don't think that was the point. Although he did ask me whether you believed Victoria. I suspect his anxiety is more about what a future bride's family might hear."

"Oh," Amara says. "Of course."

"But I stressed you were blameless, and he believed me.

Which is the most important point." Philos looks at her, with the anxious expression she has come to recognize when he speaks of her relationship with Rufus. "And perhaps, any guilt he feels might make him kinder towards you. Or I hope so." Amara reaches out to take his hand, and he holds her briefly, kissing the top of her head. "We need to wait until this evening, my love," he whispers, giving her shoulder a squeeze before moving apart. Amara watches him leave, hears the latch click, then rests her head against the wall and closes her eyes.

Surfacing from sleep, Amara feels like she is buried beneath layers of mud. She can feel the weight of someone's hand, pushing at her shoulder, and panic jolts through her, her body remembering the brothel. She flails out, hitting nothing but air.

"It's me. I didn't mean to frighten you."

Philos is staring down at her, his face lit by the flicker of the oil lamp, and she is lying in the warmth of her own bed, the room in darkness. Still the panic does not entirely recede. "What happened?"

"Nothing has happened." Philos strokes her hair from her face. "I was going to leave you to rest, but you've been asleep all afternoon." Amara struggles to sit up, and he helps her. "You look so pale. Are you sick?"

Sick and terrified, Amara thinks. "No." She moves closer to him, so that they are sitting beside one another, knees touching. "But I need to tell you something." She cannot bring herself to say the words, so instead, she takes one of his hands and holds it against her stomach, looking at him.

He stares back, momentarily puzzled. Then his face is lit by understanding, and she hears his sharp intake of breath.

"Are you sure?" he asks, his eyes so wide they shine white in the lamplight. She nods. "Do you think..." He falters. "Do you think it's mine?"

"I know it is."

"How can you be so certain?"

"Firstly, I lie with you constantly, and with him only occasionally. But mainly..." She breaks off, worried about his reaction. "Do you remember in the study, two months ago, when I was frightened because I hadn't used any contraceptive."

"Yes, of course. I hadn't even realized you used one in the first place."

"Well, afterwards, I started wondering if maybe it was such a mistake after all. That perhaps I should stop using it with you but keep using it with him. Because if I fell pregnant, then Rufus would be more likely to let you stay, as I would need the help of a reliable steward to care for the child. And also..." She swallows, embarrassed. "Also, we have so few choices. I don't know if we will manage to be together, or if I might lose you. But this way I won't lose you completely."

"You *meant* for this to happen?"

"Can you forgive me?"

"Why would I need to forgive you for wanting my child." His eyes are bright with tears. He blinks, wiping his face, but the tears keep falling, and she is worried he might start sobbing. Amara takes Philos in her arms and holds him, one hand cradling the back of his head, the other stroking his shoulders, the same way he comforts her. "I'm not allowed a family," he says. "I can never call myself a father. I'm not even a man. And you want to have a child with me."

The words cut through Amara, knowing every one of them is true. "I'm not sure how you got me pregnant, if you're not a man," she says, her voice light, hoping to make him laugh and succeeding.

He moves away from her embrace, so he can look at her, and she sees the anxiety in his eyes. "But this is so dangerous for you."

"Hundreds of women give birth every day. I'll be fine." Amara smiles, but she is frightened too. They both know hundreds of women also die in childbirth. It is, after all, what killed his wife, Restituta. "I will be fine," she repeats, leaning forwards to kiss him. "I promise. And it's early yet, I'm not even showing. When the time comes, I will ask Drusilla for the midwife who delivered Primus."

"But you're taking such a risk for me—"

"No," she interrupts. "Not just for you. This is for me, too. I want to have a child by a man I love. This might be the only chance I ever have to do that."

"How do you think Rufus will react? Obviously, he will believe the child is his." Philos stops, and Amara can tell from the expression on his face, that he has reached the same point as her. "The child will think I'm just a slave. They will never know I'm their father. We can never tell them."

"But *we* will know." Amara tries to smile again, to pretend she is not upset, but finds she can't, and instead, without warning, she is suddenly crying so hard she can hardly breathe. Philos holds her, trying to calm her, but she cannot stop.

"It's alright," he says in Greek, stroking her hair. "It's alright, my love. It's alright." Hearing him speak her own language, even mangling it with his heavy Italian accent, reaches Amara in a way that Latin cannot.

"I love you," she replies in Greek, still crying. "I love you."

"I love you too. Please try not to be so upset. It will be alright, I promise."

"Rufus." Amara finally controls herself enough to say his name clearly. "What if he refuses to let you look after the child? What if he makes you go with him?"

"He won't. And whatever happens, I promise I will do everything I can to stay with you." He interlaces his fingers with hers. "With both of you."

Amara nods, allowing herself to be comforted, letting Philos draw her back onto the bed. She closes her eyes and wills herself to believe she is safe, even though their lives depend on the whims of a man who cares less for her with every day that passes.

38

Well, well, forgotten her flute-girl days, has she? She doesn't remember but she was bought and sold, and I took her away from it all and made her as good as the next.

Petronius, The Satyricon

The smell of the bar is no easier on Amara's stomach early in the morning. Britannica forces bread on her, watching while she chews, nodding at her with a look of ferocity that is perhaps supposed to be encouraging.

"Stop staring like that," Amara says. "You're putting me off."

"Better than be sick."

"Just keep an eye out for Fabia."

They are sitting half-hidden in the shadow of the stairwell of the almost empty tavern. It is Nicandrus's voice, loudly ushering Fabia to a table, that first alerts them to the old woman's presence. By the time he has brought Fabia around the corner, and she sees them, she is trapped, blocked from escaping by Nicandrus brandishing the hot bowl of stew at her back. He gestures for her to sit, and Fabia's shoulders sag in defeat.

"You look well," Amara says, as the old woman slumps down opposite. Britannica smiles in agreement, revealing her missing teeth.

"How kind of you to see me, daughter."

"Are you enjoying your new mistress? A shame you didn't think to share the happy news of Felix's betrothal."

"Please." Fabia licks her lips, for once not touching her food. "He would have killed me."

"Victoria may cost me everything. You could have found some way to warn me."

"It's Felix. Please. My life means nothing to him. And my Paris…" Fabia trails off.

"What about Paris?"

"Felix has set him on me as a spy. My own son. I pray you never know what that feels like."

Amara ignores the plea for sympathy. "Tell me what's happened since Victoria came back."

Fabia starts to spoon in her stew, but without the usual enthusiasm. "He took her to his new bar to celebrate. He's showing her off everywhere, claiming her as his freedwoman and wife." Fabia's mouth twists, as if she has tasted something bitter. "You blame me. But you think Beronice didn't know? She didn't warn you either." Pain lodges in Amara's chest, as indigestible as the dry bread Britannica has been pressing on her. There was a time she trusted Victoria and Beronice as her own sisters. "It won't last," Fabia mutters, wiping stew from her chin. "He always turns on her eventually. I'm sure he only managed to restrain himself all these months because you would have seen the bruises."

Amara thinks of the smell of pomade on Felix's skin, his slicked-back hair, and worse, the greed in his eyes when he took hold of her. "Victoria is not the one he wants," she says. "Though I wish she were."

"He says he will destroy you." Fabia bows her head, not meeting Amara's eye. "And he means it."

"I know."

"I see him dead first." It is the first time Britannica has spoken since Fabia arrived.

"Do you know how many men have tried to kill him?" Fabia hisses. "What makes you think *you* can manage it?"

"Fabia, please," Amara says, taking the old woman's hand. "I don't blame you for staying silent before. But I beg you to tell me everything you know now."

"He has people watching your house." Fabia's voice is so low Amara can barely hear.

"He means to attack me? Or attack the house?"

"Victoria knows all your bookings, doesn't she? She's been bragging about it to him for months."

"He means to attack the flautists?"

"I can't be sure." Fabia takes her hand back, her lips pursed. "It's not as if he shares his plans with me. But that's how he normally works. Striking at a rival's earnings first."

"Thank you."

Fabia shrugs. "If he has had me followed here, I am already dead. So I might as well tell you." She wipes the last scrap of bread around the bowl then stands to leave. Her expression, when she looks at Amara, is unforgiving. "You should have said yes to him."

Amara's neighbourhood feels different on the walk back. She does not expect to see anyone she recognizes. That's not how Felix works. He has a large enough network to draw on – she knows whoever is spying will not be familiar to her. Or else, they might be all too familiar: perhaps one of the shopkeepers she nods to each day, paid or threatened to give information.

If it were not for Britannica, Amara would feel even more afraid. As they walk side by side, Britannica has her hand on her knife, her eyes constantly roaming their surroundings. But even though the Briton is a formidable fighter, she is alone, and surely no match for a gang of thugs. The house, as they approach, no longer looks like an unassailable fortress of luxury, the way it once did when Amara longed to escape here from the brothel. Instead, she looks at the wooden shutters on Virgula's store and thinks how easy it would be to start a fire under cover of darkness, to burn everyone in their beds.

"I think we should start keeping the door locked all the time," Amara says to Juventus, when they slip inside.

"Not now. The Master is coming to visit." Juventus sucks his teeth, looking her body up and down. Amara knows that her stomach is still flat, but Juventus seems mesmerized by her breasts, which are not only sore but swollen from the pregnancy. The doorman opens his mouth, a lascivious expression on his face, but then catches sight of Britannica and closes it again, keeping any further remarks to himself.

Amara fetches her harp and sits in the garden, afflicted by weariness as well as fear. She wonders if Rufus is tired of all this too, whether he finds it hard to be near her, now everything that was genuine between them has died. At least she has finally become more skilful at playing the instrument he gave her. The melody she chooses flows in time to the murmur of the fountain, the rich notes of the harp as soft as the spray. It soothes even Amara's nerves.

Rufus's shadow announces his presence before he steps into the sunlight. They acknowledge one another with a look, but he does not come closer, instead, standing to watch her a while. She can tell from his face that he is enjoying her playing, and she prolongs the melody as long as possible, plucking the final refrain over and over, until the notes die into silence and only the ripple of the water remains.

He sits beside her. "That was beautiful." She bends her head, expecting him to kiss her, but he does not. "Philos told me Victoria brought the pimp here."

"I'm so sorry," Amara murmurs. "I never wished to embarrass you. She will never set foot here again, I promise."

"I warned you against her. You should never have bought her."

"You were right. I'm sorry."

"A lying whore like that will say anything." Rufus is looking at her from the corner of his eye, trying to gauge what she knows or believes.

Amara covers her face with her hands. "Victoria told the most terrible lies. I couldn't bear to hear her insult you. Please forgive me for ever trusting her; I'm so ashamed." Between her fingers, Amara sees his posture relax. Rufus puts an arm round her, and she nestles in close. Then he is kissing her, his hands less gentle, and she knows he is looking for a different type of relief.

Afterwards, Rufus is unusually affectionate. They are reclining on the couch in her dressing room, and he is holding her tightly, the way he always used to. Amara knows she has satisfied him. She took every possible opportunity to give him pleasure, even though her body has become so sensitive, sometimes she does not even like Philos touching her.

"I remember the first time I made love to you in this house," Rufus says, lazily stroking her flank.

Amara remembers it too. Her amazement at all he had done, the gratitude, so overwhelming it felt like love. And Philos, standing in the shadows when Rufus lifted her into his arms. She can recall his presence at that moment so clearly. Had she felt something for him, even then? She turns to kiss Rufus, to tell him she loves him, but then she sees the guilt in his eyes. His nostalgia is for a relationship he knows is over. Fear grips her, and the words spill out. "I'm pregnant."

"*What?*" Rufus almost knocks her off the couch in shock. It was not, admittedly, how she had planned to tell him.

"I'm carrying your child."

"How? When?" He is staring at her in horror, eyes wide as an actor's mask.

Amara looks down, twisting the material of her discarded tunic in her fingers. "I haven't bled for two months. I didn't want to alarm you, unless I was sure."

"Alarm me?" Rufus is shouting. "You've no *idea* how bad the timing is. You could not have chosen a worse possible moment!"

"I'm sorry." She pulls the tunic up to cover herself, wrapping her arms protectively around her stomach. "I didn't mean to upset you."

Rufus breathes deeply, making an effort to calm himself. "I shouldn't have shouted. But this is not... ideal."

"I don't expect you to recognize the child. Not formally. But I hoped it wouldn't displease you this much."

"Of course I can't recognize it! My father will be beyond furious if I start parading some little Greek bastard around the place." He hunches over, as if he might be sick. "Two days ago, I got engaged. And now this."

"You're engaged?"

"The bride's family is very traditional." Rufus makes no effort to spare her feelings. "I'm sure they will be overjoyed their precious daughter is marrying a man who just got a concubine pregnant."

"But they must know you have a mistress."

"Nobody minds a man having a few girlfriends before he marries. They even tolerated my foolishness over you at the Floralia. But not *this* sort of indiscretion."

Rufus has his head in his hands, still leaning over the couch. Amara tentatively strokes his back, and when he doesn't shake her off, she gently kneads his shoulders. "I promise you I won't make this difficult," she says, her voice soft. "I don't want to bring you shame, I never did. I can live quietly with Julia. You don't have to pay much, just enough for me to survive. Philos would be a suitable servant to care for the child, and educate it. Beyond that, I needn't trouble you at all."

He sighs, his shoulders sagging. "You're a good girl. I'm sorry if I said anything unkind." He pauses, letting her massage him. "I suppose that would be one way of limiting the damage."

Amara is desperate to press him further, to make him promise to give her Philos, but she cannot draw too much attention to that part of her plan, not yet. "I will move whenever you need me to."

"I don't mean to throw you out." Rufus finally sounds embarrassed. He sits up, shrugging her hands from his back. "There's no enormous rush." His eyes, when he looks at her, have some of the kindness she remembers from earlier days. "I suppose, at least, this shows my father I can give him an heir. So it's not all bad." He sighs again, more heavily this time. "I just thought you knew how to be *careful* about that sort of thing."

"Nothing works perfectly," Amara says, truthfully enough.

Rufus is staring at her stomach. She wonders if he is going to reach out and touch her, to lay his palm against her skin the way Philos does. Last night, she had fallen asleep while Philos held her like that, lulled by the warmth of the gesture. Now, she is tense, waiting to see what Rufus will do. It is a relief when he turns his back on her, picking up his tunic from the floor.

Amara also dresses, covering the body Rufus so recently enjoyed, unable to fight off a growing sense of shame. "No need to get up." Rufus raises his hands to block her embrace. "And no rush. But maybe speak to Julia. Just to see when one of her apartments will be free."

Rufus leaves, and she draws her legs up onto the couch, curling herself into as small a space as possible. She did not feel the euphoria she expected when Rufus raised no objection to her taking Philos. Instead, Amara's feelings are closer to grief, knowing that they will always be under threat, unable to acknowledge one another, their lives strung together by nothing more than a fragile fabric of lies.

39

There is indeed some truth in that line of Callimachus: 'To little people, the gods will always give little.'
Artemidorus, The Interpretation of Dreams

Amara has never sat with Phoebe and Lais in the tablinum. There was never the need for the formality, and perhaps too, she did not want to remember Felix, to sense the echo of his position as pimp. The two women stand close together, facing Amara across the desk. Lais looks wary and Phoebe afraid.

"I have cancelled all the remaining bookings, including the party tonight," Amara says. "The risk to you both is too great."

Phoebe breathes out with relief, but Lais stiffens, understanding the implications. "Are we to be sold?"

Amara sees Lais tighten her grip on Phoebe's hand. "No. But you will have to leave this house. Drusilla will take you to her new home by the port. Her patron enjoys music, and she believes his household is large enough to absorb you both." Amara does not add what else Drusilla said: *If not, I will sell them.* "I'm very sorry. I had hoped that you might both work for me longer, that you might even find patrons."

"Like you." Lais smiles, but Amara sees the dislike in her eyes.

Lais's hatred does not anger Amara; it only pulls her back further into the past. She looks at the women before her, the women she has sold to so many men, and sees herself and Dido standing before Felix. "I pray to Pallas-Athene, to the patron goddess of Attica, that you are never separated." She turns aside, so they cannot see her emotion, and waves her hand to dismiss them. "Josephus will come to collect you this afternoon."

When they have gone, Amara does not move from her chair. She stares straight ahead, the painted doves on the lintel wavering as she blinks the tears away. The chest below the window to her bedchamber blurs into a dark shape, like a figure crouched on the floor. "Victoria," she says aloud to the empty room.

Tears stream down Amara's cheeks, and she wipes them away. It would be so much easier if she could hate her friend, rather than feel this endless, bottomless grief.

Philos still comes to Amara's room in secret at night, the pair of them now drawn together more by fear than passion. They sit huddled together on the bed, leaning their backs against the wall, repeating the same conversation they have had so many times before.

"I can't be worth all that much, with this," Philos whispers, gesturing at the place where his brand lies under the tunic. "He could never sell me at a public auction. That type of mark takes *thousands* off a slave's value. I think you should just ask for me as a gift."

"But then there's no proof you no longer belong to him, is there? Won't that make it harder for me to free you?"

"You wouldn't be able to do that for years anyway. It would look far too suspicious."

"But if I don't free you, what's the point?"

"The point is I would be with you; I would be a father. That's more important to me than being free. The child changes everything, Amara."

"Rufus can't say no, can he?" Amara has asked Philos this same question hundreds of times. "He didn't seem to mind the idea of you coming to look after the child; he didn't say no to me then. Surely, he has to agree. He has to say yes to me. He *has* to."

"Don't get upset," Philos says, putting his arms around her, pulling her close. "It's not your fault, whatever he does."

Philos's words do not calm her. She can feel the panic surging through her body as she grips on to him, staring into the shadows over his shoulder. Neither of them are worth much to anyone other than each other, and yet, this does not mean they will have a greater chance of escaping notice, or punishment. Amara has not felt this crushing sense of powerlessness since she was herself enslaved, and although it shames her, sometimes she wishes she did not love Philos, that she did not have to face the consequences of choosing a man who is not free.

In the morning, she turns to where he was lying, even though she knows that side of the bed will be empty.

She reaches out, placing her hand on the cold blanket. It must be close to dawn. The room is still dark, only the birdsong tells her it is no longer night. She hears the scrape of the front door as Juventus opens it to the street, a familiar, soothing sound. Amara closes her eyes, hoping to drift back to sleep, then opens them wide. Juventus is shouting.

Her feet slap onto the cold tiles. She flings a tunic over her head and hurtles out of her bedroom. Martha is standing waiting for her, eyes wide with alarm. Together, they run across the atrium to the door. Juventus is no longer shouting. Instead, he stands with Philos, both of them talking in low, urgent voices.

"What is it?" Amara turns from one man to the other.

"On the doorstep," Philos replies. "Don't look…"

But Amara is already rushing to the door. She sees Britannica's back; the Briton is kneeling over something on the pavement. Amara takes a step closer.

Fabia. The old woman has been dumped on the street, lain across Amara's threshold in a grotesque parody of a guard dog. She is not moving. Beside her, someone has chalked a message. *Infelix*. Unlucky.

Amara looks swiftly to the side – Virgula's store is shut, the street still empty – and scuffs out the writing with the sole of her foot. "Is she…?"

"Inside," Britannica hisses. "We bring her in. Help me."

Juventus, Britannica and Philos carry Fabia inside, nobody speaking. A dark red stain is left on the pavement where the old woman was lying. They lie her down in the atrium. Amara kneels beside her and takes her wrist. "Alive," she breathes.

"We have to stop the bleeding." It is Martha, standing close. "Strip her. Let me dress the wound."

Amara stares up at her maid, surprised by Martha's stillness, her lack of fear. "I will strip her," Amara says. "Fetch some wine. And whatever linen you think you can use as a dressing." Martha hurries from the atrium as Amara bends closer to the old woman's face. "Fabia, can you hear me?" There is no sign of consciousness, but Amara continues speaking to her, as if she might hear. "We are going to remove your clothes. I will get you new ones, if they tear." Britannica hands her a knife. Amara's father was a doctor, but her knowledge of how to treat a major injury is still slight. Her hands shake as she rips away the flimsy, blood-soaked tunic.

Fabia's body is so stained it takes a moment for Amara to find the source. It is a deep cut to her upper arm, still oozing blood. Martha has returned and hands Amara the flagon of wine. She pours it over the wound, pressing the skin to part the lips of skin. More blood seeps out, mingled with the wine. Fabia moans in pain. "Paris."

Amara goes cold. She does not know if Fabia is calling for her son, or naming the man who attacked her. "You're safe," she murmurs, as the old woman slides back into unconsciousness.

Martha is kneeling, inspecting the cut, speaking quietly to herself in Hebrew, a frown on her face as if trying to remember. "I think she has lost too much blood," she says to Amara. "But I will try." With the same rough fingers as Martha dresses Amara's hair, the maid rips the linen, wrapping it around Fabia's arm above the cut, then picks up a wooden spoon she must have brought from the kitchen.

She twists the linen with the spoon to tighten the band, digging deep into Fabia's flesh. The old woman moans again. "It is to help you," Martha assures her. "I will loosen it later." When the tourniquet is in place, she starts ripping up the rest of the linen, bandaging the wound, round and round, until red no longer drips through it onto the floor.

"How often have you done this?" Amara stares at Martha and her swift, brutal movements.

"More times than I can remember, before we fled to Masada. And after that, do you think my people just sat and waited for the Romans to kill them, like dormice in a jar? They died, rather than surrender. May God forgive me for my own cowardice." Martha looks up, and for the first time, Amara sees her. Not the heartsick, silent maid, dragged hundreds of miles across the world to serve, but the woman she must once have been, whose name Amara does not even know. "Ask the Admiral of the Fleet about the brutality of Rome's soldiers, if you do not believe me. Ask him why Jerusalem is now nothing more than ashes." Martha's face is filled with loathing. Amara remembers her serving Pliny in this house, how Martha stood beside him while he tasted the food, giving no sign of what she must have felt. It is perhaps lucky the maid did not poison him.

"I believe you," Britannica says, squatting down beside Martha. The two enslaved women look at one another. "Fabia will live?"

Martha strokes Fabia's hair, more gently than she has ever touched Amara. "If she does, it will only be by the will of Almighty God."

"We should move her to a bed." Amara turns to Philos and Juventus. "Are you able to carry her to Victoria's room?" The men lift Fabia carefully, laboriously taking her up the stairs, Juventus cursing softly as he nearly stumbles.

"It would have been closer to take her there." Martha points to Amara's rooms, where they all know the empty couch lies.

"Rufus," Amara replies. "I don't want him finding any trace of her."

The maid nods. "I will not tell." Her voice is quiet. Martha looks between Amara and Britannica. "Not for you. Not for the old woman. But because I owe *them* nothing."

Amara is with Fabia when she dies in the night, Philos sitting beside her. Fabia never regains consciousness. Her son's name, spoken in the atrium, the only word she gave before passing over to the underworld.

"Felix must have known she told me," Amara whispers, still holding Fabia's hand, even as her skin grows cold, "when Phoebe and Lais did not arrive at Cornelius's house."

"You can't blame yourself. Felix was always going to strike."

Amara says nothing. She feels guilt over Fabia, for what she forced her to tell, and yet she knows it would be no easier to see Phoebe or Lais lying here. Grief burns her eyes. "Victoria."

"Victoria won't have known what Felix would do."

"Perhaps." Amara lays Fabia's hands on her sunken chest, leaning over to kiss the old woman on the forehead. She did not love Fabia, not the way she loved the other women at the Wolf Den, and yet she cared for her. It hurts, knowing that Fabia's hard, brutal life ended like this, with yet more suffering. She prays by all the gods that it was not Fabia's own son who killed her, that instead, Fabia called on Paris for comfort. A sob escapes from her, and Philos lays his hand on her back.

"I will send for her body to be taken outside the town walls in the morning," he says. "We can have her cremated. Her spirit will be at peace, more than she ever was in life."

"Thank you." Amara leans against him, and he slips his arm around her. "We have to leave this house. It will be safer at Julia's complex. All the guards. It's much better protected than here."

"I know."

They sit together in silence, watching over the dead woman. Oil lamps set on the table beside the bed cast their trembling light on the unmoving body, now a senseless mass of fabric and shadows. Death does not feel like an auspicious omen. But it is the reason why Amara will have to call for Rufus, to ask him, finally, the question she and Philos have discussed so many times. Within days, Philos might be released. Or they might be ripped apart.

40

Rivers are analogous in one way to slaves' masters and to judges, because they just do what they want at their own discretion without answering to anyone.

Artemidorus, The Interpretation of Dreams

The house with the golden door is at its most beautiful in the warm glow of early September, but now Amara knows she is leaving, the place feels less substantial, as if the building itself were no more real than one of the paintings on its walls.

The message is sent, calling for Rufus. Amara wanders the house, trying to decide where it is best to receive him. Every room holds a difficult memory. In the end, she decides on the garden. Her hands are trembling too much from nerves to play the harp, so instead, she sits, heart pounding, while she waits.

"You called for me." Amara rises as Rufus strides towards her. There is little warmth in his face, but he looks at her body closely. Perhaps he is hoping to hear she miscarried.

"I have spoken to Julia," she says, as Rufus sits on the

bench beside her. "I thought it better to move as soon as possible. Without any fuss."

Rufus nods. "That might be best. I don't really think I can continue visiting here. Or not when your condition becomes obvious." He takes her hand in his, stroking her fingers. "I'm sorry it has to end, little bird. I promise I have never loved a woman the way I loved you."

Amara's own voice shakes with emotion, though not for the man holding her hand. "I will always love you. Which is why I know I have to let you go." She allows herself to sob then, giving way to all the pent-up terror, the guilt and the grief.

"There, my darling," Rufus soothes, perhaps pleased to be the object of so much heartbreak. "You know I will still look after you. Not like this. But I won't allow you or the child to suffer."

Amara grips his hand. "I don't deserve you."

"I will pay a year's rent to Julia. And a small allowance for you." She waits to hear the amount, but Rufus does not elaborate, and Amara cannot press him over it, not when everything hangs on her next question.

"I was thinking," she says, her heart beating so hard, the thud of it feels like a drum, trapped in her ribcage. "Perhaps I could take Philos to help look after the child. He is educated, and I know he is trustworthy, which will matter when I am so very alone."

"I suppose that's not a bad idea. You know he helped care for me when I was a boy?" Amara shakes her head, as if this information is new to her. "I'm happy to lend him to you a while longer, though I will still need him several hours a week, as before."

The hope that had been rising in Amara's heart plummets back down into panic. "Lend him?" Her voice sounds breathless. "Couldn't you... couldn't you make a gift of him to me?"

"You'll be taking plenty of presents I've given you, all the jewellery. And there's an allowance. Or don't you trust me?"

"Of course I trust you! I just think I might need him for several years – it takes so much time to educate a child. And one slave isn't so much to ask."

"He isn't just *one* slave," Rufus says testily. "He knows my family's entire business, has done for years. Philos probably does more work in an hour than three other servants do in a day."

Amara has known Rufus long enough to recognize when he has made up his mind, when he is on the edge of losing patience, but she is too desperate to leave the subject alone. "Please, my love." She tries to smile. "It would mean so much to me. The last gift I will ever ask from you." She kisses his fingers.

"There was a time you never asked for gifts." Rufus takes back his hand, looking at her with distaste. "When we first met, you never asked for anything – you were grateful just to love me. Or so it seemed."

"Please." It is impossible to keep the edge of hysteria from her voice. "Please do this for me."

"You're so transparent. Do you think I don't know what this is about?" He stands up, and Amara stares, terror expanding in her chest. "You think you can keep Philos a few years and then sell the boy on, don't you? That because he's so valuable to my business, he must be worth something. Well, sorry to ruin your little scheme, but he's *branded*. You'd hardly get any money for him at all."

Panic overwhelms Amara. She grasps at Rufus, pulling at his arm. "I don't want to sell him! Please, if that's what you think, I'll buy him from you or sign a contract. I just want him to look after the child. Please. I'm begging you. *Please*."

"I've said you can borrow him!" Rufus shouts. "And that's an end to it, don't try my patience." Amara's legs feel unsteady, and she sits back down. The garden blurs, a roaring in her head drowning out the thud of her heartbeat. She grasps the bench, leaning over to stop herself from blacking out. "I understand your condition, the funny notions and moods it can give a woman." Rufus's voice is gentler. "I don't want to argue, little bird." She feels him sit beside her again. He starts to stroke her back, making her stiffen. "Let's not spoil the last days we have together." Amara knows that she needs to control herself, to force herself to sit up and smile, to thank him for his generosity. But she cannot move or speak. "Fine then." She hears Rufus pause after he gets up, knows he is standing beside her, but she keeps her eyes screwed shut, her head between her hands. His footsteps slap, hard and impatient, as he leaves the garden.

The fountain continues its gentle murmur long after Rufus has left the house. Amara remains where he left her. Then she feels the stir in the air brought by another's approach, the warmth of a hand on her shoulder, and knows Philos is before her. She feels him crouch down. If she looks up, his face will be level with hers.

"Amara." She does not answer. "I heard how hard you tried." Philos lifts her chin with his fingers. The resignation on his face is like the cold flat of a blade against her heart. "Not everything is lost – we may still have years together. More than many are ever granted."

It is an effort to drag her voice through her throat. "It's not enough."

"It's what we have." Philos reaches out to stroke her face, but Amara does not respond. All she can think of is how badly she has failed him. Even the terrible risk she has taken with her body, her life, has done nothing more than buy them a handful of years. He kisses her on the forehead, neither of them caring who might see. "Any time I have with you is still more happiness than I ever imagined."

Somewhere beneath the suffocating layers of guilt, Amara senses the sharp edge of her anger. "It's not enough," she repeats. "How can you call it happiness? A half-life, constantly hiding in the shadows, everything resting on the goodwill of a man who could destroy us any moment he chooses."

"My life has never been anything else." Amara knows it is true. Her belief that she could free Philos and outwit Fate a second time hangs between them, as insubstantial as smoke. He takes her hands in his. "I'm sorry. I tried to warn you."

Philos is still crouched beside her, and the guilt in his face pains her more than anything else. "You have nothing to be sorry for, *nothing*." She grips his fingers more tightly. "We can try again. It might take a few years, but I'm not giving up. I won't rest until you are free, even if it takes everything I have."

★ ★ ★

Amara stands in the atrium, choosing the same spot where she once stood with Dido, the pair of them watching the house being assembled. Now it is being taken apart. Most of the furniture has already gone; all the rooms upstairs have been stripped bare, the couches removed from the dining room. Rufus has offered to lend her some furniture to take to Julia's apartment, but the new place is so much smaller, most of it won't fit.

Martha has already left, absorbed back into Rufus's household along with the brass table, the lampstands and the silver mirror. Amara watches Britannica and Philos carry the last of her bags across the atrium, placing them down carefully by the door. When the three of them have left, Juventus will remain at the house, alone, guarding it from thieves, until the new tenant arrives, and he too is called back into Rufus's service.

Amara looks up. The square of sky lets in the light and warmth of the September sun. From here, the heavens look impossibly far above her. A flock of sparrows fly over, small black arrows set against the vibrant blue, and she thinks of Pliny, when he compared her to birds which cannot sing in captivity. This house has been a haven compared to the brothel, but Amara is starting to believe she will never be free.

"Ready?" It is Britannica, not Philos, who calls to her.

"I think I will take one last look at the garden," Amara replies, surprised at how calm her voice sounds. She walks towards the light, grateful neither Britannica, nor Philos, offer to accompany her.

The heat hits her before she walks into the sunlight. Amara steps out onto the baking paving stones. White, yellow and purple flowers bloom in the herb garden she planted with Philos, and their scent sweetens the air, reminding her of her father's house. She is sad to leave the plants she has tended so carefully, but they are not the reason for her final visit. Amara looks up at Dido. The painter, Priscus, did his job faultlessly, and yet, for the first time Amara regrets that she immortalized her friend in such a brutal way. She hears Victoria's voice in her head, remembers how she turned aside in horror. *What have you done?*

The sun is scorching, beating down on her head, yet Amara does not move. She gazes at Dido, trying to screen out the scene of death she had painted around her. How little Amara cares, now, for vengeance against Felix. As if it ever mattered. As if it would ever have brought Dido back. Amara places her hand over her stomach, which is just beginning to show the first signs of swelling. She prays to the goddess Diana, in the guise of her friend, asking for protection for her child, for Britannica and for Philos. For the people who matter more to her than freedom, more than her own life.

Amara turns her back on Dido for the last time, the gentle murmur of the fountain and her own footsteps the only sound as she walks into the shade of the atrium. She joins Philos and Britannica at the door. They will both accompany her to Julia's complex before returning to the house for her belongings. Britannica did not want to risk Felix attacking Amara when their hands were full.

Amara gives Juventus a coin, pressing it into his palm. "Thank you for your service."

Juventus looks down to check the amount, nods at her in thanks, then stows it beside his belt. There is no love between the pair of them, but in the end, no great animosity either. The porter steps past Amara to perform his last act of service. He draws back the bolts, the metal scraping against the wood, and yanks the door inwards, letting in the light and noise of the street. Amara, Britannica and Philos step out onto the pavement. For a moment, Amara is mesmerized by the bustle, her eyes scanning passers-by, searching for Felix or Paris. There is no trace of them, but that does not mean she is safe. She thinks of Fabia, lying bleeding on the very stones where she is standing, and shudders.

Amara turns to take one last look back into her house, but all she sees is the door swinging towards her. She hears the bolt slam across from the inside. The wood panels rise, impossibly tall, with their brass skin of studs, as impenetrable as any wall. Her time at the house with the golden door has ended.

AD 76
NOMINALIA

41

The sin is sweet, to mask it for fear of shame is bitter
I'm proud we're joined, each worthy of the other.

Sulpicia, Roman woman poet

The room is small and dark. Wintry light filters through the shutters, letting in the sound of the street below. Amara feels a familiar rolling pressure against her stomach. The baby is moving. She lays her hand over the taut skin, wondering if the being beneath feels the answering pressure of her fingers. The exhaustion of pregnancy has been a source of unwelcome surprise, the energy she once took for granted sapped by the life growing inside her.

She can hear noises from the room below. Britannica must be back home with the morning's bread. Leaning on her elbow to take some of the strain, Amara levers herself out of bed. Her belly is enormous now, a constant pressure under her narrow ribcage. Sound and the freezing February air stream in when she opens the shutters. She peers down onto the street far below, the tops of people's heads passing beneath her like fish in a stream. A peddler is bellowing near the entrance to the Venus Baths, shoving his wares in the faces of anyone who passes close enough. Amara ducks back into the shade of the bedroom, crossing the rough wooden floor, and makes her way carefully down the stairs.

Britannica is busy at the small brazier in the corner, heating water for their daily draught of hot mint and honey. She glances up at Amara. "How is Fighter?"

Amara is amused by Britannica's passion for the baby, her unerring belief she is carrying a warrior. "Kicking," she replies, sitting on a stool.

"Good." Britannica sits beside her, setting down two steaming cups on the small wooden table. "I hear Philos go out early. Before dawn."

"He's working for Julia this morning. He wanted to get her accounts done before he has to be with Rufus."

"Lucky she pay him."

Amara gives a tight smile and picks up a cup, blowing on the hot liquid. Rufus's allowance is not as generous as they had hoped. Julia knows it and is bending the rules by paying Amara for Philos's labour, rather than his true owner, Rufus. At Amara's instruction, the money is given directly into Philos's hands, not hers; she remembers how it felt when she was enslaved, not entitled to anything she earned. Philos is supporting his family with money he has made himself, and that's what he deserves to feel. Rufus's words come back to her, making the sweet drink taste bitter. *Philos does more work in an hour than three other servants do in a day.*

"I could make you money." Britannica sips from her cup.

"I've told you; I'm not selling you as a gladiator. When I can free you, *then* you can fight."

Britannica reaches for the bread, handing Amara a chunk

and taking one for herself. "You need to get outside today. Walk to make the baby come."

"I will spend some time in the garden." Amara looks down at the crumbling hunk in her hand. It is a constant source of tension between them both – how little she dares leave this darkened house. Just walking down the street is enough to make her sweat with fear, constantly searching for familiar features in the crowd, in case Felix, or one of his henchmen, is following. It has been like this since Fabia's murder, more than six months ago, and anxiety for the child she is carrying is a much heavier burden for Amara than simply protecting her own life.

"In the garden, you just sit. Need to move," Britannica grumbles, and as if to illustrate her point, she rises, picking up a broom to sweep the floor. She darts it vigorously by Amara's feet, forcing her to shift them. "You think when Fighter is here, you feel safer out? What you do? Stay inside forever?"

"Don't. Just leave it, please." Amara leans back against the wall, turning away. Ignoring Britannica is not easy. This room is even smaller than the one she and Philos share upstairs. The walls are painted in blocks of colour, with the occasional tiny bird to break up the monotony. There is no atrium, no dining room or study, and the windows let in very little light. Yet, Amara is still happier staying inside than wandering Pompeii. It is not only about her safety. In this house, her relationship with Philos is real. Outside, she cannot acknowledge him, and instead inhabits the role of the abandoned concubine.

"Then go to garden." Britannica clunks the brush at her feet. "Now." Amara gets up, clutching her cup, but her attempt to stomp furiously out of the flat turns into a lumbering waddle.

Livia is chatting to one of the other tenants when Amara reaches the garden. The sky is a dull, heavy grey, and the stone path shines, still wet from the earlier rainfall. Amara picks her way along it carefully, not wanting to slip.

"Darling!" Livia exclaims, waving at her. "Flavia has been telling me about the most shocking theft at the painters. Her poor husband had half his pigment stolen. Imagine."

"How dreadful," Amara murmurs. She still struggles to remember the names of all Julia's tenants, some of whom she suspects are not entirely delighted to rub shoulders with an unmarried, pregnant freedwoman.

"Just as he was about to start a new commission," Flavia says, hands fluttering in distress. "Now everything has been delayed."

The breeze brings with it a damp mist. Amara glances at the canal, the surface of the water dimpled by drizzle. Livia notices too. "You should get under cover," she says, taking Amara's arm. "You don't want to catch a chill in your condition." The gesture does not exclude Flavia, but it does not invite her either.

"I had better get on," Flavia says, nodding to them both. "Sorry to have kept you."

Livia's grip is firm as she steers Amara towards the colonnade. "You should be careful, coming out in the damp. Julia will fret when she gets back from the baths. Perhaps you should pop over there to warm up?"

"I barely got wet," Amara protests. "And Britannica just made me a hot drink." She waves the cup at Livia.

"Good. I'm glad *somebody* is looking after you." Livia

pulls Amara into one of the rooms off the garden, sitting her down on a stool by the brazier and pulling another up for herself. "His new bride is nothing to look at, you know," she says in a low voice, and Amara knows immediately who Livia means. The respectable girl Rufus has married, barely more than a child, or so Julia told her.

"I hope they will be happy," Amara says.

"*I* don't. Or not him anyway." Livia snorts. "I always thought he was the most disingenuous boy. You'd be much better suited to somebody older, darling, someone who knows how to appreciate a woman."

"Maybe I don't want a man at all," Amara says. "You and Julia manage perfectly well."

"Careful," Livia says, but there is a trace of laughter in her voice. "Not everyone is so fortunate. All of us have to compromise. Everyone except Julia, that is."

"Not you?"

"Without Julia, I would have no freedom at all. She is everything to me." Livia looks uncharacteristically serious. "Women are rarely blessed with a choice, Amara, and I know how lucky I am. You would be wise to let Julia guide you, and to trust her."

"Of course," Amara says, dutifully bowing her head. She does not allow Livia to see the unease that flickers across her face.

Dusk has fallen and Amara is already in bed by the time Philos arrives home. She can hear the murmur of his voice below, the scrape and clink of bowls as Britannica serves him the remains of the soup she brought in for them all.

It's likely the only food Philos will have eaten all day. Amara considers getting up to join them both, but her head aches, and her body is unbearably heavy and cumbersome. Instead, she lies in the dark, waiting for the sound of Philos's footsteps on the stairs, the gentle creak of the door as he tries to slip in without disturbing her. The light of his lamp creeps into the room before him.

"That was a long day."

He walks over to the bed, setting down the lamp and bending to kiss her. "I hope I didn't wake you."

"No, I was only resting." She watches Philos take off his tunic, draping it over her clothes which already lie on a stool, before he extinguishes the light and climbs beneath the covers. The feel of his skin against hers is comforting. He holds her, resting a hand on her stomach. "I think the baby's sleeping for once," she says, knowing he is hoping for the reassurance of movement under his fingers. "I'm sorry you were kept working so long."

"The election means Rufus is leaving even more for me to do than usual. It won't last forever." All the hours Philos works, yet he is only paid for a handful of them. Years of his life, taken.

"Does he ever ask…?"

"No. He's too busy with his new bride. And that's safer. The less attention he pays to you, the more likely he is to leave us alone." Philos curls himself more tightly around her. "You've not had any pains or anything, have you? It must be very soon. You're *enormous*. Like a dormouse fattened up for the Saturnalia."

Amara laughs, as he intends her to. "Very flattering, thank you." She places her hand over his, their fingers interlacing.

"The midwife says it's likely to be soon." He squeezes her hand, and Amara can sense his fear, the dread she knows he feels at the approaching birth. A dread she shares. "I was thinking," she says. "Maybe in the house, when we are alone, we could use our real names."

"No." His answer is so swift she is taken aback. "It's too dangerous. Imagine if one of us used the wrong one by mistake? How suspicious that would look."

"I suppose." She waits, hoping he will at least ask for her name, or share his own. He doesn't. "Don't you want to know what my father called me?"

"Only if you want to share it."

It is not the most inviting reply. Amara hesitates, then speaks in Greek. "My name is Timarete." The sound of her own name, of who she really is, brings a lump to her throat.

"Timarete," Philos repeats softly, and she is touched by the effort he makes to pronounce each syllable correctly. "Honour and virtue. That's what it means in Greek, isn't it?"

"Yes. My father's hopes for the name influencing my character went somewhat awry."

"That's not true. Timarete is beautiful. It suits you better than Amara." He leans over and kisses her on the cheek.

She waits, hoping now he will share his own name. But he is silent, only stroking her hair, perhaps offering affection in place of the knowledge he does not wish to give. "Can't you tell me what your parents called you? I'd like to know."

"I was named by my owner. It's not the same."

"But it's still the name you knew as a child. You must have felt some attachment to it. More than to the one you have now." The name Terentius gave him.

Philos stops caressing her hair. "Can we leave it, please. Or am I not allowed to keep *anything* to myself?"

"How unreasonable of me to want to know the name of the man whose child I'm carrying," Amara retorts, hurt by his rejection. "It's not exactly a terrible thing to ask." She pulls away, hunching over, arms cradling her stomach. There is a long pause.

"It's Rufus."

"You can't blame *everything* on him."

"No. That was my name. So I think it's rather obvious why I couldn't keep it."

Amara turns to face him, struggling to shift herself with the weight of her belly. "I'm sorry."

"Don't be. You're right – it's not a terrible question to ask. I just don't have a happy answer to give you."

"I only asked because I know Philos was..." She stops, not wanting to make things worse by mentioning the man who abused him for so many years.

"Terentius gave Greek names to all his favourites. I suppose I should be grateful another boy was already stuck with Eros, though I always hated Philos, at least until I met you. Now I quite enjoy hearing you call me *beloved* in your own language." Amara kisses him, and he smooths his thumb against her cheek. "Sometimes, I think about when our child is older, when we won't be able to be like this anymore, because we will have to pretend, even in the house, that I'm nothing to you. And when that happens, you can still tell me you love me, every time you say my name."

Amara holds him, glad of the darkness that hides her tears.

42

*To see one's face reflected in a dish signifies fathering
children with a slave girl. But if this dream is seen by
someone who is himself a slave, we must conclude
the dish reflects his own slavery.*

Artemidorus, The Interpretation of Dreams

Her pains start in the deepest hours of the night. They
rouse Amara from sleep – the claws that clamp down
on her, then release. She stares into the dark. Nothing. Then
the pain hits again, and her eyes widen. Not agony, but a
warning, the distant rumble of thunder before a storm.

Philos is sleeping. The slow, steady rhythm of his breathing
like a caress. She does not wake him yet, but instead presses
a little closer to the warmth of his body, drawing comfort
from his presence. It was a lie, what she once told him, that
this child was as much for her. Amara had no desire to be a
mother when she fell pregnant, no desire for all the changes
to her body, the risk to her life, the shadow a dependent
child will cast. And yet, over the months, something shifted.
The love she feels for Philos – that constant, painful ache in
her chest – began to take in the life she is carrying.

Pain surges again, and she gasps. Philos stirs. He murmurs her name, a question half dragged from sleep.

"I think it's starting," she whispers.

In an instant, he is fully awake. He sits up in the bed. "Are you alright? Do I need to send for the midwife?"

"No." She takes his hand to reassure him. "We can wait until morning. This stage lasts hours, when the pains are still far apart." His breathing is no longer steady, and even in the darkness, she can see the fear in his eyes. "I'm not frightened," she says. It is almost true. She has dreaded this moment for so long, yet now it is here, she feels relief.

The hours of the night pass, and it is only the two of them in that dreamlike threshold between her old life and her new. Between the birthing pangs, Amara is able to talk and move as if nothing is happening, but slowly, the pains grow on her, the spaces shortening. She becomes restless, walking around the room to ease the discomfort, or sitting upright in the bed, panting. The child inside her is awake, and when she is still, Philos rests his hand on her stomach, as if he might comfort them both.

Dawn approaches, and they both lapse into silence, knowing that after he leaves to fetch the midwife, they will not see each other again until it is over. He dresses in the grey darkness, birdsong and the rumble of carts drifting in from the street. Philos no longer looks afraid; his face is unnaturally calm when he crouches by the bedside to kiss her goodbye. "It will all be well," he says. "I will send Britannica up to you now, before I go for the midwife. And after that, I will be downstairs the whole time. It is what Rufus instructed."

Amara nods, not allowing herself to show any emotion

either. Nothing that will acknowledge that they might not see each other again.

Pain hits her in time with the gentle click of the latch as he leaves, and she has to stifle a groan. Sweat dampens her skin. She wills the panic beneath the surface, closing her eyes and breathing deeply as the pressure fades again. In the lull between pangs, she hears the murmur between Philos and Britannica downstairs, then the heavy thump of the Briton's steps on the stairs.

"What you need?" Britannica is breathless, her face bright with anticipation. How she might once have looked on the eve of battle. It immediately makes Amara feel stronger.

"Some bread, the hot mint and honey. I need to eat while I can, to get through this."

Britannica nods, heading back down the stairs. Amara goes to the shutters, opening them, the breath hissing through her teeth as another pang hits. She clutches the window ledge until it passes. Sunrise is casting its pink glow, staining the rooftops a deeper shade of orange, the mountain a hazy blue in the distance.

She resumes her pacing, up and down the tiny room until Britannica joins her again. The Briton hovers, watching her eat and drink. "You want me to stay with you? For the birth?"

"Yes, please stay." Amara trusts that Valentina the midwife is good at what she does – she came with the highest recommendation from Drusilla – but she still does not want to be left alone with near strangers. A pounding from below makes her start. "That's her," she whispers to Britannica. "She's here."

★ ★ ★

The thunder that woke her in the night is nothing to the storm that engulfs Amara as she is drawn, inexorably, into the agony of childbirth. There are times she wants to claw a way out of her own body, digging her nails deep into her thighs, crouched on Valentina's enormous wooden birthing chair. The midwife's two nameless attendants try to soothe her, stroking her back, murmuring platitudes about the healthy son she will bear her patron. Amara cannot bear their touch, cannot bear the feel of fabric on her skin, keeps pulling off the blanket which Valentina has draped over her knees to protect her modesty.

"I'm a whore," Amara snarls, when Valentina tries to cover her yet again. "I don't give a shit about that!"

The midwife, no doubt used to all manner of behaviour in the birthing chamber, does not persist, nodding at one of the attendants to remove the blanket from the floor where Amara has hurled it. "It will be very soon now," she says, her voice deep and calm. "You need to stop fighting yourself."

Amara screams as another wave of agony rips through her. It is not only her body which is opening, the pain is searing her mind apart, emptying it of everything but that brutal, unstoppable rhythm. Valentina is kneeling between her knees. "Next time, I want you to push as you feel it coming, push with everything you have." The midwife's words are barely over before Amara is screaming again. Surely death itself would be less terrifying than this. "You are still fighting against yourself. Ride the wave when you feel it coming, push the pain out of your body."

"I can't," Amara moans. "I can't."

She feels someone grip her hand, the pressure on her finger so hard, somehow it reaches her. "You are strong,"

Britannica says. Amara looks at her, keeps staring into the Briton's eyes as the next wave builds, then turns all her focus on the pain. She screams, not with terror, but with rage, pushing down with the ferocity that has always ensured her survival.

"Keep going," the midwife says. "You are doing it – the baby is almost here." This time, when she feels the wave coming, Amara pushes down with all her strength just before it hits, obliterating the agony. She is no longer at the mercy of the storm, but mastering it. "You're nearly there. You are doing well." Amara does not allow herself to feel the exhaustion which clings to her like sweat. The pain builds again, and she uses every last reserve of strength to push, clutching Britannica's hand so hard she hears the Briton cry out. The child kicks hard inside her, then slides into Valentina's arms.

A moment of stunned silence, followed by a howl. Valentina laughs. "Angry, like her mother."

Amara is so exhausted, she almost does not have the energy to lean forwards to see her own child. Her daughter. She tries to look at where the midwife is crouched, but there is fire between her legs, burning as she moves. "Is she healthy?"

Valentina has laid the baby on a blanket on the floor, inspecting her, massaging her limbs, poking at her. The child wails furiously at every prod. Amara winces at the sound. "She is healthy," Valentina says at last. "I cannot see any defect. There is no reason to dispose of her." Amara reaches out, wanting to hold her, but Valentina hands the baby to an attendant, also crouched near Amara's feet. "Lean back in the chair and breathe out slowly for me." Valentina presses down firmly on Amara's stomach, the cord taut in her hands. "And again." A weight shifts through Amara's body, as the heavy burden she has been carrying for so many months slides from her. The midwife smiles in relief. The most dangerous part of the labour is over.

"Please, I want to hold her."

"I will bring her to you in the bed, after she has been bathed."

Desperate to see the child, Amara tries to stand, but to her shock, she cannot. All the strength left her body with the birth. One of Valentina's attendants caresses her shoulder, murmuring at her to wait. Water splashes Amara's skin – the woman is cleaning her. It is then she sees the blood. There is so much of it: pooled across the floor, splattered on her own legs, soaked into blankets. The aftermath of violence. Amara thinks of Felix, of all the blood he has spilled, yet his strength, his power, is a shadow. It takes nothing to end life, everything to give it. The attendant mistakes the look on Amara's face. "That's all from the birth," she soothes. "You are not bleeding too heavily now. The worst is past."

With Britannica's help, she staggers to the bed, yet more linen wrapped around her body to staunch the flow. She watches as Valentina massages oil and fenugreek onto her baby's delicate skin, before gently sponging it off with water. The child shouts in protest, and Amara's body aches with longing. By the time her daughter is finally brought to her, tightly swaddled, Amara is close to tears.

The baby's tiny face is red and rumpled, her mouth squashed into a pout, blue eyes wide and blinking. She looks both strange and familiar. Amara strokes her daughter's head, covered with soft down, and tears stream down her face.

Britannica leans over to look. "Like a frog," she says, grinning. Amara snorts, and the two women give way to their relief with a flood of mirth that borders on hysteria. Valentina exchanges glances with her attendants.

"Will your patron wish me to call on him in person?" Valentina's choice of words is careful. The baby will never legally have a father, but Rufus's informal recognition and support at least means Amara retains some vestige of her status as a concubine.

"No, I think not. He asked to be informed by his steward." Amara thinks of Philos, waiting downstairs, and tears again threaten to overwhelm her.

"What message shall I give the steward to take from you?"

"That he has a healthy girl and, if he is willing, I propose naming her Rufina. In honour of her father."

In the hours after Rufina's birth, Amara cannot sleep, in spite of her exhaustion. There is no wet nurse – she could not afford one – and so instead, she rests the baby on her own breast, trying to encourage her to feed. Valentina dispenses advice, and lotions, in case Amara's milk is late or her breasts become sore, while the attendants burn incense to sweeten the air. Britannica brings Amara stew and holds the baby, murmuring words of encouragement at the small being who she still calls Fighter.

It is a long, agonizing wait before Philos can visit. Amara sends Britannica to fetch him the moment Valentina has left, her heart thudding as she hears his footsteps hurrying up the stairs. Then he is standing in the doorway, and in spite of all the uncertainty they face, at that moment, Amara feels nothing but joy.

Philos sits beside her, slipping his arm around her shoulders and pressing a kiss to her forehead. She can feel the intensity of his relief.

"Do you want to hold her?"

He nods, staying completely still while Amara carefully transfers Rufina into his arms. "She's so *tiny*." Philos stares at the child, as if he is unable to believe what he is seeing. He holds her with such tenderness that Amara's heart, already bruised from all the emotion, aches even more. "You didn't pass any message on for Rufus about your own health. I had to ask Valentina if you were safe, and she *promised* me you will be fine. She swore it. You are fine, aren't you?"

"Yes, just very tired."

"You can sleep now. I'll look after her; you rest." He bends to kiss Rufina then gazes at her, awestruck. "She's so perfect."

"Britannica thinks she looks like a frog."

Philos laughs. "Maybe a bit. But a perfect frog."

"She certainly kicked like one on the way out." Amara eases herself downwards so that she is lying, rather than sitting, on the bed. Philos is humming softly to his daughter, and she watches them both, her shattered body finally relaxing now he is here. She closes her eyes, telling herself it will only be for a moment, before falling deeply asleep.

43

*Show me a man who isn't a slave; one is a slave to sex, another
to money, another to ambition; all are slaves to hope or fear.*

Seneca, Letters from a Stoic

The first night after the birth is the last unbroken sleep
Amara is granted. The savage rhythm of the baby's
nights drags her to a state of exhaustion beyond any she
could have imagined. Rufina's screaming wakes them
hourly, and by the third night, when Philos yet again hands
her the baby to feed, Amara sobs and tries to hide her head
under the blanket.

Philos is also hollowed out by exhaustion, no longer light
on his feet, but staggering clumsily to dress himself as he
struggles from the house at dawn, working solidly until
nightfall, when their torment begins again.

The days of celebration and family visits that would
follow the birth of a child if Amara were married, or rich, are
instead a strange state of seclusion. Britannica waits on her,
even learning how to wash and swaddle Rufina, ensuring
Amara has nothing to do other than feed the baby or sleep.
Julia, too, makes Amara feel less alone. Her landlady visits

every morning, bringing Amara gifts of food or toys, and a few days after the birth, Julia insists Amara join her in the garden.

They sit together, heaped in blankets, the baby sleeping peacefully on her mother in cruel contrast to her wakeful nights.

"You must decide who you will invite to the naming ceremony," Julia says, reaching out to sip the sweet wine on the table beside her.

"I wasn't sure it would be appropriate for me to hold one."

"Nonsense!" Julia waves her glass for emphasis, the dark liquid splashing against the side. "If you are worried about the size of the flat, I am happy to host it." Julia is too polite to mention that Amara might also be afraid of the cost.

"You are so kind, but you've done too much for me already."

"Amara, you are going to have to learn to be more like my mother. Never turn down a gift. It's hard enough bringing an illegitimate child into the world, without standing on pride."

Rufina sighs deeply in Amara's arms, a contented, snuffling breath. Julia watches, an unusually soft look in her eyes, as Amara settles her.

"What was she like, your mother?"

"Ah." Julia gazes across the garden, as if picturing another figure standing there, and although she smiles, her expression is shaded with melancholy. "She was the best and the worst person you can imagine. But it's fair to say she taught me everything I know, and not a day passes when I am not grateful to her."

"Did your father always support her?"

"He did. Though she never got over the bitterness when he ceased to use her as a concubine and pensioned her off. I must have been about ten at the time. Before that, she was a great pet of his, and her life revolved around his happiness. He gave her this house. I can remember him here, in the garden. When he arrived, he would fling out his arms and expect us to come running, to hang off his every word." She laughs, seeing Amara's expression. "It wasn't only for show. I did love my father. And as his only surviving child, I have enjoyed privileges which are unimaginable for most illegitimate daughters."

"Did your mother love him?"

"Yes, which was unfortunate. He had bought her when she was very young, and later freed her as his concubine. He was always generous, but my father really did not deserve the godlike worship my mother lavished on him. No man does. A mistake she was later determined her daughter would not repeat." Julia takes another sip of her wine. "A mistake you did not, perhaps, make with Rufus."

"I thought I loved him once."

"Until you learned of the contract?" Amara nods, not wanting to share the real moment her affection died. "I must admit that surprised even an old cynic like me. But you are quite safe now that he is married. He cannot revoke your freedom. And eventually, perhaps soon, you will find another patron."

Julia's meaningful look makes Amara uneasy. She has no intention of leaving Philos, but can hardly say so, given Julia knows nothing of the relationship. "I'm sure men will be flocking to the door of an abandoned concubine with an infant daughter."

Julia laughs. "How naïve you can be. Do you not think proof of fertility makes you valuable? And you are hardly abandoned, darling. For all his faults, Rufus still recognizes you. You have the admiral's name. And I like to think *my* friendship does not count for nothing."

"It counts for everything. Truly, I do not know what I would have done without your support."

"She's not obliging you to *gush* over her, is she?" It is Livia's sharp voice behind Amara, and she turns her head as Livia saunters over and bends to look at Rufina. "Hello, little frog," Livia says, her face dimpling with an affectionate smile. She sits next to Julia, leaning against her, and Julia lays a hand on Livia's knee. "I hope you don't mind, but I got your steward to sort out a contract for me this morning. Very helpful boy, isn't he? And rather nice eyes."

"As long as you paid him," Julia answers on Amara's behalf.

"Of course I paid!" Livia looks affronted. She helps herself to Julia's glass of wine. "He told me once the election is over, he will be responsible for caring for the child."

Amara knows from this that Livia must have given Philos a determined grilling, since he never volunteers anything about their lives. "Yes, that's true. He once helped educate Rufus."

"Really? I wouldn't have thought he was old enough. He's awfully pretty."

"I hope you didn't flirt with the poor boy." Julia is looking at Livia with her eyebrows raised. A charged look passes between them, close to amusement but darker. Livia smiles.

"You know I'd never do that." She lays her hand over Julia's. The gesture is so intimate that Amara looks down at Rufina, fussing over her, pretending she hasn't seen.

That evening, when Amara tells Philos about Julia's proposal to host a naming ceremony, he is surprisingly keen on the idea. They sit together in the bed, Philos with his arm resting behind Amara's shoulders, the oil lamp casting long, wavering shadows over the walls. The frescoes in this room are the cheapest type, geometric patterns of black and white, and it is hard to tell paint and shadow apart. Rufina is clamped to Amara's breast for one of her incessant feeds, her tugging both uncomfortable and a release from the pressure of the milk.

"Anything that asserts she is freeborn will make life easier." Philos gently strokes his daughter's toes which are bound beneath the swaddling. "I never imagined a child of mine wearing a *lunula*." There is reverence in the way he says the word. It is the necklace that will signify Rufina's free status, placing her in a different category of human being to her father, and even to her mother, who carries the taint of past enslavement.

"I feel bad that Julia is buying it all though."

"She wouldn't offer unless she wanted to," Philos says. "And I must have saved them a fair amount. Their last contract with the bath's wine supplier was a terrible deal."

"Livia said you helped her today."

"That was for a personal purchase. She certainly likes the finer things in life." Philos sounds amused rather than judgmental.

"I think she took rather a shine to *you*."

He laughs. "I don't think I'm her type. And not just because I'm a slave."

Amara smiles, but the casual mention of his enslavement feels like he is pressing down on a wound which never heals. "I was thinking," she says, shifting the baby to her other breast, "when Rufina is a little older, we should try again to free you. I can ask Rufus as a gesture of thanks for your work in looking after her. Or offer to buy you again. Maybe Julia would lend me the money?"

"We can try that. But I also think we should enjoy the time we have now, rather than constantly agonize over the future." Philos caresses her shoulder where his hand is resting.

"You work so hard, and you are given so little for it."

"But it's enough for us to live on, when you add in Rufus's allowance. And we are together, in relative safety. Many married people don't even have this much."

"I asked Valentina about the midwife training. She wasn't very encouraging."

"Perhaps she doesn't like the thought of competing with a doctor's daughter." Philos kisses her on the temple. "You only gave birth a week ago, my love. I think you are allowed a little time to collect yourself before you start hustling to deliver other people's babies."

Amara chews her lip, anxiety gnawing at her. "But her dowry."

"She's five days old!" Philos laughs. He moves himself, so that he can look into her face, cupping her cheek with his hand. "I know why you worry – I do understand. But she isn't going to have your life, or mine. I promise."

Amara has told Philos about her own journey to slavery, the dowry her parents never saved, forcing her mother to sell her after her father's death rather than see Amara starve. The start of her long, brutal journey to Pompeii, to Felix. "I can't bear that you're not free," she says, unable to keep the words back, even though she knows how much it will hurt him. "Sometimes it feels like I can't breathe."

"I know." He rests his free hand on Rufina, the other still soft against Amara's cheek. "That's why Julia's protection matters so much." Philos does not finish his thought, but Amara still hears it. *In case I am taken from you.*

44

But those you see with figures like to each
And faces like both parents, these have sprung
From the father's body and the mother's blood...
By two hearts breathing as one in mutual passion,
And neither masters the other nor is mastered.

Lucretius, On the Nature of the Universe

Rufus does not attend Rufina's naming ceremony, nor does her real father. Amara is not sure whether this is easier, whether seeing Philos as an unacknowledged slave at his own daughter's Nominalia would have been even more painful than his absence. She had half-expected Rufus to be the one who gave her the lunula, but instead, her former patron sends a lavish platter of fruit and a toy horse on wheels. It is Julia who gives the precious necklace that signifies the baby's freedom – a small crescent moon on a delicate chain. It is made of silver, and seeing the charm against her daughter's skin, Amara feels a slight easing of the pressure on her heart. She starts to believe that Philos is right: this child will not repeat the lives of her parents but will have her own.

The priest chants prayers to purify the child and burns offerings of grain and wine on Julia's altar. He makes predictions for Rufina's future based on the direction of the smoke: a happy marriage, numerous children of her own. Amara suspects the patter is the same for every child's ceremony; no doubt it's what the priest promised her own parents years ago in Aphidnai.

The gathering is very small: Julia, Livia, Britannica, Drusilla and Primus. Amara cannot help but picture those who are missing. She imagines showing her child to her parents, how her mother would have fussed, how her father would have smiled. She imagines too the happiness of seeing Dido hold her daughter. She tries not to think of Beronice or Victoria.

It is several months since Amara last saw Drusilla, but the presence of another child makes the occasion more relaxed. Primus is busy enjoying Rufina's presents, especially the horse on wheels which he clatters back and forth across the tiles. Amara was half-afraid Drusilla would not come, and suspects if the invitation had not been from Julia, she might well have stayed away. Amara is no longer someone it is valuable to know, not to mention she still owes Drusilla money. As it is, Drusilla gives no sign of the cooling of their friendship, but holds Rufina with the ease of a mother, rocking her and smiling.

"Did your parents have eyes this colour? So pretty."

"My father," Amara lies. "But I suspect hers are just an infant's blue. No doubt they will darken in time."

"She has your mouth," Drusilla says, her own curling in a mischievous smile. "I hope she is spared her father's nose."

Julia laughs. "Dear Rufus. He's no Adonis. We must certainly all pray the child follows her mother."

Amara smiles, accepting the compliment. It is too early to see what Rufina will look like – her face is still more frog-like than human – but Amara cannot help seeing traces of Philos. The delicacy of the baby's features, the wide spacing of her blue-grey eyes, giving her a look that is almost feline. *Her eyes will turn brown,* Amara tells herself. "How is married life treating you?" she asks Drusilla.

"Ampliatus has just bought me a loom," Drusilla replies, with a smirk. "To impress visitors with my womanly accomplishments. Though he's yet to wear anything I've woven on it. Even *his* devotion doesn't extend *that* far."

"Are you talking about Papa?" Primus, like all small children, has a gift for eavesdropping. "He promised to play knucklebones with me later."

"And he's adopted Primus."

Julia claps her hands, and all the women exclaim their congratulations. Drusilla nods her head in acknowledgement, her pleasure obvious. Amara is pleased for her but cannot help feeling a stab of envy. Everything about Drusilla proclaims her wealth. The rich fabric of her tunic, the delicate rose scent she wears and, perhaps most of all, her air of contentment. She looks like what she is: a woman who has secured her child's future and her own.

The first weeks of Rufina's life pass both quickly and slowly. The days drift, blending into one another. Philos is gradually able to spend more time at home, and there are moments, when Amara is with him and Britannica, that she can pretend they are a family. At Britannica's insistence, Amara also starts to venture outside Julia's complex. She starts with a brief morning stroll through the marketplace by the arena which backs onto Julia's garden, first with Britannica, then increasingly on her own.

Each day grows a little easier. By the time Rufina is two months old, Amara has become complacent. She wanders the market, weaving between the food stalls, her heart lifting at the sight of so much life around her. She chatters to her child in Greek, lifting her up to see a stall of leather goods, pointing to its hanging charms, the seller smiling indulgently. Hermeros is still selling flowers at the edge of the square, but she does not approach him – the memory of her visits here with Victoria are still too strong.

When she reaches the arena, she pauses to look up at the huge building, sun glinting behind it. Swifter than thought, an arm grips her waist, and she feels the press of something sharp against her ribs. The shock is even greater than the terror.

"Don't scream."

She swivels to see him. Felix's face is calm, broken only by a charming smile, as if he were greeting a dear friend. "I'm not going to hurt you. Not if you are quiet."

"Let go of me." She means to sound commanding, but her voice is a whisper.

"We're going to sit on that bench over there." Felix nods his head to the seat she once shared with Victoria, set against the vineyard wall.

"No." Amara grips Rufina, her chest heaving, panic rising.

"Don't get hysterical." His voice is reasonable, even soothing. "I promise I won't hurt you." He pokes the knife harder against her ribs. "Not unless you resist me."

Amara walks with him across the square, her breath coming in stifled gasps, as if she were drowning. Felix steers her, all the while keeping up a steady, smiling commentary on the stalls they pass – as if he might be helping his exhausted wife to a seat to rest herself.

"That wasn't too bad, was it?" he remarks pleasantly, as they sit beside one another. His arm is still around her, the knife hidden under his cloak.

"What do you want?"

"That's not a very friendly greeting. Aren't you going to ask after Victoria, enquire how my business is doing?"

"Fuck you."

Felix laughs. "I've missed you, Amara."

"If you keep me here, Britannica will come looking for me."

"I've no intention of *keeping* you. I have my own lovely wife now. She gave me a message, by the way, when I told her I was seeing you. Do you want to hear it?"

"I'm not interested in anything Victoria has to say."

"She begs your forgiveness." Amara says nothing, and his expression hardens. "Did you really think I'd leave you alone, that I'd let you laugh in my face? Not that it's only me you're laughing at." Felix throws his head back, as if contemplating the tendrils that trail over the wall. "Can you believe there was a time I once saw you as a rival? What a fool. There you were, spreading your legs for a slave. A *slave*." He laughs so hard, his arm shakes, and she is terrified he will cut her with the knife by accident. "You're even more stupid than my wife. What did he say to you, to make you throw your life away?"

Amara forces herself to keep her face impassive. "I don't know what you're talking about."

"Is that his bastard?" Felix nods at Rufina. Amara clutches her daughter closer, trying to shield her from view. "After Victoria told me, I must admit, I thought it was a fucking lie. That penniless boy who used to pick you up from the brothel. *That's* who you chose?"

"Whatever Victoria told you, it isn't true."

"Is that how you want to play it?" Felix strokes the side of her ribs lightly with the flat of the blade, until she is sitting rigid, her eyes fixed on his. "Do I have your full attention now?" His voice is soft. When Amara does not answer, he presses the knife a little closer.

"Yes," she gasps.

"Good girl." Felix smiles, and hatred sticks in Amara's throat like an olive stone, bitter enough to choke her. "The first time Victoria showed me around your *lovely* home, I was intrigued to see that chest in the tablinum, set right under the window to your bedchamber. I'm sure you know the one I mean. Just the sort of chest a girl like Victoria might be able to stand on, if she wanted to get a good look into your room and see what you were up to at night. Especially since it turns out you were thoughtful enough to keep a lamp burning in there, lighting up the whole bed." Felix is still staring into her eyes, and Amara knows she is incapable of hiding her fear.

"Victoria protested, but she always does what I want in the end," Felix shrugs. "You shouldn't hate my wife too much, you know. She kept your secret from me for more than half a year. She only decided to betray you after I told her how you used to fuck me when you came round to pay the debt, how I thought you would have made a better wife than *her*. So as you can imagine, when she came out with her lurid tale, I thought she might have invented the whole thing out of spite." Felix leans closer to Amara, and she shelters Rufina, not wanting any part of his body to touch her daughter. "But do you know what convinced me? I made her repeat exactly what she saw that night. Not once, but hundreds of times. She described the way he fucked you in such excruciating detail, as if she were watching the memory unfold in her head. And each time, her account was the same. Because it was true." He sighs, a long, contented exhale. "We both know Victoria isn't smart enough to memorize a complicated lie like that. To tell me exactly how he touched you and when." Felix shudders in disgust. "Though I thought she must have invented the *weeping*. Is that really what you do? Cry over him, when he's finished?"

Amara wills herself to stare back at Felix without flinching, without betraying the nausea that threatens to overwhelm her. "It's *all* a lie."

"I can see why you might stick to that. Considering what would happen, should it ever be uncovered." Felix smiles again, his face crinkling with amusement, so that anyone watching would never imagine he is threatening her. "How much is Rufus paying to support the bastard his slave got on a whore?" Amara turns her face away and does not answer. "How much would you pay *me* to keep my mouth shut?"

"You really are a fool, if you think Rufus would listen to anything you have to say."

"I agree – he might not at first. But after he has read the letter a few times, I wonder if it might start to add up. I wonder how Philos got his current position, whether you asked to keep him. Whether you ever said or did anything that might look suspicious. At the very least, I think we can agree posh boy would *question* Philos. And slaves are always questioned under torture. Your lover wouldn't look so fucking pretty after that, even if he managed to keep his mouth shut."

Amara's eyes are burning. Rufina has dozed off, snuggled against her breast, as if her mother's wretched arms were a place of safety. "How much do you want?"

"I think a monthly payment of twenty denarii would cover it."

"We'll have nothing to live on!"

"That's what happens when you throw yourself away on a slave, I'm afraid. Perhaps you might have been wiser to accept another man's offer, rather than fucking a nobody." It is the only reference Felix has made to her rejection, but Amara can feel the anger in the way his body stiffens. His rage that she chose a *slave* over him. "And then there's your lovely daughter to think about." His voice is soft, as if he were crooning an endearment at the baby.

"Don't touch her."

"Such a pretty lunula she is wearing. What a shame if she were to lose it."

"Nobody has the power to enslave her. I'm a freedwoman."

"That hardly matters, if her paternity is exposed."

"A child is *always* free, if her mother was free at the time of birth," Amara snaps. "Don't try and play fucking games with me."

Felix grins, savouring her confusion. "You really don't know, do you? We're not in Greece now, Amara." He is on the verge of laughter, and his unfeigned delight chills her. "I will leave her father the pleasure of explaining the situation to you." Felix leans in close, knife pressing against her again. "And when he has, I think you will find the price I asked is cheap. So cheap in fact, I might have to raise it at some point in the future." Felix stretches out his hand towards Rufina, and although Amara tries to twist away, she is trapped by the knife and is forced to let him rest the tips of his fingers on her daughter's head. Fear and hate twist so tightly round her heart, Amara is unable to stop the tears that sting her eyes from falling. "Every day of your life, Amara, you will know I have the power to destroy everyone you love." Felix takes back his hand. "Be here this time next week to pay me. Same spot, same day. And don't bring the British bitch." He slides his arm away from her, standing up abruptly, and walks off into the crowd without looking back.

Amara is not sure how her legs carry her back through the marketplace. She crosses Julia's garden with her head down, hoping her friend will not see her, knowing she will be unable to hide her distress. It is not only the threat but the sudden sense of exposure that makes her feel ill. All those moments of vulnerability with Philos laid bare, seen through Felix's scornful eyes. Her fingers fumble with the latch to her flat, and when she is inside, she collapses on a stool by the table. Her jerky movements wake Rufina who starts to howl. Amara tries to undo her tunic to feed her, but she is shaking so much that the baby is red-faced with rage before she manages it. As soon as Rufina is clamped to her breast, Amara starts to sob, is still sobbing when Britannica arrives back with their meal.

"What happen? Fighter is sick?"

"Felix," Amara gasps. "He knows. He knows about Philos. Victoria told him."

"*Victoria.*" Britannica bares her teeth, a look of utter ferocity on her face. "I tell you she better dead!"

Amara leans her head in her hand, still sobbing, unable to contradict her. "Felix said she begged my forgiveness."

"I forgive her," Britannica snarls. "When crows pick out her eyes." She kneels on the floor beside Amara. "Let me kill him."

They look at each other. There is no pretence between them that Britannica's suggestion is anything but tempting. "It's too dangerous. Victoria would know who did it. She would seek revenge."

"I kill them both."

Amara shakes her head. "I have to pay him." Britannica swears in frustration. "I can't risk losing you; I can't risk the murder being linked to me. It's not that I doubt you, but it's too dangerous."

"When you change your mind, I do it." Britannica rises from her knees and towers over Amara, watching her and the baby. "And now, how we pay him?"

"I will sell the harp Rufus gave me. That will buy us a few weeks."

"It was for Fighter's dowry."

"This is more important," Amara says, turning her face away in shame. "If I don't pay Felix, she won't have the chance to get married, have a dowry, anything!"

Britannica smacks her palm against the wall. Her body is contorted with frustration, all the vengeance she cannot enact. "Is like being back there," she says. And Amara knows exactly which place Britannica means.

Amara and Britannica barely speak for most of the afternoon. They are united by a sense of helplessness but little else. It is not only the money which crushes Amara's spirit, but the threat to Rufina's safety. Felix's words play over and over in her mind, and she keeps stroking her daughter's lunula, as if the charm will work its own magic protection.

It does not help that Philos is kept working until late. Amara hears him come in, the cheerful tone of his greeting, the low rumble of Britannica's reply, and his exclamation of shock. When he bursts into the bedroom upstairs, Rufina is asleep in the cot, Amara sitting up, arms tight around herself.

"Britannica said Felix threatened you." Philos sinks down on the bed beside her. "Please tell me he didn't hurt either of you."

"He didn't. But he knows about us. Victoria told him *everything*." She grips his hand. "He wants twenty denarii a month, or he will tell Rufus."

"But that's almost everything we have!"

"I know." If Amara had hoped seeing Philos would make her feel better, the look of defeat in his eyes only worsens her sense of powerlessness. "Felix said something else. About Rufina. That if it became known you were her father, she could be enslaved. But that's a lie, isn't it? He was just torturing me. A child always takes a mother's status at the time of the birth, *everyone* knows that." At first, she takes his shocked expression as proof Felix has lied, but when Philos only stares, lips parted, and offers no reassurance, she starts to panic. "It's not true, is it? Tell me it's not true. A child always follows the mother."

"Usually."

"What do you mean, *usually*?"

"It can sometimes be revoked," Philos says, his expression more serious than she has ever known it. "If a freed or free woman has an unauthorized relationship with another person's slave, their union can be declared illegal. That means their children are enslaved to the father's owner." He balls his hand into a fist, pressing the knuckles against his lips. "I thought you *knew* this."

Amara gapes at him. "Rufina would be enslaved? She would belong to Rufus?"

"Hortensius." Amara lets out a cry of distress. "But that's not going to happen." Philos grasps hold of her arms, to hold her steady. "We'll pay Felix. Nobody is ever going to find out." Amara only stares at him, eyes wide with fear. "And even if we were discovered, it's a legal process. I cannot imagine Rufus would want the scandal, especially now he's been elected. It would be so much easier to kill me and leave the child alone. That's why any involvement from Julia, any public recognition of Rufina's free status; it all helps protect her."

"But she can't be enslaved. She can't be! I would *never* let Hortensius take her." Amara remembers the way Rufus's father ran his hands down her body, grasping, as if she were standing in the slave market. Imagines him owning her daughter. "I would die before I let him touch her."

"Hortensius won't take her," Philos says, trying to calm her down. "She's safe here. Nobody's going to touch her. She's free."

"When you go to work for Rufus, I can't stand it, I can't *bear* that he owns you. But it would kill me if she were enslaved."

"It's not going to happen." Philos kisses her. "I promise you."

"I should have killed Victoria. Britannica was right."

"Of *course* you shouldn't have killed her. Don't be ridiculous. If anyone's to blame, it's me." Amara knows what he is going to say and tries to interrupt, but he presses on. "I never imagined you didn't know all the risks we faced, and I'm sorry. I wish I had not brought so much pain into your life."

"It's not your fault." Amara puts her arms around his neck, pressing close to him. "I don't blame you for any of it." She wants to reassure him further, to say that she does not regret loving him, that she could never regret having his child, but at that moment, with the image of Hortensius in her mind, she cannot bring herself to say the words.

45

Mistress, I ask you to love me
Pompeii graffiti

The harp buys them a month. In that time, they cut back drastically, saving as much as possible to make the pain of each payment less severe. Philos loses weight, and in spite of his protestations, Amara suspects there are days he goes without eating to spare them the expense. Money is not the only hardship. Felix's threat seeps into every area of their lives. It puts a strain on Amara's friendship with Britannica, makes her constantly anxious for her daughter and corrodes the sense of safety she always felt in Philos's arms. When her body has recovered enough for her to make the first tentative moves towards intimacy, Amara cannot shake the sense of Felix watching. It is as if she has been dragged back to the earliest days of their relationship, and if it were not for Philos being so loving and patient, she suspects she would have lost the ability to feel any pleasure at all.

The few moments that Amara feels the darkness lifting at home are when she watches Philos bathe or swaddle their baby, entirely absorbed in love for their daughter. His stillness soothes Amara, even though she hates the reasons he is able to stay so calm. She knows his stoicism is enforced by a lifetime's lack of control – the understanding he acquired in childhood that the only things he would ever master were his own emotions.

At Philos's insistence, Amara spends increasing amounts of time with Julia, allowing the relationship to cast a protective shadow over Rufina. As the weeks pass, Amara begins to spend more evenings with Julia and Livia than she does at home. Julia always introduces her as the admiral's freedwoman to guests, making her full name known: Gaia Plinia Amara. In spite of herself, Amara comes to enjoy these evenings outside the darkness of her flat, without the constant, exhausting needs of her daughter. She reclines in Julia's outdoor dining room with the other guests, without having to worry about the expense of the food, the cost of the wine. Her only obligation is to be charming, and with Livia's encouragement, she starts to play the lyre in company again, grateful that she kept the instrument back from sale.

When Amara gets home at night, creeping into bed beside Philos, he asks her about the guests Julia invited. In the darkness, it is hard to read his expression, but she can feel the tension in his body and hear the tightness in his voice. They never discuss the obvious, but Amara knows Philos is not so naïve that he will not have understood what the easiest route out of their financial distress would be, the safest way to diffuse the threat that hangs over their child. They don't need to discuss her former life as a rich man's concubine. Instead, the past rests beside them in the bed, as tangible as a third, silent presence.

Amara keeps up her pursuit of Valentina, and her

approaches to the midwife for work are not entirely fruitless. Valentina's manner softens a little after Amara calls on her, bearing Pliny's valuable scroll on plants, along with several herbal remedies to ease sickness which her father taught her. But for all her efforts to ingratiate herself, Amara knows learning a new trade will be time-consuming, with little chance of earning what she needs quickly enough to keep Felix at bay.

It is May, not long after the Lemuria, when Amara sees a familiar figure reclining in her landlady's company. The jolt she feels is not so much from Demetrius's presence, which she has long dreaded, but from the lack of warning Julia gave her that he would be joining them. Amara knows she has been outmanoeuvred. Julia gestures at Demetrius, no doubt telling him of his prey's approach, and he turns. The Emperor's freedman is older than she remembers, though the intensity behind his dark eyes is the same.

"Congratulations on the birth of your daughter," he says, rising to greet her. His gaze sweeps over her now voluptuous figure, too polite to linger on her breasts. "Motherhood suits you."

"Rufina is a dear little thing," Livia remarks. "We're all awfully fond of her."

Amara places a hand to her heart in acknowledgement of their compliments but is relieved that Demetrius does not express a desire to meet her child. She is not sure she could bear for Philos to bring her out. "Are you here to visit your estates?"

They sit down together, Julia retreating to the opposite couch where Livia is already reclining. "Among other duties." He glances at Julia. "It is always a pleasure to see old friends."

"Will you be staying long in Pompeii?"

"It depends if I'm welcome." His words are for his hostess, but it is to Amara he directs his answer. She feels the heat go to her face and knows it must look as if she is blushing with pleasure, rather than anxiety.

"As if you even need to ask, you ridiculous man." Julia flicks her wrist affectionately at Amara. "Darling, would you mind playing something for us? I'm sorry to impose, especially when you've only just arrived, but I've had the most trying day, and your voice is *so* relaxing."

Julia is not even attempting to be subtle, and if she were not under such pressure, Amara might even laugh at the shamelessness. "Of course," she murmurs, but before she can rise to retrieve her lyre, one of Julia's servants has brought it to her. At that, Demetrius looks at Amara and raises an eyebrow. There is warmth, not mockery, in his amusement, and in spite of herself, she smiles back.

"I hope you're not this peremptory with all your guests," he says to Julia. "*I'm* damned well not going to start warbling for you. Too many years have passed since I was obliged to sing for my supper."

Amara glances at him, surprised. Surely Demetrius isn't referring to his past as a slave? He is reclining expansively on the couch, smiling at Julia and Livia who are curled around each other, contented as a pair of cats. Nothing about his manner suggests a man who just made a shameful confession. Perhaps it was simply an expression, not a sign he was once forced to *entertain*.

The strings of the lyre are taut under Amara's fingers

as she plucks them, making sure the instrument is in tune. She starts to play Sappho's hymn to Aphrodite, a song she always performed with Dido and Drusilla, and one she knows so well there is little danger of making any mistakes. To her relief, Demetrius begins chatting with Julia rather than fixing her with his unsettling attention.

She listens to him talk about his estates, suspecting that Julia's questions are designed to show off his wealth, just as she has contrived to show off Amara's skills at entertaining. From the conversation, it seems that Demetrius not only owns vineyards and olive groves, but also a large fishery off the coast. Amara tries to concentrate on her performance, doing her utmost to block out the endless litany of riches.

Julia and Livia press Demetrius to talk about his life in Rome too, but he is tight-lipped about his business for the Emperor Vespasian, only offering the blandest praise for his master. His discretion reminds her a little of Philos, or even Secundus. Service always leaves its mark. She finds herself wondering, in spite of herself, how Demetrius came to be owned by the Imperial family, how he gained his freedom, whether he was enslaved in Greece, or whether, like her, he was born free.

The topic which never seems to exhaust him is the transformation of his adopted city, Rome. He takes pains to describe the new Temple of Peace and the ongoing construction of the Flavian Amphitheatre. "You could fit Pompeii's arena inside, perhaps ten times over," he explains to Julia. "The scale of it is unimaginable. All the wealth of the great Temple from Jerusalem has gone into its construction." His words set off an echo in Amara's mind, recalling her old maid, Martha. *Ask the admiral why Jerusalem is now nothing more than ashes.* Amara strums the strings of the lyre, no longer singing, so that she has a better chance of hearing what is being said. "You might not recognize the city you once visited," Demetrius continues, nodding at Julia and Livia. "Its greatness is unlike anything I ever expected to witness. And I say that as a man who grew up in the shadow of the Temple of Zeus."

"You are from Olympia?" Amara cannot help interrupting. "You grew up in the sacred city?" Demetrius nods, not looking displeased by her interest, but not volunteering more either. "My father always wanted to make a pilgrimage there," Amara says. "To see the statue of Zeus, before he died."

"You are from Attica," Demetrius replies, in Greek. It is a statement not a question, and Amara does not know whether he guessed from her accent or because he learned this from Pliny. "They say Pallas-Athene always leaves her mark on those from her own kingdom. I wonder if that is true of you."

In her mind's eye, Amara can see the glass statuette of Attica's patron in her parents' house. Pallas-Athene, goddess of wisdom and strategy, more beloved than any other immortal in the city of Amara's birth. The goddess Amara abandoned in favour of Venus, the patron of Pompeii. As perhaps Demetrius also once abandoned the gods of his fathers. "I've heard," Amara replies, in Latin, "that the Temple to Minerva in Rome, rivals anything to be found in Attica."

Recognition passes between them. "As Rome surpasses Athens in every respect," Demetrius replies. At that moment, Amara could almost be looking at her own father. The familiar, crooked smile he reserved for when talking about the power of Rome. *Everything they have is borrowed from us, Timarete. Always remember that.*

"Greeks," Livia says, rolling her eyes. "You're all insufferable with your sneering. As if we don't know what you're up to."

"Since Rome's dominance over Athens is not in doubt," Demetrius says, amused, "I think you can spare us our little jokes." He smiles at Amara. "And you are right about the temple on the Capitol. Though it is only one of many wonders in the city."

Amara bows her head, suddenly nervous, not wanting him to extend an invitation to take her there.

"You should see the work being done on *our* Temple of Venus," Julia says. "We may not be as grand as Rome here in Pompeii, but there are still a few sights worth seeing." She stands. "Perhaps you will join us, Amara?"

Amara looks out across the garden, at the lengthening shadows. "I will need to feed Rufina," she says sadly, as if reluctant to turn down the invitation.

"Your former patron did not supply a wet nurse?" Demetrius looks displeased, though it is hard to tell if his disapproval is aimed at her or Rufus.

"It's no matter. You can join us later, darling," Julia says to Amara, cutting across Demetrius's question to spare her embarrassment. Amara bows deeply to them all, and as she walks away, she hears Julia's muttered reassurance to Demetrius. "*Such things are easily rectified.*"

Philos is home when Amara returns, Rufina sleeping upstairs. The sight of him, sitting bent over some wax tablets in the small, darkened room, makes her chest constrict. She bends down to kiss him, and he looks up at her with a smile.

It is the type of open exchange of affection other lovers take for granted, but which is still precious to them both.

"Have you eaten?" She moves to the brazier, desperate to do something for him.

"I'm not especially hungry. Why don't you take it?"

"I'm eating later, with Julia."

"Then I'll have it, thank you. Though leave some for Britannica."

"Is that more work for Rufus?"

"No, better than that. Julia passed me some accounts to look over for a friend of hers. So it's paid work."

"Oh, wonderful," Amara exclaims, though her heart sinks at the thought of how much they now owe their landlady and how furious Julia is going to be when she declines Demetrius. She stirs the food, a rabbit broth Britannica bought yesterday, which they have been attempting to stretch over two days. The congealed fat starts to loosen as the liquid heats. Now is the moment she ought to tell Philos about Demetrius, so that they can plan together how to handle the matter. She glances over at the table. He is looking at the tablets again, a frown creasing his forehead. It is impossible not to notice the dark smudges under his eyes, the air of exhaustion that wraps him round like a cloak. A splash of broth lands on her hand from the bubbling pot. Amara sucks in her breath and moves the pot from the heat. Philos does not look over as she spoons it out into a bowl. It smells a little ripe.

She sits opposite him, setting down the dish. "Thank you so much." He closes the tablets and smiles at her again. "I remember a time you told me it made you uncomfortable when I served you. Now it makes me uncomfortable to eat while you have nothing."

"I've had plenty already today, I promise." At Amara's reassurance, he finally picks up the spoon. "I remember that day. It was the afternoon I decided to buy Victoria, after Fabia visited." Amara thinks of all that has happened since and sighs. "I wish I had listened to you."

"You loved her. It was easy enough for me to tell you to leave Victoria there. I doubt I would have listened to that advice either." Amara thinks of other advice Philos has given her, which she also ignored. The time he begged her to leave him. If she had not allowed love to guide her then, what would her life be like now? "You look very melancholy," he says. "I hope you're not blaming yourself. You know *I* don't."

Philos is gazing at her, his kind grey eyes filled with nothing but concern. It makes her feel afraid. Not of Julia, or Demetrius, or even Felix, but of herself, and the pain she knows she is capable of inflicting. In her mind's eye, she is no longer looking at Philos, but at Menander, when she smashed the lamp at his feet. She scrapes back her stool. "I will just check on Rufina," she says, her voice choked. Philos is left, startled, while she hurries for the stairs.

Rufina is asleep but seems to sense her mother's presence when Amara leans over the cot, taking in a deeper snuffling breath, stirring in her loosened swaddling. Amara sinks to the floor, wrapping her arms around her own knees, unable to bear the suffocating sense of love. It hurts, how much she cares for this child, this tiny person who was supposed to free her father, but who only trapped her mother.

"It's alright." Philos's voice is soft as he crouches beside her. He puts an arm around her shoulders, and she buries her face in his chest, sobbing. He strokes her hair, shushing her. "What's wrong, my love?"

"I'm so afraid of losing you." It is only half the truth, but as much as she can bear to say.

Philos continues to stoke her hair, his chin resting on the top of her head. "What's brought this on?" Amara does not answer but instead cries even harder. "Whatever it is, you know you can tell me."

Amara longs to tell him about Demetrius, to confess the terror she feels. Whatever decision she is going to be forced to make, she needs to ask Philos's advice, or at the very least warn him about the other man's existence, about the looming threat and opportunity presented by another patron. And yet, would it not shame Philos, if he became complicit in selling her? Surely no man wants to admit he is willing to prostitute the mother of his child, even for his family's survival. Perhaps it is kinder to make the decision alone. Amara clings to Philos, her face still buried in his chest.

"Forgive me," she says, her voice muffled in his tunic, so she doesn't have to look in his eyes. "There's nothing in particular. I don't know what came over me. I've just felt so emotional since Rufina was born." She sits up, wiping her face, and forces herself to smile. Their baby starts to cry, disturbed by all the noise, and Amara scrambles to her feet. "I had better feed her. You go and finish dinner." Her back is to him as she bends over the cot. Philos rests a hand on her shoulder.

"Only if you are very sure you are alright. I can always stay with you both."

"I'll be fine. I promise. Please go eat." Amara does not turn as he leaves. She sits on the bed, feeding their daughter. The black-and-white lines on the wall blur as she stares, distorted through a veil of tears, turning the world grey.

46

But tears cannot put out the flame;
They inflame the face and melt the spirit
Pompeii graffiti

Demetrius is sitting alone in the outdoor dining room, looking out at the garden. Amara has a brief moment to study him before he sees her, the relaxed way that he sits, his complete ease in his own company. Wealth and power rest on him, as light as the folds of his luxurious tunic. She presses a hand to her cheek. Her eyes are still hot from crying earlier, but the dusk should hide any blemish to her skin. Amara has played so many parts in her life, she tells herself this is only one more mask, perhaps no harder to wear than any other.

Demetrius glances up when she joins him, a wry look on his face. "Julia insisted she was too tired to eat. A suggestion even more subtle than her behaviour earlier." He speaks in Greek, and Amara notices his voice is deeper in his native language. It also makes his tone harder to read.

"I can leave if you prefer."

"You cannot possibly imagine that would be my

preference." He stares steadily into her eyes, not with desire, but appraisal. She does not look away. "I understand from the admiral you once worked in the town brothel. You don't act like that sort of whore."

"Is your experience of brothel whores so extensive?"

"I meant no offence." He smirks at her irritation. "But your story is somewhat outlandish. Pliny's explanation that he hired you to assist him in his research would be laughable from any other man, but I've known him long enough to be familiar with his insatiable curiosity." Amara almost smiles at this description of her benefactor. Demetrius watches her. "You're fond of him, aren't you?"

"Fond does not begin to express the gratitude I feel."

"And what about your young patron? The man who fathered your child."

"I am also indebted to him."

"But not so fond of him as you are of the admiral." The corner of Demetrius's mouth dimples in a smile. "Pliny told me you begged him to take you on as his secretary, in the most passionate, *desperate* terms." Amara does not drop her gaze from his, even though her cheeks blaze with mortification. "If I had not seen you with him in Misenum, I would never have believed that tale, even from Pliny. A brothel whore trying to bribe the Admiral of the Roman Fleet, not by offering him the use of her body, but her mind."

Amara does not allow herself to show any trace of the embarrassment she feels. "I'm glad the story amused you."

"I've been in service my whole life. Believe me, I am not laughing at you." He pours her a glass of wine, takes one for himself. "Why did your last arrangement end? And don't fear I will judge you for disparaging your former patron – I prefer honesty."

"It was an arrangement based solely on his passion for me. And when that was spent, so was his patronage. Is there any other reason for such things to end?" Amara sips the wine. Something about Demetrius's coldness soothes her. "His family's desire for him to marry also played a part."

"Did you love him?"

"Do you love the woman who serves you as a concubine in Rome?" Amara stares, so he can be in no doubt she is subjecting him to the same scrutiny he has applied to her.

"I am grateful to her. And my gratitude now takes the form of a pension, for all the years she served me in the past." He swirls the wine in his glass. "But you avoided my question."

"Because I think you are quite intelligent enough to work out the answer for yourself."

Demetrius snorts. "A politician's answer." He gestures at her to sit beside him. "Come here." It is only a few steps from one couch to another, but Amara is in no doubt about the line she is crossing. Her movements are fluid, betraying no sign of hesitation. She has banked up her grief and guilt, forcing them to a distance, behind a wall of ice. She will feel everything later. Demetrius rests his hand upon her thigh, warm and heavy. "I don't propose an arrangement like your last, based on absurd romantic expectations. But you intrigue me, *Plinia* Amara. I should like to see if we might suit one another. I suggest you come with me to Stabiae for a few weeks, and if we please each other, I will take you to Rome. If not, you may return to your life in Pompeii."

"What about my daughter?" Amara asks the question calmly, because the thought of leaving Rufina, of what that will truly mean, is a pain she has not even begun to comprehend.

"I am happy to cover the rent, the cost of a wet nurse, everything, to ensure she is cared for here in your absence. Julia tells me you have a reliable steward. We can pay him whatever you believe is required." Demetrius moves a curl of her hair, tucking it behind her ear so he can see her better. "Believe me, whatever sum you name, will be a trifle."

Amara knows this is not a compliment on her worth, but a statement of his wealth. "And will I be allowed to see her?"

"*If* we decide to enter an arrangement, then I'm sure I can spare you a month or so each year to see her and set any affairs you have here in order." She stares at the floor, conscious of him watching her, able to see every expression. "I can give you until tomorrow to consider my proposal, if that is necessary."

"*No!*" Demetrius raises his eyebrows in surprise. Amara curls her hand into a fist, the nails biting her palm. In her mind's eye, she can see Philos working at home, Rufina sleeping, and the thought of leaving them both is an agony beyond endurance. If she goes back now, she will never have the strength to give Demetrius the answer her daughter needs. "I mean... no, that will not be necessary." She bows her head. "I am, of course, honoured to accept your proposal."

Her turmoil has not gone unnoticed. "You don't sound very enthusiastic." His voice is sharp.

Amara forces herself to look at Demetrius, to stare

directly into his eyes. "It is simply that such a change in fortune... is somewhat overwhelming."

Whatever he sees in her face must reassure him. "If you are certain," he murmurs, no longer hiding the desire in his voice. She only has a heartbeat to prepare herself before he takes hold of her, a moment to prevent herself from instinctively pushing him away. Perhaps Demetrius senses her reticence, or at least he does not grab her. He leans forwards and kisses her softly on the lips, running a finger along the base of her throat. His hand is warm as he lays it against her breastbone, and she knows he will feel the pulse thumping under her skin. His touch is not, in itself, unpleasant. She kisses him, crushing her guilt, blocking out memories of Philos, trying not to think about how different it feels to hold the man she loves. Demetrius becomes more passionate, pulling her body closer, and her training with Felix resurfaces. She has given pleasure to so many men – the movements, the way to touch another... all of it is ingrained. But as he starts to push the tunic from her shoulder, she stops him. "I'm not a brothel whore anymore." She presses her finger firmly against his lips, as if to seal them shut. "You can wait until Stabiae to enjoy me."

There is a note of command in her voice, a return to the coldness she showed earlier. When he smiles in response, Amara knows she did not misjudge him. Demetrius moves apart, picking up his wine. "Very well, my darling," he says, a hint of amusement in the way he pronounces the endearment. "As you wish."

★ ★ ★

Amara is awake long before the light starts to filter through the shutters. She had been unable to tell Philos last night. He had wanted to make love to her, and she was too selfish to refuse, knowing it might be the last time he ever touched her with that much tenderness, the last time she would ever feel that close to him. When she had wept that she was terrified of losing him, it was not a lie, even if she did not deserve his reassurance.

She looks now at her lover's profile, the steady rise and fall of his chest. Over his sleeping form, she can see Rufina through the slats of the cot, her tiny mouth pursed in a pout, her lashes lying thick against her cheek. Amara had never imagined it would be possible to feel love like this. Had not believed, after she lost her parents, that she would ever have a family again. The desire to touch Philos is so overwhelming she lays her hand gently on his shoulder. He must have been close to waking, because even that slight pressure causes him to stir. He opens his eyes, looking straight into hers, and smiles.

The words Amara had meant to say, the confession she knows she must make, evaporate at the sight of his happiness. She cannot bear to tear her family apart, not yet. Instead, she bends to kiss him, promising herself she will tell him later. They get up quietly together, not wanting to disturb Rufina, who has mercifully started sleeping for hours at a stretch. Philos hands Amara her tunic, lifting her hair out from the back after she slips it on, caressing her shoulder as he arranges the curls. When they are both dressed, Amara wakes their daughter to feed her, trying not to think about how soon she will have to abandon her baby.

"I'm working for Livia today," Philos says. "Britannica is expecting to spend the day with her fighter. Will you be with Julia, as usual?"

"Yes. She has a guest staying." Amara pauses, again trying to find the words that might prepare Philos for the revelation which will rip through them, but he bends to kiss her lightly on the lips before she has a chance to say more. She wonders, watching him leave, if he suspects something but does not want to know.

Amara manages to get through a morning with Julia, Livia and Demetrius without showing any sign of the anguish in her heart. She accepts her friends' congratulations – and Livia's innuendos – with grace, grateful to have plenty of practice at hiding her feelings. Julia's excitement compensates for her own frequent lapses into silence, and Amara forces herself to smile until her cheeks ache, while the others casually dismantle her family's life in Pompeii. Julia suggests Amara travel to Stabiae as soon as a suitable wet nurse has been found for Rufina, which Livia declares cannot take more than a couple of weeks. Amara nods in agreement, the thought of leaving her daughter sitting like a stone in her chest.

A heavy downpour drives them all from the garden, and it is with a sense of dread that Amara finds herself alone with Demetrius in the library, after Livia suggests he might care to hear her read. "After all," Livia drawls, with a mischievous backwards glance, "it worked *wonders* for the admiral."

The sound of the rain, cascading onto the roof, drowns

out the beating of Amara's heart as she and Demetrius stare at one another. The older man has his back to the window, its feeble light casting him in relief, like a statue in the Forum. Amara reaches for the imperious tone of the night before, hoping she can again control him with coldness. "What shall I read for you," she says in Latin, turning to search through the scrolls lined on Julia's shelves.

"Nothing." The Greek word stops her from moving, as Demetrius walks towards her. He is standing so close, the sharp lavender of his pomade cuts through the soft scent of the rain. She looks up at his face, at the lines etched deep into the skin, and the hollows under his eyes. He notices her scrutiny and raises an eyebrow. "Yes, I'm old," he remarks drily. He runs a finger gently down her cheek. "Like Hades and Persephone."

There is self-mockery in his voice, as well as authority, and Amara finds she does not know how to read this man, or how to respond to him. She falls back upon the obvious, on what she learned from Felix, but he catches her wrist before her hand can reach him.

"No. I want to touch you."

Amara lets her mind slide to blank when Demetrius pushes her gently against the wall, his hand drifting up between her legs. Somehow, it makes it worse that he is touching her like a lover, not with the thoughtless, grasping fingers of the men at the brothel. She shivers when he undoes her tunic at the shoulder, exposing her breasts to the cold air, intent on his doomed quest to give her pleasure. Amara allows her eyelids to flutter shut, running through the repertoire of moans she learned from Victoria, willing it to be over. Demetrius's own breathing becomes ragged, and she opens her eyes to check how close he is, then gasps in shock.

Philos is standing frozen in the doorway, a bundle of wax tablets clutched in his arms and a look of horror on his face. Their eyes meet, anguish taut between them, before he turns and walks away.

47

Not always is a woman feigning love
When she sighs and clings to a man in close embrace.
Lucretius, On the Nature of the Universe

Amara draws on reserves of deception she did not imagine she possessed in order to get through the rest of her encounter with Demetrius. Her gasp is disguised as a cry of ecstasy, and her shaking masquerades as the aftermath of pleasure. It is such a convincing performance she barely needs to touch her new patron to tip him over the edge. But instead of having the leisure afterwards to collapse against his conquest, Demetrius is obliged to hold Amara upright to control her trembling. The intensity of her reaction seems to surprise and please him. "I hardly think we need to consider Stabiae a trial," he murmurs, drawing her closer. "I want you in Rome with me."

It feels to Amara as if a hundred years of smiling and false laughter must be endured before she is finally released to return home. She knows, as soon as she enters the kitchen and sees Britannica's drawn face, that Philos must have said something.

"He is with Fighter," Britannica says, pointing at the ceiling. "I never see him like this."

Amara runs up the stairs, panic rising, and pushes open the bedroom door. Rufina is in the cot, asleep, and she looks round wildly for Philos. He has his back to her, leaning against the window to look out at the street, as if he longs to escape.

"How long have you been entertaining Julia's guests," he asks, without looking round. "And when were you going to tell me?"

"That was the first time. I swear to you. I swear it."

He turns to face her. "I don't know if I believe you." She can tell from his voice that it is not an accusation, but a statement of fact.

"I promise you it's true, Philos, I promise. And I *couldn't* refuse him today, not without offending Julia. You know how much our lives depend on her, how Rufina's life depends on her. I'm just sorry that you saw..." Amara cannot continue. Instead, the scene plays through her mind as Philos must have seen it, the half-naked body of the woman he loves, writhing at the touch of another man. She puts her hand to her mouth. "I'm just so sorry."

"I used to collect you from the brothel," Philos says quietly. "It's not as if I don't know what you've been forced to do. And I've never, at any point, felt anything but heartbroken for you. But today..." He swallows, as if unable to bear the memory. "I can't get the image of you out of my head. You sounded as if you were *enjoying* it."

Blood rushes to Amara's cheeks, and she clasps her hands into fists. "I was *not* enjoying it. I'm a prostitute. How do you think women like me get clients to pay? By crying and begging them to stop? By fighting, like Britannica, and getting our teeth knocked out?"

"I'm sorry." Philos's face crumples at the sight of her obvious distress. "I shouldn't have said that." He crosses the room, tentatively reaching out to her. She throws herself into his arms, clinging to him, though she cannot help but notice he is not holding her as closely as usual. She becomes conscious that she smells of lavender, the scent Demetrius left on her skin. "How long is he staying here for?" Philos whispers. "Will you have to... see him again?" In the long silence that follows, Amara stares at the wall until it feels as if the geometric patterns of black and white will sear themselves onto her vision. "How long is he here for?" Philos repeats, his voice less gentle this time.

Amara lets go, stepping out of the encircling protection of his arms. "He is going to be my patron."

"But you've only just met him." Philos stares, incredulous, until she sees the pain of understanding bleed through the shock. "How long have you known this man for?"

"I met him in Misenum."

"*Misenum*? When you visited Pliny? But that was *months* ago!"

"Nothing happened back then, I promise! And yesterday is the very first time I've seen him since..."

"Yesterday. When you were crying and saying you couldn't bear to lose me. That's when you accepted him as your patron, isn't it?" Philos's face is cold. "Anything else you might have forgotten to tell me?"

There is no way to soften the words, no way to escape their impact. "He is taking me to Rome."

Philos sits down slowly on the bed. "Rome," he repeats

stupidly. "You're leaving me and going to Rome. With *him*."
Amara knows, seeing his look of disgust, exactly what
Philos is picturing. "I don't even know this man's name.
Who is he?"

"His name is Demetrius." Amara's tears start to fall, and
it hurts to speak each word, knowing the destruction she
is wreaking, but still, she carries on. "He is an Imperial
freedman. He is one of the richest men in Campania. He
will pay you to look after Rufina. He will pay our daughter's
dowry. And if Rufus ever agrees to sell you, he will give me
the money to buy you and set you free."

Philos is staring at her, and she can see her own grief
mirrored in his face. Then he closes his eyes, as if that will
shut out the pain. "It's not that I don't understand why
you've done this, Amara. Believe me, I do. But it's *how*
you've done it, that's so hard to forgive."

"Philos, please…"

"My whole life, I have had no control. *No fucking
control.* Not over myself, not over what happens to the
people I love. And I know you understand what that feels
like. Which is why I cannot understand how you could ever
behave like this. To lie to me, to keep so many secrets, to
leave me no choice. As if I were of no account. As if you
owned me. Is that what it feels like to you? Do you think
that because I'm a slave, and you are free, you have the right
to dictate our lives? To dictate *my* life?"

"No! I don't think of you like that; I don't feel like that…"

"Then why have you acted like you do?" He is gazing at
her, as if she is a stranger.

"I didn't want to shame you," Amara bursts out. "I
thought you might be grateful to me for making this

decision alone. For sparing you the humiliation of agreeing to hand me over to another man."

"You think finding you with him today *spared me humiliation*? That I should be *grateful* to you for that?"

His contempt cuts through Amara, making her cruel. "I'm only doing this because there's nobody else in this family to make any fucking money! What do you imagine is going to protect our child? Do you think my parents' *love* was enough to save me from slavery? I would have traded their love for a dowry, a thousand times over. Nothing means anything without money. *Nothing*."

They stare at one another, and Amara feels sick, unable to take back what she has said, what she has implied about Philos's worth. "You sound like Felix," he says. He gets off the bed, walking to the stool where his cloak is lying, wrapping it around himself, his hands shaking with anger and distress.

"Philos, please, don't walk away from me. Please, talk to me…"

Philos explodes. "*Now* you want to talk?" he shouts. "When you've already decided everything? What do you want to fucking talk about? Or are you just going to sit there and tell me how I'm expected to live my worthless life in your absence."

He strides to the door. Amara gets up to run after him. "You can't just leave like this! Where are you going?"

He whips round to face her. "I'm going for a *walk*. Is that allowed? Or will you send me back to my master for disobedience?" Rufina starts to cry, and Amara sees him hesitate, disturbed by their daughter's distress. She reaches for his arm, but rather than draw him closer, the gesture only reignites his anger. Philos holds his palms up, warning her not to touch him, and walks out of the door.

Amara hears his footsteps thump down the stairs as she bends down to pick up their howling daughter. She undoes her tunic at the shoulder and latches Rufina onto her breast, feeling the tug of the baby's hunger. Rufina is squirming in the swaddling, and so she unbinds her, feeling the warmth of her daughter's body against her own. Amara strokes her baby's head, soft with dark, downy hair, and feels her heart split open. The thought of allowing a stranger to feed and comfort her child, leaving nothing but emptiness in her arms, is a torment unlike anything Amara has ever known.

The milk soothes the baby, and after her feed, Rufina sprawls contentedly across her mother's chest. Not wanting to disturb Rufina by weeping, Amara lays her on the bed and curls around the small body, biting into her own clenched hand to stop herself from making a noise. Rufina gurgles, waving her tiny fists and kicking her feet, oblivious to her mother's distress. Amara watches the baby's movements, pressing down on the darkness in her own heart, allowing the blankness to creep in, knowing from long, bitter experience that the only way to survive is to bury the pain, and to keep walking, wherever Fortune leads. She moves closer, so that her child's perfect face is a breath away from her own. "You will never have your mother's life," she whispers, placing a finger near her daughter's hand, so that the tiny fingers curl around it. "You will never have your father's life." Amara kisses Rufina's forehead. "You will be free."

48

The women who have avenged
Herculaneum graffiti

Livia's prediction of finding a suitable wet nurse in a fort-night proves overly optimistic, but only by a week. Of those twenty-one days, Amara's last in Pompeii, Demetrius is present for the first five, and it is this which drives the wedge still deeper between her and Philos. The scent of lavender lingers in their home, and when she and Philos look at each other, there is no escaping their shared knowledge of what she is doing each day, no way to deny the secrets she kept from him. Philos moves into the small storage room off the kitchen, to sleep on the floor beside Britannica.

His politeness towards Amara, his scrupulous discussions about how she would like him to raise Rufina, feel even colder than his anger. There is only one moment when his self-control falters, when he tries to thank Amara for the sacrifice she is making for their child, but when she responds with tears of her own, swearing that she will always love him, begging him to believe her, Philos gets up and leaves the room.

The last few days are the worst, the hours slipping through Amara's fingers like sand. She had imagined wanting to spend every waking moment with Rufina, but instead, she finds it increasingly painful to see her baby, knowing she will have to leave her, and after the wet nurse arrives, Amara cannot bear to be in the house.

Britannica's friendship, her largely silent presence, is Amara's greatest comfort. And it is Britannica who helps Amara with the most dangerous of her final acts in Pompeii: a return to the Wolf Den.

They arrive at Felix's bar, not the brothel, and the place reminds Amara of the tavern Felix once took her to – a tiny, grubby hole, dark even in the daylight. A woman is bent over the counter, cleaning the surface. She looks up to see Amara and Britannica standing in the doorway, blocking out what little light remains, and cries out. It is Beronice.

"Gallus!"

Summoned by Beronice's shriek, a familiar figure emerges, feet first, down a ladder in the corner. Gallus scowls at the sight of the two former she-wolves and jerks his head at Amara. "What do *you* want?"

"That's not a very pleasant greeting for old friends," Amara replies, walking to the counter. "What else would we want, but to see our darling Beronice? And Victoria, of course. Perhaps you could send for her."

Gallus steps in front of Beronice, shielding her. "My wife is not your slave."

"No," Amara says. "She's yours."

"Perhaps you go fetch Victoria yourself?" It is Britannica this time, addressing Gallus. The Briton's hand is on the hilt of her knife, and she looks straight into the eyes of her former tormentor, without a trace of fear. "We don't like to wait."

Amara keeps watch on the customers behind them while Britannica fronts up Gallus. Two drinkers are gawping from the corner, but neither man looks like they would be keen to join a fight. She and Britannica deliberately picked a quiet time of the morning to visit. There is still no movement from the married couple at the bar. Britannica's fingers curl around her dagger as if about to draw. The Briton is taller than Gallus, and in much better shape. Amara has no doubt who would win a knife fight, and nor it seems has Gallus. "Go fetch her," Felix's freedman barks at his wife. Beronice scurries past her former friends and out into the street.

"You'll fucking regret this," Gallus snarls at Amara.

"I doubt that," she replies, deliberately echoing the way Felix speaks, the clipped cadences of his voice. Amara smiles at Gallus's look of startled recognition.

The brothel is only a few paces up the road, but Beronice is still an uncomfortably long time. Amara and Britannica wait out in the street rather than in the enclosed space of the bar. They have no doubt that their former master will turn up with his wife, their bigger worry is if he also brings an ambush. Eventually, Felix and his two women return, and Amara feels her chest tighten when she sees Victoria, whose head is now covered, incongruously, with the veil of a respectable married woman. But this is not what makes Amara catch her breath. Victoria's hands are clasped protectively over her stomach. She is pregnant. Felix sees Amara's reaction and smiles.

"Here to offer your congratulations?" he asks, bowing

to his two former whores. Britannica bares her teeth and hisses. "Still the same lovely manners, I see."

Beronice puts her arm protectively around Victoria. "She told me what you did." She looks accusingly between Britannica and Amara. "How you threatened to *butcher* her like a pair of thugs."

"Yet here she is," Amara says. "Alive and well."

"Unfortunately," Britannica adds.

"I don't think it's very wise for you to stand here on the street insulting my wife," Felix remarks, kissing Victoria on the top of her head, "not if you want to return home in one piece." Victoria says nothing but casts her eyes down to the pavement.

"Then we'll stand in your fucking bar and insult her there instead," Amara snaps. "There are things we need to discuss."

Amara sees the rage flicker in Felix's eyes, even though his smile does not waver. He flourishes his arm towards the entrance, in an exaggerated gesture of welcome. There is a pause when he and Britannica stand together at the door, neither willing to expose their unarmed back to the other, but then Felix deliberately turns to walk over the threshold, as if taunting the Briton with the target between his shoulder blades. At the sight of the neighbourhood's notorious pimp and loan shark, the two customers still lurking in the bar clear up and leave. Felix nods to Gallus. "Wait outside in the doorway. We're not to be disturbed."

Victoria and Beronice huddle by the bar, while Amara and Britannica stand against the wall opposite, their former sisterhood irreparably broken. Felix is between them, commanding the centre of the room. "Out with it, then," he says to Amara. "This had better be worth my fucking time."

"I'm not paying you any more money," she replies. "You will accept this and swear not to harm my family."

Felix laughs. "And how will you be enforcing this demand?"

Britannica draws her weapon, a long, vicious-looking dagger. "You touch Rufina, I kill you."

"I remember what happened the day I first used a knife against you, bitch," Felix says. Not deigning to reach for his own blade. "Do you?"

In her mind's eye, Amara sees Britannica in the brothel again, Felix holding a blade to her face, his hand grasping her thigh in an unspoken threat of sexual violence. It was the only time Amara ever saw Britannica afraid.

"I am Senovara of the Iceni," Britannica says, stepping forwards, her weapon raised, her intention to fight unmistakable. She cocks her head at Felix, like a hawk trained on its prey. "You will obey her, or die."

Felix draws his weapon. They circle one another in silence, each watching the way the other moves, both stripped down to the very essence of who they are: two remorseless killers. At the edge of her vision, Amara is conscious of Victoria weeping into Beronice's arms, but she does not look. She cannot take her eyes from Britannica's face, willing her friend to succeed, not daring to imagine her defeat.

It is Felix who makes the first move, a feint to test Britannica's response. She dodges him easily, retaliating with a swipe of focused aggression which nearly hits his arm. And then it seems to Amara that the pair are in constant motion, striking at one another so fast she cannot see if anyone has been hit. Their dance is both ugly and graceful, propelled by a savagery and speed which is horrifying to watch.

Amara cries out as Felix aims a blow which she is certain will be fatal, and yet, Britannica evades him, melting from his grasp like smoke. Felix charges before Britannica has time to fully recover her stance, driving her towards the tables at the back. He strikes again, and Amara fears this time he will surely hit home, and yet, Britannica springs backwards, leaping up onto the table behind her. In the split-second of surprise that she gains, Britannica aims a kick at Felix, hitting him hard in the face. He sprawls backwards onto the floor, and she falls upon him, knocking his weapon wide, her knee at his chest, her knife at his throat.

"Yield to me."

There is complete silence. Even Victoria is too shocked to continue weeping. Amara walks slowly to where Felix lies on the floor, blood smeared on his face. He looks up at her, and it is to Amara he addresses his answer, not Britannica. "I will never yield to you." She opens her mouth in shock, and he smiles. "Not what you were expecting? I swore by all the gods to destroy you. You will continue paying, Amara, because every penny you give me reminds you that *I own you*. I will always own you. You don't like it?" He flicks his eyes towards Britannica. "Then let her kill me. And what do you imagine will happen then. Do you not think I have your secret written into my will? That if you murder me, you will destroy your own child?"

"He is liar," Britannica snarls.

Felix is still staring into Amara's eyes. "She knows I am not lying," he replies.

"Let him up," Amara's voice is choked with rage. "I can't risk it."

At first, it seems Britannica is not going to obey. The anger on her face, at being denied the kill, is frightening to see. And yet, she moves, doing as Amara has asked. Victoria rushes towards Felix as soon as he is standing, but he shoves her away. "Don't fucking touch me," he spits, and Amara knows, looking at the way Victoria quails, that Victoria will suffer later for her husband's defeat.

"I will pay you," Amara says. "But if you harm Philos or Rufina, if you do not keep your silence, I will not only kill you, but your entire family." She looks over to where Victoria is standing, clutching her stomach in fear. "Your child for mine," Amara says to her. "As payment for your betrayal."

"You certainly have a high regard for the British bitch's killing abilities," Felix says, wiping the blood from his face and inspecting the red smear on his palm. "But it seems unlikely *one woman* could inflict so much carnage. She got lucky today, but how might it be if she faced not only me but my whole household? Do you really think she could kill Paris, Gallus and Thraso, single-handed? And then there's always the tragic possibility she might be set upon in a dark alley. I wonder who your protector would be then?"

"My brothers avenge me, if you touch me," Britannica says to Felix. "We are sworn to each other. They know of you already."

"You don't have any fucking brothers," Victoria says, eyes wide with fear, "not unless you plan on raising the dead."

Britannica smiles her gap-toothed grin and pushes the

tunic high up her arm to where the pale skin is freshly tattooed with black. The mark of a gladiator. "I have many brothers now. To die for vengeance is honour for me."

"You sold her as a *gladiator*?" Felix is unable to hide his surprise.

"She pledged herself," Amara replies, edging towards the door. Britannica is beside her with her dagger drawn, the safety of the street just a few paces away. "Perhaps you shouldn't have discarded her so easily. There is always a price to pay for underestimating a woman."

EPILOGUE

Now we come to examples of changing Fortune,
which are innumerable. For what great joys does she
bring except after disasters, or what immense disasters
except after enormous joys?
Pliny the Elder, Natural History

The boat does not move as swiftly as Pliny's quadrireme to Misenum. The small merchant vessel is not going to carry them for the whole journey, only as far as Puteoli. From there they will travel the rest of the way by road. The wind whips at Amara's hair. She watches the coast pass by, the giant bulk of Vesuvius looming over the bay, its peak piercing the clouds. They are approaching the harbour at Pompeii, but the ship does not slow.

Venus stands on her giant column, the guardian of her city. Amara thinks of the plea she once made to the goddess at the Vinalia, all that time ago, with Dido. *May men fall to me as this offering falls to you, Greatest Aphrodite. May I know love's power, if never its sweetness.*

From here, on deck, she can see the city walls, the Temple of Venus, and beyond that, hidden from view, are all the streets she has walked, the Forum, the Wolf Den, Rufus's house with the golden door, Julia's garden. Somewhere, in Pompeii right now, Philos is with Rufina. The people she loves most are in this city, and those she hates more than death. Amara says a silent prayer, not to Venus this time, but to the deity to whom she owed her first allegiance, Pallas-Athene. *Grant Philos wisdom, Grant Britannica victory, Protect Rufina, I beg you, goddess of my fathers, goddess of my heart.*

Amara places a hand to her chest. There is no danger she will give her heart away. There is nothing left of it to give. The last words Philos said to her, before she left for Stabiae, turn over in her mind. They had only had the briefest moment alone, and he had taken Amara's hand, the way he once did in the street, his thumb pressed to hers. *You will be better off without me.* She had understood then that he still loves her. But the thought brings her little comfort now, when she is leaving him behind. The boat dips, and she is splashed with spray, its touch cold on her skin. She does not flinch.

"Lost in thought, my darling."

Demetrius comes to stand beside her, looking out across the bay. Then he turns, observing her face without tenderness. The coldness in his eyes matches her own. Even here, set against the elements, the vast blue of the sea and sky, with the mountain behind, she can feel his pull. She remembers the words she said to Philos. *Nothing means anything without money.* Hatred coils around the remains of her heart – not for Demetrius, but for herself. She smiles. "I'm thinking of the future."

He points towards the stern. "Then you should face that way."

Amara obliges him, turning her back on Pompeii. A group of slaves are huddled on deck in front of her, guarding their luggage. She raises her eyes to the sky, watching the gulls wheel high above them. In spite of herself, something in her spirits lifts. She has left behind her daughter, her lover, her heart. But she is alive; she is unafraid. And she is travelling to Rome, the most powerful city in the world.

Acknowledgements

I am deeply grateful to the whole team at Head of Zeus, not only for their support for this book, but also during the publication process of *The Wolf Den*. Thank you above all to my wonderful editor Charlotte Greig, who was an endless source of encouragement and advice: it has been such fun to work together. Thank you also to Kate Appleton for your tireless work on publicity, and to Jade Gwilliam, Jessie Sullivan, Lottie Chase and Dan Groenewald for your amazing support in selling and marketing Amara's story. Thank you, too, to Madeleine O'Shea, who encouraged me to make Philos a central character: I'm looking forward to working with you again on the next stage of the journey. Also huge thanks to Katrina Harvery, Anna Nightingale, Clare Gordon, Clémence Jacquinet and Matt Bray.

The cover art for the trilogy is extraordinary – thank you Holly Ovenden, for bringing my words to readers through your brilliant designs.

The support from booksellers has been an absolute joy. I am beyond grateful to everyone at Waterstones who supported *The Wolf Den* as book of the month, and to all the independent bookshops who have championed the novel. In particular, thank you to Dan Bassett at Cribbs

Causeway for your friendship, and to Revekka Maria at Piccadilly for your kindness in having me in store, and all your interesting ideas about Amara's Greek heritage.

I'm indebted to fellow authors who have supported my writing in so many ways – including Buki Papillon, Laura Purcell, Nikita Gill, Caroline Lea and Jennifer Saint. In particular, working with Jenny Saint on joint events and then sharing so many thoughts, hopes and ideas together has been a real highlight of the past year. Thanks also to archaeologist Dr Sophie Hay for all your support, friendship and advice – especially on Julia Felix, the real woman behind the character in my book. And to Dr Jane Draycott for sharing your fascinating work on Roman domestic medical practice. I'm also extremely grateful to everyone who has reviewed my work on bookstagram, in the press and beyond. An especially big thanks to Liv Albert, Gen McMenemy, Jenny Williamson and Kate Armstrong for having me on your fabulous podcasts.

Homeschooling loomed large for me in the past two years, as it has for many other parents. I am grateful to my wonderful son Jonathon for putting up with so much, and for being the most cheerful, imaginative little person. Now you get a book with your name on, and it's even blue! Thank you to my mother Suzy Kendall for enabling me to write, by giving me the precious gift of time, and for being the world's best grandmother.

I'm lucky to have amazingly supportive friends and family, whose love has meant so much, even during a time when we could not always see one another. Thank you to Andrea Binfor, Lingling Hu, Dan Jones, Samira Ahmed, Kristina Holt, Trilby Fox-Rumley, Bethan Francis, Anna

Sahalayeva, Eugenie Harper, Tom Harper, Ruth Grey Harper and Alexander Harper. Thank you also to my work family at ITV News Anglia – especially Chris Warner, Gary Mabee and Neil Barbour, who kept me sane while reporting the pandemic.

Thank you to Liza DeBlock, Kiya Evans, Shabnom Khanom and the whole team at Mushens Entertainment. I cannot believe how many countries *The Wolf Den* is now travelling to, thanks to your incredible hard work and determination.

My biggest thanks goes to Juliet Mushens, who has not only been (as always) an exceptional agent, but also a very dear friend. I cannot thank you enough, Juliet, for all you do for me. This book was shaped by your insight and advice, while your generosity with your time, your kindness and your humour, has meant the absolute world. All those emails, DMs, phone calls and memes – I appreciate every single one.

About the Author

ELODIE HARPER is a journalist and prize-winning writer. Her story 'Wild Swimming' won the 2016 Bazaar of Bad Dreams short story competition, which was judged by Stephen King. She is currently a reporter at ITV News, and before that worked as a producer for Channel 4 News. The first book in the Wolf Den trilogy, *The Wolf Den*, was a Waterstones Book of the Month for fiction and a *Sunday Times* Top 15 bestseller.